Never Far Away
By Anie Michaels

Edited by
Krysta Drechsler

are assumed to be the property of their respective owners, and are used only for reference. There is no implied endorsement if we used one of those terms.

Dedicated to

All the readers who fell in love with Ella and Porter in Never Close Enough.

I could not ask for more supportive readers and wish you all knew how deeply your kind and encouraging words touch me.

I wrote the first book for me, but I wrote the second one for you.

Prologue
Ella

Thickness. Heaviness. Thoughts were trying to make their way to the surface, but Ella's brain was full of confusing liquid, rushing her thoughts from side to side, making it hard to keep them straight. Ideas were treading through dense murkiness, floating to the top, trying to form into words, but no words would come out of her mouth. She heard a deep and unfamiliar voice. It warmed her immediately. Velvety heat flowed through her when she heard it.

"There you are, Babe. I've missed that mouth." She listened, trying to place the voice. Then she felt the most gentle and soft kiss right on the corner of her lips. Who was kissing her? And why did it make her heart flutter?

"You are so beautiful," the mystery voice again. She felt her eyes scrunching in confusion. This wasn't Kyle. Why was he putting his mouth on her? "Ella? Baby?"

She tried to fight her way through; she didn't know this voice, but she felt it. Whoever it belonged to obviously knew her. His voice was so soothing and it sounded full of gentleness. She needed to see whoever it belonged to.

As she tried to wake up, all of a sudden, there was loud commotion everywhere. More voices, more people, lots of footsteps and people touching her. And then the voice.

"I'm right here, Ella. I'm not going anywhere."

Like lifting hundred pound weights with her eyelids, she struggled, but finally the light crept in – blinding light. Her hand instinctively came up to block it. She wanted to see, but the light was too bright. And why did her hand feel like it was full of sand? It fell back on the bed with a thud and her eyes snapped shut as her head fell to the side.

"What are her oxygen levels?" Another unfamiliar voice, but this one did nothing to her heart. It was cold and clinical.

"She's at a ninety-eight, Doctor." Doctor? "Her heart rate is elevated, but not too high."

"Ella? My name is Doctor Andrews. You're at OHSU. You're going to be ok. If you can hear me, can you try to open your eyes?"

OHSU? Ella knew that was the hospital. Why was she in the hospital? She tried to pry her eyes open again and another sliver of light shone through as she blinked a few times. She saw blurred figures standing around the bed she was laying in and then she saw another fuzzy person enter the room.

"Ella, you're awake!" Her mother.

"Ma…Mah…Mo…" Her throat hurt tremendously and every sound she made felt like sandpaper scraping up the inside of her neck. She swallowed hard. "Mom?" Ella was shocked by the sound of her own voice. Gravelly and weak.

"I'm here, Sweetie. Everything is going to be ok." Her eyes closed again and she felt her mother take her hand. "Why isn't she waking up?"

"This is totally normal, Mrs. Sinclair. It will take a little while for her to adjust and she still has the sedative in her system making her groggy. So far, she is responding wonderfully. She's moving and talking, all good signs." Ella could hear them, but she had no energy to try to open her eyes again and talking hurt too much. For a while Ella listened to all the people in the room fuss over her and every few minutes she would open her eyes, trying to get use to the light. Eventually, the pain lessened and she was able to look at her mother.

"Ella," her mother said with tears in her eyes, "we were so scared."

"It's ok," Ella whispered, wincing. "Water?" Ella pointed to her throat. A nurse brought her a cup of water with a straw. The water felt and tasted better than anything she could remember, like an icy, numbing salve running down her throat.

"What happened?" Ella squeaked.

"Oh Ella, don't worry about it right now. Just focus on getting better. Your father and sister are waiting outside to see you."

"Megan? I want…" Ella took another sip of the cool water. "Can I see her?" Her mother looked to the doctor and he gave a nod to one of the nurses. A minute later Megan came in the room and Ella smiled at her. Megan's mouth curved up in a smile and tears welled up in her eyes.

"Ella, I am so glad you are ok," Megan cried, as she gave her a gentle squeeze. Ella felt her eyes closing again, but wanted to talk to her mother and sister. It was useless to try and keep them open; they weighed a million pounds. She rested for a few minutes and when she opened them again she was looking at the smiling faces of the women she loved the most. Then she realized someone was missing.

"Where's Kyle?"

"Don't worry about him, Ella. We've got everything taken care of." Ella's eyebrow's scrunched up in confusion. She shook her head a little, not understanding what her mother meant.

"Where is he? Is he outside? Can I see him?" Her mother's face went from concerned, to angry, to shocked, to confused. Megan took a step forward and placed her hand on Ella's shoulder.

"Ella, we told the police what happened and they are looking for him. But don't worry, we won't let him near you."

"What are you talking about? What do you mean they can't find him? What happened to him? Is he ok?" Panic coursed through her and she could hear the machine monitoring her heart beeping more rapidly. "What do you mean? He didn't do anything to me." Ella felt the fog trying to take her brain over again.

"We know he hurt you, Ella. Porter told us what happened," Megan said softly.

"Porter?"

Megan and her mother exchanged worried looks.

"What is going on?" Ella demanded, trying to sound authoritative, but failing when her voice came out at a whisper still.

"Ella might still be dealing with some confusion. It is totally normal. Try not to add to her confusion by overwhelming her," the doctor said to her mother and sister. "Ella, do you mind if I ask you some questions?" Ella shook her head.

"Do you know how old you are?" Ella raised an eyebrow at the doctor and thought he was asking her pretty stupid questions.

"Twenty-nine."

Her mother took in a sharp breath and held it.

"Good. Now, what month is it?"

"March." This time Megan reacted and brought a hand over her mouth to stifle a shocked cry. Ella's eyes fluttered between the doctor, her mother, and her sister. Something was wrong. "What is it?" Ella looked to the doctor for answers and he smiled at her reassuringly.

"Ella, what is the last thing you remember? Tell us what you did yesterday." Ella blinked at him. It was a simple question, but she found that the answer was buried by heavy muck in her mind. She was going to have to dig and wade through mental mud to dig up the memory he asked for. She closed her eyes and tried to bring up the events of the day before. She thought hard and long, and finally images came to her mind. Megan was there, and they were walking past stores, and they were outside.

"Megan and I went shopping downtown. We had lunch at Rockbottom Brewery," Ella looked over at her sister.

"Very good, Ella. Why don't you get some rest now?"

"Is Daddy outside?" She asked.

"I'll send him in," Megan said, sounding sad. Ella watched Megan leave the room then her head fell to the side again, feeling heavy and droopy.

"Mom?" Ella asked softly.

"Yes, Baby?" Her mother answered as she brushed her hair out of her face.

"Who is Porter?"

Chapter One

Ella

Ella looked out the window of her boutique clothing store, Poppy, and was excited by the sunshine filtering through the glass. June in Portland usually brought the long awaited sun. It rained nine out of the twelve months in a year. And although Portlanders were magnificent rain contenders, they really cherished the sunlight. When the good weather rolled through the city it seemed as if everyone came out of hiding. You could see a million different kinds of people walking down the sidewalk in front of her store and people watching was always a good way to pass the time.

She found that since she had so easily lost six weeks of her life, it was also easy to lose herself for a few minutes during the day. She was constantly zoning out and drifting away, only to be pulled back to reality by someone talking to her or asking her a question, interrupting her intense gaze at nothing in particular.

She was still completely baffled that she couldn't remember six whole weeks of her life. Why six weeks? Why *those* six weeks? What if something really important had happened during those weeks and she had no idea? What if she had won the lottery? Or maxed out a credit card? Or booked a really expensive, yet fabulous, trip around the world? Was she missing her own vacation right now because she couldn't remember planning it?

The thoughts of why, or what, were all-consuming sometimes and she always felt a nagging in the back of her mind constantly berating herself for not being able to recall those six weeks. Although, it seemed there was always a silver lining. Along with any good things she couldn't remember, she also couldn't remember the bad. Her family had a hard time telling her about Kyle and, to be honest, she had a hard time believing what they told her. How surreal it had been to have her family tell her something so totally unbelievable about the man she loved. But then she had no choice but to believe them because he had mysteriously disappeared. A small wave of sadness swept over her, but she brushed it off, reminding herself that it had been two months and it was time to stop being sad over something she couldn't control, least of all remember.

She turned as a man and woman came into the shop. She smiled brightly at them as they made their way into the middle of the store.

"Hi, welcome to Poppy. Enjoying the sunshine?" She asked. Her eyes darted back and forth between the woman and the man. The woman smiled back at her.

"It is so pretty out; I hope the sun sticks around this time."

"Me too," Ella responded. She let her eyes linger on the man, hoping to catch his eye so she could engage him in conversation. It had become her new obsession. Every man over the age of twenty she came into contact with, she tried to make him speak. She was on a seemingly never-ending quest to find the voice. He had only said a few words to her right as she was waking up, but she would never forget the voice that had spoken to her or the lips that belonged to that voice.

Ella took a few steps towards the couple and spoke directly to the man who was wrapped up in his phone at the moment.

"Is there anything in particular you are looking for?" Her eyes bore into him and she hoped he could feel her eyes burning into his forehead. It must have worked because he looked up at her and mumbled a disinterested remark at her.

"Uh, no. We're just looking." He went back to looking at his cell phone while the woman continued browsing.

Disappointment washed over Ella and her shoulders slumped slightly when his too high-pitched voice immediately answered the question she asked herself hundreds of times a day: was this him?

The voice she heard that day had been deep, raw, and full of love. She had wondered about the love in his voice for two whole months now. How could someone besides Kyle speak to her in such a way that made her feel like he loved her? After weeks and weeks of arguing with what she heard, she finally gave in and just accepted that what she heard was most definitely love. Aside from actually uttering the words at her, everything else she could remember about those few moments she had with him ached with love; the way he touched her, the way his words caressed her, and the way he kissed her.

Her family insisted that no one else had been at the hospital but them, but Ella knew better. What she didn't know was why they lied to her about it. Her mind mostly tried to convince her that if they kept something from her it was for her own good, but there were times when she was so angry and frustrated with them. She deserved to know everything about what had happened to her, the good and the bad.

"Ok, well, if you need anything let me know," Ella said to the woman, flashing a forced but hopefully convincing smile at her. She walked over to a table that displayed soft blouses of bright colors for summer and began folding the shirts into neater piles, trying to pass the time while her mind kept wandering back to the mystery voice. Eventually, she knew she would go crazy thinking about it, but there was nothing she could do to stop herself. It was a result of reverse psychology. Her family basically told her she could never know who he was, so it was all she thought about, obviously.

She heard the door open again and a very genuine smile played across her face as her little sister came walking into the store. Ella could tell ever since she woke up missing six weeks of her life that Megan struggled with keeping information from her. Megan did what their parents thought was best and they had developed a "Don't ask, don't tell" motto around the whole debacle. It would be really easy to be mad at Megan, but she couldn't bring herself to hold it against her.

"Hey, Megs. How are you this morning?"

"Loving the sunshine, Fella. We should close up shop and hit the Saturday Market. It's a perfect day for strolling along and browsing," she said with a lazy voice.

"Right. Which is exactly why we need to be here, making sure people have the opportunity to browse in my store." Ella gave her sister a big grin.

"Fine. Slave driver," she said with a laugh and continued into the backroom. Ever since Ella had been in the hospital her sister started taking shifts at her store when she could to help out. Megan majored in business and graduated from the University of Portland just the week before. Megan's fiancé, Patrick, landed a job at a reputable company in the city. Ella was thinking about asking her sister if she wanted to help her expand her business, but hadn't found the right opportunity yet. Megan seemed content working for her at the moment and Ella was enjoying spending all the time with her sister.

When she returned from the back, Megan started looking through some of the new merchandise Ella put out that morning. There were perks to owning a clothing boutique, but sometimes it was more of a hindrance to the wallet. Even though she spent more money on clothes than she would ever admit, Ella loved being able to bring in unique and unknown designers that she liked and felt sometimes like she was helping out designers who were trying to get their name out there. It was thrilling for her when a designer she supported became well-known in the fashion world. It was validating for her and cemented for her what she had already known: that she had an eye for fashion and was doing what she was meant to do.

"This dress is amazing, El. You should save one for Kalli."

"Already did. She's coming by later." Kalli was the wardrobe manager for a movie being filmed in town. She came by the store before her accident, but before Ella could get better, the movie wrapped and Kalli left. A couple weeks later she came back for another film and came by the store to see if they could work together. Everything worked out well and Ella's store supplied many pieces for the female lead in a new romantic comedy that would be out the next year. The most rewarding part of the whole situation was the friendship she'd developed with Kalli.

Kalli was fun, witty, gorgeous, and thirty as well. She lived in Seattle, but was in Portland for the duration of the shoot of the movie. One of the things Ella liked most about Kalli was that she had no idea what happened to Ella in those six weeks she lost. Spending time with her was easy and free of the tension she sometimes felt around her family. Ella and Kalli talked about what had happened to her, but it wasn't something they dwelled on. Ella loved that they could spend time together and that she felt normal around her. Plus, they were able to visit the set and met some pretty famous people. That wasn't bad either.

"Good. Kalli will love it. How's it been today?"

"Pretty steady. It's early yet. Once everyone has had their coffee they'll be out and we'll get busy. Hope you're ready."

"Born ready, Sis." Megan's phone pinged and she pulled it out of her pocket. A worried look came over her face as she looked at the screen. She glanced over at Ella. "I'll be right back," she said as she walked into the back.

These were the moments that Ella hated. Knowing something was being kept from her and also knowing Megan had no choice in the matter. She tried to push back the dark cloud that had just stolen her sunshine.

Chapter Two

Porter

No matter how many days passed, waking up alone in his now-too-big bed made every morning a constant reminder that he was still without her. The first week he was alone, he couldn't even bring himself to sleep in the bed. The vanilla scent, that had been somewhat comforting when he thought they would only be separated by miles, was now a painful reminder that what separated them was so much more.

The last eight weeks were a nightmare and he sank deeper and deeper into a darkness that honestly scared him. Multiple times since the accident he found himself in his truck, sitting outside her store, waiting for her to walk past a window or walk down the street. Every time he caught a glimpse of her blonde hair, or her blue eyes, it calmed him in a way but also dug the hole in his heart a little deeper. It was bittersweet. Sometimes he wished he would lose his memory too. But then he thought about not remembering how she felt underneath him or how her hands felt on his skin, and he knew he would rather spend an eternity remembering for the both of them than spend one second not knowing their love.

Reading her letter on the beach was the last push he needed to make the decision to finally go to her. He grabbed his phone off his bedside table and texted Megan.

How is Ella doing today?

It took a few minutes for Megan to respond, and he was considering calling her when she sent him a message.

She is doing well. I just got to the store and she is in a good mood.

***Great. I am going to drive there to see her today. I just
wanted to give you a heads up.***

Immediately after the message was delivered his phone rang
and he knew it would be Megan. He answered the phone, trying
to contain his aggravation.

"Don't try and talk me out of it, Megan. I've waited long
enough to see her."

"Porter, I know you think it's best for Ella to know about you,
but I don't see how upsetting her right now is going to do her any
good. She's adjusting well; she's moving on."

"Moving on? Megan, I love her. And she loves me, or used to
love me anyway. Why do you want her to move on?"

"I don't *want* her to move on, Porter. But if she hasn't
remembered you by now, I'm not sure that she ever will. Plus, if
she remembers you, she has to remember Kyle and frankly I think
she's better off not remembering what that asshole did to her."

Porter took in a deep breath. He understood what Megan was
saying and it was true that the chances of Ella remembering what
had happened between them were getting smaller by the day.

"Megan, I don't know how to function without her. It's killing
me knowing that she's there, living her life, not knowing that I am
dying to be with her. I understand she might not remember me,
but why shouldn't I at least get a chance to get to know her
again?" He heard her hesitate on the other end of the line and
then she let out a deep sigh.

"If my parents find out about this they will not be happy. My
mom has done nothing but worry about Ella for the last eight
weeks, Porter. I don't want to upset her even more."

Porter laughed. "This won't be the first time Ella and I have
kept something from your parents."

"Very funny."

"Listen, I am going to get ready and then drive over. So you can either choose to be there or not, but I am coming. I promise I won't tell her what happened between us. I just need to talk to her."

"Fine. I will be here. I don't feel good about this, just so you know. I am agreeing to this under duress."

"Noted. Lighten up. Nothing can get any worse than it is right now. Not for me anyway."

"I know this has been really hard on you, Porter."

"I'll be ok. I just need her in my life again, even if we have to start over."

"Well," she let out a loud sigh "You better hurry up and get here then."

"See you in a few hours, Megan."

"See you then, Porter."

Every time Porter drove up to Poppy he had to push back the terrible memories of the night of Ella's injury. The flashing police lights that lit up the dark night, the barricades that kept him from her, watching the ambulance pull away, not knowing that she had been in there, hurt and alone. He hoped that today, actually speaking to her, he would be able to replace the bad memories with good ones.

He parked his truck along the street and then looked in the windows of Poppy, hoping to catch a glimpse of her before he went in. Megan walked in front of the window, a worried look across her face, and she was checking her watch as she looked out onto the street. He knew Megan was caught in the middle and he was sorry that this was causing her stress, but there was nothing in the world that was going to keep him from Ella now. He was so close and he made up his mind.

He took one look in the rear view mirror, made sure he looked decent enough, and then got out of his truck and headed towards the store. Megan caught sight of him as he walked towards the door and he could see the tension forming across her face. A little farther behind her he could just make out Ella. She stood with her back to him talking to a customer. Her blonde hair cascaded softly down her back like a waterfall the color of wheat, landing right between her shoulder blades. His fingers ached to move her hair to the side to taste her neck and feel the goosebumps he knew his mouth could cause on her skin. He wanted to place his nose in the crook of her neck and let her vanilla scent permeate through him. He walked up to the door, pulled it open, his eyes never leaving the golden trail of her hair.

"Hi, welcome to Poppy. Can I help you with anything?" Megan's nerves were evident in her voice as she made a lame attempt at treating him like a stranger. He gave her a sideways glance and mouthed the word 'Smooth' to her. She shrugged her shoulder and gave him a look that said she was giving it her best attempt. His eyes went back to Ella.

"No, thanks. I'm just looking," he said, perhaps a little louder than necessary. He thought he saw Ella's back straighten and her shoulders might have pulled back a little. She slowly turned around and he was entirely mesmerized by her movement. When her eyes met his, he felt as if a piece of his soul fell back into place. He spent the last eight weeks keeping his distance from her, watching her from afar, but to have her eyes locked on him brought him a sense of peace. Even if she didn't say anything to him or even acknowledge him, every dark thought or breakdown he had since her injury was worth it just to see her eyes and have her look at him.

"Good afternoon," Ella quietly and softly said to him. He fought to remain calm and worked doubly hard to keep his breathing even. Her voice, something he'd longed to hear for so long, was almost sweet enough to bring him to his knees. He reigned himself in, knowing that if he went all "I'm your long lost boyfriend you can't remember" on her, she'd think he was crazy and send him away. For just a moment, he was second guessing his decision to come here and see her. But then she smiled at him. Her smile was powerful enough to steal the air right from his lungs. Then she cocked her head to the side and looked him up and down. Her eyebrows scrunched in a little and he couldn't read her face enough to figure out what was going through her mind.

"Hello," he answered her hesitantly. How was he supposed to speak to her without letting her know that he loved her more than anything? He couldn't be held responsible for the words that might come out of his mouth. He wanted more than anything just to tell her he loved her.

"Are you looking for anything in particular today?" She smirked at him, like she knew something he didn't. He couldn't help but smirk back and gave her a questioning look. Of all the responses he imagined happening when he was finally in the same room with Ella, this was not remotely close to any of them. He pictured her looking right through him, not giving him a second glance, completely unaware of who he was. In one of his imaginings, she miraculously regained her memory just by the sight of his face and ran into his arms, professing her love for him. In yet another scenario, she admitted to knowing who he was all along but had decided to stick with the amnesia story to avoid breaking up with him, feeling as though their relationship was moving too quickly for her. This Ella, the one sending him sly glances and smirks, was a little confusing and he wasn't sure how to proceed.

"Um, not quite. I was looking for something for a while, but I think I might have found it. Thanks." He heard Megan let out a loud groan from across the room.

"Megan," Ella said without taking her eyes off of Porter.

"Yeah?"

"Please go in to the backroom and find the inventory reports from this week last year."

"What? Why?"

"I want to compare the number of scarfs we have this year to how many we had at this time last year," she said without blinking. Megan looked back and forth from Ella and Porter, her eyes darting between them. She let out a loud and obviously annoyed breath and retreated into the backroom. Ella started walking towards Porter, looking a little unsure of her next words.

"She didn't seem too happy about that," Porter said, trying to fill in some of the uncomfortable tension that was flowing between himself and Ella.

"I don't even have inventory reports from last year. She will never find what she is looking for. It will take her about five minutes to figure it out, so we don't have much time." She was right in front of him now.

"Much time for what?"

"Porter."

She said his name and he was sure his heart stopped beating and started racing within the very same moment.

"How do you know my name?" He whispered, shocked by the continual realization that Ella, his Ella, used his name.

She pointed a finger up at his face with a new menacing look on her face. "How do you know who I am?" She asked, demanding information from him.

"I am not sure how to answer that," he said honestly. His hand ached and begged to touch her face. She was so close and damn it if he couldn't smell her sweetness. Vanilla wafted all over him.

"There is a coffee shop two blocks south of here. Meet me there tonight at six."

Confusion lit up his face. She wanted to meet for coffee? How was any of this happening? He looked back and forth between the stockroom door and Ella's face. He shook his head, trying to hide a small smile. As if there was ever any question, whatever Ella asked of him of course he would give it to her.

"Ok, but don't tell Megan," he said, glancing back towards the backroom.

"So you know Megan too?" She asked, narrowing her eyes.

Porter was so confused by what was going on, about how she

could possibly know his name, but not know who he was? How could he answer her questions without breaking the promise he'd made to Megan not to tell her what had happened? Instantly, as if a switch flipped in his mind, he knew that he was irrevocably tied to Ella. If he had to go back on his word to prove to Ella that they were meant to be together, that was something he was willing to do.

"We'll talk later. I will be at the coffee shop," he said with conviction.

"Ok then. You had better leave before she comes back."

"See you at six." He turned around and left Poppy, wondering how, after all these months of being away from her, it was possible to walk away from her again. It hurt physically. His chest ached, and his head felt light and dizzy. He had no idea where their meeting would take them or what he would have to reveal to her, but anything was better than being kept from her indefinitely.

It was five minutes until six and Porter waited at the coffee shop, hoping that Ella would still show up. He also hoped that it would be just Ella, that Megan hadn't gotten word of their meeting and decided to tag along to make sure he kept his word. He watched as people walked past the coffee shop's front window, not really paying much attention to anyone in particular until one couple caught his eye. The man and woman walked hand in hand, both smiling and laughing. The man stopped, pulled the woman back into his arms, and said something into her ear as his arms wrapped around her waist. His eyes dropped away from them and looked down at the table, not wanting to intrude on their personal moment but also wanting to avoid the dark feelings that usually came over him when confronted with people happily in love.

"Hello, Porter." Her sweet voice flooded his senses and made everything in the room look brighter. Hearing her say his name again, as surreal as it was, made a little bit of his tension float away.

"Hello, Ella," he said as he looked up to her.

"So, you do know my name," she said giving him a questioning look.

"Yes, I know your name and you know mine."

"Interesting, isn't it?" she said, but then paused and looked towards the counter. "I'm going to get a tea. Do you want anything?"

"No, but please let me get the tea." She nodded at him and sat down in the chair across from him.

"Peppermint, please," she said with an unsure smile. He went to the counter and ordered her tea and smiled because he had learned something new about her; she liked peppermint tea. He brought the steaming cup back to the table, carefully set her cup down in front of her, and took a seat in the chair he vacated.

"So, Porter, tell me how you know me." Her eyes burned into his. She was looking at him so fiercely and he found it a little difficult to even form words.

"I don't really know where to begin. Why don't you tell me how you know who I am?" He tried to stall.

"I heard you talking to me when I was waking up in the hospital." Her voice was small and quiet, and she looked down at her cup of tea, seemingly avoiding his eyes. Porter worked hard to make it seem like her words hadn't affected him. And then he proceeded to run through his mind what he could have possibly said to her as she was waking up that had stuck with her that entire time.

"What did you hear?" He asked softly.

"I heard a man, you, tell me that I was beautiful. Then you kissed me and told me that you weren't going anywhere." She looked up at him, saying his words back to him, staring him straight in the eye. Her eyes begged him to confess, to tell her that he was that man. He was torn. If he opened this door, there would be no going back. He would never be able to un-tell her. For better or worse, she would know the truth. The decision became easy in a moment of clarity. Of course she deserved the truth. If he owed her anything, it was the honesty of what had happened between them. Whether or not she would ever remember, or whether or not she would feel anything for him ever again, he could never lie to her. "It was you, wasn't it?" She asked him one last time and it shred the last piece of his resistance to tell her.

"Yes. That was me." The rush of her breath was audible and it made an invisible fist squeeze his heart.

"You loved me. I heard it in your voice. I felt it when you kissed me." She whispered fiercely, her words spitting out at him. "You told me you weren't going anywhere, and then you left and I never heard your voice again." She breathed hard and Porter wanted nothing more than to reach across the table and take her hand. But he knew now wasn't the time. Mostly, he wanted to correct her. She assumed he didn't love her anymore, but nothing was farther from the truth. His love for her was bigger and more encompassing than ever. It was engrained in him now, a part of his make-up. Loving her was just as necessary as breathing for him. He didn't do it only by choice; he did it for survival. "Only that's not true. I've heard your voice every day since. I hear your voice in my sleep, while I'm awake. I listened to every voice I've heard hoping that I would find out who you are. Now that I have, I can't figure out if I am happy to have solved the mystery or royally pissed off at you for disappearing. I guess I am leaning towards the latter."

"You have to believe me that leaving you was never my decision or even my choice. I never wanted to leave you. Everyone thought it was in your best interest, for you to heal."

"That's bullshit," she said flatly. Porter laughed, glad to see she was still the spitfire he remembered.

"I agree."

"How do you know me?" She asked again, with more insistence this time. He took a deep breath in and, just like jumping in a cold pool on a hot summer's day, he knew it was going to sting and be uncomfortable but hoped the end result would be a relief.

"A week before your accident, we met at my mom's bar. You had come to the beach after finding your boyfriend with another woman and you were drowning your sorrows, so to speak. Your car battery died, so I gave you a ride to your rental house." Porter ran his fingers through his hair, trying to figure out how to tell her what had happened between them. In all the scenarios in his head that included them speaking to each other she always remembered him. He felt pretty stupid that he hadn't considered the fact that he might have to explain their relationship. "Anyway," he continued, "after a few days of meeting up and getting drinks, I asked you out on a date." He looked up at her hoping she would be giving him some sort of reassurance, but her face was blank.

"And this all happened a week before the accident?"

"Yes, well, ten days to be exact," he replied.

"What happened between us?" She pleaded with him through her eyes, begging him to give her something.

"We spent ten amazing days together, falling in love, and making plans to be together." He paused again, trying to find the right words. "When you woke up and didn't remember me, or us, I didn't really know what the next step should be. And I definitely didn't have any say in your care. I had only met your parents *because* of the accident. They felt like it would be better for you to recover with as little stress as possible and to them that meant that I should stay away." He looked down at his hands, mostly because he didn't want to look at her face. He didn't want to be telling all of this to a stranger; he wanted to be reliving it with his Ella. "I called your mom every day for weeks, trying to convince her to let me see you, that I could help in some way. I texted Megan constantly, trying to get any updates from her that I could." He shook his head and looked back up at Ella and her blank eyes. Frustrated, he let out a loud and exasperated sigh. "Maybe this was a mistake. I should go."

"Wait," she said, placing her hand over his. "Please. Don't leave."

Chapter Three

Ella

The last thing Ella wanted was for him to leave her again. She heard his voice in Poppy and immediately her blood ran heated through her veins. She was sure she would have to search for him, but then he just appeared in her shop. She would have known his voice anywhere. At that moment all she wanted to do was listen to his voice forever. That was until she turned around and saw him, and then she realized she wanted to spend forever looking into his chocolate eyes. He was the kind of handsome that made women weak-kneed and swoon. His dark brown hair matched his eyes and his strong jaw made his face look all kinds of manly. Somewhere, deep inside of her soul, she knew exactly why she felt like he loved her at the hospital: because she knew she would have fallen in love with him in an instant. Something pulled her towards him and if she didn't stay grounded, they would collide.

"I asked my mom and Megan many times who you were. I *knew* someone was there with me, I felt it. But no matter how many times I pleaded with them, they would never give me any information. Eventually I gave up on asking."

"I never left your side at the hospital. I was there every day," he paused, realizing that all of this information might be overwhelming for her. "I am sorry if this is confusing for you."

"You have no idea how confusing this is. I don't think 'confusing' as a word really encompasses how bizarre it is to deal with amnesia. I woke up to a strange man kissing me, who wasn't my boyfriend, but was kissing me regardless. And everyone just tells me that I was imagining things, that it must have been the medication," she laughed a little as she looked out the window. "I might have been drugged but that kiss, small as it was, felt more real to me than anything since." She shook her head and raised her eyes up to meet his again. "Every day something pops up, something that is tied back to those six weeks of memory I lost. It is a struggle every day to try and figure out what's real, what's probably not true, and then there's what my gut tells me about you." Ella saw him swallow hard and then he spoke softly with a tentative voice.

"What does your gut say about me?"

"It says to trust you." A small smile crept across her face and his relief was evident to her as he let a sigh past his lips. "I know this sounds crazy, but I've been looking for your voice in every man for eight weeks now. When I heard your voice in the store, I knew it was you. I knew you had come to find me and that you would have all the answers I was looking for."

"I'll tell you anything you want to know. I'm tired of hiding things." Ella cocked her head at him and thought hard about her next question.

"Will you tell me what happened to me the night of the robbery?" She was looking him directly in the eye and she saw his eyes flash anger. Once they softened slightly he ran his fingers through his hair and she liked the way it looked after he'd rumpled it.

"It was Sunday afternoon and you had left my house about two hours earlier. I was in my shop working on my boat and you texted me that you had made it home safely. We joked around a little, and then you said you would call me when you were going to bed." She watched him take in a shaky breath as he seemed to be gathering strength to continue on. "About a half hour later, maybe forty-five minutes, you called me. You were crying and upset. You told me that Kyle had been at your apartment and that he had hurt you. You never told me the whole story. You were upset and I just wanted to get to you. I never got all the facts." His head fell into his hands and he was breathing in ragged breaths. "I was so upset with myself for letting you go back home alone. I'm still upset about it. None of this would have happened if I had just stayed with you. I never wanted to let you go."

Ella drew in a ragged breath. She wasn't expecting him to be so emotional about her accident. Everyone in her life had been putting on a brave face, but no one had let her see how upset they had been about the accident. Sometimes she felt guilty for feeling depressed or angry about her injuries since no one else was. Everyone was so focused on her moving forward, no one wanted to help her *deal* with the fact that she had been shot and lost her memory. So hearing Porter and all his frustration and hurt made her feel close to him. She reached across the table and placed her hand over his again, this time holding on and gently rubbing her thumb across the back of his knuckles.

"I'm ok, Porter. You aren't responsible for what happened to me."

"I know you don't remember us, but I will always be responsible for you," he whispered. He took his hand from her and rubbed both his hands over his face. "I'm sorry. I didn't come here to make you uncomfortable. I know this must be awkward for you."

"It's ok." She didn't want to tell him that his words touched her. She wasn't supposed to feel so connected to someone she technically didn't know. "Can you tell me what happened next?"

"I drove to Poppy and the cops were already there. They told me you were taken to the hospital and when I got there I learned about your injuries. I also ran into Kyle. I beat the shit out of him," Porter let out a little laugh and it made her smile. "He left the hospital and never made another appearance, which was probably best for his safety." He paused again, and his next words were heavier and full of reflection. "I stayed by your side, every day, until you woke up. When you started opening your eyes I called the nurses and they made me leave the room. When I finally was told what had happened, that you had lost your memory, the decision had already been made that I wouldn't get to see you. Even the doctor agreed. Ever since then, I've been living off the minimal updates your mom and sister have been sending me."

"It sounds like you've been really upset by all of this."

"Can I be honest with you? "

"Please."

"This is wrecking me. It's an odd situation to be in and I have no idea how to navigate these waters. But to have someone you love so much ripped away from you, and to know that they are still out there living their life but you can't be a part of it," he took in a deep breath and then continued, "it's the worst thing that's ever happened to me." His words cut at her and she believed that he was hurting. She could see the pain painted across his face and she could feel the sadness radiating from him in waves. She was compelled to reach out to him, but felt that he would just pull away again. She wasn't sure how to navigate the waters either; she didn't even remember how to swim.

"Where are we supposed to go from here? I mean, what is supposed to happen next?" She asked him hesitantly.

"I have absolutely no idea. I have been so focused on just getting to speak to you. I hadn't thought about what we were going to do once I'd gotten to talk to you. But whatever happens from this point on, it's up to you. I don't want to put any pressure on you whatsoever. I just wanted to see you again and make sure you were doing all right."

The pressure his words were putting on her made her feel heavy like stone. She was never good at taking the lead and didn't feel comfortable saying to him everything that was running through her mind. How do you tell someone you don't really know that you want them to want you? That you want to spend time with them, lots of time? She could only rely on her gut and her gut was telling her there was a reason she felt inexplicably tied to him.

"Can I ask you a question that might make us both uncomfortable?"

"Of course," he said immediately.

"Do you still love me?" She watched her question sink into him and could almost see her words land on his shoulders, weighing them down.

"Ella," he said softly. "When we met, we spent one week

together in some sort of bubble. Real life wasn't affecting us. We were determined and convinced that we could surmount any obstacle that was thrown our way. We were reckless and excited by each other."

Ella could feel the brush off coming; he was explaining their feelings away, like they were a fluke.

"I spent ten days getting to know you, but then I spent eight weeks away from you. Two whole months of complete separation and isolation."

"I understand," she whispered, wanting to stop his explanation before he got to the point where it would hurt her.

"But I love you more today than I ever have, Ella. Every day. Every. Single. Day. My love for you expands. I'm not ever going to be complete unless you are with me."

As her eyes swept up to his face, she could see the hope still shimmering in his eyes. He still wanted her. When everything in her life was up in the air and she was unsure of anything, this little sliver of hope made her feel confident that Porter was something she could be sure of. She took in a deep breath and it was the first time in weeks that she felt relief.

"If you're not opposed to it, I'd like to spend some time with you," she said, trying not to sound needy. How do you tell your boyfriend you don't remember that you want to date him without sounding needy? She was needy. She needed him to help her feel normal again.

"I am definitely not opposed to that," he said as released a breath, smiling.

Ella's phone buzzed in her purse and she read a text message from Kalli, reminding her that they were supposed to meet to go over some clothing options.

"Are you free tomorrow? The Saturday Market is open and I haven't been yet this season. We could walk around and eat at the food trucks for lunch," she said hopefully.

"That sounds great. Want to meet around eleven?"

"Sure. I will meet you at the waterfront at eleven, then."

They both stood up and headed to the exit. Once they were both outside, Ella gently grabbed Porter's arm and looked him in the eyes.

"Thank you for coming and finding me. I can't imagine that the last eight weeks have been easy for you, but in some ways I am glad that I wasn't the only one affected. It's nice not to feel completely alone, even if only for a moment." She slowly and tentatively moved towards him and pulled him into a hug. She wrapped her arms around his waist, hands clenched, not wanting to feel too much too soon by allowing her finger tips to run along his back. Her cheek came to a rest on his chest and she felt his body tense at her touch. For a few agonizing moments she stood there alone in a hug, wondering if she had overstepped some invisible border. Then she felt him relax and his arms wrapped around her shoulders. Shivers were sent down her spine when his nose found her hair and she heard him inhale.

"You still smell the same," he whispered.

"I wish I could say the same," she mumbled into his shirt. He did smell good, though, of wood and soap. "I guess I will see you tomorrow, then," she said as she pulled away from him.

"Do you need a ride home?" He asked.

"No, thank you, I am headed back to the store."

"Isn't it closed?"

"Yes, but I have some things I need to take care of." She saw in his face he was instantly concerned, and his brow was scrunching and coming to a point between his eyes. "What's the matter?"

"It bothers me to think of you there after hours and at night." Ella cocked her head to side and studied him. Her entire family had been completely and ridiculously over protective of her for the last two months, and it had become overbearingly irritating. But for some reason, when Porter put on a protective front it made her feel cherished.

"I will be ok. I'm actually meeting a friend there. I won't be alone and I won't be there for long, either." Porter drew in a deep breath and stuck his hands in his pockets.

"Ok then, I will see you tomorrow." She watched his eyes until he had turned around heading in the opposite direction of her store.

Ella made it to Poppy and as she was unlocking the door, she saw Kalli come around the corner. Kalli's face lit up with a genuine smile that Ella had no choice but to return; Kalli's friendly and sweet nature was contagious.

"Hey, Lady," Kalli said in greeting. She nearly always called every woman she spoke to "lady". It was a quirk that Ella found endearing.

"Hey yourself. Ready to check out that dress I was telling you about?"

"Always."

The two of them went into the store and Ella punched in the code for the alarm system, making sure she armed it for safety while they were still in the store. Kalli told Ella about some snafu that had occurred on the set of the film she was working on as Ella was walking through the store, taking off her sweater and setting her purse on the counter.

Kalli was one of the new developments in Ella's life for which she was grateful. Kalli had a way of making Ella completely forget that she was living with a void in her mind. It was refreshing to be around her because Ella never had to wonder if Kalli knew more than she was letting on, or if she was keeping something from her. Kalli was simply real, friendly, and good. They had quickly formed a strong and powerful friendship. As she spoke she brushed her auburn hair over her shoulder, and then mindlessly twirled the small and delicate diamond stud that adorned her ear. Her hands were constantly moving, whether she was talking with her hands, gesticulating wildly, or simply fingering the hem of her shirt. If she stayed still for a whole five minutes she might have turned to stone, or so it seemed.

"I mean, I can't help it if one of the extras stupidly spilled coffee on the lead's shirt. I can replace it, but I can't turn back time and take it back, ya know?" Ella was forced back into the conversation by her question.

"Definitely." Ella smiled because she knew Kalli could find a way to complain about almost anything, and nearly did. But generally her frustration had a short lifespan, and once she got the words out of her mouth you could almost see the tension melt away from her. Ella didn't mind being a sounding board for her, because the comfort she got from their friendship outweighed this slight character flaw by no comparison. "Ok, so I received this dress in a shipment and I think it would be perfect for the movie." Ella grabbed the dress off of a rack behind her and held it up for Kalli to see.

The dress came to just above the knee, was gathered at one shoulder with a shimmery applique. It started as a light blue at the gather and gradually moved into a midnight blue towards the bottom.

"Oh, Ella, I love this," Kalli said as she tucked her hair behind her ear. "Ombre is totally hot right now and the one shoulder look is really sexy. This would be perfect for the gala scene. We shoot that in two weeks."

"That's exactly the scene I thought of when this dress came in."

"Can I take it to the set for approval? I really think they'll like it."

"Of course. Not a problem," Ella said with a smile. She grabbed a garment bag from under the counter and began to put the dress in.

"So where were you coming from when I saw you unlocking the door?"

"Oh, um, I had just met a friend at the coffee shop up the street."

"A friend?"

Ella knew she was digging around and contemplated not telling

Kalli about Porter. But then she realized she couldn't really tell her sister about their meeting, so by default Kalli was the only other person she could talk to about what was happening.

"Listen, I really need to talk to someone about this, but I don't want to put you in a bad position with Megan. I need this to be kept between us, so if that's something you feel comfortable with, I would really love to tell you about it." Concern instantly came across Kalli's face and she took a few steps towards Ella until she was close enough to put a hand on her shoulder.

"Ella, of course you can tell me anything. I promise I won't tell Megan unless you give me the ok."

Ella looked down at her hands which were wringing together in a nervous manner. She let out a loud breath and decided she needed to talk to someone about Porter.

"Do you remember me telling you about the man I heard when I was waking up in the hospital?"

"You mean 'The Voice'?"

Ella tilted her head and narrowed her eyes at her reference, not sure if she liked the way it sounded coming from Kalli's mouth. To Ella, the voice she had heard in the hospital had been sacred. And even though she was being completely sincere, hearing her refer to it as if it were part of some urban legend sort of irritated her.

"Don't say it like that, Kal. It happened. I heard it and now I have proof."

"What are you talking about?"

"The man whose voice I heard in the hospital came into Poppy today." Ella got a little satisfaction when Kalli's eyebrows shot towards the roof and her eyes became as wide as the "o" her mouth was making.

"You're joking."

"Never would I joke about this."

"That is a good point. Are you sure it was really him?"

"Well, for one, I would have recognized his voice in an instant. I heard him speak and my whole body responded to his voice. My stomach dropped, my breathing went all crazy, and I had to focus just to turn around without falling on my ass," Ella said, remembering the way her body had been so quick to let her know of his presence. "And two, he told me who he was."

"Oh my gosh, Ella. This is huge. What did he want?"

"He wanted to see me. He said that he's been trying to convince my mother and sister to let him see me since I woke up, and it seems as though he just got tired of waiting for their permission."

"And Megan never told you he was trying to see you?"

"No, but that isn't her fault. Megan is very much in the middle here. My mom is worried about me. I can see why she wasn't sure if it would be good for me to see him, but I can tell that him being in my life is going to be good." Ella couldn't help the smile that was finding its way onto her face and she could feel the blush tagging along with it.

"What did you guys talk about?"

"I asked him to tell me about the robbery and I asked him what had happed between the two of us."

"What did he say about the two of you?"

"Not really a whole lot, actually. Nothing too specific. He basically said that for the ten days leading up to the robbery, we had met and fell in love." What she didn't tell Kalli was that she got more information from the way he said the words than from the words themselves. The way his words made her feel was even more powerful than just the content.

"He's in love with you?"

"Apparently," Ella said as she shrugged her shoulders.

"This all seems a little weird, Ella. Some guy shows up in your store and tells you that he loves you, but you don't remember him at all? Isn't that a little suspicious?"

Ella couldn't disagree with her. It was weird. But nothing about her life right now was normal. Ella rubbed her hand up and down Kalli's arm.

"Everything is going to be ok. I know he's here for a reason and I intend find out what all of this means, if anything."

"You're going to see him again?"

"We're going to The Saturday Market tomorrow."

"Well, at least it's out in public. Do you want me to go with you?"

"No. I want to spend some time with him alone and see what he has to say." She also wanted to be alone with him to focus on the way her body seemed to be connected to his. She needed space away from everything to just let him be with her.

Chapter Four

Porter

Last night was the first in weeks that didn't haunt Porter. When he walked into his house, he was no longer accosted by images of Ella that made it difficult for him to breathe. She was still everywhere, but instead of gripping his heart and weighing him down, the memories made him smile as he remembered her in his kitchen wearing his clothes, or leaning up against his wall, dressed in lace, waiting to be ravaged. He went to sleep in his bed, wasn't tortured by her scent, or the emptiness of the bed. He was comforted by the way he could still feel her hugging him from only hours earlier.

His meeting with Ella couldn't really have gone any better and he was sorry he hadn't taken the initiative to do it sooner. He told her most of everything there was to tell and she hadn't called him crazy or run away from him, but seemed to understand him. He felt like she was waiting for him to find her.

His drive to Portland the next day to meet her was vastly different than the day before. He was no longer nervous for what the future held, but hopeful and excited. Something about the way Ella had embraced him yesterday made him feel like there was still something between them, even if she didn't remember the all-consuming love they had experienced together.

He parked his truck and walked along the waterfront when he saw her leaning against the railing looking out over the river. Her hair was down and every few seconds it fluttered in the breeze coming off the water. The June sun was illuminating her golden hair and radiating off the cream-colored skin of her shoulders. She wore a purple tank top with khaki shorts and he felt a tug in his stomach at all the bare skin she was showing. She hadn't seen him yet and he enjoyed taking a few extra seconds to admire her.

"Hello, Ella," he greeted her once he'd felt like he'd gotten a good enough look at her.

"Porter," she said as she looked up at him, holding one hand up to shield her eyes from the mid-morning sun. "I'm so glad you could make it. I've wanted to peruse The Saturday Market for a few weeks now and it's always more fun with someone else."

"I've never been."

"Really? Well, you're in for a treat, so long as you aren't put off by the acquired taste of the Portland Hipster. They seem to run rampant in these parts," she said with a smile.

"I think I can manage," he smiled back.

The Saturday Market was a permanent fixture on the waterfront of Portland and hundreds of people came out every weekend to spend an afternoon browsing. Vendors of every craft imaginable came every weekend to set up their booths and sell their goods. You could find street performers, food trucks, psychics, palm readers, and the ever-present hipster. Porter stuck close to Ella, stopping with her when she paused to admire handmade clothes and frilly things she would like to decorate her house. A few times she spoke to the vendor about their products and offered a card, telling them to come and see her. He was proud to see her networking confidently. In their ten days together, he never really got to see her in her element and it was very attractive. And he was pleased when she would stop with him to take a look at pieces of woodwork that caught his eye.

"Oh, do you mind if we stop here?" Ella asked him, motioning towards a particular jewelry booth. He smiled at her and motioned with his hand that he would follow her. "I really am a sucker for jewelry, especially stuff that isn't really typical or mainstream. All this handmade stuff is so fun to look at." She fingered through trays and trays of rings, all laid out with no real order. "Oh wow," she said with raspy voice, holding up a single ring.

"Find one you like?" Porter asked.

"This is perfect," she said quietly with awe and she tried to put the ring on the middle finger of her right hand. "Damn, it's too small."

Porter caught the eye of the vendor who ran the booth and waved his hand at him. The vendor approached with a smile.

"Hi, can I help you with something?"

"Yeah, do you happen to have this same ring, only a little bigger?" Porter asked, showing him the ring.

"Let me check," the vendor replied. Porter took a second to look at the ring. It was silver, and there was hardly anything to it. It was an arrow that wrapped around, but never met in the middle, and actually overlapped a little creating a sort of coil around the finger.

"Isn't it beautiful?" Ella asked him. He met her eyes and smiled, but didn't answer because he didn't really have any thoughts on it. It was a ring. "The arrow makes me think of going in one direction. Kind of like, forcing your way through everything that stands in your way, and heading in the direction you were meant to, regardless of anything that poses an obstacle. Most importantly, going in the direction *you* want to, and not letting anyone else shoot your arrow for you."

Watching her eyes light up, giving the ring more meaning then even the artist could have probably intended when he made it, made Porter's heart swell for her even more.

"It suits you," he said softly.

"Here we go," the vendor said as he returned. "Try this one on." Ella slipped it on her finger, gliding it all the way down.

"Oh, it fits!" She smiled happily and she started reaching into her purse.

"I've got it, Ella," Porter said as he pulled his wallet out of his back pocket.

"We've got a matching men's ring," the vendor said with a smirk, his eyes darting between the two of them. Ella laughed nervously and Porter shook his head.

"We'll just take hers today. Thanks for looking for this one for her."

"Porter, you don't have to buy it for me," she said placing her hand on his arm.

"I know. I want to. You should have seen your face when you described it to me. That ring was made for you and I want to give it to you."

"Thank you," she said, blushing slightly.

"Are you ready for lunch? Dodging all these hipsters is making me hungry." Ella laughed and he was immediately reminded of the gulf that was still between them. Her laugh, something that he had taken for granted, shot through him. He would do anything to hear her laugh every day for the rest of forever. He only hoped that being here with her was helping get closer to getting them back to the spot where her laugh was a constant in his life.

They sat on a bench near the river, dining on food truck cuisine, which tasted way better than it sounded.

"So, Porter, you know what I do for a living. Tell me, what is it that you do?"

"I'm a contractor. I mainly do residential work, building houses, remodeling jobs, stuff like that."

"Sounds tiring," Ella said as she bit into her gyro.

"Well, it's more paperwork then you'd imagine. Plus, I own my company, so a lot of the time I'm in more of a supervisory role. But there are certainly days when I come home worn out and sore."

Ella looked at him with squinty eyes. "We've had this conversation before, haven't we?"

"What conversation?"

"The 'what do you do' conversation."

"Yeah, I guess we have. Why?"

"This must be really boring for you, hearing things about me you've already heard, and I am just pleasantly enjoying our conversation completely clueless."

"We spoke about a lot of things before your accident, but we by no means covered everything. I don't mind repeating myself and I could never tire of hearing anything about you. Don't put too much pressure on yourself and try not to think about stuff like that. I just want to get to know you again."

"Tell me something you never told me before," she asked with a smile.

"Ok, well, I don't usually tell people this because it makes people angry. But, I don't like dogs."

"You don't like dogs?"

"Nope, never have."

"That's really weird. Who doesn't like dogs?"

"I don't *hate* dogs, I just don't want one as a pet."

Ella starting laughing. "Why not?"

"They are really high maintenance. I feel like a pet should blend into the background. I shouldn't have to rearrange my day to take care of a pet. Dogs take a lot of work and I just wouldn't ever commit to one."

"Interesting," Ella said once she finished laughing.

"Tell me something about yourself you wouldn't want to tell anyone," Porter said, liking the way their conversation was going. Ella brought a finger to her chin in contemplation.

"Ok, but this is going to make me sound really bitchy."

"Well, I definitely didn't sound like a prince with my dog-hate speech," he replied with a smile.

"True," she said. "But promise you won't hold it against me."

"Promise."

"Ok, well, I sometimes lack the ability or even the inclination to sympathize with people." She scrunched up her brow, looking nervous to be revealing this unattractive trait.

"What exactly does that mean?"

"Basically, when people are complaining, mostly people I don't know, I have a tendency to think they are just whiney and I get irritated by them easily. Like, I feel people should just shut up and move on." She dropped her face into her hands. "I'm the worst person on the planet."

"It's ok. That's how I feel when people talk about their dogs," Porter said, hoping to get a smile. She did smile, but she also smacked him on his arm.

"That's not funny."

"So you don't tolerate whiners. There are worse things you could have said."

"I guess that's true." They were quiet for a few minutes while they finished their meals.

"Can I ask you something? You might not like the question," Porter asked.

"Sure."

"What do you know about your break-up with Kyle?"

"Ah, Kyle," Ella tucked her hair behind her ear and took in a deep breath. "I've been told that on my birthday I came home from work and found him with someone else." She started fidgeting with the hem of her shirt and was looking down at her hands as they worried the fabric. "My mom said that we broke up on the spot, that he packed a bag and left that evening. She also told me that he came and went picking up his stuff. By the time the store was robbed he was completely moved out, but that we had a fight that night."

Porter watched her as she said the words, wondering what, if anything, he should tell her about the situation.

"I guess he wasn't too happy that I wouldn't give him another chance and he came over to try and convince me that we should be together," she took a breath in and let it back out. "Kyle was never a violent guy, so I don't understand why he would put his hands on me. I almost don't believe it happened. It's all third-hand information. I don't remember it and no one has seen Kyle since I was in the hospital." Ella looked back up at Porter, and he saw that her eyes were thoughtful and a little confused.

"It happened. I heard your voice when you called me. You were terrified."

Ella stood up and took a few steps away from the bench.

"I don't understand why my parents and Megan would go to such lengths to tell me a story that is so completely different than the truth. It just confuses me even more."

"I'm sorry," he said as he went to stand in front of her, wanting to look her in the eyes. "I don't want to undermine your parents; it seems to me they were just trying to do what was best for you."

"I know," she whispered. "I just wish I could remember." Porter took a step closer to her and placed his hand on her cheek, urging her to look up at him.

"Your confusion might go away if your memory comes back, but a lot of other stuff comes with it. Do you want to remember the robbery? Do you want to remember walking in on Kyle? Maybe there's a reason your mind is choosing to block all of that out."

Ella's hand came up to rest on top of Porter's.

"What about my memory of you? This isn't fair to *you*." Porter's other hand came up to frame Ella's face and he pulled her closer, their faces only inches apart.

"Don't worry about me, Ella. I can make you love me again; I'm not worried about that. Do I wish that I could hold you right now? Do I wish I could kiss you? Yes, damn it, I do. But there's time for that. Right now I just want you to get to know me and trust that no matter what, I will always be here for you." He looked into her eyes, hoping that she was not only hearing what he was saying, but feeling it as well. Her hands came up to rest on his chest, pulling gently on his shirt.

"You can kiss me if you want to," she breathed. Porter's heart raced in his chest and he dreaded the words he knew he had to say to her.

"I'm not sure that's a good idea, Ella. As wonderful as it would feel to put your lips on mine, taking them away might kill me. The next time I kiss you, I want to be able to do it for hours. To make up for the weeks of kisses I've missed. I just don't think we're there yet."

Ella dropped her forehead to lean against his chest, rested on him for a few seconds, and then stepped away from him, and turned back towards the market.

"Please don't be angry with me," he said to her back.

"I'm not angry, Porter. I'm disappointed and irritated. I'm tired of everyone making decisions for me. I'm tired of being treated like I'm sick and need protecting. Tell me, how long did you wait to kiss me the first time we met? Were you playing the chivalrous gentleman then, Porter? Because the last time I checked, you said we fell in love in a week. Was there no kissing? Did we sit on opposite sides of the couch? I'm not a baby and I don't appreciate being treated like one." She finished and he couldn't help but smile at her, reminded of her firecracker tendencies. "What the hell is so funny, Porter?"

"Nothing. I was just remembering that you, actually, kissed me first."

She tried to hide the shock on her face, but recovered quickly.

"Well, don't hold your breath for that to happen again."

Porter took a few pointed steps towards her, never removing his eyes from hers.

"Don't worry, you'll get your kiss," he said playfully. "In all honesty Ella, I just don't want to mess this up. I've already lost you once. I really couldn't live through losing you again." He watched a smile try to play on her lips, but she fought it.

"I'm not broken, Porter. Please don't treat me any differently than you would any other woman you'd take on a date."

"You think this is a date?" He asked with a smile and he was thankful when she smiled back.

"Well, we had a meal, and you bought me a gift. That's pretty datey." He reached down and linked his hand with hers. They started walking back the way they had come from.

"Ok then. It's a date. And for the record, we have had this conversation before."

"When?"

"The second day we knew each other. We went out for a drink and you told me that you wanted to go on a real date with me."

"It sounds like I was pretty aggressive. I don't usually kiss the guy first or ask them out. You must have really intrigued me," she shot him her brilliant smile.

"I think we were both drawn to each other equally," he said carefully, trying really hard not to allude to the fact that he remembered them being irrevocably tied to each other, both emotionally and physically.

"That's probably the most unflattering thing I've ever heard someone say about me," she laughed. "Really? 'Equally drawn to each other'? Let's hear it, Porter. Tell me the dark and dirty details about our weeklong tryst." He stopped walking and pulled on her hand so that she fell into his body. He leaned down and placed his mouth on the shell of her ear.

"First of all, it wasn't a tryst. Every moment we spent together was us building something we wanted to last a lifetime. Secondly, there was plenty of mutual gratification. We couldn't get enough of each other and when our week together was over, it killed us both to let each other go. For the record, I know your body better than I've ever known anyone's and you were pretty fucking familiar with mine. So, don't think for a minute that I don't want you because every moment that I'm not touching you is torture." He pulled away from her and saw a shocked look on her face. She cleared her throat and he saw the blush creep over her face.

"You've got some mouth on you, Porter."

"We've had that conversation, too."

"Oh shut up," she said with a smile as he led her back to the market.

Once she had gotten her fill of the market, Porter walked Ella to her car, dreading the fact that he was going to be apart from her. He gave her hand a small squeeze and tried to focus on the fact that since he'd first laced his fingers with hers, neither one of them had broken their connection. Just holding her hand would have to be enough to tide him over for a while.

"So, now that our first, but not really first, date is out of the way, am I going to be able to see you again?" Ella asked as they approached her car. She sounded shy and he felt a smile pull at his lips. They stopped and faced each other on the sidewalk.

"Of course. Do you still have the same phone number?"

"I do."

Porter pulled out his cell phone and sent a text to her number he saved in his phone. The same number he'd looked at countless times willing himself to be strong and not contact her. His smile grew thinking about the fact that they were here, together, exchanging phone numbers again.

"There. Now you've got my number, don't be afraid to use it."

"I won't be," she said. He was a little surprised when she leaned towards him and lifted up to put her arms around his neck. He immediately wrapped his arms around her waist and let his face rest in the crook of her neck, breathing in her scent again. When he felt her pull away, he tried not to groan out loud; he wanted to hold her forever. "Thank you for the beautiful ring, Porter. I love it."

"I'm glad. I had a really good afternoon with you, Ella. I hope I didn't scare you away with everything I told you. I've never really been very good at filtering my mouth. I usually just say whatever I'm thinking."

"Honesty is exactly what I need right now so, no, you didn't scare me away."

"Good, well, I'll let you get back to the rest of your day." He took a step back from her and before he turned away he gave her wink. He was rewarded with her radiant smile and a laugh. She shook her head and got into her car. He idly wondered if there were still jumper cables in her trunk with a big red bow on them, and how they would have been explained to the woman who wouldn't remember receiving them. He shook his head at the thought, because it simply didn't matter.

Ella

Ella decided to stop by Poppy after she left Porter and his devastatingly handsome face. He had held her hand most of the afternoon, and it made her feel young and giddy. His hands were large and rough from his work, she imagined. The feeling of his callouses scratching along her hand made her skin prickle more than once. Had his hands been all over her body? He had painted a really hot picture of the two of them being together. What would it be like to let his hands roam wherever they wanted? She shook her head and smiled because she knew what it would be like: amazing.

She was fairly certain that even if they didn't have this unusual history, she would still be terribly drawn to him and she would probably make a fool of herself falling for him. She caught a glimpse of herself in the rearview mirror and saw the smile plastered all over her face. She liked the way she looked when she was happy. She hadn't seen a smile on her face a whole lot lately.

As she strolled into Poppy, she noticed that Megan was behind the counter and she was talking to Kalli. As she approached she noticed Megan's eyes glance up at her, and then she did a double take and her mouth fell open. She closed it quickly with a loud snap.

"Oh, shit," Megan said.

"What?" Kalli asked, looking between the two of them.

"Yeah, what?" Ella was confused.

"You were with him, weren't you?" Megan said accusatorily.

"What?" Ella was confused by her tone and her question. "Who?"

Megan came around the counter and came towards Ella until she was standing right in front of her.

"You know who, Ella."

Ella looked between her sister and her friend and decided it was dumb to be hiding Porter from them. She was an adult and she had every right to see whomever she wanted.

"Are you talking about Porter?" Ella asked icily. Megan's eyes shot up at the use of his name.

"Damnit. He promised me he wouldn't tell you who he was."

"I knew who he was." Shock moved across Megan's face like lightening.

"What do you mean you knew who he was? You remember him?"

"Yes, I remember him from the hospital, after I woke up. He was there for just a minute, but I remember him. But nothing from before the accident."

"What did he tell you?"

"Everything. But you can't be mad at him. He's just doing what he feels is right. Just like you. I'm tired of everyone tiptoeing around me. I can handle it, Megan. Trust me. Porter will be good for me." Megan's eyes lingered on Ella's for a few seconds as she seemed to mull over what she had said.

"Listen, as your sister I just want to say this: Porter is very hot. And I am sure he is equally charming and sweet. But just because he shows up here and tells you that you used to be in love with him, it doesn't mean you are obligated to him."

"Obligated? Megan," Ella let out an exasperated sigh. "Where is this coming from? Why are you so against him? I have said hardly anything about him and you're already rooting against him? Why?"

"You've been through so much, Ella. We're all worried about you. I just don't want something bad to happen to you again."

"So I'm not allowed to date?"

"Ella, the last time you dated Porter, it was like warp-speed dating. You guys went from zero to fucking in like, a matter of hours." Ella's eyebrows shot up.

"That doesn't sound too terrible," Kalli said, smiling at Ella.

"Wait, really?" Ella was intrigued.

"Yes, really. I mean, it was really like two days, but come on. You had never acted so irrationally before."

"But was I happy? He tells me I was happy."

"Deliriously so," Megan exhaled loudly.

"How much did I tell you about him?"

"Enough to know that he rocked your world, in and out of the bedroom. And I know that he really fought for you when you weren't sure you should continue to see him."

"Why didn't I want to see him?"

"It wasn't that you didn't want to see him, you just were afraid that the distance would be an issue."

"It seems that my brain is actually the issue now," Ella said dejectedly.

"Honey, don't worry about your memory. It's out of your hands, and stressing about it won't help any," Kalli said as she rubbed circles on Ella's back affectionately.

"Porter would never let anything stand in his way, now that he's made himself known. I'm surprised you're upright right now."

Ella laughed at her outrageous sister.

"Meaning?"

"That you should be horizontal and totally satisfied."

"I am not going to pretend to disagree with you. I told him that he could kiss me and he told me that he wouldn't kiss me until we were ready. It all seems a little backwards."

"Do you want him to kiss you?" Kalli asked.

"That seems like a ridiculously rhetorical question. Of course I want him to kiss me. Once you see him, Kalli, you'll understand."

"Just checking. I wasn't sure if you were still having all the same tingly feelings for him this time around that you did last time," Megan said, shrugging her shoulders.

"There are definite tingles."

"Well," Megan said, sounding resigned. "What's next in the Ella and Porter saga?"

"We are not a saga," Ella said as she rolled her eyes at her sister.

"Oh, yes. You are."

"Well, we exchanged phone numbers and we are going to talk. We'll see how things go, what happens next."

"I foresee lots of time on your back, Ella."

"Shut up, Megan," Ella said smiling. "You're just jealous."

"Oh no, Porter's got nothing on my Patrick."

"I'm feeling terribly left out here, guys." Kalli said with a frown.

"Listen," Megan said as she pointed a finger at Kalli. "I refuse to feel one iota of sorry for you since you work, every day, with that hot actor. You get to take his shirts off and measure him, and generally just be near him. So zip it." Kalli cocked her head to the side and thought about what Megan said. A grin slid across her face slowly.

"You know what? You're right. My job is awesome. I know his inseam."

"You are both ridiculous. I'm going home," Ella said with a smile.

That evening Ella heard her phone ping and saw a text message from Porter.

I hope you had a good rest of your evening. And I hope I'm not being too forward texting you so soon after our second first date.

Ella grinned at her phone and sent him a message back.

Not too forward at all. I was hoping to hear from you. Glad I don't have to wait the obligatory three days like girls usually have to. What are you up to?

Nothing really, working on my boat, drinking a beer. You know, man stuff.

Are you literally working "on" a boat, or like, fixing a boat?

Building a boat. You're damn cute.

Well, how the heck am I supposed to know? But you're pretty cute yourself.

Glad that bump to your head didn't mess up your taste in men.

Ha. Ha.

So, when can I see you again?

Do you want the reserved girl answer? Or the real answer?

How about you give me both and I will see which one I like better?

Reserved girl: I am not sure, I'm pretty busy with work these days. Maybe call me next week sometime and I'll see what works.

Bullshit. Next.

Ella took a deep breath in and exhaled loudly. Mustering all the courage she could, she typed out her real answer.

Real Answer: As soon as possible because I cannot stop thinking about you or your lips that you refused to use on me.

Shit, Ella. I'm two hours away and you send me that? That's cruel. And so hot.

You did this to yourself.

I'll take that. Can I see you next Saturday? Maybe we could go hiking? That could be fun.

I won't tell you that I just groaned because that's six whole days from now. I will just say "Sure! Sounds great!"

Sorry, but I really do have to work ;)

Me too. Well, I will tell you in my reserved voice that I will see you next weekend, but my real voice says don't be a stranger. I'm available for texting all week!

You're going to get tired of hearing from me.

I'm pretty sure that's not possible. Talk to you later, Porter.

Sweet dreams, Ella.

Chapter Five
Porter

Porter knocked on Ella's door right at nine am Saturday morning, as promised. He waited a minute and when she didn't come to the door he knocked again. Finally, her heard footsteps coming from inside her apartment and then the door opened. There stood Ella, hair falling crazily around her face with soft lines of sleep still fresh on her cheek, obviously just waking up. His eyes wandered down from her face and when he saw that she was wearing his tee-shirt; he couldn't help the strong and immediate possessive feelings that came over him.

He was immediately inundated with images of Ella in his room wearing that shirt after their first night together and then again the night before she left. That shirt went home with her to remind her of him and all this time she'd been wearing it not even knowing it was his or where it came from. He wasn't sure if he was comforted by the idea of her wearing his shirt unknowingly, or if it bothered him.

"I'm so sorry, Porter. I overslept. I promise I will be ready to go soon. Come on in." She looked down at herself and he saw when she realized she was just wearing a tee-shirt, as she pulled down on the hem trying to cover what she could.

"It's fine. I can wait in my car if you want."

"Don't be silly. Come in. I will be quick."

Porter walked into her apartment and looked around at her space. Even though he knew she had shared this apartment with Kyle, it was seeping with signs that Ella dwelled there. Poster sized prints of vintage Vogue covers adorned her living room walls. There was a mannequin used for clothing design in the corner with long strands of different colored pearls around the would-be neck. The entire apartment was decorated in shades of cream and pale pink. It was a drastic contrast to Porter's own decorating style, but it radiated 'Ella' and made him smile.

He heard the shower come on in her bathroom, and he tried to find something to occupy his thoughts so that his mind didn't wander to Ella in the shower with hot water cascading down her body.

Along the wall there were pictures hanging in varied heights and he took some time to peruse them. Most of them were pictures of Ella with her family, a lot of them taken many years ago. One picture featured Ella, looking to be under ten years old, holding a baby wrapped in a pink blanket. He assumed the baby was Megan. Ella had two blonde braids coming down the sides of her face, and her eyes were the same piercing blue he had come to rely on.

Another picture looked to be taken at a wedding and Ella was in a stunning black dress, smiling in the way that made his heart thump harder, only behind her, with his arms wrapped around her middle, was Kyle. They both looked spectacularly happy and the sight of her hands covering his, with their fingers linked, tore at his heart. He wasn't accustomed to feeling jealous. He knew this was an old picture that perhaps she just hadn't gotten around to removing from her wall, but it still bothered him that Kyle was in her apartment, while he was still trying to break back in to her heart.

He heard the shower turn off and got out of the hallway because the last thing he needed was to see Ella traipsing around her apartment wrapped in a towel. He had plenty of self-control, but wasn't a masochist.

He wandered back into her living room and sat on her plush cream colored couch with small pink pillows.

"I'm so sorry again, Porter. I will hurry," she called from the back of the apartment.

"Ella, really, it's no big deal. No rush. The trail will still be there no matter what time we leave. I packed us a lunch. I figured we would get hungry and I thought we could have a picnic." Porter smiled at the memory of the only other picnic they had together. His mind was flashing images of Ella straddling him under a sleeping bag on the beach.

"That sounds great. Thanks." Ella came down the hallway and he took in her appearance. She was wearing shorts again, this time some purple athletic shorts, with a black, form-fitting tank top. She had a towel wrapped like a twisty cone on top of her head, keeping her hair up. She sat down next to him on the couch to put on her shoes, her thigh brushing up against his, her closeness never far from his mind.

"I've never been on this trail before. I'm excited. Thank you for inviting me."

"You've never been to Multnomah Falls? It's one of the most popular tourist attractions within fifty miles of Portland. How can you call yourself a Portlander and not go there?"

"Hey, I never said I hadn't been there. I have been there many times, but I have never hiked the trail. When I was younger, I was always afraid to go to the top because of the old legend about the Native American couple who fell from the top. Then, when I was old enough to realize that I was being silly, I just never made it back. The falls are beautiful though."

"Well, it's not a really difficult hike, but the views are spectacular."

"Just let me dry my hair and we can go."

She walked back to the bathroom and he heard the buzzing of her blow-dryer. A few minutes later she appeared, fresh-faced and looked ready to go.

The June sun was out in full force and even though it was bright enough for sunglasses and sunblock, it was early enough that there was still a chilly bite in the air. They started their hike and were currently weaving through throngs of people, trying to make it past the popular viewing point that didn't require any real hiking, just a place for people to come and admire the majestic waterfall, and feel the cool mist of the water as it crashed onto the rocks below.

"That area down there," Ella said as she pointed towards where the water was pounding into a pool formed at the bottom, "it used to be open to the public. Megan and I would come here with my parents and we would swim down there. A few years ago, that big boulder there fell from the top. They closed off all the areas close to the falls to make sure, if anything like that happened again, no one would get hurt." A smile formed across her face. "I will always feel privileged that I got to swim in those waters; we got to explore this beautiful place before they had to close it down."

"Sounds like a great memory."

"It is. Tell me a memory from your childhood," she gave him one of her shy and simple smiles.

"Well, I guess my favorite memory would be the one time my dad took me deep-sea fishing when I was twelve. It was a birthday present to me and I had wanted to go out for years, but my mom always thought I was too young. She had irrational fears of me falling overboard and drowning. Finally, my dad convinced her that I was old enough and he signed us up to go out on one of those tours you see signs for along the highway in Lincoln City."

"I've always seen those signs! I've always wanted to go on the whale watching tours!" Her excitement was contagious.

"Well, maybe we'll go sometime," he said as he flashed her a bright smile. "I remember being on the boat for a while before they stopped and let us throw out our lines." Porter took a few moments to bring the memory to the front of his mind. Sometimes he had a hard time visualizing his father's face; it had been so long since he'd seen him. But this memory was so vivid, he closed his eyes for a moment to try and burn it into his mind forever.

"My dad was an avid fisherman, but deep sea was new even to him. I swear he was almost as excited as I was. I remember just sitting on the boat, in our cool anchored chairs, built to keep you onboard as you reeled in a fighting fish, and we talked about everything. He gave me advice about girls. He told me about his dad, whom I was never able to meet. We talked about sports, I mean, everything. He wasn't lecturing me and he wasn't trying to tell me what to do. We were simply talking.

"All of a sudden there was a pull on his pole and his line started zooming out of his reel. The men who owned the boat started shouting instructions at my dad to pull up hard and crank the turn. Pull and crank. Pull and crank. My dad went at it for about ten minutes and I was on the edge of my seat. The excitement was overwhelming. My dad looked over at me and said, 'Porter, get over here and reel this fish in'. I couldn't believe it, but he handed me the pole and I must have worked on that fish for twenty minutes. Pulling and cranking. The whole time my dad was behind me, pulling me back by my shoulders, giving me more strength to reel it in.

"When that fish finally got close enough to the boat for us to see it, my dad started hollering and clapping his hands. The owners handed him a giant net and eventually the fish was close enough for my dad to swoop down with the net and get it on board."

Porter looked over at Ella and realized he had been talking for a very long time, and she hadn't said a word.

"That is an amazing memory, Porter," she said softly.

"The fish ended up being a thirty-four inch tuna and it was a beast. My dad was so excited, and I remember him hugging me and telling me how proud he was of me – for a stupid fish. But looking back, I think he was talking about more than just the fish. I think he was proud of the man I was becoming and I hope he still is."

Porter felt Ella's hand slip into his and he laced their fingers together as he looked over at her.

"I'm sure your dad is very proud of the man you've become."

They continued up the winding path that zigzagged up the side of the mountain, passing people who were walking at a more leisurely pace, and also politely smiling at the hikers coming down from the top of the trail. All kinds of people were drawn to the beauty of the falls, teenagers out enjoying the sunny weather, older couples staying active, and even young families were hiking the trail. Porter watched as a few dads passed him carrying small children on their backs. He noticed how proud and doting some of the fathers seemed to be, making sure the babies still had sunhats on, or if they had fallen asleep on their father's backs, making sure they weren't in a position that would cause them pain when they woke up. He also noticed the way the mothers of these children looked at the fathers.

Obvious love. Not lust, not even infatuated love, but love simple and overt. The love he saw directed at those men who coveted their children was astounding, and for the first time he felt a little hollowness deep within him which he knew was the longing for a family.

He knew it wasn't an accident or coincidence that these feeling would transpire as he was holding Ella's hand. It was only a matter of time before he started thinking about their future, hoping she was onboard for everything he hoped they would experience together.

The image of Ella's belly round and full with his child suddenly grasped his heart and he knew that someday he wanted exactly that.

About thirty minutes later, they made their way close to the top. Of course, on such a beautiful Oregon day, there were a lot of people who had come to hike the falls and it had become a bit crowded near the viewpoint that looked out over the edge of the falls.

"Let's take our picnic and follow the water back a bit. We can find a spot not so crowded and wait until everyone leaves for lunch."

"Sounds great. Lead the way," Ella said.

Making sure not to let go of her hand, he led her off the trail and back along one of the smaller creeks that bled into the massive waterfall. There was a thick canopy of trees, which Oregon was notoriously not short on, and the sunlight was being cast through the spaces between branches and leaves. Small rays of golden sun were illuminating their path and the sound of the trickling water was ethereal. They were probably about a quarter mile off the main trail when he found a small area on the edge of the water with two big and flat rocks that would be perfect to sit on.

"This looks good here," he said looking towards her.

"Perfect."

Porter took his backpack off and started unloading. He handed Ella the blanket which she spread out over the rocks and they took a seat. As he unloaded their lunch he saw her looking around, taking in their surroundings.

"It's so beautiful here. You know, I've always heard you're not supposed to go off the trails. Every year lots of hikers get lost around here and all you hear from rescuers is to stay on the trails." She gave him a look that said 'this is dangerous, but I kind of like it'.

"Don't worry, Ella. All we did was follow this creek. We just follow it right back to the trail. I wouldn't let anything happen to you. Although, I can think of worse things than being lost out here with you." She turned her head slightly and looked at him from the corner of her eye.

"Me too."

As they ate, they talked about their week. Ella told him about the actress from a Hollywood movie coming into her store with Kalli for a fitting, which she described as 'the most exciting moment of her life, ever.' He told her about his work on his latest project of a house rebuild on the beach and about the progress he'd made on his boat over the course of the week. He did not mention that he used working on his boat to keep himself from going insane with thoughts of her, and to keep him from driving to Portland every night to see her and finally make her his again. She didn't need to hear that.

"So," Ella began when they'd finished their meal. "Tell me about us, Porter." Taken a little off guard, Porter cleared his throat and took a drink from his water bottle.

"What do you mean?"

"Well, you've alluded to the fact that we were, um, well, intimate, with each other," she said and even though he wasn't looking at her, he knew she was blushing.

"That's correct."

"Well, I mean, I guess I'm just wondering, what it was like."

"Can you be more specific?" He became uncomfortable, not really sure what kind of information she was looking for.

"Ok, well, the first time was, obviously, really soon after we met, right? Was it like, a one night stand?"

"No." He responded immediately and unequivocally.

"Were we a couple by then? Already?"

"No," he said less surely.

"Throw me something here, Porter. You are very handsome and terribly charming, but I am still trying to wrap my mind around how I came to sleep with you thirty-six hours after I met you." Porter took a pause to formulate the best response he could come up with.

"I'm not going to downplay the highly unusual circumstances that brought you and me together. You were a broken-hearted beauty who needed someone to help you that night. And I might have stepped into some sort of hero role, unintentionally. I can't miscount the beach and the effect being somewhere as romantic as the ocean can have on two people. So, yes, we were both acting, perhaps, a little out of character, being influenced by the situation we found ourselves in. But the fire with which we consumed each other was neither pretend, nor was it the product of our surrounding circumstances. We wanted each other. No, we needed each other that night."

Porter was looking at the water, so he couldn't see the look on her face as he said those words, but he heard her sharp and ragged intake of breath.

"Porter," she whispered. He looked over at her. "How can you say those words to me? How can you think those thoughts, and tell me these words, and be so far away."

"I'm right here, Ella. I'm never far away." What happened

next should have been in slow motion and nearly felt like it was. Ella leaned towards him, turning slightly so that she was facing him, and with her hand wrapped around the back of his neck she pulled his face towards hers until their lips met. Porter's face contorted, almost as if he were in pain, and in some ways, he was. Kissing Ella would undoubtedly cause him immense pleasure, but bring him more pain as well. For now, unless she remembered him and how much they loved each other, he was kissing someone else. All these thoughts were infiltrating his head: doubt, worry, fear, apprehension. He felt her lips on his, but couldn't give in to her. It wasn't fair to either one of them. She felt his reluctance and pulled away, but only far enough to breathe words into his mouth.

"How was my need for you then different from now, Porter? What is the difference? Do I need to be more broken than I am right now? I feel pretty damned broken right now, Porter. You are supposed to love me, but so far, I only feel slightly rejected and majorly pissed off."

"You think that when I kissed you before it was because you were broken? I'm not looking to clean up after anyone, Babe," he said with harshness. "When I kiss you, I want to know it's because you feel something for me. Not because you THINK you're supposed to be kissing me."

"What the hell do you think I'm trying to do here?! You think I don't want you? You think this isn't confusing as hell for me, either? I've been trying to tell myself all along not to get involved with you just because I supposedly had before. Well, fuck that, Porter. What if every time I see you my heart beats faster? What if every time you're close to me I want you to be closer? What if every time you hold my hand I imagine your hand on my body in a million different places?"

Porter's breath quickly rushed in and out, their eyes still trained right on one another's.

"If this happens, Ella, it happens one hundred percent. I will not settle for anything less than every single part of you. No more hiding from anyone and no more going entire weeks without being together. I want you and I will have you. That's what kissing me means right now." His words floated through the air and landed right on Ella's lips. He waited an eternity for her to respond. When she finally moved, it was to pull him back in. She paused right before their lips met again, and with closed eyes whispered, "I'm yours if you're mine."

"You're mine," he growled and crashed his mouth into hers.

The electricity and thunderous exchange between Porter and Ella was in complete contrast to the serene and peaceful surrounding they were currently in. The fire raging between them threatened to burn the forest down.

His hands found the familiar groove that fits his hands perfectly, behind her ears, as he framed her face, pulling her in closer. He brought her over to him, and she climbed atop him, straddling his legs, her own hands finding his face as well.

Their kiss was frantic at first, almost angry. Both of their need and desire coming through and burning on their mouths. He tugged on her bottom lip, and she dug her nails into his shoulders. Tongues stabbing, drilling into each other. Each of them fought the other, trying to prove with their mouth that they, in fact, had the most feeling invested in this kiss.

Porter pulled away first, not wanting to kiss her in anger anymore. This wasn't the first kiss he had wanted with her, but he was thankful for the contact regardless.

"Why are you so mad?" He asked, trying to catch his breath.

"I'm angry that I missed out on what we were. I can feel how much you loved me and I am mad that I can't remember the most epic love of my life."

"Now who's far away?" A slight smile played across his lips.

"What do you mean?"

"Well," he said as he tucked a stray hair behind her ear and flicked his nose against hers. "Here we are again. What we had before, although it was, up until now, the best ten days of my life, was exactly that. Ten days. I can give you ten more days. I can give you ten years. I want to give you a lifetime, Ella. Don't let something we can't control affect what's between us."

"Why are you mad?" She asked after a long pause.

"I'm mad because you won't let me kiss you the way I want to."

"How do you want to kiss me, Porter?"

"Like this." He quickly maneuvered her so that she was laying on the blanket covered rock. He laid her down softly, covered her body with his, and wrapped his hands around her wrists, pinning them above her head. He ran his nose from the crook of her neck, all the way up to her earlobe, breathing her in.

"Vanilla," he whispered. She quietly moaned at the vibration his voice made on her neck. He took her earlobe in his mouth, tugging and pulling on it with his teeth. When he finally made his way to her lips, his kiss was feather soft and left love dusted all over her mouth. He started the kiss simply and slowly, lightly rubbing his mouth over hers, not a kiss really, but a marking. This was his mouth now. It became an actual kiss when he used his tongue to tease the seam of her lips and when she opened for him it was with complete surrender. He felt her giving in to him, letting him take her wherever he was going, trusting him to tell her the story of their love with his lips.

Suddenly his tongue filled her mouth, and the urgency with which her tongue slid against his made him move his hands from her wrists and slide down her arms and come to her face again. They breathed rapidly, their heartbeats thundering through their veins, keeping rhythm to their lips dancing.

Porter waited weeks to feel Ella's skin beneath his hands, to be able to put his lips to hers, and in this moment, he couldn't be happier. As her legs fell open, it allowed his body to get even closer to hers and he fit snuggly in between her knees, just like he remembered.

His hands came down from her face and while one hand twined its fingers with hers, the other was trailing down her shirt, between her breasts.

She arched her back and pressed herself into his hands, asking to be touched. He moved his lips from hers down to her neck.

"Ella, I've waited so long to hold you like this," he mumbled into her neck. His hand played with the hem of her shirt and as his fingers slid just under the fabric, teasing the part of her stomach above her shorts; he heard her whimper. "You sound just as eager as me." He moved his lips along her neck, trying to taste every part of her exposed skin.

"I haven't been touched like this in so long, Porter. Please don't stop."

For just an instant Porter halted, knowing that Ella was talking about Kyle. Of course she didn't remember when they'd had their hands all over each other eight weeks ago. It only took a moment for the thought to pass, as he resumed trailing his tongue along her collarbone.

"Tell me what you want me to do," he growled. "Tell me how you want me to touch you."

Ella

Ella pulled back to look at Porter. She had never had someone be so bold and upfront with her while kissing. He wanted her to tell him where to touch her? What in the world for? Every other time she'd been with a man, especially Kyle, they pretty much already had a road map that had very few pit stops before they reached their final destination. But, here Porter was, turning her on in such a way that she had never imagined, and he was asking her what she wanted? She thought she might as well give it a try.

"I want you to touch my breasts, Porter."

He grinned at her and slid his hand slowly up her stomach, watching her as he did. She knew he was waiting for a reaction, and because she was stubborn, she held out as long as she could. She didn't flinch when his fingers grazed the edge of her bra and she tried not to make a noise as his rough hand slid over the cotton of her sports bra. When he pulled the cup down exposing her breast she tried to stifle the gasp that left her, but she lost the battle when his thumb gently rubbed over her nipple. A long and loud moan escaped from her mouth. Then her eyes betrayed her by rolling into the back of her head and closing, trying to absorb all the sensations this one hand was giving her.

"Is this what you wanted?" He asked her with a smug smirk.

"Yes," was her immediate and involuntary answer.

"I've been waiting to see you beneath me like this, to feel you in my hands. You feel damn good, Ella."

"Now, I want you to kiss me again." He smiled at her.

"Anytime, Baby." His lips came down on hers gently, and the combination of his swirling tongue and his fingers rubbing and pulling on her breast was explosive. She wrapped a leg around his waist, pulling him in closer, feeling him between her legs and wanting as much friction as she could manage.

As if he could read her mind he thrust gently against her, the fabric of his shorts doing nothing to hide his arousal, which had her moaning again at the pressure.

Ella took her hands out of Porter's hair and ran them up along his forearms and biceps. As her hands ran along the muscles that wrapped around his shoulders and bulged in the sexiest way, she whimpered again. Porter pulled away and laughed.

"What's so funny?" She asked, out of breath.

"You and your fascination with my arms." She looked at him with a puzzled expression.

"We've talked about your arms?"

"Yes. Extensively."

She smiled, mainly because this might have been the first thing he revealed about their time together that she could completely understand him knowing. Obviously if they were intimate, there was no way she could be with him and not comment on his arms. They were her weakness. She still blushed a little.

"I like arms," she said shyly.

"Yes, and I like that you like my arms." He bent down and placed a chaste, swift kiss on her lips, quickly righted her sports bra, and lifted off her.

"Where are you going?" She demanded.

"Well, I'm going to take you to see the falls? Why?"

"What if I wasn't done here?"

He smirked again and she could tell she was feeding his ego.

"Babe, there is nothing I would like more than to continue this…exploration…but I will not have our second first time be on a big rock by a creek." Ella looked around and the expanse of trees and shrubbery.

"Are you afraid the birds will watch?"

"No," he said as he grasped her hands and hauled her up so she was pulled against his body. "I'm simply biding my time. When we are finally together again, it's going to be an all-night affair. Not a quickie in the forest," he said, flicking his nose against her again. She couldn't find reason to argue with his logic, so she just grabbed his hair and pulled him in for another simmering kiss, if only to make him regret ending their tryst in the forest too soon. She pulled away right when she felt him lose his control a little. Smiling, she said, "Let's go check out those falls!" She heard him groan and then yelped when he smacked her ass.

They picked up the remains of their picnic and started back towards the falls. Porter held her hand again, which only made her smile widely as they carefully stepped over rocks and fallen tree branches.

Suddenly her vision blurred slightly and she stumbled, luckily falling right into Porter, who caught her.

"Whoa, you ok?" He brought her face up to his and looked her in the eye.

"Yes, I think so," she said as she blinked a few times to try and clear the cobwebs that seemed to be in her vision. "I just need a minute."

"Ok, here, sit on this log," he moved her slowly so she was positioned above the log. "Sit," he ordered. She obeyed. She closed her eyes and dropped her chin down to her chest, breathing steadily as she tried to relax. When she opened her eyes, everything was clear again.

"That's better. That was really weird," she said looking up at Porter who had concern etched across his face with worry lines creasing his forehead.

"Are you sure you're ok?"

"I feel fine; my vision was just blurry for a moment. I'm ok now." She stood up and took his hand again. "Come on, let's go look out from the view point." She tugged on his hand and he reluctantly followed her.

"Ok, but if you start to feel badly, we're leaving."

"Ok, deal."

His plan had worked and by the time they made it to the lookout the crowd had thinned to just a few tourists, making the viewpoint much more enjoyable. Ella stepped up to the railing and gasped at the view.

They were hundreds of feet up the bluff and the viewpoint was, quite literally, hanging off the edge of a cliff, giving Ella the illusion of being dangled over the edge. Looking out farther, she could see from both sides of her trees lining her vision until they gapped and then opened up into the gorge of the Columbia River.

Ella has always known she lived in a beautiful place, but views like this cemented in her mind that Oregon rivaled other famous cities for its gorgeous landscapes. She felt lucky that she could drive for thirty minutes and see this breathtaking view anytime she wanted. The view was only enhanced when she felt strong and warm arms cage her in as Porter came from behind and placed his hands on the railing next to hers.

"Thanks for bringing me here, Porter. This is beautiful."

"Mmmmm," was all he said as he nuzzled his nose into her neck, sending shivers all over her body. She leaned back into him, letting him take her weight, enjoying the feeling of being so close to him.

"How many women have you taken up here?" She smiled as she asked, not really expecting a serious answer. He lived more than two hours from here and she knew it wouldn't be a popular date destination for him.

"I've only ever been here by myself, and only a few times. Before you came along I never really dated anyone. Not more than one or two dates anyway." She turned her head to look at him.

"Why not? You seem like a hot commodity." She smiled at him, but he didn't seem entertained. He shrugged his shoulders.

"I don't know," he said, finally meeting her eyes. "I guess I was waiting for you." She swallowed the lump in her throat and tried to maintain a regular breathing pattern, even though her heart was racing and electricity was coursing through her.

"So, then, the wait is over?" She asked shyly. He reached a hand up and ran the back of his fingers over her cheek.

"Babe, it was over for me the day you walked into my life. There will never be anyone but you." She turned in his arms and her hands found their way to the back of his neck as she pulled herself up to kiss him. She loved how his silky brown hair slid between her fingers as she ran her hands through the strands at the nape of his neck. His hands gripped her hips and dug into her skin and she was a little surprised that his roughness only heightened her need for him.

Suddenly, like lightening had cracked in her skull, blinding pain shot through her head right behind her eyes. She pulled away from Porter, covering her eyes with her hands, drawing in deep breaths through her teeth.

"What is going on, Ella?" He asked, gripping her by her shoulders. The pain in her head eased a bit to a throbbing ache.

"I don't know. I just got a terrible headache. Like, there's a rock concert going on inside my brain headache."

"Ok, well first your eyesight's blurry, now you're getting headaches; I think it's time to go."

"I'm sorry, Porter. I don't want to ruin the afternoon." She really didn't; she loved spending time with him, and she didn't want to scare him, but her head was killing her. Even the sunlight was causing her pain.

"Don't worry about me, Ella. Let's get you back to my truck."

"Ok." They walked slowly down the trail. So slowly, in fact, it took about three times longer to get down than it had going up. He kept asking her if she was ok or if she wanted to rest. She put on a brave face and soldiered on, but in reality she felt like she was living through someone drilling into her head with power equipment. It was unbearable.

The pounding in her head was getting worse. Two or three times as they were walking, she became dizzy and the blurred vision came back. She didn't want to let on to Porter how freaked out she was by the whole thing, so she continued down the path trying to seem like nothing was wrong and they eventually made it to his truck.

On the drive back to her apartment, Ella kept her eyes closed and her head against the passenger window. It might have looked like she was sleeping, but she was actually using every part of her body to keep herself from crying, or being sick, or both.

Porter kept his hand on her thigh, every few minutes asking her if she was sure she didn't want to go to the hospital.

"No, Porter, please just take me home." That's all she could get out of her mouth before the nausea took over and she clamped it closed again.

She vaguely registered when they pulled up to her apartment, and he helped her in, using her keys to unlock the door. She went straight for her bedroom and slowly crawled into her bed.

"What can I do for you?" He asked, sounding worried and helpless.

"Excedrin, in the bathroom. Water," was all she could manage. He brought her what she asked for and after she swallowed the pills, he set her glass down on her bedside table.

"I'm going to be in the living room, Ella. Let me know if you need anything."

"No," Ella groaned. "Please, lay with me." She felt the mattress dip, and his warm body came up behind hers, spooning her, covering her from head to toe with his body. She couldn't form full and complete sentences, but she could feel a tiny bit of relief as she relaxed into him. She let his warmth carry her off to sleep.

"Ella, Baby, can you wake up for me?"

"Mmmmm," Ella moaned, still feeling sharp pains radiating through her brain.

"Baby, I am sorry, I have to go. My mom is having a problem

at her restaurant. Megan is here. I called her to come take care of you. I will call you tomorrow ok?"

"Mmmmm," was all she could manage. She heard Porter head towards the door where Megan was standing.

"Just keep an eye on her. It came out of nowhere and she could hardly even talk. She took some Excedrin a couple hours ago. I'm hoping she just sleeps it off. Please call me if she gets worse."

"Porter, she'll be fine. She's not the first person to have a headache."

"Well, you didn't see her. I'm just worried about her."

"I know and I love you for it. But honestly, I've got it. Go rescue your mom. Meet your hero quota for the day."

Ella felt Porter's lips on her temple.

"I love you," he said to her in the quietest of whispers, almost as if he didn't want her to hear it, but she definitely had. And if her brain hadn't been trying to escape out of her tear ducts she might have had something to say about it, but she just let the words wash over her and fell back asleep.

Chapter Six

Ella

Ella's brain was still foggy throughout the night. The pain seemed to be ebbing away with the help of the medicine. When she woke up and was finally able to speak to Megan it was past eleven at night and she told Megan she could go home. Megan put up a little bit of a fight, but eventually agreed to leave as long as she promised to call her back over if she started feeling poorly again. Ella drank a glass of water and headed back to bed.

This time though, when she fell asleep, it wasn't as restful. Her mind was full of images, all of them hazy. Even in her sleep she could feel herself trying to make it through the fog and capture whatever was weighing down her mind. Slowly, images became clearer, and the first thing she could see was Porter. In her dream she opened up a door and Porter was on the other side. He smiled at her and she felt the floor drop out from under her. She wanted to run to him, bring his body in to hers, and use her hands to feel every contour of his body. Finally, she noticed his white shirt with blue sleeves. A baseball shirt. God All Mighty.

Everything went swirling again and then she was in a new room, still with Porter, but this room had a fantastic view of the ocean and a magnificently gorgeous king-sized sleigh bed. She admired the beautiful bed and Porter was behind her, kissing her neck. She wanted him on that bed and she felt like she was going to get what she wanted when he pulled the zipper to her dress down her back. She looked down at the dress as it pooled at her feet. Was she really going to have a sex dream about Porter?

Before she could even get onboard with that idea the fog was back, but this time when it cleared she sat in front of a fire on the beach making smores with Porter. His arms wrapped around her from behind helping her hold up a stick with a marshmallow on the end, both of them laughing when the white fluff turned into black char, melted off the stick entirely, and fell into the red hot flames.

In the next instant she was lying on a four-poster bed, white chiffon curtains surrounded her. When she looked up, all she could see was Porter and his gloriously naked chest holding himself over her. She immediately realized that the rest of him was naked, and furthermore, so was she. She glanced up at him, wondering how they got into this room and this ridiculously romantic bed when he gently flicked her nose with his, continued to trail his nose down her neck, and stopped to breathe shivers into her ear.

"I love you, Baby," he said as she felt him slowly push into her, filling her completely. She no longer had time to question what was happening between them because she was quite literally in the middle of it and it was fantastic. As he slowly and deliciously pumped into her she found herself using her hands to pull him even closer, trying to get as much of him into her as possible. She breathed him in, licking his neck to get his taste in her mouth. She heard him groan as her fingernails bit into his skin. She drowned in him and as he filled her lungs, she could think of no better way to go.

He reached between them, to the spot where they were connected, and slowly started circling her clit. "I've been waiting for you, Baby," he said as she arched her back, recklessly plummeting into a pool of pleasure so deep she would never be able to climb back out. "I need you with me, Ella. Come back to me." At his words, she experienced the most consuming and violent orgasm she'd ever had. She came so hard she was pulled from sleep and slammed back into the reality of her own bed where she was very aware of the fact that she was all alone.

The fogginess had followed her out of the dream and confusion had come along with it. She breathed heavily, still trying to recover from the phantom orgasm, and her brain was working overtime. She felt like all the pieces of her brain were mixed up in her head; she wanted to shake it to make the wayward pieces fall back together again. It was that ultimately annoying moment in life when something is so very frustratingly on the tip of your tongue and you just can't get your brain cells to connect with each other.

She breathed faster and now panic was beginning to take over as well. She felt as though something was coming and she had no idea what she should be preparing for. Images and colors flashed through her mind. She heard Porter's voice and waves violently crashing onto the shore. She reached a pinnacle of panic, holding her head between her hands, rocking back and forth on her bed, crying, when suddenly – peace washed over her. All the pieces fell back into place. A clarity she'd been lacking for eight long weeks finally settled in her mind, and she found herself gasping for air while smiling and laughing. She had one thing on her mind: Porter.

Ella had never been so happy to experience déjà vu in her life. The last time she had been racing to the beach sobbing, they had been devastating tears. This time, the tears she cried were happy tears mixed with excitement and nervousness. Two hours felt like twenty minutes and she found herself at Porter's house ringing his doorbell at four in the morning. He wasn't coming down fast enough so she started banging on the door with her open palm, laughing and crying at the same time.

Finally she heard thumps coming from inside and she knew he was coming to the door. When the door swung open, Porter first looked totally confused. Then he switched gears and looked worried and panicked.

"Ella? What are you doing here? Are you ok?" His hands came to her shoulders and were running down her arms like he was looking for injuries.

"I'm fine, Porter. I'm fine," she managed between laughing sobs.

"Why are you crying?" He asked, pulling her into his living room and closing the door behind them.

"Porter," she started and had to stop to cover her mouth when more tears and sobs came out.

"Ella, please, tell me what's going on," he pleaded as he pulled her into his arms. She let him hold her and buried her face in his chest, relishing in the familiarity. She took in a few deeps breaths to calm herself.

"Porter," she started again. "How do you think I made it to your house?" She shook from the adrenaline pumping through her system.

"You drove your car?" He answered like a question because he didn't understand what she was getting at. She took in one last big breath.

"How did I know where you live?" She pulled back to look him in the eyes. When he grasped exactly what she was telling him, she saw his realization come across his face.

"You remember?" he whispered, as he placed his hands on either side of her face. As she nodded her head, with rivers of tears streaming down her face, he began to frantically grasp at her. First her face, then her neck and her shoulders, trying to just feel her to make sure she was really there and really telling him what he was hearing. "You remember me? You remember us?" His voice was high pitched and just as frantic as his hands.

"Yes, Babe, I remember everything," she said as she let him feel as much of her as he needed. He crushed her to him using his hands to guide her legs around his waist so that he was carrying her. He walked up the stairs and into his room. They approached his bed and he sat on the floor with his back leaning up against it, her legs still wrapped around his waist. He still breathed rapidly and she quietly let him come to terms with what she had revealed to him. He finally pulled back from their hold and again gripped her face in his hands.

"Ella, I need you to promise me that you are going to be completely honest with me for the next five minutes. No matter how you think I will feel about what you say, I just need to know that you will be one hundred percent honest." She nodded at him.

"Of course," she said and saw a little bit of relief come over him, but not enough to ease his nerves.

"You've been through a lot over the last few months, and I cannot even begin to imagine what you're feeling or even thinking at this moment. The last thing I want to do is put added pressure on you, or pile expectations on top of what you've remembered. I will probably go to hell for asking you this now, when you've just remembered everything and haven't had any time to process what's happened to you. But I can't wake up another day and live in this state of flux anymore. And whatever you decide is fine, I'll accept anything you have to say. I just can't go on like this. Please, Ella, I need to know how you feel about us. I need to know what you see happening between us. I need to know if I should finally move on and let you go."

He looked at her and his eyes pleaded with her. Not asking her for any answer in particular, but the desperation in his voice made it clear to her that the last eight weeks had done the most damage to him, not her. She now could see the dark circles under his eyes that weren't there eight weeks ago. She noticed the lines around his eyes she didn't remember from before. She put her hands over his that seemed to be holding on to her for dear life.

"I love you, Porter. I finally found my way back to you and I'm never going to let you go." As her words sunk into him, she watched recognition came over his face of what she had said. And then he broke her heart into fragments as he began to cry.

He wrapped his arms around her waist, pulled her in close, and his face found the crook of her neck. Then he began to sob. Gut wrenching and heaving sobs came from this strong, capable man. Tears soaked the shirt she had on, but she dared not move more than to caress his back and stroke his hair as she gently told him that she loved him. That everything was going to be ok now. He keened and rocked back and forth and at some point she began to cry along with him.

She wasn't sure how much time had passed. Minutes or hours, it didn't matter. She would have held him forever if it had made up for any of the hurt he had gone through when she didn't remember. When he had finally stopped the wracking sobs and his lungs stopped hitching every time he tried to take a breath, he silently held her, his face never leaving her neck as the sun rose and light flooded through the giant picture window of his bedroom. She felt him take in a deep breath and let it out slowly, his breath whispering over her neck. He pulled his face back from her and looked at her face, his hands running over her hair.

"I can't believe you're here and that you remember. I had almost given up hope," he said in a whisper.

"I'm here, Baby, and I'm not going anywhere." She kept her eyes on his as she slowly leaned in towards him, asking him for permission to put her lips to his. She stopped before their lips met, unsure if he was ready for the contact. He answered her by closing the space between them. The kiss swept through her, slow and sweet like honey. Her hands, forever drawn to his arms, glided along the muscles of his shoulders. His hand moved into her hair, gently tugging on her tresses, while the other hand had snaked around her waist, gripping at the curve of her hip. "Please, Porter, tell me we can be together right now. I need you to make love to me," she wasn't opposed to begging him; although she didn't think it would be necessary. She needed to connect with him, more now than ever. He didn't answer; he just lifted her with his ungodly strength and laid her gently down on the bed.

His eyes never left hers as he peeled off the shorts she'd worn on their hike the day before. For an instant she regretted not changing or showering before she left for his house, but thinking back on their perfectly sweet and emotional reunion, she wouldn't have changed a thing. She sat up quickly and removed her tank top. She grabbed the bottom of her sports bra and pulled it over her head, She felt Porter's gaze on her naked torso.

"I've imagined you here, in my bed, so many times since you went away. It was torture even sleeping here, Ella."

"Come over here and make new memories with me, Porter." He pulled his shirt off before he came to rest over her body on his enormous bed. The feeling of his chest resting upon her breasts was heavenly. The small smattering of hair on his chest only added to the goose bumps that were taking over her body.

Porter wasted no time paying close attention to the spot on her neck that drove him crazy. He feasted on her, slowly lapping at her skin. He moved his velvet mouth down her neck and left a trail of kisses down her throat and between her breasts. He placed slow and wet kisses down her body, stopping when he came to the top of her underwear. He peeled the top of them down her thighs, using his thumbs to rub all along the outside of her legs, causing her body to convulse with pleasure. He had them off in seconds and she was left naked, completely at his disposal. He made his way back up to her mouth, stopping only to bury his nose in the apex of her thighs, lovingly nuzzling her swollen sex. She gasped at his brazenness and her arousal was catapulted into overdrive. She grabbed at the waistband of his shorts and pushed them down to his feet, not taking the time he had to worship her body, but frantically trying to simply free him so that she could feel all of him on her.

His mouth found hers and the fire between them was fueled by their new nakedness. Legs tangled, arms entwined, and his body found all the nooks and crannies of hers to fill. There wasn't a part of his body that wasn't melting into hers. She felt his thickness between her thighs and reached down to stroke him.

"Oh God, Ella."

"Even when I didn't remember you, I missed you, Porter. I knew you were missing from me; I could feel it," she said as she lazily slid her hand over his hardness. "I'll never understand why my head couldn't remember, but my heart never forgot."

His hands smoothed over her ribcage, grazing over her stomach. He looked down at where her hand was holding him and then his eyes met hers again. As his eyes bored into her, she felt his hand glide down her front until it reached her core. He cupped her and drove his palm into her, the friction causing her to gasp for even a single breath.

"Your body remembers me, Ella. I will always be the one your body craves. The only one it responds to. You're mine."

"Yes," she breathed.

His fingers slipped past her entry and she couldn't help the moan that escaped her. Slowly his fingers pumped in and out, trailing along the walls of her sex, finding all the spots inside her body that made her tighten in her core. She felt the familiar tingle and clenching inside her stomach that she knew would eventually come through her like an avalanche. She pulled his face down to hers and kissed him, trying to match with her mouth the intense desire he was stirring with his hands. As they kissed, her hips were tilting and thrusting, doing everything they could to allow him to have complete access to her. When his thumb brushed over her clit, her body jolted and she felt him smile against her lips.

"You like that?" He asked in a husky voice, his lips still pressed against hers. She nodded. His thumb brushed over it again, only this time it lingered and he pressed harder.

"Please," she begged.

"Mmm. Please what?"

"Don't stop," she tried to say, but it came out as a whispered cry.

"Never." His delicious torture continued as his mouth moved down to her breast. As his tongue swirled around her nipple and his hand continued to dive in and out of her, she could not stop the orgasm as it ripped through her body. Her legs shook, her hands grasped the bed, and she had no control over the moan that escaped her.

Porter slowly kissed her breast as she came down from the high of her orgasm and she ran her hands through his silky hair. Both of his hands slid up the side of her body, past her hips, over her waist, along the sides of her breasts and up her arms. He linked both of his hands with hers over her head and gave her a kiss so soft and gentle it brought tears to her eyes. She could still feel him hard between them, and his soft kiss turned into something more urgent and greedy. He broke the kiss to lean over to his night stand to find a condom and Ella grabbed his hand to stop him.

"I don't want any barriers between us tonight, Porter. I just want you. I'm on the pill and I've always used a condom. Plus, if I had anything I would have found out from the hospital. I want to feel all of you inside of me." She looked up at him with pleading eyes. "This is you and me, Porter. I want to be with you this way, only you. Bare and raw," she said as she gently placed a hand on his cheek.

"Are you sure?" He asked quietly.

"I trust you. Please, make love to me."

With their eyes locked, Porter slowly slid into her making sure he remembered the moment they became one in every way.

"Oh god, Porter," she said as she raked her nails down his back. Never really having thought that sex without a condom would feel any different, she was shocked by the difference actually feeling him was making.

"It's never felt like this before, Ella. You were made for me." She pulled him down to her, wanting as much contact with him as possible. He kissed every inch of skin he could find and she was riding the waves of pleasure he was bringing her. He put a hand under her ass and pulled her hips up to meet his thrusts, giving him an even deeper angle that had her biting her tongue to keep from yelling out.

"You're so warm, Baby. Warm and wet," he rasped out at her.

"I'm close, Porter."

"Wait for me," he ordered. She groaned and tried to keep her pending orgasm at bay. Her eyes bolted closed and she bit her lip while he found new angles and speed at which to drive into her, all of them making it harder and harder for her to hold on any longer.

"Please come, Baby. Come inside me," she whispered in his ear seductively.

"Ahh, fuck..." he groaned and drove roughly into her a few more times. She couldn't wait any longer as her orgasm rocketed through her. She felt a wave of relief as he came right along with her. Breathing heavily and resting atop her, his heartbeat frantically pulsed into her chest. She caressed his back with her hand, waiting for him to come back to her.

"Condoms suck," were the first words out of his mouth. She giggled.

"Yes, apparently they do. They also lie. It definitely doesn't feel the same." Porter flicked her nose with the tip of his.

"Felt good?"

"Amazing."

"Yes. For me too. That was definitely an experience worth having. Again and again." He nuzzled into her neck and she heard him take a deep breath. He was quiet for a minute and then quietly said, "If we fall asleep, do you promise to be here and remember me when we wake up?" He pulled back to look at her. She pushed his hair off of his forehead and smiled at him.

"Yes, let's go to sleep." He rolled off of her and pulled her back into his chest. He pulled the plush comforter up over them, and then finally reached over her and braided his fingers with hers. She felt his breathing slow and eventually even out. Once she was fairly certain he was asleep, she let herself drift off as well, cradled in the warmth of the man she forgot, surrounded by the love she nearly lost.

Chapter Seven

Porter

When the afternoon came they finally woke and Porter was put at immediate ease by the smile that Ella wore. He grabbed her and rolled them so that she was on top of him, her body draped all along his.

"Good morning, Beautiful," he said as he kissed her chin.

"Good afternoon, Handsome."

"Did you sleep well?"

"Mmm. Better than I have in months." She laid her head upon his chest and he ran his finger through her loose hair, content to just be with her.

"What would you like to do today? Do you have to go back to Portland?" She lifted her head to look at him, placing her chin on her hands lying flat on his chest.

"I think I'd really like to go see your mom."

"She'd really like to see you, I'm sure." He ran his hand along her cheek.

"The problem is, in my frantic rush to get to you last night, I never packed anything. I have no clean clothes."

"Tell you what, why don't you relax for a little while, I will run to the store, get you some clothes and stuff, and then we can go have dinner at the bar. Sound good?"

"Sounds perfect," she said as she crawled up his body to kiss him. He growled in her mouth, kissing her back.

"We'll never make it out of bed if you keep that up," he said against her lips.

"I'm ok with that," she laughed. He rolled them over again, playfully slapped her bare backside as he got up, and headed into his closet. He emerged dressed and stopped to take in the sight of

Ella in his bed, his white sheets draped over her seductively, as she was looking at her phone. She had absolutely no idea how sexy and beautiful she was.

"I've got to call my family. Megan couldn't find me this morning and now everyone is freaking out."

"Do you want me to stay?"

"No, I really want some clean clothes. You go. I'll call after I shower. Can I text you my sizes?"

"Sure, Baby." He leaned down to kiss her.

When he came back to the house and made it up the stairs, he heard his shower running and quickly stripped his clothes off to make sure he could join her before she was finished. He walked into the bathroom and was never so glad that he had built himself a walk-in shower without doors. His heart nearly popped right out of his chest as he saw his Ella, eyes closed, turned towards him, water running down the front of her body. Water was cascading over her shoulders, her breasts, her stomach, and her toned thighs. He had a lot of images of Ella burned into his mind, Ella in lingerie, Ella naked bent over the arm of his couch, Ella asleep in his bed curled up next to him, but this image is one that would be hard to beat. He watched her for a few more seconds and then slowly stepped into the shower, wrapping his arms around her from the front. He felt her startle for just a moment, catching her unaware, but then she melted into his hands.

"You made it home fast," she said as she folded her arms around his neck.

"Well, having you waiting here for me is motivation to move quickly."

"Did you get me something decent to wear out of the house?"

"Yes. But let's not talk about putting clothes on you just yet. I like the very naked and very wet version of you right here." His hands slid down her back and over the curve of her ass as he grabbed a hold and pulled her into him. Once he had her slick body pressed up against his, he moved in to take her mouth with his. She gave a sweet whimper and he felt himself harden even more between them. He felt her hands weave their way into his now wet hair and she tugged gently as their tongues blended into one another's.

He walked her back until her legs bumped against the bench seat. With his lips still pressed against hers, he murmured, "Sit." She obeyed and slowly sat down, a smile playing over her lips. He moved the shower head so that it was still raining down behind her. He knelt down in front of her, grabbed her behind her knees and pulled her towards him so that her hips rested just at the edge of the bench. His eyes took her in, splayed out for him, on display. She was perfect.

"You're mine, yes?" He asked her.

"All yours."

"Every part of you?" He teased.

"Mmmhmm," she said as she bit her lip.

"So," he said as he ran his hand up her stomach to her chest to tease her nipple, "your gorgeous breasts, those are mine?"

"Yes," she cooed at him. His fingertip trailed slow circles around the brownish-pink tip of her breast, and his thumb teased it by roughly rubbing it back and forth. She whimpered and moaned quietly, her eyes closed and head leaned back against the tile wall of the shower. His hands came down to her waist and he bent over, placing soft kisses along the inside of her thigh. His fingers slightly dug into the soft part of her leg where her thigh met her hip. His kisses inched up her thigh until he reached the V where her legs came together.

"What about this?" He asked as he used a finger to part her entry. "Does this belong to me, too?"

"Oh God, Porter, only you," she cried as his finger slid all the way into her. He then added another and her volume increased, moaning even louder.

"That's what I thought, Baby." He was hard, almost

uncomfortably so, but there was nothing he wanted more than to watch Ella fall apart here in his shower. He watched as his fingers pumped in and out of her, watched her as she writhed on the bench, trying to meet his fingers with her hips. She was shameless and it was the sexiest thing he'd ever seen. He removed his fingers from her and gently spread her knees farther apart. She opened her eyes and looked at him, her blue eyes had a gray haze over them.

"You're driving me crazy, Porter," she said. Without speaking a word, and keeping his eyes on her, he lowered his face down to her and used his tongue to spread her open. She immediately bucked against him.

"Be still, Ella," he said and was rewarded with a long and sexy moan. His tongue found her warm and wet, inside and out, eager to be licked and lapped. As his tongue explored her clit, flicking and licking, his fingers made their way back into her, stroking and pumping into her. She tried to stay still, he could tell, but her hips found ways to meet his mouth. Her hands found his hair, as she pushed his face into her, trying to drown him in her.

"I'm going to come," she cried out.

"Come for me, Ella."

"Oh, yes," she moaned, her words stretched out sounding less like words and more like groans. He continued his assaults until he was sure she had come down. When she opened her eyes and smiled at him, he stood and pulled her up to him. She wrapped her arms around him and kissed him hungrily. Her legs came up around his waist and he turned to sit down on the bench, placing her on his lap. The feeling of his cock snug up against her sex made him groan softly.

"Tell me which parts of me belong to you, Ella."

She leaned over and placed a soft kiss on his lips. Then she smirked at him.

"Your sexy arms belong to me, don't they?" She said as she ran her hands up and over his shoulder and biceps. "You have such strong and capable arms. I feel like nothing could happen to me as long as I am in your arms."

"Yes, Ella, they belong to you. What else?" He raised his hips, grinding into her, trying to give her a hint. She winked at him and wiggled her ass, causing him to exhale harshly, pushing the air through his teeth.

"Your kissable lips that tease every part of my body, those are mine." She bent down, took his bottom lip in her mouth, and then bit down hard enough to make him yelp, then soothed it by sucking it back in again. He pulled back again.

"Fuck, Ella, you're going to kill me here." She rose up on her knees. Her breasts pushed up into his face, so he took one nipple in his mouth returning the bite she'd given him. He smiled around her nipple when he heard her cry out and then used his tongue to make it feel better.

"My favorite part of you, though, definitely belongs to me." He saw her sexy smirk cross her face as she reached between them, positioned him at her opening, and then slid down him slowly, taking all of him in.

"Shiiiiit…." Porter whispered.

"Hmmm….feel good, Baby?" She rose up again, just to slide right back down.

"Yes, don't you fucking stop," he said through clenched teeth.

"Don't you worry. I've got you." After that, she took off. She kept her own pace, which didn't matter to him. She could do whatever she wanted as long as she kept him inside of her. Up and down a few times and then she would grind down on him, making him and herself cry out in pleasure. His hand roamed her body, finding her ass, helping her fit all of him in by pushing her hips down onto his lap. She slowly increased the speed at which she bounced on him and he enjoyed watching her breasts bounce as she did.

"Faster," he demanded and she complied. He gripped her hips harder, but she didn't seem to mind and he forced her to take as much of him as possible. He could tell he was filling her to the hilt, hitting the end of her channel, and she loved it. Her moans became louder, and his breathing became frantic. He needed to come in her and soon. "Come with me," another demand.

"Yes," she answered, still giving him everything she had. She finally slammed down on him and then ground down on him, circling her hips. He watched as her head fell back with a cry and he followed her into oblivion.

Her head rested on his shoulder and he pressed small kisses along her shoulder, letting his heart calm down. He stopped when he noticed the quarter sized scar she bared. He kissed it tenderly.

"Does this still hurt?" He asked as he gently swiped a finger over it.

"Not really. Every once in a while I feel some random sharp pains in my shoulder, but nothing too bad. It's all normal, I've been told."

"I'm so sorry I wasn't there for you when you were recuperating."

"Babe, you really didn't have choice, did you? I understand why everyone made the decisions they did." Her hands came up to his face and she forced him to look at her. "I'm fine, Porter. Everything is ok now. You can't hold on to the guilt. It won't do either one of us any good."

"Just promise me that you won't let anyone keep you from me anymore."

"Baby, wild horses couldn't drag me away." She kissed him on the lips. Before he had a chance to take advantage of their still connected bodies, she hopped off of him to proceed with finishing her shower.

"Did you have this type of thing in mind when you built this bathroom?" She asked him with a smile.

"Listen, when I built this bathroom, I was twenty-one. I wasn't innocent, but not even my young mind could have comprehended anything that sexy or erotic would take place in my bathroom. You outdid yourself, Babe." He slapped her ass and enjoyed the wet smacking noise it made as it echoed through his bathroom.

"I do what I can," she said as she shrugged up one of her shoulders and threw him a sexy smirk.

They finished up their shower and continued to get ready to go see his mom, stealing glances at each other, sharing innocent and not so innocent touches.

"Babe, I did not need all these clothes," Ella said as he sifted through three shopping bags full of the pants, shirts, and such.

"I know they're not the fancy clothes you're used to, but I wanted you to have enough that you could leave some here in case you ever needed something."

"Why, Porter, are you giving me a drawer?" She asked as she shimmied into some jeans. He laughed at her playfulness.

"I guess so. I mean, as much as I like you naked, it wouldn't be a terrible thing for you to keep some things here."

She walked over to him and pressed her body up against his, the lace of her bra scratching up against his chest.

"Thank you. For everything." She pecked him lightly. "You did a very good job buying me lingerie, Porter."

"I have never wandered through that section of a store before and I will tell you right now that I don't know what guys complain about. Everything I saw I pictured on you and it was amazing. You can take me lingerie shopping anytime."

"You're such a perv sometimes," she laughed. "Get dressed, Perv."

As they pulled up to Tilly's bar, Ella's phone started ringing. She saw it was Megan calling and signaled to Porter to wait a minute before getting out of the car. She answered the phone and put it on speaker.

"Hey Megan."

"Ella, where are you? Are you ok?"

"Yes, I'm fine. Why?"

"Well, no one has heard from you today and when I went to check on you, you weren't home. I called mom and she hadn't heard from you either. We got worried."

"Megan, listen, something amazing happened last night. My headache was killing me and it got worse for a little while. I tried to sleep it off, but it woke me up, and when I finally realized what was happening, I remembered everything."

"You remember? Like, *everything* everything?"

"Yes, well, I mean, I think so. I remember Porter. That's where I am, with Porter, in Lincoln City."

"So you're horizontal?!"

"Shut up, Megs. I am not horizontal… Anymore." She laughed and was blessed to hear her sister laugh as well.

"So, how are you feeling? Does your head still hurt? Do you need anything?"

"I feel fantastic, Megs. I am so happy."

"I'm so happy for you, Fella, and happy for me too. It was getting a little ridiculous trying to keep Porter from you. I'm glad you guys can just be together now, like, for real." Ella looked over at Porter and gave him a smile that stopped his heart.

"Me too, Sis." She leaned over and kissed Porter loudly on the mouth.

"Oh, god, is he there with you right now? Did I just hear you kiss him? You two are probably going to go off the grid for weeks now, huh? Making up for lost time? Well, remember to tell Mom and Dad this time. They deserve to know."

"I will call them tonight."

"Ok, well, I will let you get back to your man. I love you, Sister."

"I love you too and thank you for always trying to do what you feel is best. You're an amazing sister and I'm lucky to have you."

"Ditto!" Megan laughed as she hung up the phone.

"So," Porter started, "Your sister gave away your nickname that you so cruelly withheld from me."

"What do you mean?"

"Fella?" He raised his eyebrows at her. She laughed and threw her head back, resting it against the back of her seat.

"I guess she did. Well, now you know. Does it change the way you look at me?" She asked sarcastically.

"Sadly, not really. Yours really isn't that bad."

"Yeah, yours is way worse," she leaned over and kissed him. "Let's go, Portly." She laughed and he rolled his eyes at her. As they walked towards the bar, Porter linked his hands with Ella's and lifted her hand to kiss the back of it. It had been less than twenty-four hours since she'd shown up on his doorstep and he was still trying to get use to the idea of being able to just hold her hand – something he might have taken for granted eight weeks ago. Just before they went inside, he pulled her into him and kissed her softly.

"I love you, Ella," he whispered to her, running a hand smoothly down her cheek.

"I love you too," she answered wistfully, placing her hand over his and moving to her mouth to place a small kiss on his palm.

"Are you ready for this? My mom is going to lose her mind when she sees you."

"I'm looking forward to it," she smiled. He pulled the door open for her and she led the way in. It took roughly about four seconds until Porter heard his mother's shrill and high pitched scream from behind the bar.

"Ella!" His mother said her name over and over again, running from behind the bar all the way to the front with her arms open wide, waiting for Ella to fill them. When Tilly made it to them, Ella dropped Porter's hand and let herself be enveloped in Tilly's arms. He couldn't help the smile that spread across his face or the warm feeling that spread through his chest at the sight of his mother hugging her. Nothing compared to having the two most important women in his life together, with him, happy and healthy.

"What does this mean?" Tilly asked as she pulled away from Ella, but not letting go of her. Her eyes were darting back and forth between him and Ella.

"Last night my memory came back," Ella said, wiping a tear off of her cheek, obviously affected by the overwhelming welcome Tilly had given her. "I got in my car and immediately drove here to see Porter. And today, this was the first place I wanted to come. To see you."

Tilly pulled her back into her arms.

"I am so happy you're back, Ella. We've missed you so much." When his mother finally let her go she moved over to Porter and wrapped her arms around him as well. He bent down and took his mother's small frame in his arms and felt a little more of the tension he'd been carrying around with him melt away.

"She's really here, Porter. She came back to you. Don't let her go," she whispered in his ear so quietly, even he had a hard time hearing her. His mother pulled away from him and turned around quickly to wipe her eyes, trying to hide that she'd started to cry over Ella's return.

"Why don't you both go grab a booth and I will be over in a minute to get you some dinner."

"Ok, Mom," he said as he laid a small kiss on the top of her head. He knew that seeing Ella would affect his mom, but he wasn't prepared for her to be so emotional about it. The fact that his mother cared so much about Ella only reaffirmed the feelings he'd had for her all along.

They chose a booth towards the back of the restaurant. He let her slide in first and then slid in next to her, enjoying the idea of having such open access to her. He took his hand, placed it on her thigh, and gave a gentle squeeze. Every touch and every look he gave her was not only exhilarating, but also relieving; she was still here. He wasn't dreaming. She remembered.

"How are you feeling?" He looked over to her and asked. She rubbed her hand over his which was still comfortably resting on her thigh.

"I feel fine, Baby. Great even."

"No headaches?"

"None. I feel wonderful," she said as she leaned over and placed a kiss on his lips.

"Well, I think we should call Dr. Andrews and make an appointment to see him. I'm sure he'd have something to say about your memory coming back."

"I'll call him tomorrow morning, promise. But please, don't worry about me. I'm fine."

It wouldn't do any good to tell her that he would likely spend a lot of time worrying about her. At least for the foreseeable future, he couldn't imagine his mind not being consumed by fears that she would forget, that she would disappear from his life again, and he would be left circling the proverbial drain. If Ella had another setback, if she lost her memory, he would have no rights, just like last time. The only way it was guaranteed that he would have access to her is if she were his wife.

He looked over at her again and she flashed him her brilliant smile. One day he would ask her to marry him and even though he knew he wanted her for the rest of his life, he didn't want to propose out of necessity. He knew, also, that Ella wouldn't want that. She was convinced that she would be fine and even though he wouldn't feel one hundred percent comfortable until they spoke to a doctor about it, he was willing to try and not let his worries affect their time together.

When his mother sat down across from them, the smile she beamed was blinding and wonderful. He knew exactly how she felt.

"So," she began, "now what?"

"What do you mean?" He asked.

"Well, now that you're back, Ella, how are you two going to proceed? You know, with your relationship?" Porter looked over at Ella and she returned his gaze.

"Well, Mother, nothing really has changed for us. We love each other and I am so happy that she's back, but she still has her life in Portland and I'm here. We'll just have to make it work, like we had originally planned."

"I don't like that plan anymore," Ella said suddenly, turning to face him again.

"What do you mean?"

"I mean, I don't understand why we have to be apart. There has to be a way for us to be together. You know, really together. Unless…" she paused as her eyes went wide, "unless you don't want that. I'm sorry, I didn't mean to steamroll you right now. It all just came out." She brought her hands up to cover her face, shaking her head in embarrassment.

To hear Ella say those words, for her to admit that she wanted to be close to him, it was everything he'd always wanted from her and never thought he'd get. She had been so unsure of their relationship before, and now she seemed eager to be together on a more permanent level.

"Babe, we don't have to talk about this now. Let's just enjoy dinner."

"Why can't you talk about it now?" Tilly interjected.

"Mom, this is a private conversation I'd like to have with Ella alone."

"Well, if you're thinking about sticking around here for me, don't. I'll be fine without you."

"Well, ok, Mom. Tell me how you really feel about it."

"Porter, you've been trying to make up for the lack of your father for twenty years now. You've taken such good care of me, this bar, your company, but you've never taken care of yourself.

Don't let your notions of obligation keep you from being truly happy. I'm just saying."

"She has a point," Ella said, shooting a sweet smile his way.

"Listen, I'm not saying anything either way. I just think this is a conversation best had privately."

"Ok, just so long as you know where I stand," Tilly added.

"Noted. Now, let's just have a peaceful meal."

Ella

The last thing she had wanted to do was put Porter on the spot in front of his mother or to pressure him in any way. But the thought of being separated from him again made a knot form in her stomach and her head throb. She linked her hand with his under the table, hoping to assure him that she hadn't meant any harm. He smiled at her and her concern melted into a hot puddle that settled between her thighs. His smile was intoxicating.

"Porter?" A tallish brunette came to the side of the table Porter was sitting at and was shamelessly batting her eyelashes in his direction.

"Amy, hi."

"Hi, sorry to interrupt your, uh, dinner," she said as she gave Ella a disinterested glance. "I was hoping you could help me get into my car. I locked my keys inside again."

"Um, yeah, sure," he said as he looked back at Ella with an expression that looked a little embarrassed but mostly apologetic. "I'll be right back, Babe." He scooted out of the booth and led the way to the door. Ella could have sworn the brunette was checking out his backside as he walked towards the door. 'Let her look,' she thought, 'he's never been anything but mine.'

"Ella, I'm glad we have a few minutes alone. How are you doing, really?"

"I'm really good, Tilly. As soon as my memory came back, I mean, it's like everything is right again. I was so confused for so long. I knew something was missing and I knew it had something to do with Porter, but I couldn't figure it out."

"He was absolutely lost without you. He was destroyed. Ella, he was wrecked. The first few weeks that you were, uh, away, it was all he could do just to get out of bed each day. He called your mother daily, sometimes he made it to work, but mostly he just fell apart."

Ella could see the tears starting to form around Tilly's eyes.

"A couple weeks ago, after you were out of the hospital and seemed to be doing better, he started to get out more and showing up for work regularly. But the light in his eyes was gone. He was empty."

"I don't want to imagine what he was going through; I just wish he had come to me sooner. I know I didn't remember him right away, but I knew he loved me and I started to fall in love with him again. He didn't need to be so far away," Ella said, hating to hear about his misery without her.

"He was just trying to make everyone happy. Everyone but himself. He will forever be looking out for everyone but himself first. His tragic flaw." Ella smiled at Tilly's words.

"It's one of the things I love best about him; his ultimate selflessness."

"Yes, it is admirable, but can be detrimental, especially the last couple of months."

"Agreed. Listen, Tilly, I know this has been quite possibly the weirdest start to a relationship in the history of dating, but I need you to know that there isn't anything in the world that is going to keep me from being with him. I know that before the accident I had my reservations about him and me, but there's nothing like getting a second chance with Porter to make you realize that waiting to be together would only be wasting precious time. I was given a gift when my memory came back and I don't intend to take it for granted."

"That's good to hear, Honey. He deserves someone to love him." Ella reached across the table and grabbed Tilly's hand.

"Consider him loved. More than I ever thought I could love anyone. Truly."

"Thank you so much for helping me, Porter. You were always so considerate and helpful," Ella turned her head to see the brunette, Amy, stroking her hand down Porter's arm, the arm that definitely belonged to her.

"Baby," Ella plastered a fake smile on her face, "aren't you going to introduce me to your friend?"

Porter looked like a poor deer with headlights headed straight for him.

"Uh, Amy, this is my girlfriend, Ella." Ella tilted her head and made sure her smile didn't look like 'nice to meet you', but more like 'get your hands off him now'. Amy smiled and slid her hand all the way down his arm until it had nowhere else to go but back to her side.

"It's so nice to meet you," she gave Ella an equally frosty smile. "Porter really hasn't dated much, I mean, besides me," she laughed and gave him a longing look.

Oh. Hell. No. Ella started to scoot out of the booth when Tilly's voice stopped her.

"Amy, I'm so glad you're here. I have someone I want you to meet. I know you're always on the prowl for a new man. I know just the right guy for you to sink your teeth into." Amy's mouth opened and closed like a fish, not quick enough to find a way out of the trap Tilly had set for her.

"Um, ok, thanks again, Porter. I'll call you," she said over her shoulder as Tilly was pulling her across the bar towards what looked to be a mid-thirtyish man whose shirt was a size too small, and not in a good way.

Porter slid back into the booth next to Ella and placed his arm around her shoulders.

"Ella Sinclair, if I didn't know any better, I would say that you were jealous just then." Ella tried not to pout.

"She was touching your arm, Porter. She's lucky she still has all of her fingers attached. How many ex-girlfriends of yours are roaming around this town?"

"You know I didn't really date and I wouldn't even call Amy an ex-girlfriend. We dated a few times. Nothing serious."

"But you slept with her?"

Porter coughed suddenly, needing a drink of the water in front of him.

"Well, this is uncomfortable," he mumbled when she kept staring at him waiting for an answer.

"Let's grow up, Porter. We're both adults here. We've both had sex before we met each other. Just tell me. What's your number?"

"My number?"

"Yeah, like, how many women have you been with?"

"At one time? Or like, all together?"

"Shut up, Porter." She sent him a withering look and he was laughing at his own joke. "Seriously, I'll tell you mine if you tell me yours."

"I don't want to know your number. Honestly. Let's just assume we were both virgins when we met."

"That is ridiculous. Besides, you had to have learned your moves from somewhere," she said, trying not to blush.

"You think I have moves?" He leaned in closer, his lips nibbling on her earlobe.

Ella groaned quietly.

"Porter, when we first made love, you blew my mind. I had no idea sex with someone could be so, well, intimate." He used his index finger to turn her chin so look at him. He brushed some hair behind her ear and cupped the side of her face.

"It's only ever been that way with you." She sighed at his sweetness and leaned her forehead against his.

"I missed your words, Porter."

"I think you took them with you. I've got no use for them unless I've got you to say them to." She looked up at him again and leaned closer. Her lips came to rest upon his, not seeking heat or looking for instant passion, just a connection.

"I don't want to be without you anymore," she said against his lips.

"You'll never be without me," he countered and took their kiss deeper, using his hand on the back of her neck to pull her in to him. She let him kiss her and she gave as much as she got, but she pulled away eventually.

"I want to have a serious conversation about this. Tonight."

"Whatever you want, Babe. Let's just do it at home, without prying eyes or ears," he nodded his head towards the bar where Tilly was serving drinks and spying on them simultaneously.

"Deal," she said and kissed him quickly one more time.

Chapter Eight

Ella

Later that night, Ella found herself sifting through Porter's closet searching for something comfortable to wear to bed. She found a pair of his boxers and a tee shirt and sighed in contentment, smelling his shirt, finding his scent soothing. She quickly shed her clothes and slipped into his. When she exited the closet, she found Porter sitting up in his bed reading a book. She smiled at the sight of him, doing something as normal as reading a book. She loved that she was here with him, able to see him just reading. She wanted this every night. She wanted to share a life with him. And she wanted to start now.

"Baby? Can we talk?" Porter closed his book and set it down on the table next to the bed.

"Of course."

She walked to the bed and climbed up, then got under the covers and snuggled up next to his side. He kissed her temple and she smiled into his chest.

"Listen, Porter, I know that I've just gotten my memory back and we've just found each other again, but I am really serious about us being together. I don't want us to be separated any more, in any way. I think we've been through enough and if we can make it through the last two months, we can make it through anything."

"Ok, so let's talk specifics. What is it that you want?" He brushed his fingers through her loose hair, waiting for her response. Ella took in a deep breath, readying herself to lay everything on the line. She was going to put everything out there and it would go one of two ways.

"Well," she said, resting her head on his chest so she was looking right in his eyes, "I want to ask Megan to manage Poppy in Portland and to look into opening a new store in Salem. Even if Megan doesn't want to do it, Brittany graduated and is looking for a job. I'm sure she'd take it if I offered. I want to move to Salem and I want you there with me." She watched his face, hoping for any indication of what he was feeling or thinking. His brows furrowed a little, creating sexy wrinkled between them.

"So, you want us both to move to Salem? Where would we live?"

"Well, I don't know. We could rent a house or an apartment. I hadn't really thought too far into housing. It seems silly to think about it before we've decided what was happening." She turned her head so her cheek was resting on his stomach, and she could feel it rising and falling with his breath. "If you don't want to move to Salem, it's fine. I am going to move there regardless. It's time for me to branch out and expand; it makes sense for me. I understand if this is too soon for you, or if you'd rather just keep things the way they are, or the way we originally intended. Salem is a whole hour closer than Portland, so at least there's that." She rambled and she knew it. His silence unnerved her and she just wanted him to say something, one way or another.

"Hey, don't try and talk me out of it," he said, pulling her chin back to look at him. "Let's just think it through a little. I don't want this to be impulsive; I want it to be right, for both of us."

"Ok," she said quietly.

"So, you want us to move to Salem together. You will open another store there and I will commute to Lincoln City? What will I do with my house?"

"Well, I guess that's up to you, but I wouldn't want you to sell this house. I love this house. Do you mind the commute every day? That's two hours in a car, every day. And you'd probably have to leave your boat here too."

"I don't want to sell and I don't need to. We could still come here on the weekends. I think I would rather rent a house, an apartment would probably be too small. But eventually I'll want to build us a house." Her heart stopped as her eyes caught his. She felt the breath burning in her lungs trying to get out.

"You want to build us a house?" She whispered, a little unsure she'd heard him correctly.

"Of course I want to build us a house, Baby. I want to give you everything." He rolled over her and pressed a kiss on her lips. "Don't doubt us, Ella. I want us to be together more than anything, but I just wanted to make sure that we're doing it right." He gently flicked his nose against hers. "I've never lived with someone before. Aren't you worried you'll have to break me in?" He smiled at her.

"I'd love nothing more than to break you in," she said with a sly grin. Then she realized what he'd said. "Wait, does this mean you'll do it?"

"Of course I'll do it; that was never a question, Ella. I'd move anywhere to be with you."

"Well, you could have fooled me, I was really worried I was laying it all out there and that you were going to reject me," she said, playfully slapping his chest.

"Being with you is all I've ever wanted," he said suddenly serious.

"I know. I'm sorry it took a gunshot, a coma, and some amnesia to bring me around."

"Yeah, no more of that," he said.

"No problem."

The next morning was Monday and Ella called Dr. Andrews' office. Once she told the nurse her situation, she said the doctor would want to see her that day. To Ella's delight, Porter called his second-in-command at his company and told him he wouldn't be in that day. They both got ready to head to Portland to return to OHSU.

"Are you nervous about seeing the doctor?" Porter asked her as the Portland skyline came into view. They had already dropped her car off at her apartment and were in his truck. He casually had his hand on her thigh and every time his thumb grazed over her skin gently, she could feel the sensation shoot directly to her core causing goose bumps on the back of her neck.

"Not really," she smiled at him. "I really feel like everything is going to be ok. Are you nervous?" She asked as she reached out to take his hand, anticipating his answer.

"A little. I just need to hear him tell me that you won't lose your memory again." She kissed his hand, trying to offer him comfort even though she knew she couldn't tell him what he needed to hear.

They made it to the hospital and found their way through the maze, finally arriving at his office. His receptionist led them to an examination room and told them the doctor would be in shortly. Ella waited patiently on the examination table, while Porter paced the room. She could feel the anxiety coming off of him and it was starting to make her nervous, too. What if the doctor came in the room and told her it was likely she'd forget again? How could they make sure that if her memory went away she would still be a part of Porter's life? The only thing she could think of was marriage. He'd still be a stranger to her if she forgot, but at least her family couldn't keep him away again. Would he even want to marry her? Would she want to marry him? She smiled to herself, glad he wasn't looking at her. Of course she would marry him. Right now if he asked. But the idea of marrying him just to safeguard against something that might not even happen didn't sit well with her. She wanted to marry him because she loved him and when the time was right.

The door opened and Dr. Andrews walked in with a smile.

"Ella, so good to see you. I hear your memory has returned." He shook her hand and then turned to shake Porter's. "Mr. Masters, good to see you again too. And honestly, it's good to see you together," he smiled at them both. "Ella, why don't you tell me about how your memory came back to you?"

"Ok, well, Porter and I were out hiking and I started to get a little dizzy. We started to head home but I started to get a really bad headache. It was probably more like a migraine." The doctor was listening to her and writing notes on his notepad. "The headache got really bad and all I could do was sleep." She looked over at Porter, realizing that she hadn't told him the next part yet.

"I started having these really vivid dreams. Well, what I thought were dreams, turns out they were memories. They were all about Porter. And they were very real," she coughed a little, embarrassed to remember the phantom orgasm she'd had. "Anyway, I woke up and my headache was even worse, but then I started to have what I would call a panic attack. It was like I knew something was happening, but I didn't know what. Then, all of a sudden, I just remembered. Everything was back. The headache was gone." She looked back at the doctor.

"Well, it sounds pretty stressful. Have you had any problems with panic or anxiety in the past?"

"No. Only during the attack at my apartment before the shooting," at her words she saw Porter's head snap towards her.

"So, now you also remember the attack?" The doctor asked softly. She looked down at her hands.

"Yes."

"Ok," the doctor said and let out a loud sigh. "Here's my doctor speech: The brain is still a mystery to the medical field. For every one fact we know about how the brain works, we don't know a million things. So, the best I can give you is an educated guess. It seems as though whatever connection in your brain that was damaged when you hit your head has been repaired. That might have been the headache. The pain you felt could have been your brain making the final repairs to restore that connection, which would explain why the headache went away as soon as your memory returned.

"There are very few cases of people having retro-grade amnesia. Short term memory loss is far more common. There are even fewer cases of patients with retro-grade amnesia having their memory restored. I, personally, have never treated anyone whose memory came back. You should consider yourself remarkably lucky, Ella." His words caused Ella's eyes to tear up. Even the doctor hadn't had faith in the fact that she would remember. It became obvious to her in that moment that her love for Porter, and his for her, was the only thing that saved her. She looked up at Porter and his eyes mirrored her. He came to her side and wrapped his arms around her, rubbing his hand along her back, trying to sooth her.

"It's ok, Ella. I'm right here," Porter whispered in her ear. She took a few deep breaths and then pulled away, looking back to the doctor.

"Do you think I am ok, Dr. Andrews? Is there anything we should be worried about?"

"Well, I would like to get another CT scan today, just to check everything out and be very sure everything looks normal, which I fully expect it to. But there really isn't anything for you to worry about. Once I heard your memory had returned, having no experience with patients in your situation, I reached out to some colleagues around the region and from what I gathered, no one has ever dealt with a patient who regained their memory and then lost it again. It seems to be, as far as we can tell, a permanent fix." He smiled at her. "The brain is a miraculous and wonderful thing. We should trust that it will be fine from here on out."

Ella laughed out loud with happiness and she heard Porter release a breath he must have been holding for weeks. She looked at him and had never seen such a joyful look on his face.

"So, what I remember now, I should remember forever?"

"That should be correct." The doctor's face went from smiling back to serious. "Now Ella, although I am convinced that your brain itself is healing nicely, I am a little concerned about your mental health. Dealing with all the memories returning, the good, the bad, and the panic that accompanied them, I think it would be a good idea for you to talk to a psychiatrist. I think it would be good for you to discuss your attack and the robbery with a professional. They can also prescribe something for the anxiety, if you would want them to." Dr. Andrews took a business card out of his coat pocket and handed one to her and one to Porter. "It might not be a bad idea for you to talk to someone too." Porter took the card and nodded.

"Do either of you have any questions for me before we get you a CT scan?"

"No," Ella said, "I've heard everything I wanted to hear."

"Great, I will have my nurse get you all settled and I will call you tomorrow with the results. By the way, this man here," he said, pointing to Porter, "he never left your side while you were in a coma. All the nurses were all in a flutter over him in the ICU. He impressed a lot of people with how devoted he was to you. I know as a doctor I might be overstepping my boundaries here, but as a father, I admire him for the way he took care of you. I wouldn't want anything less for one of my daughters."

Ella was stunned by the doctor's words. As he made his way out of the examination room, he shook Porter's hand and thumped him on the shoulder, in less of a doctor way and more of a man-to-man way. Ella raised her eyebrows at Porter.

"Well, you certainly made an impression on the good doctor," she said with a smile. Then the nurse came in and took Ella to get a CT scan.

After the CT scan, Ella wanted to go to the store to check in and make sure everything was running smoothly since she made the hasty retreat to the beach.

When Porter's truck turned onto the street of Poppy, Ella's heartbeat thundered through her chest. As her store front came into view, she felt her body start to shake.

"Ella, Baby, what's wrong?" Porter pulled the truck over and scooted towards her, enveloping her in his arms. He stroked his hand down her hair, rocking her gently side to side. "Please, talk to me." Ella was still shaking, but with her face buried in his chest she tried to answer him.

"I just haven't been back to the store since I remembered the accident," she said through shaky breaths. Porter pulled her in closer to him, tightening his hold on her.

"I'm so sorry. I didn't even think about that," he said gently. "Do you want to go?" She shook her head against his shirt.

"No, it's my store. I can't avoid it. I just need a minute." So they sat there as she focused on breathing and the sensation of Porter's hand sifting through her hair.

"Can I ask you something?"

"Sure," she said as she pulled back from him.

"Do you remember who shot you?" He whispered, almost as if he was afraid his voice would break her.

"I remember seeing the man who shot me, yes, but I never saw his face."

"Could it have been Kyle?" He asked gently. Ella looked in Porter's eyes and saw the pain in them. She knew he wanted nothing more than for Kyle to be the bad guy so that he had someone tangible to blame all their heartache on.

"No. It wasn't Kyle," she whispered.

Porter placed his hand on the side of her face, stroking his thumb across her cheek.

"You're sure?"

Ella silently nodded her head. He placed a kiss on her forehead and let out a loud sigh. She knew he was upset, even with her memory coming back they were no closer to knowing who had shot her than before. She almost felt disappointed in herself. She could only imagine the hope that had been hinged on her getting back her memory.

"I'm sorry I don't remember, Porter. I didn't see his face, but I would have known if it were Kyle. I would have recognized him."

"I know, Baby. You've got nothing to be sorry for." He paused for a moment. "Do you still want to go inside?"

"Yes. I can't let the memories stop me from going into my own store. Thank you for holding me," she looked up at him.

"Always," he said and gave her a small kiss. He pulled away, got out of the truck, and came around to her side, ever the gentleman. He opened her door and linked his fingers with hers as they walked towards Poppy.

Ella was glad to see the store was pretty busy, customers perusing the racks and her two employees helping women accessorize and find matching pieces. When Brittany, her most experienced employee, saw her, a smile formed along her lips.

"Ella, hi! We weren't sure we would see you today."

"Hi, Brit. How are things going today?"

"Just great. Pretty busy for a Monday," she said as her eyes strayed towards Porter and his hand linked with hers.

"Brittany, this is Porter. Porter, this is Brittany, she is one of my valued employees." Porter reached out with his free hand to shake hers.

"Nice to meet you," he said. "I've heard good things about you."

"Really? Well that's good," she said smiling.

"We just came by to check on the store, make sure everything was going well."

"Everything's fine, promise. Do you guys have plans today?"

"Not really, we just came from the hospital."

"What?" Brittany asked, concern flashing across her face. "Is everything ok?"

"Yes. Everything is fine. Better than fine, actually. My memory came back Saturday night." Brittany's eyes went wide and her smile was back.

"Ella! That's great! I'm so happy for you."

"Thanks, I am too." Ella looked up at Porter and saw he was smiling as well. "I am just going to check my messages and then I will be out of your hair."

"Ella, this is your store. You're not in my hair," she laughed.

Ella led Porter to the backroom and she sat down at her desk looking at some papers that had been left for her.

"So, when do you actually work? You seem to come and go from here as you please," Porter asked. Ella laughed.

"I'm lucky enough that I can hire a full staff. So the store runs whether I'm here or not. I spend a lot of time here, more than forty hours usually, but I've been distracted the last couple of days." She winked at him.

"So, your store makes enough of a profit that you can fully staff and you don't even have to be here if you don't want to be? Why haven't you opened a second store sooner? It's obvious that you are very good at this."

"Fear of failing, I suppose, or being too comfortable."

"You're not afraid anymore?"

"No, the fear is still there, but the excitement and need for change is stronger. I guess I'm just ready. Besides, I feel like I can do anything if you're there helping me." He came to stand behind her and placed his hands on her shoulders.

"I'm honored to help." Just then her phone rang and she gave him a worried look.

"It's my mom," she said and then answered. "Hey, Mom."

"Ella, where have you been? We've all been worried sick about you."

"I'm fine, Mom. Sorry you worried. Listen, can I come over for dinner tonight? I have something I want to talk with you about." Her mom let out a sigh and Ella knew she still wanted to be upset with her for disappearing.

"Of course you can come over for dinner. I'll see you around six?"

"Sounds great, Mom. Oh, and I'll be bringing a date."

"A date?"

"Yes, a date," she threw a smile at Porter, which he returned and made her insides quiver.

That evening as they drove to Ella's parents' house, Ella could feel the tension radiating off of Porter and it was making her nervous in return. He drove his truck and hadn't spared a glance her way since they left her apartment. His hands gripped the steering wheel with impressive strength.

"Baby, what's bothering you?" Ella reached across the cab of the truck and gently stroked his forearm, trying to calm him down. He pushed out a loud breath and ran a hand through his hair which made Ella smile because his hair was constantly in disarray because of his habit. "What is it?" She pressed.

"The last time I spoke with your mother she basically told me to move on. She told me to give up, that you wouldn't ever remember me, or us, and that I should just cut my losses," he paused. "I just don't know how I feel about ambushing her like this. I don't know what I'm going to do if she's upset that we're together." Ella scooted across the seat and placed Porter's arm around her shoulders so that she could press herself into his side.

"First of all, my parents will probably be so ecstatic that my memory came back that will overshadow anything else. And secondly," she said as she placed her hand on his chest. "It doesn't really matter what my mom thinks about us being together. Nothing could keep me from you now. Besides, my mom isn't really the type to forbid something. I'm a grown woman. Once my mom sees how happy we are, I'm sure she'll be fine."

"I just don't want anyone to be upset. We've had enough drama already. I just want everything to go smoothly."

Ella kissed his cheek and patted his chest.

"Everything is smooth sailing from here on out, promise."

When they pulled up to her parent's house, Ella made sure she held Porter's hand in hers. She wanted there to be no mistake about their relationship when her parents saw them together. Ella knocked on the door and then opened it.

"Mom?" She called out.

"Back in the kitchen." Ella gave Porter's hand a squeeze. When they entered the kitchen, Ella saw her mother's eyes lift to take them in and confusion immediately painted across her face.

"Hi, Mom," Ella smiled at her.

"Ella, what's going on?" Her mother's voice was calm and smooth, genuinely concerned but still friendly.

"Mom, I've got something to tell you and Daddy. Is he around?"

"Ella, is that you?" She heard her father's voice as he entered the kitchen, and the same concerned and confused expression came across his face to match his wife's.

"Mom. Dad," Ella started. She wasn't really sure where to start, so she decided to just jump in. "Saturday night my memory came back," Ella said with half a smile, hoping they would understand what she wasn't saying: that she remembered Porter.

"Your memory came back?" Her mother asked.

"Yes. It was completely random, out of the blue, and hurt like hell. But it came back." Her mother's hand came to her chest and she could see tears forming in her eyes.

"It hurt?" She asked through the tears.

"Yes. It felt very much like a migraine and then it was like a thunderstorm was in my brain. The worst of it didn't last long and it was over quickly, but it did hurt." She felt Porter squeeze her hand. She looked up at him and he leaned down to place a chaste kiss on her lips.

"And it appears you've remembered Porter as well?" Her father asked.

"Yes, I remember Porter. He's the first thing I remembered," she smiled up at him. "I drove to his house immediately that night. That's why you couldn't get ahold of me."

"So, then it's true?" Susan asked and Ella could see a small smile was playing across her lips.

"What's true?" Ella asked, confused.

"That you fell in love with him at the beach?"

"Yes," and a rush of air followed as Ella finally released some of the tension she'd brought in with her. "I fell in love with him at the beach, and I fell in love with him again in Portland, before I remembered him. I would fall in love with him over and over again, I'm sure. Although, I think we'd both rather that this time it stuck."

"You've been seeing each other in Portland?" Her mother's eyes flicked between her and Porter.

"Yes, Ma'am. I'm sorry if you feel like I went against your wishes. I just couldn't stay away from her any longer." Porter said, sounding like he was bracing himself for an onslaught of anger and argument.

"Obviously, you can understand, given the circumstances, we made decisions based on what we thought was best for Ella," her father began. "It was a stressful time for everyone involved."

"Daddy, I know why you and Mom made your decisions. Porter and I are just hoping now that I remember everything and know with everything inside of me that I love this man, that you will give us your blessing to be together." Ella's parents looked at each other and seemed to communicate silently, something that can only come with years of marriage. Ella could only hope that one day she and Porter could boast about how long they'd been married, and give each other looks that communicated entire thoughts.

Ella's mother walked over to her and pulled her into a hug.

"All we want is for you to be happy and healthy. Porter proved himself to us at the hospital and every day since."

Ella pulled away from her mother and saw her father shaking Porter's hand. Her father leaned into Porter, said something quietly near his ear, and she saw Porter nodding in affirmation.

Everything worked out the way she had planned and she could almost see the proverbial light at the end of the tunnel, a point in her life in which she was happy, with a man who truly loved her, and thriving.

Her father informed them dinner was ready and served on the deck. When they walked outside they were seated and surrounded by food. Ella's mother had a tendency to over prepare.

They were deep into the meal, enjoying casual conversation, her parents trying to get to know Porter a little better, when the conversation shifted back to Ella.

"So, Ella, getting your memory back must have been a little strange. Have you remembered anything surprising?"

"Not really, but it definitely is strange. I remember the robbery and the shooting, which is a little scary, but mostly I'm just remembering little things that might seem inconsequential to most, but it's makes all the difference in the world to me now."

"Like what, Honey?" Her father asked.

"Well, for instance, before the robbery I had been thinking about expanding the store and opening a second location." She glanced over at Porter instinctually, looking for the support she knew he'd supply. Of course he knew what she needed and laced his fingers with hers, squeezing her hand gently.

"Well, that's a wonderful idea, Ella. You're store does so well and you're so good at what you do. A second store would be a good investment," her mother gave her a genuine smile. "Would the second store be in Portland? Oh!" Her mother was suddenly very excited. "East side or West side?"

"Well, actually," Ella gave Porter another look, trying to absorb all the strength she could from him. "I think I'm going to open a store in Salem."

"Salem?" Her mother asked, confused.

"Yes. It's a decent-sized city and I don't want to be too close to the other store, otherwise I will drown the market. I have to build them up separately to make sure they can survive independently of each other."

"But Salem is so far away," her mother sounded honestly upset.

"Susan, it's only an hour," her father added. Ella gave him a grateful smile for his subtle show of support.

"I was farther away when I was at college," Ella stated.

"But the plan was always for you to come back. Why are you running away?" Ella put her fork down on her plate and took in a deep breath, trying to calm the agitation that was threatening to take over.

"Mom, I'm not running away. I understand that this must be shocking for you, but you should try to be happy for me. I've spent the last two months lost, roaming around without direction or purpose. Now, I finally feel like I'm back to a place in my life where I can move forward. I can't open another store here, Mom. It just wouldn't be smart. I don't need you to like my decision, but it would be nice if I felt like I had your support." Her mother's eyebrows were furrowed with worry and the lines around her eyes were deepening the longer she contemplated Ella's plans.

"What are you going to do down there all by yourself. You'll be lonely, Ella."

"I'll be there with her," Porter answered. Ella's chest filled with warmth knowing that he had taken it upon himself to break the news to her parents about their plans to live together. She squeezed his hand and rubbed her thumb along the top of his knuckles, all of a sudden wishing they were by themselves and just spending time holding each other in bed, instead of being here with her parents.

"Porter, that's sweet of you, but what is Ella supposed to do when you're at your house? During the week when you're not visiting? She's just gotten over a very traumatic event in her life. I don't think it's a good idea to be so far away and all alone."

"Like I said, she won't be alone. We're planning on living

together in Salem."

Silence fell across the room and all Ella could hear was the ticking of the grandfather clock in the corner of the dining room. Her parent's eyes met across the table, again, conversing without words. Her mother sighed heavily.

"Porter," her father began, "Ella has a broad and profound stubborn streak."

"Ah, yes, I'm aware," Porter laughed lightly.

"Once she puts her mind to something there is little to do to try and steer her in another direction. We've learned that sometimes it is best to just let her go."

"I'm right here, Dad. You don't have to talk about me like I'm not in the room." His eyes darted over to her. Ella had had enough of people pretending like she wasn't around. All through her recovery everyone was always walking on eggshells around her, talking about her as if she couldn't speak for herself, or handle what they were going to say.

"Ella, I'm not trying to offend you. I'm just trying to explain to Porter how if someone was going to be with you in Salem we're glad it's him." Ella felt a smile pull at her lips. "You don't need our permission to move to Salem, or to live with Porter. You're a grown woman. But we're glad you've decided to do something to make yourself happy."

"I am happy. Thank you for understanding."

"Sweetie, after everything you've been through, all we want is for you to be safe and healthy. Salem isn't that far away. Plus, I think it would be fun to decorate a new house!" Her mother exclaimed. Ella laughed.

"Well, we can't do too much decorating. Nothing too extensive anyway. We are going to rent a house for now until Porter can build us our own." Ella looked over at him and smiled.

"Build you a house? That sounds decidedly permanent," her father said, sounding concerned.

"Everything about Ella and me is permanent," Porter said without even blinking, as if he were stating fact as sure as the earth revolving around the sun.

"Well," her mother stated after releasing a soft sigh, "If your father had said things like that a week after meeting me, I would have dropped everything and moved in with him too."

"Exactly," Ella said, then leaned over and placed a small kiss on the corner of Porter's mouth. "Thank you," she whispered in his ear.

"Ok," her father interrupted. "Who wants dessert?"

Chapter Nine

Porter

Porter and Ella were on their way back to her apartment when her phone rang.

"It's Megan," Ella stated as she answered. "Hey Megs, what's up?"

"Well," Porter heard her voice through the speaker of Ella's phone, "I was wondering if you and Kalli wanted to come with me tomorrow to look at a few wedding dresses."

"Of course I want to come and look at wedding dresses with you. When and where?"

"How would two work for you?" Ella held her hand over the phone and whispered to him.

"What time do you have to leave tomorrow?"

"I will probably leave early in the morning to get to work by eight."

"Two is fine with me," Ella said to Megan. "I'll put some time in at the store, then when we're done drooling over you in a wedding dress, I will just head out to Lincoln City. Does two work for Kalli too?"

"Yeah, she's off tomorrow."

"Perfect. Which shop?"

"Bridal Bliss. It's downtown, on fifth."

"Great, I'll be there. I'm so excited to see you in a wedding dress Megs."

"I will be the most beautiful bride you've ever seen, obviously." She added with a laugh.

"Obviously."

"Ok, please tell Porter I say hi and I will see you tomorrow.

Bye, Fella." Ella laughed and shook her head at her sister.

"Bye, Megs."

"So, you're going to come out to Lincoln City tomorrow?" He asked her hopefully.

"I thought that's what we decided. No more nights apart. You're here tonight, so it's only fair I should go to you tomorrow. Is that ok?" She asked, suddenly sounding worried.

"Babe, of course it's ok." He took a deep breath in and let it out loudly. "I guess I'm just still getting use to the idea that I get to spend every night with you," he said as he took her hand. His mind wandered back to the nights when he couldn't even sleep in his own bed because thoughts of Ella made it impossible to get any rest. There were days when he considered selling his house simply because the thought of walking in and knowing she wasn't there was too distressing. They pulled into her parking spot and when he turned off his truck he looked over at her.

"Listen, I don't want you to ever doubt that I want to be with you. Don't doubt that every night I want you next to me."

"I want that too, Babe. So much."

He reached out and placed his hand behind her neck, pulling her into him. His mouth took hers gently and he felt her sigh into him, her breath caressing his face. How much longer could he have survived without her? If he had never gone to see her would she have ever remembered? The idea of not being in this exact moment with Ella caused a panic within him. His panic manifested itself in the kiss and he found himself pulling her even closer. She complied and crawled over his lap, straddling his thighs. His hands grasped at her, threading themselves through her hair, sliding down her back to land on the roundness of her ass.

"Do you have any idea how much I need you, Ella? How much of my ability to breathe is dependent on knowing you're safe and you're mine?" He looked into her eyes as he brought his hands to her face.

"I love you with every small piece of my being, Porter. I'm not me if I'm not with you. That distinction was made clear as I waded through two months of wasted time, wondering what was missing. But as much as I love you, and need you, my love for you will always be second best to the way you love me." She leaned down and kissed him. He tried to return the kiss but was distracted by her words that echoed the letter she'd written him. Suddenly the letter was red hot in his wallet, singeing him through his pocket. He pulled away from her and grappled with his pants to get out his wallet, not an easy task with Ella sitting on his lap. He finally managed to get ahold of his wallet and pull it out. He opened it up and her letter was staring up at him from its designated spot, where it had been for nearly three months. Ella saw it and reached in to take it.

"Is this my letter?" She said as she eyed it. She gently opened up the envelope and pulled out the frail and worn paper, unfolding it as if it would turn to ash if she handled it too roughly.

"Yes," he answered around the lump forming in his throat.

"It looks like it's been read a lot."

"I read it every single day you were gone." He watched her open it up and saw her eyes track the words as she read. His eyes never wavered from hers and he saw the tears begin to well up. Then he watched her push them back and take a deep breath.

"I had forgotten all about this letter," she whispered.

"Understatement of the year, Babe" he laughed quietly. She playfully slapped his chest.

"You know what I mean," she smiled at him and caressed one of his cheeks with her hand. Her touch was warm and soothing. She always managed to give him exactly what he needed with her touch. Whether he needed to be calmed, or wanted to be excited, hers was the only touch that had ever affected him that way. "Why did you read it so many times?"

"It was the only thing I had left of you. Besides the memories that haunted me and my house that still smelled like you, it was the only way I could feel close to you." She held his eyes for a moment and then looked back down at the paper.

"If I had known what was going to happen to me that night, I might have written this letter differently."

"What would you have changed?" He asked, rubbing his hands up the outside of her thighs, up her waist, and back down again.

"I probably would have told you not to let anyone keep us apart. That I would be hurting just as badly as you were, perhaps just in a different way."

"Let's just be sure that from here on out we remember what we went through and use it as a reminder."

"Ok, a reminder of what though?"

He reached up and tucked a piece of hair behind her ear.

"A reminder that you and I should always stand firm that we know what's best for us, and that we will always put each other first. And that regardless of where one of us is, the other is never far away. No matter what."

She smiled at his words and leaned down to kiss him, stopping just before her lips met his.

"Sounds good to me," the end of her sentence was mumbled against his lips as he pushed his mouth into hers. He used his hands to pull on her hips and bring her body in closer to his, to feel her as close to him as possible. He could never get enough of the staggering pleasure that feeling her body against his could bring. Once he felt like the center of her body was sufficiently pressed against his own, his hands roamed her body again, seeking out the pieces of her that reacted to his touch. His hands on her face, on her back, his lips on her neck. If they hadn't been in his truck in a parking lot, Porter would have found it hard at this point to keep Ella's clothes on. Instead, he let his hands wander just along the hem of her shirt, feeling her smooth skin against his rough fingers.

She fisted his hair in her hands and he could feel her arousal start to grow, not only by the urgency in her hands, but the sexy sounds she made. Light and gentle sighs and whimpers floated through the cab of his truck and he felt himself harden between his legs even as Ella used her core to grind down on him. He hated to, but he pulled away.

"Ella, let's go upstairs," he tried to say but she kept finding ways to kiss him through his words.

"No," she said quickly between pecks.

"No?"

"I'm fine right here," she mumbled as her hands began to unbutton his jeans. He quickly grabbed her hands to stop her and pinned her wrists behind her back.

"Ella, this is not happening here. We are not teenagers. There's a perfectly good room with four walls in your apartment. Let's go." Ella gave him a hard glare.

"I remember a time when you nearly had me on a public beach. In fact, I believe you *would have* had me if the rain hadn't started." She leaned forward with her wrists still captured behind her back and her breasts pushed up against his chest, causing him to pull in a sharp breath. Her lips found his ear and she rasped, "What's the difference?"

He growled and turned his head to nip at her throat, sucking and licking, drawing out more groans from Ella that had his blood running hot and thick through his veins.

"This difference is that on the beach we were under the cover of blankets and it was deserted. We are out in the open here and anyone could just walk out of their apartment. I won't have anyone but me see you turned on." He pulled on her wrists, causing her to sit up straight. "Let me take you inside. I want to be able to make love to you and it's difficult in this truck." He let go of her hands, but only to lace his fingers through hers.

"How is anyone supposed to argue with that?" Ella smiled at him, and gave him a small kiss before climbing off of his lap. The missing weight of her did not go unnoticed as his body ached for her to return. He managed to get himself under control enough to walk her to her apartment. He took the keys from her and opened the door. They stepped inside and he dropped his small duffle bag on the floor in the hallway. He had only been in her apartment once and it was before her memory had returned. She wasn't technically his then, so he was able to argue away the urge to remove Kyle's pictures from her walls. He stared at one now and as reasonable as he tried to remain, he couldn't ignore the fact that he wanted the pictures gone.

Ella followed his eyes she walked to the picture.

"After all the years we spent together and everything we had been through, I never would have imagined that he could have put his hands on me the way he did that night." She reached up, took the frame off the wall, and studied it for a moment. "How could I have been with someone like him? How did I not see him for who he really was?"

Porter came to stand behind her, placing his hands on her shoulders.

"People like Kyle do a good job of hiding who they really are, Ella. You saw what he wanted you to see."

"People like him?" She asked. "What kind of person was he?"

"A sociopath with a death wish," Porter said through gritted teeth.

Ella turned and went into the kitchen, coming back a few seconds later with a big trash bag. She threw the picture in the bag and then continued down the hall tossing every other frame with a picture of him in the bag as well. She moved quickly and her breathing was frantic. Porter began to see the panic come over her. He went to stop her and pull her into his arms.

"Babe, stop. You don't have to do this now. Please, I'll do it for you, just calm down."

"I need to get him out of this house, Porter." Her hands came up to cover her face and she breathed rapidly now. "Everything is returning, all the memories." She buried her face in his chest and he smoothed his hand down her back, trying to help calm her. "Being with you is wonderful because we have beautiful memories, even though they are few. I am in a haze of happiness with you, Porter. But when I go back to my old life, the store, and now my own house, all the bad memories come back. I shouldn't have to be afraid of my own life," she cried.

"You're right, Ella," he said as he used his hands to pull her face level with his so she could see how serious he was. "You shouldn't have to deal with any of this, but you are. You're doing just fine. You just have to feel it all and deal with it as it comes. I'll be here the whole way and we'll get you in to talk to someone. But hear me when I say that I will never let him hurt you again, Ella. Never. You need to let that part of your fear go and give it all to me. Let me worry about that and you just let the fear go."

"Porter," she said, holding back tears, running her hand down his cheek. "Kyle held me up against that door behind you and tried to rape me." Porter turned to stone at her words. He knew something else had happened between them before she was shot, but had never gotten the opportunity to talk to her about it. If he had known the whole story, he surely would have killed Kyle at the hospital when he had the chance. His fists clenched at his sides and he tried not to let himself picture what she must have gone through.

"What do you mean by 'tried'?"

Ella took in a deep breath, looking as if she was trying to calm herself.

"He pushed me up against the door, held me there by my jaw, then he ripped… he ripped…" she let out a sob and he pulled her into his arms, shushing her and kissing her temple.

"No, Ella, it's ok. You don't have to tell me."

"I do, though, Porter," she said as she cried. "This will eat away at you just as much as it will me if it isn't out there. I don't want it bottled up inside me. It will poison me from the middle if I don't tell you. Please, let me tell you." He felt her crumbling against him and he slid her down to the floor with him. He pressed every available part of his body against hers, offering himself to her in comfort and love, hoping that she would take from him what she needed. His arms were wrapped around her shoulders, and his legs were sprawled out around the sides of her as she sat on the floor between them. She curled up into him, breathing hard and holding back sobs. He could feel the heaving of her lungs as she tried to control the eruption of emotion.

"He ripped my shirt open," she paused, trying to remain calm. "He ripped it open and then grabbed my breast so hard it left a bruise. I could taste the blood pooling in my mouth. I heard the ripping of my shirt. I could feel my teeth biting into my cheek. He would have raped me if I hadn't stopped him."

"But you did, Ella. He hurt you, but he didn't win and he didn't rape you. You kicked his ass. I saw him at the hospital. You broke his fucking nose."

She looked up at him with tears in her eyes, but a small smile on her lips.

"I did?" she asked hopefully.

"Oh yeah, he looked terrible." She buried her face in his chest again, a little calmer than before.

"It's a good thing I'm moving out of this apartment. I don't think I could live here anymore. And honestly, I don't think I could sleep here if you weren't with me."

"Well, you don't have to worry about that. I am where you are."

She looked up at him again, her eyes asking him to kiss her. He moved in slowly, making sure this was what she wanted. When she closed her eyes and moved to meet him, he knew she needed him to be there for her. He would give her whatever she needed, but didn't want to push her too far.

Their lips met and it was a softer kiss than they normally shared. Her lips were swollen from crying and salty from tears. She slowly teased his lips with her tongue and he opened for her, trying not to rush her, but finding himself needing the contact with her just as much as she seemed to need him. Although the kiss started soft and slow, it gradually moved toward longing and need. Ella moved so that she was again straddling his lap, quickly becoming his favorite way to kiss her, their bodies connected at the core. His hands ran up her back, trying to hold her to him, to give her the feeling of being protected. That was all he ever wanted, to protect her. He reached up and twisted his hands around her hair, gently but firmly pulling it back and forcing her lips from his. Her hands came behind his neck as she leaned back into his arms, allowing him to take her neck.

His mouth found the spot between her neck and shoulder that tasted of vanilla every time, and as he kissed and sucked there she let out a throaty moan. His hand traveled up the front of her body, sliding smoothly all the way from her belly button to her neck, pulling her back into the kiss.

"Porter, please," she begged.

"What do you need, Baby?"

"You, please. Make me forget." He looked at her and saw the question in her eyes. What a strange request. After everything they'd been through, hoping she'd remember, to now, in this moment, doing everything they could to wipe her memory away. Porter couldn't help but wonder if his dire need to be with her was worth the pain he saw in her eyes right now. If he'd just left her alone, moved on as best he could without her, would her memories still be buried away? If it was his fault that she was reliving this nightmare, he would do anything he could to help her forget. Using the wall to push against, he stood up, still holding her against him. He started to carry her to the bedroom when she stopped him by putting her feet back on the ground.

She reached down for the hem of her shirt and pulled it up over her head slowly, never taking her eyes off of his. He watched her as she slid her jeans down her hips, leaving her in just bra and panties. He got a small thrill knowing he bought that set for her. In any other circumstance he might have commented on how he liked her in the sexy things he bought for her, but now wasn't the time. Her hand came out and gripped his shirt. She walked backwards and pulled him with her. She moved backwards until her back was up against her front door. When the door hit her back, she cringed and closed her eyes. He saw a shutter run along her body and he ached to help her through the turmoil evident on her face.

"Tell me how I can help you, Baby." He leaned his forehead against hers, waiting for her to tell him what he could do. She didn't look up at him; she just reached for the button of his jeans and slid his pants to the floor along with his boxers. She pulled his shirt over his head and tossed it towards the living room. He finally placed a finger under her chin and lifted her face so he could look in her eyes.

"You've got to tell me what to do, Ella. I'm flying blind here and I need you to tell me what you want."

"Make me forget, Porter." She said as she reached behind her back to unclasp her bra, letting it fall to the floor. "Make love to me, here, and erase it all." She pushed her panties to the floor and stepped out of them. He continued to look her directly in the eyes, silently asking her if she was sure. She gave a small but certain nod, and he moved in to her body, pressing her against the door.

He delicately grazed his fingers along her jaw and felt her breath shutter. His mouth dropped feathered kisses from one side of her jaw to the other, trying to kiss away her memory and her pain. As he kissed her jaw, his hand came to her breast. He held it in his palm, feeling the weight of it, when he felt her take his hand off and thread her fingers through his. She placed his other hand on the opposite breast, indicating that was the one with the need. He gently, with unparalleled care, fluttered his thumb across her nipple. She made a sound that sounded like a sob and he immediately halted.

"I'm sorry, Baby. I'm so sorry," he whispered.

"Please don't stop. I don't want you to stop," she cried. He nodded, wondering if he was doing more harm than good anymore. He could only trust that she knew what she needed and that she trusted him to give it to her.

He moved his hand back to her breast and fingered her nipple again. She breathed through his touch and seemed to be ok. Keeping his eyes on her, he bent down and laid the lightest of kisses upon it. This time her eyes closed and her head tilted back, so he took it farther and pulled her nipple into his mouth, using his tongue to swirl around it. To his relief a moan of pleasure escaped her lips. He continued to use his mouth on her as he felt her place his other hand between her legs. She placed his fingers at her opening and he could feel the heat radiating from her. She pushed their fingers into her and she moaned again.

Her heat and her moans spurred him on and he felt the tension grow between his own legs. The fact that he could even become aroused was a relief to him, not being sure he could achieve any kind of erection knowing he was trying to erase an attempted rape from his girlfriend's mind. But in the end, this was Ella, and she was offering herself to him; she needed him. He responded to her body, both physically and emotionally. Despite the pressure and complication of their situation, his body would always be tied to hers irrevocably.

He continued to lave at her breast and thrust his fingers into her. Both of her hands came up to tug on his hair and one of her legs wrapped around his waist. She reached down between them and took him in her hands. He heard her sigh.

"What's wrong?" He asked.

"Nothing, I was just worried."

He placed his hand on her thigh wrapped around him and flipped his nose against hers slowly.

"Worried about what?"

"I guess I was just afraid that you wouldn't want me after what I told you."

He continued to look in her eyes and saw all the insecurity she was laying out in front of him, all her vulnerability.

"I will always want you, Ella. It's impossible not to want you. I just don't want to hurt you."

"You couldn't hurt me. It's impossible." He loved that she felt that way, that she knew he could never hurt her. Her words only made him harder and he felt himself nudge against her. She felt it too and lifted to wrap her other leg around his middle. Her arms draped around his neck and her legs hooked behind his back. With one arm around her and his other arm against the door for support, he leaned in and took her mouth. She kissed him back and all the reservations from before seemed to melt away. It was only the two of them here now and she was only with him. He gave in to the passion and let his tongue make wide sweeps through her mouth, and when she used her hips to grind into him he let out a growl that surprised even him.

The tip of his cock found her opening and he looked her in the eye as he sank into her, thrusting upwards.

"I love you so much, Ella," he said through rough breaths and a gravelly voice.

"I know. I love you too."

He pushed her hips up against the door, pinning her there with his own, and continued to drive into her. She gripped him with her strong legs and her face found the space carved out for her by his neck, the crook that she belonged in. He felt her heartbeat against his chest and knew his beated just as rapidly.

Sweat beaded on his brow, the pressure in his groin mounted. Every time he pumped into her she cried out, spurring him on.

"Oh God, please," she begged him.

"Hang on, Baby," he replied. He brought his hand down between them and used this thumb to circle her clit. Her moans became louder and more crazed, so he pumped into her harder and faster.

"Yes, please, Porter. Come with me."

Within seconds of her command, he was over the edge and taking her with him. They stilled, breathed harsh and panting breaths, their connection still intact. Once he got his breath back and felt strong enough, he placed both hands under her thighs and carried her from the door and down the hall.

"Where are we going?" She asked as she placed sweet kisses along his shoulder.

"To make more memories," he said simply.

Chapter Ten

Ella

Ella woke to the feeling of the mattress dipping down around her. Then she felt Porter's hand on her thigh. Tingles immediately coursed through her body. Her eyes fluttered open and when they adjusted she was saddened to see Porter sitting next to her in bed completely clothed.

"Are you leaving?" She croaked, her voice still asleep.

"Yeah, Babe, I've got to go if I'm going to make it to work on time."

Ella grumbled something incoherent; early mornings weren't her thing. She heard Porter laugh at her and then he brushed her crazy hair out of her face. She felt the warmth of his breath on her face and she peeped open one eye.

"Give me a kiss goodbye." His voice was soft and sexy.

She leaned up and brushed a small kiss across his mouth. He hummed in appreciation and she smiled against his mouth.

"I'll be in Lincoln City by six, I think," she said.

"Ok, text me when you leave. And I left a key to the house on your dresser."

He was leaving her a key. To *the* house. Not his house. The house. The difference in the distinction was felt way down deep in her heart. They were sharing everything now, sharing a life. The smile she already wore grew even wider and Porter's mouth mirrored hers.

"What are you smiling about?" She shrugged her shoulders, not wanting to seem like a complete and total sap.

"Nothing, just you."

"Hmmm," he bent down to kiss her again. "Drive safe. Remember to text me."

"Ok, you drive safe too and have a good day at work."

"Bye, Baby," he said and she could feel herself drift back to sleep.

Ella pulled up to her store, only this time she was alone, without Porter to help ease the panic she felt roiling to the surface. She silently chastised herself for not calling the psychiatrist the doctor had referred her to; obviously, she needed to talk to someone about her panic.

She spent a few moments in her car, breathing deeply, trying not to think about the man in the dark hoodie who had disrupted her life so suddenly. Through the window of the store she could see Brittany and the thought that someone else would be there with her calmed her slightly. When she felt like her fear was ebbing, she ventured out of the car and into the store.

Throughout the morning she had a few moments where she wasn't sure she could push the panic back and at one point she ran to the bathroom, afraid the fear was going to make her sick. She managed to keep everything under control, although she wasn't entirely sure that the girls at the store didn't think she was crazy.

When she wasn't wracked with worry or trying to maintain the façade of someone who wasn't suffering, she marvelled at how different her life had become in just the span of a few days. She recalled being in her store and spending days in a haze, when her mind would drift to thoughts about the missing weeks in her mind. Now, she knew with certainty everything that had transpired during those weeks, and she was grateful to take the good with the bad. Her mind had sacrificed her security and mental well-being to bring Porter back to her. She smiled, partly because she knew she would eventually be ok. The panic would subside and her anxiety would ease, but she would never be able to be ok without Porter. So, it was a sacrifice she was willing to make.

When it was finally time for Ella to leave for the bridal shop, she felt exhausted emotionally. Trying to maintain a calm and cool demeanor while she felt like her heart was going to pound out of her chest was more taxing then she could have imagined. The panic she felt at the apartment and the anxiety she felt at the shop were similar and eerie. In her mind she tied the two events together, which seemed logical as they happened within a few hours of each other. She had a hard time separating the events in her mind, and the longer she spent at the store the more she thought about the night of the shooting and Kyle's attack.

"Brittany, I am leaving for the day. Call me if you need anything. I probably won't be in tomorrow until at least eleven."

"Bye Ella. Have a good rest of your day!"

Ella was glad she had such dependable women working for her and she knew the store was in good hands.

When Ella arrived at the bridal store, she was relieved to feel her anxiety melting away slightly. It worried her that she knew the physical distance from the store was the reason she felt better; she didn't like having to feel afraid at her store, the business she'd worked so hard to build up and make successful.

She immediately heard her sister's musical laughter deeper in the store and she followed it to her.

"Ella! So glad you're here! Kalli and I were waiting for you!" Megan said as she pulled her into a tight hug.

"Have you tried anything on yet?" Ella asked as she moved to give Kalli a hug as well.

"No, but I've picked a few out."

"Why isn't Mom here?"

"Well, don't be mad, but I went out dress shopping with mom last week. I knew she couldn't make this trip, some school board curriculum thing, so we went alone." Megan looked at her, waiting for her to get upset.

"I'm glad you and mom got some time together and that she isn't missing seeing you try on a wedding dress for the first time."

A woman, who Ella assumed was the consultant helping Megan, approached them.

"You must be the sister and Maid of Honor?" She looked at Ella.

"That's me," Ella said with a smile.

"Great. Now that everyone's here, let's get some choices locked down and get Megan in a dress."

As they sifted through dresses, Ella found Megan deferring to her about style choices and different fabrics. Kalli had a lot to contribute and Megan mentioned a few times how lucky she was to have such sophisticated fashion aficionados at her disposal.

Ella made sure her sister didn't touch any mermaid cut dresses or any ball gowns. Kalli was a big fan of the sweetheart neckline on Megan, but didn't like her in the blush colored fabric.

Ella heard Megan squeal from the fitting room and she and Kalli exchanged excited looks. When Megan came out of the room, Ella was sure she had never seen a bigger smile on her sister's face. To see her sister so happy and in a wedding dress, immediately brought tears to Ella's eyes.

"Oh my gosh, you guys, I think this is the one!"

Megan was stunning in a creamy white, satin, sweetheart-neck gown with cap sleeves. There was no poof, no bling, no embellishment at all. It was simple. It was classy. It was perfect. The way the satin draped over Megan's curves was ridiculously flattering and Ella knew Patrick would die if he saw his fiancé in this dress.

"Megan, you look amazing," Ella said, trying to hold back tears.

"Do you really like it?"

"Are you kidding?" Kalli said. "You look phenomenal. Breath taking."

"Yes, Megan, you look like a photo in a bridal magazine."

"I always thought I'd want something a little more, I don't know, formal. This looks like lingerie."

"You've always told me how much Patrick likes you in lingerie." Ella added with a smile.

"Yes, but do I want to be up in front of one hundred and fifty plus people knowing that he's picturing me naked? I'm not sure. Plus, if the dress looks like lingerie, what am I supposed to wear on the wedding night?"

"Oh, honey. You can find something sexier than this dress. This will be the appetizer to wet his appetite." All three girls cracked up at the sales woman's forward comment.

"Ok," Megan exhaled a deep breath. "It's a definite contender, but I want to see more. I cannot commit so quickly."

"More dresses, more choices," Kalli said with a smile. Megan ambled back into the dressing room and Kalli turned towards Ella with a smile on her face.

"So, I have some news," Kalli started.

"Do tell," Ella answered, returning the giant smile across Kalli's face.

"A couple days ago I was on set and ran to the Starbucks down the street to get coffee for the team, and I met a man." The excitement radiating off of her friend's face was contagious and Ella found herself nearly bouncing up and down in her seat as Kalli was.

"I repeat: Do tell!" Ella laughed.

"I was in line to order and he bumped into the back of me accidentally. He was really apologetic and grabbed my elbow to keep me from falling," Kalli's eyes went all glazy and she was far, far away. "Ella, when he touched me, even though it was just my arm, I swear I felt it all the way in my toes."

"Oh my," Ella said, understanding all too well.

"And he is very handsome, like, lose your breath handsome."

"That's the best kind of handsome," Ella replied. "What is his name?"

"Scott," she said with a deep sigh, making Ella giggle.

"Scott is a good name; I've never met a Scott I didn't like."

"You'd like him, Ella. He's perfect."

"So, did he just bump into you or are you guys gonna go out?"

"We exchanged phone numbers after he flirted for a few minutes and bought my coffee, and he's texted me a few times."

"This is all very exciting, Kalli. You haven't dated very much since you've been here."

"I know. I'm *really* ready to go out with him, if you catch my drift," she said with raised eyebrows, leaning over towards Ella so that the sales women couldn't hear her. Ella laughed out loud and then covered her mouth quickly.

"I caught your drift. Don't worry," she said as she gently patted Kalli's knee.

Megan tried on upwards of ten more dresses, but none of them put the smile on her face like the satin one. She was reluctant to put a down payment on it until their mother saw her in it. They still had almost a year until the wedding, so there wasn't a huge rush to make the decision that day.

"I will have to come back with Mom soon."

"She's going to love it, Megs."

Eventually Megan came out of the dressing room in her normal clothes and sat down next to Ella to put her boots back on.

"Megan, do you think we could talk for a minute?"

"Sure, is everything ok?"

"Do you guys want me to give you a minute alone?" Kalli asked.

"No, Kalli, it's fine, please stay and listen." Ella took a deep breath and then looked Megan in the eyes. "Megan, Porter and I have decided to move in together."

Kalli's hand flew to her mouth in shock and surprise, while Megan's face lit up with a smile.

"Really?" Megan asked. Ella nodded her head in affirmation. Suddenly Ella was being pulled into a hug and she felt Megan's arms wrap around her. "Ella, I am so happy for you and for Porter. You guys deserve some happiness. I've never seen a man love a woman like he loves you." Ella pulled back from the embrace.

"Patrick loves you, Megs," Ella reassured her, being reminded of the conversation they shared at the beach and Megan's ridiculous insecurities surrounding Patrick's feelings for her.

"Of course Patrick loves me. I'm amazing. And I love him. There's no one else in this world that I am supposed to be with and I am going to love him for the rest of my life. But Porter, well, I've seen Porter without you. He was only meant to live if you are beside him, Fella. He was empty, lost. He had no direction and no North without you." Megan's eyes misted up with tears she was trying to keep at bay. Ella had a hard time keeping her eyes dry as well.

"Well, that's not all the news I have," Ella said, trying to steer the conversation away from the sad, and onto the exciting.

"OK…" Megan said, drawing out the word, obviously anxious about what Ella had to say.

"We are moving to Salem so I can open another Poppy."

"Oh my gosh! Ella that's so amazing. You're going to do great!" Megan pulled her into another hug.

"And I want you to be the manager of Poppy in Portland, full time." Ella felt Megan freeze in her embrace. Slowly, Megan pulled back.

"You want ME to manage Poppy?"

"Yes, I think you're the best person for the job. You did great while I was recovering and you're looking for a job, right?"

"Well, I mean, yes, I'm looking for a job, but I don't know about this Ella. What if I mess up everything you've worked so hard for? What if I run Poppy into the ground and you have to close the doors and we all end up homeless?"

Ella laughed at her sister's over dramatics.

"Megan, calm down. You aren't going to ruin anything. You are going to be great, if you accept. You already do a great job at Poppy."

"What about Brittany? She's worked there longer."

"Brittany will get a promotion to assistant manager. I really think you'd be great at this. You've got a degree in business; Brittany's degree is in art history. You're qualified. Please, you'd really be doing me a big favor by taking the job."

"You really trust me to take care of your 'store baby'?"

"Implicitly," Ella laughed.

"Well, I'd like to talk it over with Patrick, but I think I can unofficially accept," Megan smiled at Ella.

"I'm so glad, Megan. It will make being in Salem so much easier if I know you're taking care of Poppy here. You don't know how much this means to me."

"You guys are too much. You make me want a sister," Kalli laughed.

"Ok," Megan said, wiping away the rogue tear that had escaped. "Enough with the sappy."

"Yeah," Ella agreed.

"We should go celebrate tonight!" Megan nearly shouted, making Ella laugh again. Sometimes, more than others, the eight year gap between them was glaringly obvious.

"I can't tonight. I am headed to Lincoln City to stay with Porter."

"So, go out there tomorrow," Megan said with a shrug of her shoulders.

"Can't. Porter and I made a promise not to spend any more nights apart."

"That might be the sweetest and sickest thing I've ever heard," Kalli said and then gave Ella an apologetic look. "Sorry."

Ella laughed.

"It's ok. I know it seems sudden, perhaps especially to you, but we just don't want to spend any more time apart. Plus, since I've gotten my memory back, it's difficult being at my apartment alone." Megan nodded in understanding.

"Well, maybe we should all go out on Friday. It will be so fun! Patrick and I haven't been out in ages! Kalli, you could bring a date. Please?" Megan practically begged, waggling her eyebrows at Kalli.

"Ok, I'll talk to Porter about it. And this would be a good opportunity to hang out with Scott," Ella sing-songed at Kalli. Kalli blushed and nodded.

"Well, Kalli, do YOU want to get a drink tonight to celebrate my new job?" Megan asked, feigning insult and annoyance.

"You know I'm always down for a drink. But let's find a dive this time, something more my speed." Megan laughed.

"You don't like my dance clubs?"

"I did, when I was twenty-two."

"Hey! I am twenty-two!"

"I know, but I will get you up to speed with us adults," Kalli joked.

The three women stood up and Megan thanked the consultant, promising to bring her mom back to see the dress. They all hugged at the door before Ella left and headed for her car. Before starting the engine she took out her phone and sent Porter a text.

Leaving now. Should be about two hours. Do you need me to pick anything up for dinner?

No, I just need you. Here. Drive safely. No hitchhikers.

So, should I kick out the one guy I already picked up then?

Very funny. Be careful.

Always. Love you.

Love you too.

When Ella pulled up to Porter's house she was once again floored by the fact that he had built it with his own sexy, capable hands. She couldn't wait to begin the process of building their own house. Honestly, she couldn't wait to *watch* him build their house; it would be glorious, she was sure.

She got out of her car and was immediately hit by the unusual warmth that she felt. Granted, it was late June, but for it to be hot outside on the Oregon Coast was surprising. She was grateful that she had worn a breezy skirt with a sleeveless top.

She was also accosted by the screeching sound of what she thought was a power saw coming from behind the house. She hadn't been in the shop out back yet. She blushed a little at the thought of most of their time together being spent inside the house in one particular room. She ventured around the side of the house to see the big shop, big enough to house the sailboat he was building, and just as spectacularly built as the house. Of course, the buildings matched. He seemed to be somewhat of a perfectionist when it came to his work and it showed.

As she came to the entrance of the shop, two large doors like you'd find in a barn, she could see a surprisingly large boat that was obviously in the midst of creation. Porter had told her it was a twenty-five foot sailboat, but the numbers had really just flitted through her mind, not really taking hold. To see in person a boat that size and realize that the hands of this man were responsible for it made parts of her liquefy. She swallowed her arousal down, trying to maintain some semblance of a cool and unaffected demeanor. She continued in the building and all efforts to stay cool, calm, and collected were thrust back out the door when her eyes found Porter.

He was standing at a table saw, gracefully moving a plank of wood through the blade, shirtless. He was wearing jeans that clung to his ass in the most delicious of ways, and God help her, a tool belt. Every cheesy picture of a construction buff flipped through her mind, one comparing to the glistening Adonis standing before her. As he pushed the wood through the saw the muscles in his back rippled and waved. The forward and backward motions of his arms triggered his biceps to contract and bulge and Ella's ability to stand up straight was stolen from her. Her belly quivered, her core tightened, her hands painfully ached to smooth over the muscles that lined his back and arms.

Even in her hyper-aroused state, she knew it would be dangerous to sneak up on him while he was using a blade, so she used the moment to soak in the view, stowing the sight away in her mind to remember later. Once he powered the saw off, she let out a breath, still trying to take all of him in.

"I still maintain that there should be women lined up on your yard trying to win your affections. You are one seriously sexy man." He turned towards her, obviously surprised to see her.

"Hey, Babe. I didn't hear you come in," he said as he started towards her.

"Well, that's because you were operating that beast of a machine over there. You know," she said with a gleam in her eyes, "women, mainly me, would pay good money to watch you work out here, shirtless, and see all your glorious muscles flexing and thrusting." She emphasized the last word with a sexy whisper. He made his way over to her and gripped her hips.

"You want to see me thrust?" He asked with a smile.

"Always." Her wicked smile stayed on her lips until his came down on hers. Her hands, as if she had no control over them, slid all over his shoulders and down his arms. He was slick with sweat making her hands glide effortlessly over the chords of his muscles still warm from use. She rubbed on him and pulled him in closer to her. He nipped at her bottom lip and pulled away to look her in the eye.

"Ella, I'm covered in saw dust and sweat. Let's go inside and I'll get cleaned up."

"Mmm, nope. I like you dirty right now." Her hands came down between them and she started to undo the button on his jeans.

"I'm warning you, Ella. If you start this, I'm not going to be able to stop. The doors to the shop are open. It's daylight, and I will ravage you in here. But I won't put the brakes on. Your call." She kept her eyes trained right on his and slowly pulled his zipper down and cupped him over his boxers. She watched as his eyes went from a chocolate brown to almost black as lust coursed through him.

"I like your underwear, Porter," she said. He raised an eyebrow at her, half in playfulness, half in confusion.

"Good to know," he said as he flipped the tip of his nose against hers, a classic Porter move that had her heart fluttering in her chest.

"Yes, well, I'm just wondering if you'd like mine as much as I like yours." Realization dawned on him and she watched with a smile as his eyes traveled down from her face and landed right on the apex of her thighs.

"Did you put something special on for me, Ella?"

"I might have made a special effort when I was choosing certain undergarments this morning, hoping I would get the chance to be seen in them," she said in a non-committal way, shrugging her shoulder. He took a step back, putting a few feet between them.

"Take off your clothes, Ella, and let me see." His voice was deep and demanding, sending shivers throughout her body. She reached up to the buttons on the front of her blouse, slowing undoing them without removing her eyes from his. Once they were all undone, she pulled the fabric apart at the center, just enough to show the canal between the swells of her breasts and her belly button. She left it on and moved on to her skirt. She reached behind her and pulled the zipper down the back, letting it float to the ground and pool around her feet. His eyes followed the skirt but quickly came back to her. She could tell he was anxious to see her, which was only exasperated by the fact that her shirt was still covering everything she was sure he wanted to see.

"All of it," he growled.

"So impatient," she scolded with a smile.

"Damn straight, Ella. I've gone too long without you for you to be standing here teasing me. Now take it off before I ruin it by ripping it off."

His forceful demand made her blood boil and run in thick, hot, rivers through her body. He had waited for her and she would be eternally grateful for that. She reached up to the collar of her shirt and pulled it down her shoulders, letting it join her skirt on the floor. The low and throaty groan that came from his mouth was enough to set her nerves on fire. His gaze was like flame, burning her everywhere his eyes roamed.

She was wearing all white. In a white-lace bra that pushed her up in a ridiculous way which was almost misleading, although she felt amazing in it. The lace was a loose pattern that left nothing to the imagination, but was just decorative enough to be pretty. Her panties were white satin and the silky feeling of them between her legs did nothing but spur on the heat that was expanding from her center outwards.

"White, huh? I'm a filthy mess here, Ella, and you come to me wearing all white?"

"I don't mind getting dirty," she said, surprised at her own brazen attitude. Porter cocked an eyebrow at her comment. He stalked towards her with a smug grin on his face. When he was within arm's reach of her, he hooked his fingers in the dainty strings that held her panties to her hips and pulled her against his body. She felt him grip the strings with more force and yank them apart. A quiet rip she heard was the decimation of the pretty satin panties and she knew they had served their purpose well. He reached behind her and unclasped her bra; her shoulders rolled forward as she let him slip it from her body and drop it to the floor. He looked down at her naked body and she felt his eyes on every part of her.

"You are one beautiful woman, Ella," he said as his hands traveled along her body. He was feeling all of her, everything his hands could reach. One hand slid down the side of her hip while the other smoothed up her stomach, seeking out her breast. "I love the way you feel under my hands. I'm not sure I'm complete unless I'm touching some part of you," his breath was hot on her skin and his words were felt in the very core of her body. Her eyes rolled back in her head as his mouth found her neck. He ran his tongue along the soft flesh and a slight moan escaped her. His hand found her ass and hauled her even closer to him.

"Please, Porter," she begged him. She wasn't clear on what she wanted; all she knew was that he had it. "I need more," she breathed. She reached down and pushed his jeans and boxers to the floor, feeling him hard between them, making her heart rate skyrocket. He was gloriously hard and she wanted to feel him inside of her.

"This is going to be quick, Ella. You've gotten me all worked up in your virginal-white lingerie and I'm not going to go slow or last long. I'm almost a goner just standing here with your sexy body up against mine," he said in between trailing kisses up and down her neck, over her collar bone, along her breasts.

"Oh God, Porter, please," again she begged him for anything he was willing to give her. Suddenly he picked her up and carried her to a table along the far wall of the shop, hidden behind the boat. In the back of her mind she was grateful for the boat blocking the view of anyone who happened upon them, but it was nothing more than a passing thought because at that moment, she was unaware of her surroundings. She focused solely on Porter and how he made her feel, the way he made her body feel when he touched it. It was the singularly most erotic and consuming feeling – to have his hands on her body. Nothing compared and nothing would ever come close.

"Don't worry, Baby," he whispered against her lips, "I've got you." He pulled her hips to the very edge of the table and spread her legs to wrap around his hips. His lips pressed fully on to hers and he sank into her in the most deliciously slow way. Inch by inch she felt him fill her, felt every vein, every ridge. When he was fully seated in her, he tugged on her hips just to get in as deep as possible. She groaned into his mouth; the sensation of being full to the brim made her breathe faster and crave even more. He held her hips still, pulling her as close to him as possible. She tried to rock her hips against him and he stilled her with his hands. "Just let me feel you for a minute, Ella. I've missed you."

She pulled away to look in his eyes, trying to read what was going on in his head. Placing her hands on both sides of his face, she laid a soft kiss on his mouth, threading her fingers through his hair and pulling him into her.

"What's wrong?" she asked as she placed tiny kissed along his shoulder.

"Baby, nothing's wrong. I just miss you when you're not around," he pulled out of her until just the tip of his cock was left inside and then, once again, slowly pushed back in.

"This is torture. Porter, please. I thought this was going to be fast," she rasped.

"I think it feels pretty damn good. There's something to be said for slow," he said as she maneuvered in and out again. She whimpered quietly into his shoulder. As slow as he was going, she was surprised to find herself climbing to an orgasm.

He sped up fractionally and started leaving small, wet kisses over every inch of skin he could get his mouth on. Between kisses he was slowly pumping in and out, pulling her closer and saying the most wonderful words to her.

"One day I'm going to take you sailing on this boat." Kiss. "We'll make love all afternoon on the deck, under the sun." Kiss.

"Yes," she moaned.

"One day, you're going to be so round with my baby." Kiss. "I'll spend hours touching your belly and loving you." Kiss. "You're going to wear my rings, Ella. You'll be my wife and the mother of my children." Kiss.

She felt herself even closer to the edge and now tears were forming in her eyes. She knew that he loved her and saw a future with her, but to hear him plainly say he wanted to marry her and have children was comforting on another level. She'd never felt so secure or sure of her future than she did in that very moment, wrapped in his arms, connected to him on the most basic and human level. She belonged to him and he to her. They were meant to spend the rest of their lives together and she would tackle any obstacle along their journey to make sure he was by her side every moment.

"Oh Porter, I want all of that. I want your rings, and our babies, and our life. I want all of you, forever." She pulled his face to hers and kissed him fiercely.

"You're mine," he claimed her as he pushed into her again faster and with more force.

"I'm yours and you're mine," she answered, taking every thrust he gave her, relishing in the feeling of his body sliding against hers. She teetered on the edge.

"I love you, Ella," he said looking straight into her eyes, noses touching. He pushed her right over the cliff she'd been dangling from and into an abyss of shocking pleasure that coursed through her veins, hitting every nerve and firing every circuit in her body.

"I love you so much," she answered, her voice shaky from her body's response to him. He continued to thrust into her as she rode out her orgasm, speeding up, and finally finding his own release. As he spilled into her, she splayed kissed all along his shoulders and neck, unable to keep her mouth from connecting with his body. He eventually captured her mouth with his and kissed her down from her euphoric high. He brushed his hands gently down her back, calming her. She sighed into him and he wrapped his arms around her back.

"You know I mean everything I ever say to you, right?" He asked, pulling his face back from hers, making sure she could see his eyes.

"What do you mean?"

"When we're together, like this, when I'm making love to you. I mean every single thing. I'm not just saying things to say them. I want you to marry me and I want you to have my children. I don't want you to be confused by the fact that I say these things to you while I'm inside of you." Ella smiled at him, warmed by his unnecessary confession.

"Porter, you never say anything you don't mean and neither do I. I understand why you say what you do when we're connected like this, it's when we feel closest to each other. I always *feel* the same about you, but when you're inside me and I can't deny our connection, the words come spilling out of me too. I love you endlessly. I want to be with you. Not for a little while, and not until the newness of us wears off. I want to be with you until I cease to exist, because there is no me without you."

Chapter Eleven
Porter

"Babe, dinner's here," Porter called up the stairs to Ella. He placed the takeout bags on the island in the kitchen and started getting plates ready for them to eat. Ella came around the corner into the kitchen, bringing a smile to his face. She was wearing his tee shirt again and it looked damn fine on her. "Nice shirt."

"Thanks," she said as she flashed him a sexy grin. He watched her as she hopped up onto the island and sat, legs dangling over the edge. "I've got good news."

"Hit me with it," he said as he prepared a plate for her.

"Megan accepted my job offer and will be the new general manager of Poppy Portland."

"I never had any doubt," he said, glancing up at her. She was beaming. The Ella he'd met earlier that year had been hesitant and insecure with herself. The woman in his kitchen this evening was confident, excited, and in charge. He was proud of her, and happy that she had decided to make the next big step in her career and life. Even more satisfying to him was that they were making the steps together. "I think Megan is going to be a great manager. You're lucky to have her."

"Agreed," she replied with a nod. "When I was driving here this afternoon, I called a few real estate brokers and I made an appointment for Friday to go look at some store space in Salem."

"You did this while you were driving?" He asked, instantly concerned and a little annoyed that she would put herself in harm's way.

"Porter, it's called Bluetooth. Very safe, promise." He exhaled loudly.

"I'm sorry," he said sincerely. "You have no idea how crazy it makes me when I think of you being unprotected. I can't be with you all the time and I'm afraid that one of these times we're apart, something terrible will happen again."

Ella hopped down from the island and came to him, wrapping her arms around his middle. He heard her take a deep breath.

"I think we're both affected by what happened to us a little more than we have admitted."

Porter rested his cheek on top of Ella's head, breathing in the sweet scent of her shampoo. She smelled so good and she felt so good in his arms.

"I was so focused for so long on just surviving without you, I never took any time to evaluate how I was faring emotionally. I was wrecked – that's all I knew."

"I know, Babe. We're both just trying to figure this out as we go along. But I think we should both see someone. Maybe we should call that psychiatrist Dr. Andrews suggested."

"Make the appointment. I will be there," he said, placing a kiss on her forehead.

"I will." She moved away from him, taking her spot on the island again, the moment of tension passed. "I was thinking," she said between bites. "Maybe on Friday, if you can manage it, you could come with me to look at store space and then afterwards we could go look at some houses." She looked at him tentatively, like she wasn't sure of his response and was bracing for a negative reaction.

"Sounds good," he said easily. She raised her eyebrows up in surprise.

"Well, that was easy."

"What were you expecting, Ella?"

"I don't know," she shrugged. "You've missed a lot of work recently and I don't want to ask too much from you. I don't want to be a hindrance to you. But I want you to be a part of the new store and obviously our house. I feel like I'm walking a fine line here. I'm trying to be really respectful of you and how much time you've invested in us over the last couple of months."

"Don't worry about work, Babe. My company does fine if I'm not there every day, much like yours. They are capable of handling everything and I am excited to do these things with you." He came to stand right in front of her, his hips rested between her knees, pressing up against the counter. "I was even thinking of looking into getting a little contracting business in Salem. Maybe that way I wouldn't have to be in Lincoln City all the time and I could stay in Salem some days." Her eyes went wide and her mouth popped open.

"Really?" She exclaimed. "That is a great idea. To think that we could both be working and living in the same city...I don't know, Porter. It seems a little too perfect, doesn't it?"

"No, it seems like just the right amount of perfect." He felt his phone vibrating in his pocket and reached in to pull it out as he planted a loud smacking kiss on her lips.

"Hey, Mom," he said as he answered. "What's up?"

"Porter, do you think you could come down to the bar? That damn line in the dishwasher busted again, but this time there is water flooding everywhere."

"Damn it, yeah, I'll be there. But I'm not a plumber, Mom, you need to get Mitch in there to look at it."

"But you'll come, right?"

"Yeah, I'll be there as soon as possible."

"Thanks, Son."

He hung up and looked up at Ella.

"Mom's got a problem; I got to go to the bar. Do you want to come?" Ella winced a little.

"I'm actually really tired. Do you think your mom would mind if I stayed here?"

"No," he chuckled. "I think my mom minds that there is currently water flooding her kitchen." He kissed her again quickly, backing away to find his shoes.

"Stay here and rest a while. I don't know when I'll be home, but it shouldn't be too late."

She hopped off the counter and followed him to the door.

"Ok, just call me when you're on your way back."

"Will do," he said as he pulled on a light jacket. "Lock the door after me." She rolled her eyes at him and he immediately smacked her ass, hard enough to illicit a yelp. She looked at him with wide eyes, rubbing her behind.

"I'm serious. Lock the door."

"Ok, yes Sir," she said with a smile.

"Bye, Baby." He kissed her quickly and then slipped out the door, smiling to himself when he heard the deadbolt clank into place.

Ella

After Porter had left to rescue his mother, in a very Porterly move, Ella made herself at home, reading on the couch, snuggled up in a throw blanket. Her eyes started to burn and she had to admit she was more tired than she had realized. She stood to go upstairs but saw the mess in the kitchen and decided to clean up a bit so that Porter wouldn't have to deal with it when he got home.

As she walked into the kitchen, she heard a noise that sounded like it had come from the front door. It wasn't a knocking noise, but more of a bang. One bang, then nothing. It was so eerily quiet, she started to wonder if she had even actually heard anything. She paused, mid-step, between the couch and the kitchen, holding her breath so that not even the sound of her breathing could be mistaken for any noise she might hear. A solid twenty seconds went by without another noise and she started to think she had imagined everything. She started towards the kitchen again when the bang came through the door once more.

She quickly turned towards the door, not sure what she was expecting, halted still, waiting for either Porter to come in the door or for the sound to come again. She was frozen in place, unable to move. When a few minutes passed without another noise, her nerves settled again. She took a few deep breaths and walked towards the door. She rolled her eyes and silently cursed Porter. All his master craftsmanship and he couldn't put a freaking peep hole in his door? She put her hand on the deadbolt and took a deep breath in, let it out slowly, trying to release all her nerves with it. She went to turn the deadbolt, but was distracted by the shadow that ghosted by the front window.

Panic. Sheer Panic. She ran back into the living room, grabbed her phone from the coffee table, and immediately dialed 9-1-1.

"Hello, this is 9-1-1. What is your emergency?"

"Please, I need a police officer. I think there is someone outside my boyfriend's house trying to break in."

"Ok, Ma'am, stay calm. I will get an officer out to you immediately. Can I get the address?"

"Shit! I don't know the address."

"Ok. It's ok. Are you in the house?"

"Yes."

"Is the suspect in the house with you?"

"No, I heard someone outside and when I went to look out the front door someone ran by the window. I couldn't see him. Tt's too dark. But it was a person."

"Ok, can you see any mail lying around your boyfriend's house? Bills, letters, anything with an address?" Ella ran into the kitchen and looked all over the counters, which were ridiculously spotless.

"I can't find anything," panic started to flood her body, causing her voice to come out shaky and scared.

"Look in the garbage," the woman told her firmly.

Ella grabbed the cupboard door under the sink and ripped it open. The garbage can was under the counter and she pulled it out and dumped it over. All sorts of things spilled out onto the floor. Her eyes landed on a white envelope and she picked it up frantically. She turned it over, desperately searching for the information she needed.

"Ok, I got it! 558 East Tidal Road. Did you get that?"

"Yes, I did. Good job, Ma'am. Officers are on their way."

"Ella. My name's Ella," she said with a quiet whisper.

"Hi, Ella. I'm Mary. You did a good job. I need you to stay away from the windows and try to hide. Do not hang up with me until the officers arrive. Can you do that?"

"Yes," she answered, unable to keep the tears from her eyes or the strain from her voice. She went into the bathroom off the living room and climbed into the tub, sitting with her knees pulled up to her chest, silently crying.

"Ella, are you still with me?" the dispatcher asked.

"Yes," she whispered.

"Good. Have you heard anyone enter the house?"

"No," she cried. Being in the dark room by herself, unable to see anything, was almost scarier than being out in the open. She just waited for the bathroom door to swing open and for some man in a dark hoodie to point a gun at her. She felt helpless and terrified. Would this be her life from now on? Hiding from threats, crying in dark rooms, waiting for help to arrive?

She started to hear cars pulling up on the gravel.

"Ella, the officers have arrived. They are doing a sweep around the house, so I need you to stay put and let them clear the house outside."

"Ok." Tears streamed down her face. She heard sounds outside, but couldn't tell what she was hearing. A few minutes passed then she heard a knock on the door.

"Ella, the officers are at your door now. It's safe to come out and open the door for them."

"Ok." Ella stood up in the bath, legs barely able to hold her up for all the shaking they were doing. "Are you sure it's the police? What if it's the man?"

"Ella, I promise it's the officers. I have been communicating with them this whole time. Officer Barrows is on the other side of your door; he's there to help you."

"Ok." That seemed to be the only word she could muster. She walked slowly to the door, her eyes darting around the living room, looking for anything that might cause alarm or give reason to panic. Her trembling hand reached for the deadbolt and she twisted it. Then she gripped the doorknob and took a deep breath before slowly opening the door. True to the dispatcher's word, a police officer stood on the other side. One of his hands gently pushed the door open, while the other rested on the holster containing his gun.

"Hello, Ma'am. I'm Officer Barrows and I'm here to help."

"Ella, did you let Officer Barrows in?"

"Yes," Ella answered into the phone as the officer slipped past her into the house.

"Great. Ella you did a wonderful job. I'm going to hand up now, ok?"

"Ok, thank you for your help."

"No problem." Ella heard the line go dead and then turned to the officer. "I heard some banging outside and then I saw someone walking past the front windows. I panicked," She said a little embarrassed. "I might have overreacted."

"Ma'am, I need you to stay here in the living room and we are going to clear the rest of the house just to be certain. Ok?"

"Alright," Ella said and turned to find her way to the couch. She sat down and rested her head in her hands. Her breathing was shallow and her head was starting to pound. She heard footsteps on the floor above her and disembodied voices coming from all corners of the house as police officers searched the house for any intruders.

Suddenly there was a commotion outside and Ella heard yelling. She stood up before she knew where she was headed and found herself running for the door. The voice she heard outside belonged to Porter and he was more upset than she'd ever heard.

"Sir! We are still investigating and you cannot go in the house right now."

"This is my goddamn house and she's in there! ELLA! Damnit, get out of my way," Ella heard Porter yelling. She came out of the front door to see Porter being physically restrained by two police officers, struggling to make it to the house.

"Ella!" He yelled as soon as he spotted her.

"Porter!" She cried as she ran down the porch steps towards him. The officers holding Porter released him when they saw Ella coming towards them. When they finally collided, her arms went instinctively behind his neck, holding him tightly to her. His arms wrapped around her waist and his face into her neck.

"Are you ok?" He said, pulling away and holding her face in his hands, looking at her to see if she was injured.

"I'm ok, Porter. I'm ok," she said and buried her face back into his chest.

"I pulled up, and I saw the cop cars, and it was just like that night. They wouldn't let me get to you. I had to get to you." He was on the verge of frantic, and as upset as she was, he needed her right now to be ok. He needed her to be there for him, to know that what happened that night wasn't being repeated.

"Hey, Babe," she said as she leaned back to look him in the eye. "I'm right here and I'm fine."

"I can't lose you again," he whispered, his eyes brimming with tears. He looked completely broken, as if everything he'd been trying to hold together for the last three months was crumbling right in front of her.

"Porter, look at me," she said and she gently took his face between her hands. "I am not going anywhere and you don't have to worry about losing me, ever." He nodded his head at her, indicating that he had heard and understood her, then pulled her back into his chest, holding on to her tightly.

Minutes passed and they stayed in their embrace, unwilling to move for anything. At least until Officer Barrow returned to Ella.

"Excuse me, Ma'am?" Ella pulled back from Porter to look at the officer.

"Yes?"

"Can you give me a statement about what happened tonight?"

"Um, sure. She pulled farther away from Porter to speak to the officer, but Porter didn't let her go, his grasp on her waist still firm and comforting to her. Porter left and I was reading on the couch. When I got up to go into the kitchen I heard a loud bang outside, like someone had rammed into the door. I waited to see if I could hear anything else, but it seemed to go away. Then, I heard it again. I got a little freaked out, but wanted to see what it was so I went to the door to open it." Ella felt Porter stiffen beside her. He obviously didn't like the fact that she had decided to investigate. She linked her fingers with his and tried to calm him with her touch.

"Before I could get the door open, I saw a shadow move across the window, as if a man had run in front of it outside. I panicked and ran to call 9-1-1. When the dispatcher told me to hide, I went into the bathroom off the living room and sat in the tub."

"Could you identify the suspect in a line up? Or describe him to an officer?"

"Probably not. It was dark outside and I couldn't really see anything except that it looked like a person, a male."

"When we were doing our initial sweep of the perimeter of the house, we found a set of foot prints that were outside of one window and then seemed to lead to another. It would seem you did have someone on your property."

Ella's breath caught in her lungs. She could feel the fear coursing through her body, but she needed to stay calm for Porter. Her freaking out was not going to help him at all.

"Maybe somebody was just lost," she suggested.

"Ma'am, lost people don't loiter outside of private residences and look in windows. Is there anyone you know of who would want to hurt or scare you?"

"Kyle," the name was out of Porter's mouth before she even had a chance to put her thoughts together. She looked up at him and couldn't hide the shock from her face.

"Why would Kyle do this?"

"Why would Kyle shoot you? Because he's a crazy mother fucker with a death wish."

"Wait, who shot you?" Officer Barrow looked confused. Ella let out a breath. She was tired of reliving everything that had happened to her.

"A few months ago, I was in my store in Portland and a man came to the store front and shot me through the window."

"Was he apprehended?"

"No, they never caught the man."

"And how does this Kyle fit into this."

"Hours before the shooting she had an altercation with her ex-boyfriend who assaulted her and attempted to rape her."

"Was he charged?"

"No. She went in a coma, then had amnesia, so she couldn't make a statement about it. He skipped town and she just regained her memory about a week ago." The officer looked at Ella, and pointed a finger in her direction.

"You need to go to the Portland police station, file a report, press charges, and get an order of protection. I don't have any way of knowing who was outside your house tonight, but in my line of work there are no such things as coincidences."

"Fucking Kyle," Porter said.

"Is there anything else you need from me tonight, Officer?" Ella asked, growing more and more weary of the way the whole situation with Kyle seemed to always come up and impact her life.

"No, I will have patrol drive by your house a few times every night for the next few nights, just to keep an eye out. If you hear or see anything suspicious, call 9-1-1 immediately."

"Thank you, Officer," Ella said quietly.

"Can I have a word with you?" Porter asked, looking at Officer Barrow.

"Sure," he answered and the two men stepped away from Ella, leaving her alone in the driveway. She wondered what Porter wanted to talk to the officer about, but felt he wanted space from her at the moment. She wondered what it was he had to say that couldn't be said in front her. She walked back up the porch stairs and into the house, nodding at the two police officers leaving the living room and heading outside. Once she was sure everyone was clear of the house, she went upstairs to the bedroom. She saw her reflection in the mirror in Porter's walk-in closet as she searched for something to wear to bed. She stared at her face and realized she looked exhausted. Everything was taking its toll on her and it showed. She rubbed her hands over her face, trying to shake off some of the fear that had clung to her for the last hour. Her apartment in Portland held terrifying memories, and now Porter's house was tainted as well. The move to Salem was looking better and better.

She didn't want to think about who was outside of Porter's house, spying on her, scaring her. She truly didn't believe it was Kyle. What motivation could he possibly have? What was he gaining from all this? Then again, who else could it be? She didn't know who shot her, but it wasn't Kyle, of that she was sure. She exhaled loudly and pulled out her favorite shirt of Porter's to wear to bed. The gray shirt with Lincoln City on the breast was soft from washing and smelled of wood, soap, and Porter. She stripped down to her panties and pulled the shirt over her head. She crawled in the king size bed and waited for him.

A few minutes later she heard him come into the room and he paused at the doorway. She rolled over in the bed to look at him and he looked just as wrecked as she had.

Without saying a word, he pulled his shirt over his head, took his shoes and pants off, leaving him in his boxers. He pulled the comforter back a bit and climbed into the bed, reaching over to turn the lamp off on his bedside table, leaving them in the dark.

She felt him move closer to her. Once his hands found her, he pulled her gently over to him, cradling her against his chest. She curled up into him, letting him hold her, taking everything from him he was offering.

"What is going on inside that pretty head of yours?" He whispered. She exhaled, wanting to spew a thousand thoughts at him; there seemed to be so many things going on in her head she had no idea where to start.

"Will things ever be normal for us, Porter?" She mumbled into his chest.

"What do you mean?"

"Will we ever just get to be? Will we ever just have a normal week where no one is shot? Or loses their memory? Or has to call the police to scare away an intruder? All this stuff keeps happening, and only to me, and I don't know why. I was never this high maintenance before. You should probably just give up on me now; I'm not worth the trouble."

"You think I'm going to leave you because of all this?"

"No, I don't think you're going to leave me, but I think maybe you should."

"Explain that to me." She could hear the question in his voice. He was confused and looking for clarification.

"I've brought nothing but trouble to you, Porter. You've wasted so many weeks with me not even remembering you. Now I've brought some lunatic to your house looking for me. Everything was so much simpler for you before I came along. I wouldn't blame you if you wanted to go back to the way everything was before we met."

"I had nothing before you, Ella. Nothing. I was just living, day to day, surviving for nothing. You brought light into my life. Color. Meaning. I'm not living without you. I couldn't. Are things complicated and crazy right now? Maybe, but *you're* crazy if you think I'm going to just walk away from you." She felt his muscles tensing with his words. She upset him. "If you want out, just say the words, Ella. I'll let you go if it's what you really want, but you have to say the words."

"You know I don't want that," she said desperately, not liking the direction the conversation was headed.

"Damnit, Ella, I'm here. I'm right here. Don't push me away after everything. I can't get any clearer with you, any more transparent. I'm wide open to you. I want to be with you forever. What kind of man would I be if I promised you everything and then ran at the first problem or sign of trouble? Have a little more faith in me than that, a little more faith in us."

"I'm sorry," she whispered, aiming her face up at his, even though she couldn't see him. She felt his breath on her face and he was as close to her as one could be without kissing. She ached for his lips to touch hers, for him to show her that even though she had brought turmoil into his life, he still wanted her, still desired her.

He slowly ran his nose along the side of her face and then flipped his nose against the tip of hers. She felt him smile, but he still didn't kiss her.

"Tell me you won't run away from me," he whispered against her lips, just barely touching.

"I'm not sure I could leave, even if I tried," she answered.

"Tell me you won't try."

"I won't try."

His lips slowly pressed into hers and she exhaled all the tension she'd built up over the night into this kiss. It wasn't rushed. It wasn't full of passion. It was simply loving. He caressed her mouth with his gently and gingerly, as if her were expressing with his lips how fragile he felt they were in that moment. He simply kissed her, loved her. She felt one of his hands rest on the curve of her waist, and she reached up and felt the stubble on his face.

"I'd find you, you know," he said as he laid feather-light kisses along her neck.

"What do you mean?" She rasped, her heartbeat pulsing right under where his lips were caressing her on her neck.

"If you left, I'd find you. I found you once before. I'd find you again. Always." She smiled at his words.

"So you're saying there's no point?"

"Absolutely none."

"Ok."

He kissed her again, then rolled her so that her back was to his front. She felt him nuzzle his face into her hair and neck, breathing in deeply.

"Go to sleep, Baby. Everything will look better in the morning." Ella relaxed into his arms, letting herself melt into him as she had every other night they'd spent together. Her breaths started to even out and her mind started to wander. Images of the man ghosting past the window broke her from her relaxation and her body tensed at the sudden fear that shot through her body.

"Porter?"

"Yeah?"

"Did you lock the doors?"

"Yes, Babe. All the doors are locked, the sheriff is patrolling past the house, and I'm right here. I won't let anyone get to you. I promise."

She relaxed slightly at his words, and his protective hold on her helped, but she wasn't used to feeling scared. She didn't think it was a feeling to likely go away any time soon. He started to gently rub her back, massaging away the tension and fear.

"Sleep, Ella. I'm here; you're safe." She let the rhythm of his breathing and the feeling of his hands on her skin lull her into sleep.

Chapter Twelve

Ella

The next morning Porter woke her up, pulling her into the shower. They didn't say any words about what had happened the night before. He just made love to her under the hot water, slowly showing her how much he needed her. The fear from the night before was still present, but having his arms around her made her remember that he would protect her always.

While she was getting dressed, she turned to him, taking a moment to admire his shirtless body.

"You are so ridiculously hot," she said with a grin. He turned to her and smiled widely.

"Well, we make a matching pair then, because you are smoking hot as well." She batted her eyelashes at him playfully.

"I am pretty cute." He shook his head and laughed at her. "Hey, by the way, Kalli and Megan want us to go out with them on Friday night. Megan wants to celebrate her promotion by going to a club." Porter shot her a look that clearly said he wasn't interested.

"Ella, when have I ever given you the impression that I am a 'club' kind of guy?" He asked sardonically.

"Never, actually. But I definitely got the impression that you were a 'hang out with my girlfriend and maybe get to watch her shake her ass' kind of guy."

"I could get you to shake your ass for me at home," he said with a smug grin.

"You're right. That's true. Tell you what, you stay home and I'll go shake my ass for all the other guys who go to the club." She never even saw him approach her, she just knew that the next moment she was in his arms and his breath was on her face, eyes locked on hers.

"That was not the smartest thing to say," he growled at her and used his teeth to nip at her bottom lip.

"Hmm… maybe not, but I like the reaction it got out of you."

"You want me to go clubbing with you and your friends?"

"I want to spend time with you. And I think it could be fun to go to a club. We don't have to dance, but I was looking forward to pressing my body up against yours and feeling all your muscles," she smiled playfully.

"Well, that doesn't sound *all* bad. But won't we be the oldest people there? Crashing the college kids' party?"

Ella tsked-tsked at him. "Porter, don't you watch Portlandia at all? You're not cool in Portland until you're thirty." He laughed at her.

"Ok, I'll go, but you owe me big time. And I expect prompt payment."

She smiled up at him. "Anything you want, Baby."

He roughly kissed her on the lips, groaning into her mouth as her tongue slid along his.

"Don't make promises you can't keep," he rasped at her.

"I never do." With that he slapped her ass and walked away from her shaking his head.

"I've got to leave for work in twenty minutes. Is that going to be enough time for you?" he asked as he walked away from her into the closet. Her heart constricted a little, knowing he had picked up on the fact that she was afraid to be in the house alone.

"I'll be ready," she answered softly.

Twenty minutes later he walked her to her car and kissed her softly.

"I will be in Portland by seven tonight. Will you be ok until I get there?" He asked, rubbing the back of her hand down her cheek, sending chills down her spine. She put a bright smile on her face, hiding the doubt she had.

"I'll be fine, Porter. Take your time." He looked into her eyes for a moment, seemingly searching them for something. Finally, he took her lips with his again, kissing her senseless, as he had a tendency to do. She pushed away all the uncertainty and let herself feel him and everything he was giving to her. She pushed her hands up his hard chest, wrapping them around his neck, tugging his hair gently, pulling him closer. He groaned and his hands found purchase on her ass, holding her to him. After what seemed like hours of him kissing her deliciously, he pulled away.

"I had you not an hour ago and I still want more of you," he said in a voice so deep and sexy she almost pulled him back into the house.

"That's good, Porter. It will make the day go by faster," she said as she winked at him.

"Highly unlikely," he grimaced.

"Go to work. Be a man. Hammer some nails. Work out your sexual frustration." He laughed at her.

"I'd rather work out my sexual frustration on you," he whispered directly into her ear, which might as well have been a direct line to her core because everything south of her belly button constricted and ached with his words.

"Sounds like a plan for later," she answered with just as much frustration.

"Text me when you get to Portland safely," he requested.

"I will." She tipped up on her toes and placed another quick kiss right on his lips. "I love you, Porter."

"I love you too," he answered against her lips.

Ell made it to Portland and went directly to Poppy. The sun was out in full force again and there were only a few white puffy clouds in the sky. The beautiful weather made everything seem a little more tolerable and pulling up to the store, it felt a little less nerve racking than it had the day before. She still needed to take a few deep breaths to steady herself and tried not to let her thoughts drift towards the man in the hoodie. It took her a fraction of the time to get into the store, and smiled when she saw Brittany and Megan behind the counter.

"Ella, I was just talking to Brittany about all the changes happening at the store," Megan said with a bright and infectious smile.

"Are you really going to promote me to assistant manager?" Brittany asked hopefully.

"Don't sound so surprised, Brit. You do an amazing job here. Does your excitement mean you'll accept the position?"

"Of course I will! I can't believe this," she said with such a big smile, it made Ella's cheeks hurt just looking at her. All of a sudden, though, her face became sad. "Does this mean you won't be around as much?"

"Well, I won't be a complete stranger, but yeah, I won't be here every day anymore. That's what you and Megan are for. And you're going to be amazing managers. I am so excited for all this to happen. Plus," Ella added," I'll also need both of your help getting the new store running and hiring new staff."

"Ella, anything you need, just let us know. Right, Brittany?"

"Definitely," Brittany answered sincerely.

"Great. How's business today?"

"Pretty slow so far, but I think the weather will bring out all the shoppers."

"Well, I have a few calls to make, but I am here all day, so I will be out soon." Ella went into the back of the store to her desk and sat down. She pulled the business card out that Dr. Andrews had given her and tapped it on the desk a few times gathering up the nerve to call. Finally, she picked up the phone from the desk and dialed the number.

"Dr. Evans' office. How can I help you?"

"Hi, I was referred to Dr. Evans by Dr. Andrews at OHSU. I was hoping to make an appointment and I was wondering what your earliest availability was," Ella asked, trying to sound cool and collected, and not at all like she needed a psychiatric evaluation.

"Absolutely. Would this be a solo visit or is this couple's counseling?"

"Well, actually, it would be for two, but it's not actually couples counseling. Or, I don't know, maybe it is. Is there any way I could just make the appointment for two and then talk to the doctor about it?" She didn't want to divulge all her personal information to a receptionist over the phone.

"Of course. I have an opening two weeks from Tuesday, which we could work into regular meeting if you decide to continue seeing Dr. Evans. But if you're looking for a more immediate appointment, I have an opening today at four." Ella looked at the clock. It was only ten am. Porter would have to leave Lincoln City by one-thirty to make a four o'clock appointment. She knew that she was walking a thin line between 'ok' and 'not ok', and thought it best to take the appointment.

"Ok, I will be there for the four o'clock. I am not sure if my boyfriend can make it, but I will definitely be there."

"Great. What is your name?"

"Ella Sinclair."

"Great. Ella, you are confirmed for four o'clock. Please show up a few minutes early to fill out paperwork."

"Thank you."

"Have a nice day." Ella heard the line go dead. She picked up her cell phone to text Porter.

Hey Babe. I made it to Portland safe and sound. I also made an appointment with the psychiatrist. They had an opening in two weeks, or one today at four. I took the appointment today, but I totally understand if you can't make it. I just felt like, for me, the sooner the better.

Ella started checking her email to get caught up as much as she could and heard her phone ping a few minutes later.

∗∗I think it's important that we go together, if that's ok with you. Like I said, I want to be there for you, but I need it too. I will always make time for you. I will be there.∗∗

Ella melted a little at his words. Of course he would be there. She was beginning to fully understand that there was nothing Porter wouldn't do for her. It warmed her to think that he would rearrange his day and leave work early to make a doctor's appointment.

∗∗How did I get so lucky to find you?∗∗

∗∗Luck had nothing to do with it, Ella. Fate pushed us together and then we fought like hell to find each other again. Luck doesn't keep me with you, love does."

∗∗I love you.∗∗

∗∗I love you too.∗∗

∗∗You have the address right?∗∗

∗∗Yes. I will see you at four.∗∗

∗∗Ok. Drive safely.∗∗

The day at the shop went quickly. As expected there were a lot of women out window shopping in the beautiful sunshine. Sales were good and both Brittany and Megan were on cloud nine, basking in the glow of their promotions. Ella got lost in the new stock, mentally pairing tops with bottoms, matching patterns and colors. There was a lot of business knowledge and strategy that went in to running a successful store, but Ella really enjoyed the artistic side of it as well. Fashion was something she loved. Even though she knew she could never be an actual designer, as she lacked the ability to draw even a respectable stick figure, she knew and loved clothes. She had even toyed with the idea once of being a stylist, but the need for personal stylists in Portland was not paramount. As the city started to slowly grow, in both population and cool factor, more and more people were viewing Portland as a new and exciting place to be. Movies and television shows were filmed there more often, which is what continued to bring Kalli to town. More and more celebrities started making Portland a second home. Perhaps in a few years, when the new Poppy was off the ground and self-sufficient, Ella would look into getting some work as a personal stylist.

New ideas and plans kept Ella's mind consumed well into the afternoon and eventually it was time for her to leave for her appointment. As she drove to the doctor's office, she tried not to let her nerves get to her. She had never been to see a psychiatrist and wasn't sure how her first appointment would go. It did soothe her a little to know that Porter would be there. Ella laughed to herself a little at their strange situation.

Had she normally started dating a man three months ago, she could only imagine that she would probably keep the fact that she needed a shrink to herself. But here they were, with only really three weeks of actually being together under their belts, and they were seeing the doctor together. One thing was for sure: where she and Porter were concerned, nothing was ordinary.

She pulled up to the building that housed the office of Dr. Evans and was nearly giddy to see Porter leaning up against the tailgate of his truck. His blue jeans hung deliciously from his hips, tee shirt stretched against his muscles as every shirt he owned tended to do, brown hair pointing in every direction imaginable. He was looking at his phone but saw her car pull up behind his truck and gave her a heart-stopping smile. When she made it out of the car and walked up to him, she wrapped her arms around his middle, resting her cheek against his chest.

"I'm so glad you're here," she said.

"Me too."

When she pulled away, he took her hand and laced his fingers through hers. He used his other hand to open the door for her. When they found the right door to Dr. Evans office they went inside and Ella was greeted with a smile from the receptionist.

"Hi, I'm Ella Sinclair and I made an appointment earlier today over the phone."

"Right, of course," the receptionist said. "Here are the forms I need you to fill out. And I also need to know, will this be billed to insurance?"

"No, I'll be paying cash," Porter answered, before she could get a word in edge-wise.

"Perfect," the receptionist beamed a smile right at Porter. Ella noticed that the woman's eyes did a poor job of remaining on Porter's face, as she watched her rake her gaze over the same muscles Ella had admired right outside the building. Before she knew what was happening, Ella's hand threaded itself through the crook in Porter's arm, staking claim. Porter didn't seem to notice anything out of the ordinary, but Ella saw the receptionist's eyes fall on her hand laying gently on his forearm. More than ever, at that moment, Ella wanted a ring on Porter's finger, just to send a message that he was most definitely taken.

"Just bring me the forms when you are done filling them out and the doctor will be out to greet you in a few minutes."

"Thanks," Porter said, without giving her another look. Ella simply nodded at the woman as she turned to sit and fill out her form.

After all the forms were complete, a door in the office opened up and a woman who looked to be about forty stepped into the waiting room, just far enough to peek around the corner at them.

"Ella Sinclair?" Ella and Porter stood and he took her hand in his again, threading their fingers together.

"Good afternoon, I am Dr. Evans. Please, follow me." They trailed behind the doctor as she led them through the office and to a door with her name engraved on the front. She opened the door and motioned for them to go in ahead of her. "Please, take a seat and make yourselves comfortable."

They both sat in arm chairs that were opposite Dr. Evans' desk, and even though Ella knew there wasn't anything to be nervous about, she was anything but comfortable. The doctor took a seat behind her desk and shuffled some paperwork around making neat piles. She had shoulder-length brown hair that was so straight Ella wondered if it was made to be so. Her eyes were dark and hidden behind large framed glasses. She wasn't wearing any jewelry apart from a thin wedding band. Her face was friendly and when she finally looked up at Ella and Porter, she gave them a reassuring smile.

"Ella, my receptionist noted that you were referred from Dr. Andrews at OHSU. He is a colleague and good friend of mine for many years. I had him fax over your medical file. However, I have no information on you, Sir," she said looking at Porter.

"My name is Porter Masters and I am Ella's boyfriend. Medically, there is nothing really to know about me."

"Ok, nice to meet both of you," she said, all business. She brought out an iPad from a drawer in her desk and then looked Ella in the eyes. "Ella, why don't you tell me why you're here."

"Well, the last couple of months I've been put in a lot of unusually stressful situations and it seems I am having some problems dealing with the stress of it all."

"I saw in your file that you were involved in a shooting, and then suffered from retro-grade amnesia which eventually went away and your memory then returned."

"Yes, when the memories returned is when the panic and

anxiety started," Ella said, exhaling a deep breath. Porter reached over and laid a hand on Ella's thigh, giving her a gentle squeeze. She placed her hand over his and clasped her fingers around his hand, willing him to keep his there.

"Tell me about the attacks," the doctor urged her.

"Well, the first one came outside of my store where I was shot. It was the first time I had been there since my memory came back and it kind of came out of nowhere. We pulled up to the store and as soon as I saw it, my heart started beating really fast and I felt like I couldn't get enough air in my lungs. I was shaking and trembling," Ella's voice petered off and she swallowed hard. Remembering the attack was almost as bad as living through it. She took a deep breath and looked up at Dr. Evans. "I had never experienced something like that before and I was scared."

"She had another attack that same night at her apartment," Porter added.

"Did something traumatic happen at the apartment as well?" Dr. Evans asked.

"I was attacked there by my ex-boyfriend and nearly raped," Ella whispered. She felt Porter's hand tighten around hers and she noticed him clenching his other fist in his lap.

"Are you having any trouble sleeping?"

Ella thought about the question and then began to blush.

"Um, no. Not since…" Ella brought her hand to her brow and tried to hide her eyes from the doctor.

"Ella, if there is any place you need to feel comfortable, this is the place. I will not judge anything you say here. Would you like Porter to leave? Are you afraid to be honest around him?"

"No!" Ella almost yelled. "It's not him, actually, it's me. I just feel silly."

"Ok, well, just be honest. I need to know everything if I'm going to be able to help you."

"It's just that, since the memories have come back, I haven't spent a night away from Porter," Ella said, and she could feel the blood rushing to the surface of her face and knew she was blushing horribly. She also saw Porter smirking. "I sleep very well when I'm with him."

"That's good; anything comforting can be very therapeutic for patients with anxiety. How long have you two been together?" Ella and Porter both laughed lightly at the doctor's question. Ella knew eventually they'd have to explain their unique situation.

"Porter and I met a week before I lost my memory. He stayed with me the entire time I was in a coma at the hospital, but things got a little tricky when I woke up and didn't remember him."

"I was kept from her by her family, seeing as how they didn't really know me and she didn't remember me. But I constantly sought out updates on her. Eventually, after two months of not seeing her and her not remembering, I just went after her. That was about two weeks ago and she just regained her memory a few days ago." Ella watched as the doctor tried to compute everything they had just told her.

"So, for Ella, this is a very new relationship, but for you, Porter, it has been going on quite a bit longer." Porter shrugged.

"You could say that."

"Well, what would you say about it?" The doctor asked.

"I'd say that I'm just as invested today as I was the first week. Time isn't really a factor in our relationship because I was in deep from the beginning."

"So, you would describe your relationship as 'committed' then?"

"Irrevocably," Porter answered without hesitation in his deep raspy voice, making the breath in Ella's lungs steal away. Ella was even sure she saw the doctor react in a very female way to that word, spoken in the sexy way that only Porter could ever pull off.

"And you feel the same way, Ella?" Dr. Evans asked her.

"There's no one else in the world for me. Porter is it." The doctor took a pause and scribbled some things on her iPad, then looked up at Ella.

"What you are describing definitely sounds like anxiety attacks," the doctor said as she laid down her IPad on the desk. "Anxiety attacks are often a symptom of a bigger issue. In your case, the anxiety seems to be a symptom of Post-Traumatic Stress Disorder. You will need more sessions to get a formal diagnosis, but in your situation the disorder is very clear. The anxiety is only exacerbated by the sudden return of your memory. Although, it wouldn't be unheard of if someone went through your same situation, never lost their memory, and then developed PTSD. The fact that your body and mind went through the traumatic event once and then, for all intents and purposes, a second time when the memory of the events returned, only heightens the level of anxiety and the physical symptoms that accompany it."

Porter rubbed his free hand over stubble-ridden face and had a look of confusion written all over it. "Any chance you could give that to us again in layman's terms?" He asked sheepishly. The doctor laughed gently at his request.

"Basically, Ella's body is responding to the stress more than usual simply because of the memories returning. It would be totally normal for someone to have anxiety after what you went through, but the amnesia adds a new dimension to not only the symptoms, but also the treatment."

"What is the treatment?' Porter asked, pulling the question right out of Ella's mouth.

"Medication and counseling."

"What kind of medication?"

"A selective serotonin reuptake inhibitor like Zoloft or Paxil is usually prescribed."

"Are there any side effects?" Ella asked.

"As with any medication, there are side effects. Dry mouth and nausea being the most common. There isn't any chance you could be pregnant?"

"No," Ella answered quickly.

"Good. Now, Porter," the doctor said, turning her attention towards him. "Although I can appreciate the supportive boyfriend role you likely excel at, let's talk about why you are here and how I can help you. I imagine watching Ella go through all this, and then being separated from her was very difficult."

"It wasn't the best experience I've had," he said as he swiped his hand through his hair, a move that told Ella he was more upset than he was letting on. The doctor just continued to stare at Porter, waiting for him to elaborate.

"When she woke up and didn't remember me, it was like someone had taken the one thing I was living for away from me. And even if I could have functioned normally with just that happening, when they refused to let me see her, or talk to her, it was even worse." He paused and looked down at his hand that was still tangled up in hers. "I had dealt with loss before and had pretty much built a life where I wouldn't have to deal with it again. I wasn't sure I could. But then Ella came storming into my life and everything I had tried to push away suddenly was everything I wanted. Desperately." He looked over at Ella and she could see every ounce of love he had for her in his eyes.

"I wasn't prepared to have her taken from me and when she was gone it was like I was lost."

"Can you explain the loss you mentioned? What loss had you dealt with?" Dr. Evans asked.

"My father died suddenly when I was twelve."

"So, is it safe to assume that when Ella was kept from you, it stirred up past feelings of loss that you had previously associated with your father's death?"

"I guess. Although, even though this might sound disrespectful to my father, it was almost worse with Ella."

"How so?" The doctor probed.

"Well, when my father died, it was absolute. He was gone. It was hard, sad, and difficult, but there was a finality to it. With Ella, I was literally just dangling off of a cliff, waiting to either plummet to the bottom of the ravine, or for Ella to come and save me."

It broke Ella's heart to hear his words. She never wanted to be the reason he felt anything but love and happiness. Hearing his heartache brought tears to her eyes.

"There were times I didn't think I was going to make it through to the next day. Not because I would have taken my own life – I never would have left Ella like that, amnesia or not. I just really felt like the sadness would take me. I didn't know if it was possible to die from sadness, but I was sure I was going to find out eventually." Ella couldn't control the sob that escaped her and hadn't known it was coming until it had already leaked out. She quickly brought a hand to her mouth the stifle any rogue sobs that fought to get out. Porter leaned towards Ella and reached up with his hands to bring her face closer to his.

"Don't you cry, Ella, don't. I'd do it all again if it brought you back to me. I'm not the victim here, you are. I just need you to stay strong for me, Baby."

"I just feel so bad that the whole time you were drowning like that, I was just living my life. I had no idea," she whispered.

"No, you were fighting your way back to me. We were both struggling."

Ella nodded. "I was looking for you, even when I didn't know who you were."

"I know. Your heart knew me."

They sat there for a minute, foreheads pressed together, calming each other with their deep breaths and soft touches.

"Porter, let me ask you this," the doctor said. "Are you afraid you might lose Ella a second time?"

"I won't let that happen again," he answered forcefully.

"What do you mean by 'again'?"

Porter clenched his fist again, and Ella heard his breaths coming faster and harder.

"The first time she was taken from me, it was my mistake. I never should have let her go, at least not alone." Porter ran his fingers through his hair, dispelling the air from his lungs in a loud rush. "I knew, I *knew*," he said as he slammed his fist into his own thigh. "I knew something wasn't right. My gut was telling me not to let her go home, not to let her out of my sight. I dismissed it, thought it was just my mind just wanting to be near her. We'd spent the week together, surely I was just lusting after her. I told the nagging voice in my head to go away and that it would be crazy of me to demand she stay with me. But damnit, that's exactly what I should have done." Porter leaned forward, resting his forearms on his legs, placing his head in his hands.

"Even if I had driven a little faster, gotten to the store twenty minutes earlier, I could have stopped that bastard from shooting her."

"When your father died, did you have feelings of guilt around his death as well?" Dr. Evans asked. Porter looked up at her with a confused look on his face. His brow crinkled near the bridge of his nose and he looked lost in thought.

"I suppose. I mean, I was twelve. I remember thinking that I should have done something differently that day, should have changed something to make it so that truck hadn't wrecked into his. But I think that's a perfectly acceptable reaction for a boy to have when he's lost his father."

"I agree. But I'd like to remind you that you haven't lost Ella," the doctor said, waving a hand towards Ella. "She's here, and for all intents and purposes, she's fine. She's going to continue to be fine. There are lots of things that could have gone differently, but they didn't, and it's no one's fault. Well, perhaps aside from the actual person who shot her." The doctor turned her attention back to Ella.

"Ella, is there any reason Porter should place blame on himself for your injuries?"

"No!" Ella exclaimed, vehemently. "Porter, I don't feel that way at all," she said turning to him. "And I'm not sure I understand why you feel that way. Someone did this to *us*, not to just me. I was the one who was physically injured, but you were hurt in other ways as well. Please, Baby, you have to allow yourself to let the feeling of guilt go. I don't blame you, couldn't blame you. You've done nothing but take care of me and protect me from the very beginning."

"Porter, I think Ella makes a good point," the doctor added. "In order to heal from all this, you need to start considering yourself a victim as well. Now, that doesn't mean you need to wallow, but you need to feel it *with* Ella and try not to remove yourself from what happened. Like she said, it happened to you too. If you spend time and energy on feeling guilty, you'll be wasting time and energy that could have been spent on other things. Like love and being with Ella without the confines that the guilt brings upon the relationship."

"What does that mean exactly, Dr. Evans?"

"Well, if Porter is constantly feeling guilt over his perceived blame for your injuries, he cannot be fully invested in the relationship. The guilt and the blame will always be lurking under the surface and eventually he might start to resent the fact that he cannot be fully happy with you, that he will always have these feelings." Ella looked over at Porter and noticed he was deep in thought.

This was not what she had anticipated. She had been prepared to defend her relationship with Porter, to explain that even though they hadn't actually been together for a significant amount of time, that their commitment to each other was solid. She still believed this to be true. However, to hear the doctor tell her that Porter's issues with his guilt may, in the end, cause them to drift apart, made her pulse race. She couldn't lose Porter, wouldn't. As if a switch had been flipped, something within her snapped into place, some piece that had been missing. There was absolutely no way she was going to let someone else's action come in between them. Porter had fought so hard for her and now it was her turn to fight for him. To fight for them.

"I don't resent Ella for any of this," Porter said, quietly.

"And that's good," the doctor started. "But that doesn't mean that after a prolonged period of feeling guilty, you might not start to resent the relationship." Porter turned to look at Ella.

"I could never resent you for anything that's happened. None of it was your fault."

"None of it was your fault either, Porter. You need to listen to Dr. Evans. I need you to listen to her and to listen to me. I can't lose you, Porter. This is important." Porter was quiet for a moment, obviously lost in thought. He turned towards the doctor with a question.

"Dr. Evans, can I ask you something?"

"Sure. Go ahead."

"As we stated earlier, Ella and I met and fell in love rather quickly. Her family had a hard time accepting our relationship because of the timeframe. I have absolutely no doubt that Ella and I were supposed to meet and fall in love at the beach. My life is changed because of her and I wouldn't go back for anything. What I want to know is this: From your professional standpoint, are there any issues that could arise from Ella and me entering into our relationship so quickly and continuing to move forward with each other."

"What do you mean by move forward?" Dr. Evans asked with her head cocked to one side.

"Well, I mean advance in our relationship. Ella and I are going to move in together and we're going to build a house. Do you think it's too soon?" Dr. Evans contemplated Porter's question and seemed to move in her seat to make herself more comfortable.

"When I think about healthy and stable relationships, I am not thinking about length of time together or how long they've been dating. I think about communication, mutual respect, and intimacy," the doctor explained, looking both Ella and Porter in the eyes. "If you feel like Ella is someone you want to be with and she reciprocates those feelings, as long as you both have those things, there shouldn't be any concern with the amount of time you've been together. You are placing other people's expectations and confines of traditional relationships on your own and that could cause harm where there is no need or concern for it. Let me ask you this, Porter. Do you feel obsessive towards Ella? Are you finding it hard to focus on work or your day to day activities? Do you find yourself making rash decisions or doing things that are uncharacteristic of yourself in order to see her or be with her?"

"I think about her all the time, but not in an obsessive way. I think about her in a loving way. Just about how lucky I am to have found her and then found her again, despite all the obstacles. I think about our future, whether it be in the distance or what we're going to do that evening. I think about how beautiful she is and how I've never wanted to be with anyone like I want to be with her." Porter paused for a moment, and Ella grasped his hand tighter. "I have rearranged my life for her, but only because it isn't my life anymore – it's ours."

Dr. Evans looked over at Ella and let Porter's words sink in. "Ella, what about you? Are you obsessive about Porter? Are you making rash decisions?"

Ella looked over at him. She could see in his face how much he needed to hear that what they were doing wasn't crazy. That even though they had all the odds stacked against them, they would make it through to their forever.

"The only thing out of the ordinary about our relationship is the time factor, that our feelings for each other have progressed so quickly. Besides that, and the whole amnesia thing," Ella said with a wave of her hand, "everything is as it should be. We are enjoying each other, getting to know each other, learning about each other. The only difference between what Porter and I have and any other relationship, is that I know, with more surety and certainty than I have ever known anything else, that there is nothing I am going to learn about Porter that will change my mind about being with him forever. I know all the important stuff. At this point, the rest of it is just noise."

Ella saw him smile at her, knowing that he remembered speaking those exact words to her at the beach house. It was true then and it was still true now. When he had spoken those words, it was her who needed reassurance, and now it was Porter who was looking for her to give him the assurance he needed. Ella would do anything to make sure he knew she wasn't going anywhere.

"You kids are going to be fine," the doctor said with a smile. Ella couldn't help but smile back at her because she knew the doctor was right.

Chapter Thirteen

Ella

With a prescription in hand, Ella left the doctor's office with Porter following close behind. The doctor suggested that Ella come back for weekly appointments to try and help her transition into taking the medication and dealing with her anxiety. Dr. Evans said she didn't feel Porter needed to come back immediately unless his feelings of guilt or blame didn't start to decrease soon, or something else became an issue for him. They made it out to the sidewalk and Ella paused as Porter came to stand in front of her.

"Well," Ella said. "That was more exhausting than I had imagined it would be." She took a step into him and rested her cheek against his chest. She felt his arms come around her neck and she snuggled in a little closer. She couldn't help but smile a little at his scent of soap and wood. It was a scent she would love to smell over and over again. She inhaled deeply and felt his chest shake a little with laughter.

"Everything ok down there?" He chuckled.

"Yes. You smell good."

"Are you hungry? It's about dinner time," he said, brushing some hair back from the side of her face.

"I could eat. Want to go back to my place?"

"No, I have other plans."

"Oh you do?" She said, as she pulled back far enough to give him a questioning look.

"Yes. Leave your car here. We'll come back for it later," he said matter-of-factly, and took her by the hand, leading her to his truck. She didn't argue or mind. He opened her door for her and she loved the feeling of his hands on her hips as he lifted her into the cab. Would she ever tire of feeling his hands on her body? She hoped not. She watched him walk around the front of the truck, and when he got in, she let her eyes graze all the way down his body noticing how his muscles were evident through his shirt.

"Enjoying the view?" Porter asked with a smug grin.

"Immensely," she returned his smile. "Where are we going?"

"Out to dinner."

Ella took his short answer and decided it was all she was going to get out of him, so she decided to just enjoy the ride. She unbuckled her seatbelt and scooted down the bench seat until she was right next to him, and she laid her hand on his thigh, resting her head on his shoulder.

"Buckle up, Ella," he said, sounding more demanding than pleading. Ella rolled her eyes towards the ceiling of the truck, feigning annoyance at his protective nature. In reality, she thought it was sexy as hell when he worried about her. She would never take for granted that when she was with him she always felt safe.

As he maneuvered the truck down the highway, Ella took the opportunity to admire one of her favorite spots in Portland. Driving towards a tunnel, completely surrounded by trees and brush, once you emerge from the other side all you can see are skyscrapers. The sudden and immediate transition from greenery to cityscape is something that always amazed Ella. It spoke volumes about the city of Portland as a whole; you were never far from a completely different landscape. If you drove an hour from the city in any direction you could encounter an ocean, rivers, a mountain, endless fields of crops, waterfalls, not to mention the windsurfing capital of the world. You had to be completely lazy and blind not to notice everything that surrounded Portland.

"I love this tunnel," Ella said quietly as they drove out the East end to a different kind of forest made of buildings instead of trees. "I love the juxtaposition. One second you're surrounded by trees, then bam, buildings and bridges."

"I never really noticed that before," Porter said thoughtfully. Ella shrugged her shoulders and smiled at him. They traveled in silence as she took in the sights of the city and the boats on the river. The fourth of July was quickly approaching, and she could see preparations being made on the waterfront for the annual Blues Festival.

Ella couldn't keep herself from cringing as Porter squeezed his giant truck down the narrow and busy streets of downtown. Every time she covered her eyes and made scared yelps, Porter chuckled and patted her on the thigh.

"You think I'm going to hit something with my truck?" He laughed.

"It's just so big. I don't know how you control it the way you do." Porter looked over at her and waggled his eyebrows. It took her a moment, but she finally realized what she had said and slapped him in the chest. "You know what I mean!"

"I'm an expert at getting big things in tight spaces," he said, not even trying to hide his smile. Ella pulled away from him, trying to put a frown on over the smile that was surely taking over her face.

"What are you, fourteen?" She teased. Porter shrugged as he pulled into an available space on the street to park.

"I'm a guy, Babe. I call 'em like I see 'em. We're here," he said as he pointed across the street.

Ella looked up to the Rock Bottom Brewery, one of Ella's most favorite restaurants in Portland.

"Babe, I love this place."

"I know. I asked Megan where I should take you."

They hopped out of the truck and headed towards the restaurant. Ella hadn't been there in months and she was already perusing the menu in her mind, thinking about what she would order. When they walked in they were met with the sounds of a busy restaurant: plates clanking, people laughing, doors from the kitchen swinging open. The restaurant was made entirely of a dark wood and even in the brightest of late Spring evenings, you could still feel the dark golden light reflecting off the wood creating the aura of an intimate setting. Ella loved that you could find any type of person here: Business women and men, college students, families, and the ever-present hipster. It was the beer that brought everyone in. Portland was famous for its beer and Rock Bottom definitely upheld the reputation.

A young brunette hostess brought them to a table with a small candle lit on the surface. After they sat down Ella ordered her favorite beer and Porter took the same.

"I can see why you like this place," Porter said, smiling at her. She melted at his smile. After such an emotional afternoon with Dr. Evans, it felt good to see him happy, even if his worries were only suspended for the moment. She reached across the table and took his hand.

"I love you," she said, only making him smile bigger.

"I know, Babe. I love you too."

"I just want to make sure you understand that. I know things are difficult, but I love you and nothing will change that, ever." He rubbed his thumb over her knuckles, sending small shivers throughout her body.

"Ella, I don't want you worrying about me. I heard what the doctor said, and I've taken it in. But nothing in the world could make my love for you turn into something resentful. The only thing I resent is that it took thirty-two years for you to come into my life."

Ella bit on her bottom lip, trying to walk the fine line between trusting what he was saying and making really sure he understood where she was coming from.

"Just promise me something," she asked, begging him with her eyes.

"Anything."

"Promise me that you'll talk to me about what you're feeling in regards to the accident and your guilt. I don't want that to come between us."

"Done." He said quickly in agreement. Ella was skeptical.

"Porter, I'm serious."

"So am I. I have no reason to hide any of this from you, that's not how I operate."

"Ok."

"Can we just have a relaxing meal now? I want to enjoy a dinner with my girlfriend and just let the stress of the last couple hours fall away."

"Done," she replied with a smile. His smile returned, just as she'd hoped it would. With the touchy subject behind them, they spent the next hour chatting and eating what Ella thought to be the best bacon cheeseburger she'd ever had. They managed to learn things about each other that hadn't previously come up in conversation between them. Ella almost felt guilty that she had no idea when Porter's birthday was, but immediately pulled out her phone to program a reminder for October first. He did the same for hers on April tenth, although they laughed about how neither one of them could ever forget her birthday.

"Best and worst day of my life," Ella chuckled.

"More good than bad though, I hope," Porter said, caressing her hand again.

"Of course." She smiled at him sweetly.

"Are you about ready to go?" He said as he signed the receipt the waitress had left on their table.

"Yes. Are we going to pick up my car?"

"No, Megan picked it up while we were eating."

"What? Why?" Ella was supremely confused.

"Don't you worry about it. I've made plans. Trust me." Well, how could she argue with that.

"Ok. What's next?"

"It's a surprise," he said looking directly into her eyes, his voice low and sexy. Excitement ran through her body with his sultry words. He stood up and held his hand out for her to take. She gripped his hand tightly, trying to contain her rapid pulse. When they made it out to the truck he opened her door for her and again took her by the waist and lifted her onto the seat. He placed his hands on either side of her knees, keeping her legs hanging out of the truck.

"Since it's a surprise, you're going to have to keep your eyes closed." She smirked at him, his playfulness welcomed by her. "However, I don't trust you not to peek, so we're going to have to resort to drastic measures." He pulled a bandana out of his back pocket and started folding it up to be long and narrow. Ella's eyes darted between the bandana and his face.

"You're going to blindfold me?" He didn't answer, just nodded his head, never removing his eyes from hers. "Are you serious?" Again with the nodding. She'd never been blindfolded before, well, except during piñatas at birthday parties in grade school, but she very much doubted this type of blindfolding was anywhere near that realm. Letting a man blindfold her wasn't anything she'd ever experienced before. He continued to let his eyes burn into her, waiting for what? Her permission? Her acceptance? She decided that if there was anyone on the planet she trusted enough to let them blindfold her, it was Porter. She closed her eyes and bowed her head towards him, giving him the surrender he seemed to be looking for.

She felt him wrap the cloth around her head and gently tie a knot in the back.

"Is it too tight?" He asked quietly. She shook her head. His fingers left the back of her head and traced lightly over her cheeks and she felt him urge her face forward. She felt his lips connect with hers and she was instantly lost in the tender way his kissed her. The excitement she felt by his blindfolding her coupled with the gentleness in his kiss had her reeling. He pulled away but left his forehead resting up against hers.

"You kill me with that mouth," he rasped. His comment made her smile.

"Where are you taking me?" she whispered.

"Oh no, I'm not telling. We'll be there soon." With that, he nudged her knees inside the truck. She felt him reach around her to buckle her seatbelt and then close her door. The truck fired to life and the roar and vibration of the engine only intensified her climbing arousal.

"Hang on, Baby," he said. Ella could hear the smile in his voice.

Porter

It surprised him how much he enjoyed blindfolding Ella. He wouldn't consider himself a sexual deviant by any means, but he would be lying if he said that Ella completely trusting him with her body and safety, giving herself up to him like that, didn't totally turn him on. The entire way to his surprise destination, he kept stealing glances at her. Her small frame dwarfed even more by the size of his truck, she looked a little abandoned on the other side of the truck. At a stoplight he reached over and grabbed her around the waist the haul her to his side of the seat. She yelped in surprise, then laughed as she laid her head on his shoulder.

"We're almost there," he whispered in her ear. He enjoyed watching her shiver and saw the goose bumps appear on her neck.

"This better be a good surprise," she mocked complaint.

"I hope you like it," he answered honestly. To be fair, he wasn't sure she'd like it at all. She might think it over the top, or unnecessary, but there was this pestering need he felt inside to do this for her. And, of course, there was a little bit of payoff for him as well.

He pulled up to the sidewalk in front of a big posh building.

"I'll come around and help you out," he told her. When he came to the valet, he threw him the keys and then held his finger up to his mouth to indicate to the young man not to say anything to ruin his surprise. He opened Ella's door and helped her climb down from the truck, not being able to resist placing a small and innocent kiss on her lips as she got her bearings.

"Ready? Take my hand and I promise I won't run you into any walls," he said as he took her hand in his. She held his hand tight and kept him close, banking her forehead on his bicep, putting complete trust in the fact that he wouldn't lead her astray.

He walked through the lobby of the Hilton Hotel in downtown Portland. Lush furniture and green plants lined the elaborate room. He saw the woman behind the counter give him a knowing smile. Perhaps he wasn't the first person to lead a blind folded woman through her hotel. He pushed the button on the elevator and when Ella heard the ding announcing the arrival of the car she perked up.

"Is that an elevator?"

"Yup, take a few steps on, Babe. We're going up." He led her on to the elevator and then pushed the button for their floor. As they stood alone in the elevator Porter couldn't help but run his nose along the side of her neck. A small groan escaped from her.

"Porter," she breathed, "where are we?"

"Does it matter?" He said with his lips brushing against her skin.

"Um, kinda. How do I know we're not in an elevator with a bunch of strangers? Wait, are we in an elevator with a bunch of strangers?" She sounded a little panicked, but it didn't stop her from moving her head to the side so he could get at more of the skin on her neck. He continued to lay kisses along her bare skin, taking small nips at her, trailing small bites up and down.

"We're all alone," he said as he wrapped his arms around her waist, moving his hands up her back and pulling her into him. They passed a few more floors and he was glad that their ride was uninterrupted by any other passengers. Once the doors opened he pulled her out and led her down the hallway to their room. He saw that she was biting her lip, obviously still a little worried about where he could have taken her. He pushed his keycard into the lock and pushed the door open. When they entered the room he took a moment to make sure everything was perfect. When he was convinced that she would love it, he slowly took the blindfold from her head. Now it was his turn to wait.

She blinked a few times, trying to acclimate to being able to see again. When her eyes finally opened and she took in what she was seeing, her mouth turned into a sweet smile and he hand came to her chest, covering her heart.

Laid out, on the floor of the posh hotel room, was a blanket, with two sleeping bags rolled up on the side, a bottle of champagne, two champagne flutes, and makings for smores. Porter came up behind her and placed his chin on her shoulder.

"Remind you of anything?" He asked, hoping she remembered that night as vividly as he did.

"Yes," she whispered. "Our picnic. On the beach." She turned and brought her hands up around his neck. "That was the first time I told you I loved you."

She looked up at him with her crystal blue eyes, smiling, and running her fingers through the hair on the nape of his neck. He flipped his nose on the tip of her nose, then pressed his lips to hers.

"That was one of the best moments of my life, hearing you say those words to me."

"Mine too."

"Sorry I couldn't make this happen at the beach, but as I remember, you had a problem with the visibility factor at the beach. So I thought perhaps you would appreciate the privacy of the hotel room." She turned and looked around the room, still taking it all in. He saw when she took in the giant picture window that overlooked all the skyscrapers that lined the night sky, twinkling lights and all.

"Wow. Porter, I've never seen the city like this before. It's so beautiful. Definitely a change of scenery from the beach, but I like it just as much." She turned back to look at him. "How did you pull all of this off anyway?"

"Well, I left work early and came here with all the supplies, then while we were at dinner Megan and Patrick came to help get everything set up."

"This is very sweet, Porter, but I don't need all of this."

He could tell she was worried about his work, and how much he must have spent on the hotel room. He placed his hands on her waist and brought his face down level with hers.

"I was thinking all morning about how stressful the last week had been for you. And I know that there aren't many places you feel safe at the moment."

"I feel safe with you," she interrupted him.

He kissed her for that.

"I'm glad you feel safe with me, but I want you to feel safe all the time. This morning you had to leave early because you didn't want to be at my house alone and I know you have issues being at your place. I just wanted, even if it's just for tonight, to give you a place without any negative memories, where we can relax and enjoy each other." He kissed her again, this time she leaned into him and he brought his hands up to her face to hold her right where he wanted her. Eventually he remembered the one part of this surprise that was one hundred percent, completely, and undeniably all for him. He pulled away from her with a smile.

"There should be something for you in the bathroom. Go check it out."

She gave him a crooked eyebrow and slowly pulled back from him, then headed towards the bathroom. While she was gone he spread the sleeping bags out on the floor, lit the few candles that were spread around the room, turned the lights down, and opened the bottle of champagne. When he heard the bathroom door open he turned to see her. He knew what was waiting for him, but what he couldn't have anticipated was the way seeing her affected him.

She stood in the doorway and the candlelight dimly cast a golden hue on her that only complimented the creamy color of her skin. In contrast to her milky skin was the black lace that she wore. She rested her hip against the doorjamb of the bathroom, her hands behind her back, allowing him an uninterrupted view of her perfectly sexy body. She had pulled her hair down and it was falling softly down past her shoulders. She was absolutely everything he could ever want in a woman. From the way she was stubborn about the stupidest things, to the way she seemed to *need* him. He doubted he would ever be able to fully explain to her how he felt, so showing her was the next best option.

"Ella, you're breathtaking." She smiled at him and then, lifting her hip off the doorjamb, slowly walked towards him. His eyes made no apologies as they roamed over her body. He was equally turned on by the sight of her gorgeous breasts which were deliciously pushed up in black lace, as he was by the simple vision of her bare feet. In his mind, shoes came off once you were trying to get comfortable. If Ella's feet were bare, she was at home. It made him happy to know that she was at home when she was with him. His eyes moved back up from her feet and he admired the piece of lingerie he'd picked out for her. The black lace stretched seductively over every curve she had, clinging to the very parts of her body he wanted to get his hands on. The top and bottom of the negligée were lined in a soft pink lace, bringing out a softness against its black counterpart. The combination of the soft pink and sexy black did very arousing things for Porter.

"You could have a future in lingerie, Porter. If I decide to open a store just for sexy undergarments, I could bring you on as a buyer," she teased as she got closer to him.

"That might be counterproductive for us, Babe. I would probably spend more money on samples than you'd make selling it."

"Porter?" She said, stopping a good six feet from him. "Why is it that I am in this beautiful negligée which, by the way, feels very luxurious against my skin, and you are still fully clothed? That seems hardly fair." She put on a fake pout which only made him smile. He reached up and started slowly pulling at the buttons on his shirt.

"You'd like to see me in less?" He teased.

"Baby, if it were up to me and socially acceptable, we'd be naked one hundred percent of the time," she said as she sauntered towards him again. "Well, at least if we were at home. I wouldn't want any other women to see you without a shirt on. You're lethal shirtless. We can't be responsible for the toll your bare chest and arms would take on the population." As she came to stand before him, she helped him undo the very last button of his shirt. He watched as she laid her palms flat on his chest, moving her hands up to his shoulders, pushing his shirt down his arms. "That's better," she said as she leaned forward and placed a kiss right over his heart.

He ran his hands over her shoulders and down her arms. When he reached her hands, he linked his with hers and then pulled her hands behind her back causing her to fall into him, pinning her lace-covered breasts against his chest. Her face lifted up to his and he could see soft light flickering in the blue of her eyes. He was lost in her and he knew he would never find his way out. He closed his eyes and leaned his forehead against hers.

"Sometimes," he said so quietly it was almost a whisper. "Sometimes, the urge to hold you as close to me as possible is so overwhelming, I have to remind myself that I can't just keep you all to myself forever. I just want to cling to you, feel you next to me at all time, feel you pressed up against me, making sure that you're mine, and that you're safe."

"With you is the only place I want to be, and the closer the better."

His lips found hers and, like always, they seemed to melt against his perfectly. Everything about her body lined up perfectly with his. She *fit* him, was made for him, was his. As he pressed their mouths together with even more fervor, she leaned into him more. He released her hands to cup the sides of her face, bringing them both deeper into the kiss as his tongue slipped past the seam of her lips. She opened for him willingly and he savored the taste of her. He felt her hands peruse up his back gently teasing his shoulder blades.

"Do you want some champagne?" He asked, kissing down her neck, his most favorite spot.

"Mmm….," was all she could muster in response.

"What does Mmmm mean?"

She pulled back and looked him in the eyes.

"I'll take whatever you want to give me."

"Well, in that case, you get champagne. I want you relaxed and worry free."

"Being here with you gets me halfway there already."

He placed a quick kiss on her lips.

"Good, I'm glad. Take a seat," he said motioning towards the sleeping bags on the floor. He poured her and himself a glass of champagne and handed it to her. He took a seat behind her, wrapping his legs around her as she leaned her back up against his chest. He took one moment to nuzzle in and smell her hair, his lips smiling against the back of her neck. He brought his mouth to her ear and lifted his glass up in a toast.

"To second chances, moving forward, and loving without regret."

Chapter Fourteen

Ella

The rest of the week had continued with little excitement, but more happiness and contentment than Ella could remember. Being with Porter every night was something she had quickly grown accustomed to. Friday had come and true to his word, Porter had taken the day off to look at houses and shop space with Ella. She had insisted that they drive her car, sighting many instances where Porter's large truck nearly decimated many smaller cars in Portland.

"I don't want to cause any accidents, and I definitely don't want to spend the day cringing and hyperventilating because I'm a terrible passenger," Ella said with her hand on the doorknob, ready to leave but hoping to convince Porter to see her point.

"Fine," he said dropping a kiss on her lips. "You drive and I'll control the radio."

She eyed him suspiciously. "What kind of music do you listen to?" Even to her the question seemed ironic. In her mind she chastised herself for not knowing what type of music the man she was going house hunting with listened to.

He winked at her, a smile spreading slowing across his face that still had the dark stubble from the day before. "I guess you'll just have to weigh your priorities carefully. Do you want to drive? Or are you willing to risk your ears for the next hour?"

She continued to look at him through slitted eyelids. "Fine." When they got to the car and Ella started to pull out of the parking lot of her apartment Porter was flipping turning the dial on her radio and stopped on a classical station. He sat back in his seat and gave her a satisfied grin. She pulled onto the highway and laughed. "You think this is going to bother me? I made it through college listening to classical music while I studied. I could listen to this all day."

The soft classical music was the perfect backdrop to the hour-long conversation they had as they drove towards Salem. Ella told Porter stories of her childhood, a few involving Megan, but most were just tiny pieces of her life. She told him about the time she was in the third-grade play and she forgot her one and only line and then tripped over a microphone wire. She told him about her first kiss which happened her freshman year of high school during a dance. She told him about her dog, Scruffy, and how he had been with her from when she was five until she was seventeen.

In between listening to her stories, Porter told her stories of his own. She listened to him talk about playing baseball in his yard with his father. She also heard about his first kiss which happened to be inside his mother's restaurant one night after it had been closed down.

"You broke into your mother's restaurant?" Ella stated, shocked.

"No, I had a key."

"How old were you?"

"I don't know, old enough to drive I guess. Sixteen? Seventeen?"

Ella thought seventeen was a little old for a boy to have his first kiss. "Were you a late bloomer? How did you make it to seventeen without being kissed?" Porter shrugged his shoulders.

"Probably the same way I made it to thirty-two without having a serious relationship. I just wasn't interested. I was too focused on making sure my mom was taken care of and that the restaurant was running smoothly. I didn't have much time for girls."

"So what made you go to all the trouble of sneaking into your mom's restaurant with a girl if you weren't interested?"

He tilted his head at her and drew in his eyebrows. "I was uninterested in a girlfriend, but I was still a seventeen year old guy. I was pretty desperate. I think she only wanted to go out with me so I could get her access to the bar though. She was pretty drunk before we got to the kissing."

Ella pouted at him. "Your first kiss was with a drunk girl?" He shrugged again.

"It could have been worse. My first everything could have been with that drunk girl. Besides, it was only one kiss. It didn't last long and it wasn't great. But it was an experience."

"Good point. So, who is running Porter Enterprises today?" He laughed at her.

"Porter Enterprises?"

"Well, along with the type of music you like, I also don't know the name of your company."

"Masterson Construction. It's kind of a play on 'Masters and Son'. I wanted to make sure I gave my dad a little credit. It was his life insurance that got me started in the business. But I also didn't want to deal with explaining that Dad was gone. So, I thought Masterson was a good compromise."

Ella reached out for his hand and laced her fingers with his. "It really is Porter. I love that name." She took a deep breath, trying to let her feelings settle a bit. For as manly and rugged as Porter made himself out to be, he was also vulnerable and fragile at times. It was confounding to Ella. The juxtaposition of the protective and almost caveman-like persona she was use to and the inner child who just missed his father sometimes took a moment to reconcile in her mind. "So, who is manning Masterson Construction today?"

"That would be Matt. I've known him for about ten years. He was the first person I ever hired when I started my own company. He moved here to be with his girlfriend Brook, who is now his wife." Ella heard Porter's voice drift away and knew his mind was working something out. "He is definitely the closest friend I have. Actually, I'm surprised you haven't met him yet. I think out of everyone I know he's the one who has been the most understanding about why I am the way I am."

"What do you mean?" Ella probed.

"He knows I don't date. He's never tried to set me up with anyone and he doesn't push the subject. I've told him about what happened to my dad, and he knows how I am about my mom. In fact, he's stepped in a time or two when something's happened at the restaurant and I was unavailable. He's gone over there, no questions asked, and just helped her. I am so grateful to him for that. He's never once questioned my decision to remain single or made me feel like less of a man because I wasn't sleeping with a different woman every weekend." He let out a little laugh and sighed through the end of it. "His wife would kick his ass if he did."

"I think I'd like to meet these friends of yours," Ella said softly.

"I'm sure they're dying to meet you," he said while giving her one of his brilliant smiles.

A few hours later Ella and Porter returned to her car.

"I cannot believe we just signed a lease on a house," Ella said excitedly.

"It's only temporary, Ella. Soon I will find a good plot to start building and we can build our dream house together."

"Trust me, I'm excited for that to happen too, I just can't believe we found a house on our first trip, and one that was immediately available too. How'd we get so lucky?"

"It was about time some good stuff started happening for us," he replied dryly.

"I guess you're right. But you like the house, right? You didn't just take it because I wanted to?"

"No, Babe. I liked it enough. It's no three-story craftsman on the beach, but it'll do," he said with a wink. "Now let's go look at this storefront you're so excited about." Ella was nearly bouncing in her seat. The storefront she'd seen on the internet looked perfect for her store. The real estate agent had assured her it had everything she was looking for.

"Promise me you'll be honest when you see it? I want your truly honest opinion," she pleaded with him.

"Definitely."

When they pulled up to the store front Ella couldn't contain her smile. The store had a white awning that made it look quaint from the street. She had always wanted an awning at the Portland store, but it didn't fit with the urban feel of the street the store was located on. This street in downtown Salem had more of a intimate feeling to it. It felt more personal. Not only did it have an awning, but it also had display windows, another thing she'd always wanted. She could already see mannequins in the window with different ensembles for the different seasons.

"Ok, Ella, this is the one I was telling you about," Rachel, the real estate agent, said excitedly. "I think it has almost everything you've been looking for. Unfortunately it isn't already wire for security like you had requested, but that's something you can easily take care of once you take ownership. Let's go inside a look around."

Rachel was an older woman, probably in her sixties, and she was all business. She was friendly enough, but she didn't engage them in small talk and was very professional. It was refreshing for Ella to be around another woman who didn't openly gawk at her boyfriend. Rachel earned points for that in Ella's book.

The inside of the store was as expected. Large and empty. The previous owners had gutted the place, and she preferred it that way. She could let her imagination run wild with an empty canvas. She was regretting not bring a pad and paper with her. Rachel must have noticed her concerned look on her face because she reached into her briefcase and handed Ella a legal pad and a pen.

"Wow, you're good," Ella said as she took the pad and paper.

"I've been doing this a long time. I recognize the look of inspiration when I see it. Your fingers were almost miming making a list."

"Thank you," Ella said as she started making notes. She spoke her thoughts out loud as she jotted them down. "We would need to build a backroom and stock area, fitting rooms, and shelving.

The floors need to be replaced. Hard wood maybe."

"Cherry. It would warm the space up," Porter chimed in. Ella turned and smiled at him.

"You think it's cold?"

"Yeah, but it's an empty room right now. We can make it right. Portland can handle the starkness of Poppy; the concrete floors, the dark walls. It fits. Here though, I think you'd want to go with something softer." She smiled because it was like he was reading her mind.

"Hardwood floors. Cherry wood. Butter yellow walls. White shutters around the mirrors. Shabby Chic. Drapes on the fitting rooms, not doors."

"Will you call it Poppy?" He asked.

"I don't know yet," she said, contemplating everything. "I think it might be good to call it Poppy, to draw in the people who already know the store in Portland and would want to shop here. But part of me wants to make this store different. A different vibe. I've been toying around with the idea of still using the name of a flower though. That way the stores are tied together, but this one could have its own unique look and feel." She shrugged her shoulders. "It's just an idea."

"It's a good idea, Ella." Porter said, wandering back to the other end of the room. "Is this space already have complete plumbing? I'm not a plumber." Ella laughed to herself at Porter's constant insistence that he doesn't *do* plumbing.

"Yes, the whole space has complete plumbing and electrical," Rachel said cooly.

Porter looked at Ella. "Do you know what this means?" He asked, his eyes wide, eyebrows raised.

"Yeah, that is was meant to be and we were supposed to find this place?" Ella said laughing.

Porter looked back at Rachel. "I don't do plumbing or electrical."

"Babe," she heard Porter yell through the house. "Are you almost ready?"

"For someone who didn't really want to go, you sure are eager!" She yelled back through the bathroom door. Within a few seconds she heard a small knock on the door. She smiled and rolled her eyes simultaneously. She cracked the door just enough to see his gorgeous brown eyes peering at her through the crack.

"May I help you?" She asked, smiling sweetly at him.

"I think the real question is, may I help you? What do you have going on in there that's taking so long?" Ella shrugged her shoulders and added 'grumpy when kept waiting' to the ever growing list of things she was learning and loving about Porter.

"Give me five minutes. I'm almost finished." His eyes glowered at her and he turned and walked away. She laughed, shook her head at him and closed the door. Even though he'd spent most of his adult life single, he seemed to be falling into the typical 'relationship guy' role with few problems.

Ella needed to finish up a few things before they headed out to the club. Megan convinced them to celebrate at an actual dance club, which Ella wasn't terribly excited about as she preferred dive bars, but Megan was so excited it was impossible to say no. She was also excited to let loose for a night and spend some time doing normal couple things with Porter. It bothered her a little that their relationship thus far had really been unconventional. She loved the way they met and would treasure their past because it only led them to where they were now, but she'd be lying if she said that it wasn't a little stressful at times. They needed a night of fun out with friends and with each other.

Ella took just one more moment to make sure she was put together properly. Her hair was down with big barrel curls floating past her shoulders. Her make-up was a little more dramatic than she was used to, but she wanted to fit in at the club and thought the smoky eye look complimented her outfit. She was wearing a pair of black trouser shorts that came down to about mid-thigh. They were short enough to show off her legs, but not short enough to be inappropriate. Her top, a simple button-up white, cotton tank, was tucked into her shorts. She threw on a chunky silver necklace and silver bangle bracelet. Just to add a splash of color she chose bright red pumps which matched her red lips. She turned her body every which way just to make sure she looked presentable from every angle and when she was satisfied she looked her best, she pulled the door open just to find Porter standing at the end of the hall.

She saw him leaned back against the wall looking terribly bored, but tremendously hot. He added some gel to his normally unruly hair and the effect was maddening. He looked sharp and sexy. He wore her favorite pair of jeans that hugged his thighs and made his ass look amazing. His arms were hugged tightly by his maroon button up shirt, his sleeves rolled up to his elbows. The red of his shirt made his brown eyes pop and the chocolate color was so delicious she found it difficult to pull her gaze from them. The sight of him was arousing and she knew she was going to have to keep women off of him all night. It was a task she was happy to take on, seeing as how she didn't plan on leaving his side.

"Porter, I stand by all my previous comments. There is no way on this earth you made it to thirty-two years old and remained single. I think you must have been really irritable or a complete asshole before we met. You are, by far, the sexiest man I have ever seen. I'm not sure I even want to go out anymore. Let's stay home," she smiled at him as she wrapped her arms around his waist.

"Oh no. You spent an hour in that bathroom getting ready while I waited patiently. We're going out. You remember how sexy you think I am at this moment when you try to get me to dance. All sexiness evaporates when I try to dance." He took her by the hand, pulled her out from his body, and made her spin around. "But we don't have to worry about dancing because there is no way I am letting you out on a dance floor in this." He pulled her back to him suddenly, her hands coming to rest on his shoulders.

"I really like Possessive Porter," she whispered up to him.

"Well good, cause Possessive Porter is your date for the evening." He bent down to her and as his lips touched hers, it was as if he'd branded her. Heat torched through her veins and she gripped his biceps to keep herself upright. He pulled away as quickly as he'd swooped in and she couldn't help but laugh at the bright red lipstick that was now covering his mouth.

"Come on Possessive Porter, we should probably clean the lipstick off you before we go."

It had been years since Ella had been to an honest-to-God dance club. She was worried to a certain degree that she'd be the oldest woman there, but she was surprised to see quite a few women who looked to be in their thirties. She wasn't interested in feeling like a chaperone. Porter had her by the hand and led her through the crowd to where Megan and Patrick were seated at a tall table against a wall that lined the dance floor. Ella felt the bass of the music thumping through the floor and when she got to Megan, she was forced to yell in her sister's ear just to be sure she could hear her.

"Hey, Megs!" She shouted.

"FELLA!" Megan yelled as she jumped from her stool to give Ella a wobbly hug. Ella gave Patrick a look over Megan's shoulder that said 'She's already drunk?' Patrick just smiled and shrugged his shoulders. If there was one thing Ella knew about Patrick, it was that he loved Megan. He was secure enough to let her be her wild self, but man enough to not take any crap from her either. There were times they fought as hard as they loved, and Ella had always been a little jealous of how passionate they seemed to be about each other. No one could handle Megan like Patrick could, but no one could love Patrick better than Megan.

Ella watched as Porter reached out towards Patrick to shake his hand. Patrick shook his hand and then they did the weird, mannish, half-hug thing that guys did. Porter said something in

Patrick's ear and she watched Patrick nod his head. Porter slapped him on the back and Ella smiled as she watched Porter make friends with her future brother-in-law.

"You started the party without us," Ella said in Megan's ear.

"I only had a few drinks to warm up. It's fine! Once Kalli gets here, we'll all dance and have a good time!" Ella smiled and took a moment to remind herself that Megan was just twenty-two. She was still in the 'I can drink every weekend if I want to' stage of life, while Ella was in more of the 'I'll take a glass of wine or two with dinner every now and then' stage of life. She decided to let Megan enjoy her promotion party, knowing that Patrick would never let anything happen to her.

"Is Kalli bringing that Scott guy?" Ella asked.

"I'm not sure. I know she invited him, but I'm not sure if he's coming."

"Have you met him yet?"

"No. She's been keeping him to herself," Megan answered with a wink.

Ella felt Porter come up behind her. She felt her body respond with warmth as he placed his mouth right near her ear.

"Do you want something to drink?" His voice sent vibrations along her neck that made her shiver.

"Yes, can you get me a vodka sour, please?" She asked sweetly.

"Sure," he said, as he placed a small kiss just below her ear. "Stay here. I'll be right back." He walked towards the bar and disappeared in a sea of people, most of whom were gyrating and rubbing various parts of their bodies against each other.

"So," Megan sang in Ella's ear. "You and Porter?" She made it sound like a question.

"Yeah?" Ella answered, not really sure what Megan was getting at.

"You're good? I mean, happy?" Ella smiled at her sister. She was always worried about her and there were times she thought Megan would have made an excellent big sister.

"Megan, I am deliriously happy, really."

"Good. You guys look good together. It never occurred to me, until just now, that the only time I ever really saw the two of you together was when you were in a coma." Megan laughed, sensitive sister moment over. Ella had to laugh too.

Just then Kalli came up to their table.

"Kal!" Ella exclaimed. She stood up to hug her friend and realized it had been a while since they'd seen each other. "I've missed you."

"Ella, I've missed you too." Ella pulled away and smiled at her. Kalli made her way over to Megan and gave her a hug as well. Then she pulled up a stool and sat down in between them.

"Where's your date?" Megan asked.

Kalli rolled her eyes in frustration.

"He's a little hot and cold, I'm afraid. I invited him and he said he'd try and make it, but I'm not holding my breath."

Ella frowned and rubbed her hand up and down Kalli's arm, trying to comfort her.

"Maybe he'll surprise you and show up," Ella offered hopefully.

"We'll see," she said and then her eyes darted up behind Ella and went wide with shock.

"Here you go, Babe," Ella heard Porter say in her ear as a glass appeared in front of her. She had to hide the smile that came from watching Kalli react to Porter. Yes, he was hot.

"Porter, this is my friend, Kalli," she said motioning towards her friend with her mouth open still. "Kalli, this is my boyfriend, Porter." He held out his hand to Kalli and she placed her hand in his. Ella knew what his handshake felt like, firm and strong. Powerful. Just like him.

"Kal," Ella said, trying to get her attention. When Kalli's eyes returned to hers, Ella mouthed the words 'close your mouth' at her. She promptly snapped her jaw shut and started blushing.

Megan laughed loudly at Kalli, the alcohol obviously having an effect on her.

"Let's dance!" Megan shouted.

"You guys go ahead. I don't want to be the fifth wheel," Kalli said with a frown.

"Don't be a Debbie Downer!" Megan said. "Come on ladies. We're dancing. Let the boys guard our purses." It became obvious to Ella that there was no arguing with Megan this evening and the woman wanted to dance. Ella quickly took a gulp of her drink and then turned to Porter who already had one eyebrow raised at her.

"I have been nominated as the purse bitch, haven't I?"

Ella kissed him on the cheek and said into his ear, "Take care of my purse now and I'll take care of you later." She pulled back from him and saw a smile on his face. Megan grabbed hers and Kalli's hand and began to drag them towards the dance floor. They stood in the obligatory triangle that women always seemed to form when dancing as Ella strained to hear the lyrics to the song beyond the thumping bass. It was some poppy princess song she didn't recognize, but the melody was catchy. She smiled as she watched her sister sing the lyrics word for word, eyes closed, enraptured in the music.

Ella let the beat take her over and felt her hips begin to sway to the beat. Her hands came up over her head and she happily swayed back and forth with the rest of the crowd. The girls continued to dance and every once in a while Megan would point out a couple that were nearly having sex on the dance floor and they would all laugh and wrinkle their noses. Whenever Ella snuck a peek back at their table to check on Porter, he had his eyes on her. Sometimes he was simply watching, making sure she was alright. Other times he looked pissed, usually when a guy was trying to get one of the girls to dance with them. Megan and Ella did a fabulous job of shooing guys away, or sending them to Kalli if they were cute enough and didn't use an opening line that made them roll their eyes.

One brave guy approached their sacred triangle motioning towards the table where Porter and Patrick were sitting.

"There's two guys at that table taking their job of possessive boyfriends very seriously. I'm hoping they belong to you two and that *you*," he said motioning to Kalli, "are free to dance with me."

"Oh, um," Kalli stammered.

"She's available," Megan said, gently shoving Kalli towards the interested man. Kalli stumbled into him, but regained her footing with the help of his hands bracing her arms against him. Ella saw him whisper something in her ear and Kalli gave him a twinkling smile. She tentatively placed her hands on his shoulder and he rested a hand on the small of her back. Ella smiled as she watched them, glad he had perhaps eased her mind about Scott not showing up. With Kalli occupied, Ella shouted to Megan that she was going back to the table for a drink.

She walked up to the table as Porter and Patrick were engaged in conversation. Without missing a beat or even looking in her direction, Porter opened an arm to her, allowing her to sidle up to him. They were in tune with each other and everything about it made her heart sing. She watched his jaw move as he spoke with Patrick, noticing the stubble that had grown in over the course of the day, wanting to feel it scrape along the side of her neck. The thought of the scratchy skin roughly scraping over the inside of her thighs made her belly flip and her core heat. He turned to her in between sentences and gave her a wink, as if he could hear her thoughts. She blushed and pressed a kiss to his neck just below his jawline.

Ella looked around for Megan, wondering where she had wandered off to. She finally saw her dark brown hair over at the bar.

"I am going to go get another drink. Want anything?" She asked the guys. Patrick declined, as did Porter. She leaned up to kiss Porter's cheek and made her way to the bar. By the time she made it there, Megan has disappeared again and Ella felt a twinge of frustration. The bartender came over to her quickly and asked for her order.

"Vodka sour, please."

"Coming up," he said automatically. When he handed her the drink she gave him Porter's name to add it to the tab and he nodded at her, moving along to the next customer. Ella took a sip of the drink, enjoying the sweet and sour taste that flooded her mouth. Vodka sour was one of the first drinks she ever ordered when she had turned twenty-one and she always seemed to return to it, never wanting to try anything else if she wasn't sure she'd like it. She looked back towards their table, but an enormous group of women had clouded the path back to Porter. One woman in the middle of the group was wearing a blinking sash that said 'Bride' on it and the rest of the women were all wearing matching tiaras. The bride-to-be looked completely trashed and Ella laughed, thinking about how the woman might feel the next day. Not wanting to contend with twenty drunken bridesmaids, she went around the group of women and took another route that led her along the far wall of the club.

She weaved through the crowds of people, holding her drink slightly above her head, trying to avoid having it knocked around and spilled. She tried to politely say "Excuse me," a few times, but was met with irritated glances and people grumbling as she tried to make her way through. She sighed a little as she made her way past a couple groping each other against the wall. She tried to keep the disgusted look from her face, but was caught off guard as a hand grasped her around her arm.

She yelped as she felt her body being yanked to the side, coupled with the cold blast as her drink came down on to the front of her shirt, the sting of the ice cold liquid soaking into her top stole her breath. Before she could see who had a hold of her, she was thrust down a dark hallway and pushed face first into a wall. Two strong hands grasped her arms, pushing her into the wall, making it impossible for her to move. Her face was smashed against the brick wall, the sharp edges of the grainy stone scraping along her cheek. Fear licked through her veins. She was paralyzed by it and could do nothing to try and free herself.

A body pressed up against her, forcing her even further into the wall. A small whimper of fear made it past her lips, but nothing more.

"Ella."

She immediately began to struggle against the voice, a voice so familiar, so unforgettable. Her body revolted against his as it remembered the last time he'd had his hands on her. She opened her mouth, finally feeling the urge to scream, but his hand clamped over it, squeezing hard, muffling her cries.

"Ella, not this again. Be quiet and I won't hurt you. I don't want to have to hurt you." She tried to hold back a sick laugh as she realized the irony of his words while her face was being smashed into a wall. She felt him still against her and slowly the pressure on her mouth weakened, as if he were testing whether or not she would scream if he removed his hand. She breathed fiercely. Her breath rushed in and out of her nose, hitting his hand and making a muffled sound. She shouldn't be able to hear her own breath over the loud music, but she focused on the sound of her breath in and out, trying to remain calm.

"No screaming," Kyle said as he slowly took his hand from her mouth. She ran her tongue over her lips, trying to bring some life back to her mouth after his harsh pressure on it. "You're hard to get alone these days, Ella."

"What do you want, Kyle?" She rasped. He laughed and she could feel him shaking his head at her.

"Don't pretend to be concerned with my wants or needs. Just listen." He pushed harder against her arms splayed on the wall and brought his mouth right to her ear. "I want your word that you will forget what happened between us, Ella. I know your *boyfriend* is pushing you to go to the cops, but I want you to drop it." His fingers squeezed her wrists a little harder and she let out a cry laced with fear. The fear was starting to take her over.

"You're lucky the cops didn't catch me outside of your

boyfriend's house the other night. We'd be playing a different game right now if I'd been taken to jail." She squeezed her eyes tight as his knee came up behind her and pressed into her bottom, nudging her legs open, and pressed into her. Tears threatened to spill out.

"That was you outside the house? You were trying to break in?" Her words were fast and shaking.

"I was trying to get you alone so I could convince you to just let it go."

"Was it you who shot me?"

He was silent for a moment.

"No," he finally answered.

"I don't believe you," she said.

"Yes, you do. You told Kalli you didn't think it was me."

"How do you know Kalli?" Then everything became clear and the fear she had for her own safety was suddenly overshadowed by the fear she had for her friend. "You're Scott."

"Well, Kalli thinks I'm Scott," he said with a laugh. Ella was going to be sick. To think that Kalli had been dating Kyle, had spent time alone with him, let him into her apartment, all because of her. She fought back the bile that threatened her throat.

"I'm telling you right now, Ella, let all of this drop. Tell your boyfriend you don't want to press charges. Tell your sister and Kalli to just let you move on and I will leave you alone. I will disappear and you will never have to see me again." He moved close to her again.

"But I swear to fucking God, if you go to the cops and report me for *anything*, I will do my best to make you and everyone you care about pay for it." He laughed again and it sent shivers over her entire body to hear so much evil in him. He ground his hips into her bottom again, and she cried when she felt that he was aroused.

"It seems you've become quite the slut lately. Didn't wait very long before you shacked up with your latest victim. Go use your whorish talents to convince your boyfriend to let everything drop." She took a deep shuttering breath.

"How can I believe you? How do I know you're telling the truth?"

"I've got no reason to lie to you about this. I've taken everything I wanted from you. I've used you up already. You're not worth anything to me anymore." It shouldn't have hurt her to hear him say those words, but it did.

"You're a sick fuck," Ella said sharply before she could weigh the consequences it might hold.

"Well, you've got me there I guess," he laughed. "Remember this though, Ella. I might be a sick fuck, but I also don't give a damn anymore. Don't give me a reason to make things worse than they already are."

With those parting words, she felt him move away from her quickly and before she could gain stable ground she tumbled to the floor. She watched the back of him as he walked away from her, not looking back once.

She was on her hands and knees, her wet shirt clinging to her, and all she could feel was her heartbeat pounding through her body, radiating in her brain. She heard crying and knew the cries were hers, but she couldn't register what was going on around her. She felt the concrete beneath her hands, the flat surface providing no comfort to her knees. She tipped over so she was sitting on her hip, her head hanging with her chin to her chest, breathing at a frantic pace trying to expel all the fear from her body with sobs. She must have been sitting there long enough for the other's to start to worry because she eventually heard her sister's voice over the music.

"She's over here!" Megan yelled to someone. "Shit. Shit. Shit. Ella? Are you ok?"

Suddenly big, rough hands were on her face, pulling her up to look into the eyes that usually made everything better. Her heart dropped when she realized that right now, she felt the urge to push him away. She was tainted. Poison. She didn't want him to get hurt because of her.

"Baby, what the hell happened? Are you hurt?" He ran a finger over her cheek that had been pressed against the wall and she cringed at the stinging. She couldn't speak; she could only plead with her eyes for him to understand that she needed equally for him to hold her tight and walk away. The words she couldn't say made their way out of her in the form of more cries and sobs.

He lifted her up by her arms and placed her back on her unsteady feet.

"What the hell, Ella?" He looked down at her shirt. She lowered her head and noticed that the drink had caused her shirt to become practically transparent. She watched Porter unbutton his shirt and place it over her shoulders. In the back of her mind, she thought about how good he looked in just the plain white tee shirt he was now wearing and how when they walked back through the bar all the women would begin to ogle him for it.

"Are you ok?" He asked, bringing her face up to look at him.

She said nothing.

He bent over and wrapped an arm under her legs and caught her upper body in his other arm, carrying her through the club. She let him take her and she rested her head against his chest. He passed Patrick on his way to the door.

"Patrick, make sure Kalli gets home safely, ok?"

"No problem. We'll take her home."

"No!" Ella screamed, all of a sudden coming to life. "You have to take Kalli home with you and Megan tonight. Please. Make sure she stays with you," Ella pleaded, panicked to think that no one would be with Kalli. "Where's Megan?" Ella asked as she tried to wriggle free from Porter's hold.

"I'm right here, Ella."

"Megan," she said as she managed to get her feet on the floor. "Please, take Kalli back to your place tonight. Don't let her go home alone or with anyone but you."

"Ella, what's going on?" Porter asked. Ella looked at him, but couldn't bring herself to say anything to him.

"Promise me," she begged Megan.

"I promise. But Ella, you're scaring me."

"Patrick," Ella said, turning to him. "Take them home, now."

Megan's eyes darted back and forth between Ella and Porter. She looked just as confused as he did.

"I'll go get her," Megan finally resigned.

"I'm taking you home," Porter said firmly. Ella wanted to run away, to make sure that everyone was safe, but that she was nowhere near them. She had brought on all the terrible things that had happened to them and now Kyle had threatened all of them. How could she trust that he would keep his word? How could she trust herself to do what he asked? Staying away from Porter would be an impossibility; even if she could manage to tear herself away from him, she was sure he'd never allow it.

"Maybe," she began to say to Porter, trying to resist the urge to fall apart. "Maybe you should go home with them too."

She'd seen a lot of things in Porter's eyes before. Mostly she'd seen unyielding love, warmth, and affection. A lot of the time his eyes went chocolaty with lust and desire, swirling with passion. A few times she'd seen his eyes fill with annoyance or irritation. But she'd never seen the angry blackness that filled his eyes at her words.

"*We* are going home, Ella. Let's go." He grabbed her arms and started leading her out of the club. She could have resisted, but she didn't. She wanted to leave but she wasn't sure she wanted him to be with her, for his own good. As soon as they made it out of the building and on to the sidewalk, she pulled her arm from his grasp.

"Porter, I'm serious. Go with Patrick. Or go back to Lincoln City. I'm fine. I'll be fine," she said through hiccups that were a leftover symptom from the crying. He moved so fast, she almost didn't see him, but he was so close to her she had no room to breathe her own air. His face was nearly touching hers.

"Get. In. The. Truck. Now." He demanded.

"No," she whispered as she shook her head, still looking him directly in the eyes. He turned around and rested his hands flat on the hood of his truck. She could see his chest heaving in and out, trying to reign in his anger. She flinched at the loud bang that came when he slammed one of his balled fists against the hood, denting the very center of it. Her nerves were shot to hell and the loud noise immediately cause her yelp. She started crying again. He moved with superhuman speed again and her face was in his hands, his forehead pressed against hers.

"I'm sorry, Baby. I'm not trying to scare you. Please. Don't push me away right now. Don't. Please let me in. Let me help."

She tried to shake her head but he still held it in his hands.

"What happened in there, Ella? Why are you so scared?"

She pressed her lips together, smashed them together so hard she could feel the indentions forming on the inside of her mouth from her teeth. Her instincts urged her to tell him, but the fear of something happening to him was the overriding factor that kept her from giving him what he wanted.

"I can't be with you right now," she whispered.

"I can't be without you," he whispered back.

She knew he wasn't going to let her out of his sight. She sighed loudly and put her hands over his which were still on the sides of her face. She gently pulled them down until her face was free and she leaned away from him.

"It's not good for us to be together."

"Why would you say that?" She could think of no lie to tell him, couldn't bring herself to utter something that wasn't true.

"Because I love you."

Chapter Fifteen

Porter

"Please get in the truck, Baby. Let me take you home." Something had happened in that hallway; he knew it. What he didn't know is why she wouldn't tell him about it and why she was now nearly hysterical talking nonsense about them not being together. She looked at the ground and finally nodded her head in agreement.

"Do you have any of the pills the doctor gave you for your panic attacks?" He asked gently.

"No," she shook her head. "But I'm not supposed to take them with alcohol anyway. Besides, this isn't a panic attack." She turned and headed towards the truck. He silently followed, racking his brain for anything he could say to try and bring her back around.

She was silent all the way back to her apartment and she sat as far away from him as possible, which killed him. When they finally parked in front of her apartment, he noticed that her breathing became hilted and quickened. He wasn't surprised, seeing as how sometimes just seeing her apartment triggered her anxiety. He slid across the seat to her side and she looked at him with wild and frightened eyes.

"It's never going to end, Porter," she said between labored breaths. "I'm trapped and I've trapped you."

"Shhh, Baby. Calm down. We're not trapped. We're fine. Let's just go inside and go to bed." His concern for her was growing, and he thought he might need to find Dr. Evan's business card and call the emergency number on it. If she didn't calm down soon, he was going to have to do something. The ER wasn't out of the question either. He was thoroughly and completely worried about her, but he didn't know what to do about it besides hold her. "Do you think we could just go inside? We'll lie down and try to just forget about everything for a little while and sleep? Everything will look better tomorrow, I promise." She gave him a look that read 'doubtful', but eventually moved to get out of the truck.

He unlocked the door and opened it for her, flipping on the lights after she walked in. He watched her walk to the back of the apartment and go right into the bathroom. He exhaled loudly as he closed the door and rubbed his hands up and down his face. He walked into the bedroom and stripped down into his boxers then put on a pair of sweats. He sat on the edge of the bed and waited for Ella to emerge from the bathroom.

When he heard the door click open, he raised his eyes to the door to see her enter the bedroom. She had taken off all of her makeup, leaving her face raw from washing but also red from crying. Her hair was pulled up into a messy bun, with strands falling down every which way around her face. She had taken off her clothes and was left standing in front of him in only panties and his unbuttoned shirt. He knew she was in the middle of some sort of crisis, but he couldn't help his eyes from wandering up and down her body. Instead of becoming aroused though, which he was fully expecting, he become protective and possessive. Someone had hurt her tonight and he wanted to know who. Someone had caused the pain that he saw so clearly etched across her face.

She fidgeted with her fingers, playing with the buttons on his shirt.

"I took one of the valium the doctor prescribed to me. I don't think I drank enough alcohol to really make a difference. Right now I just want to go to sleep and forget everything."

"Ok," he said, apprehensively, half expecting her to ask him to sleep on the couch. He wasn't sure which Ella he was dealing with at the moment: the one who said she loved him or the one who said they shouldn't be together.

"Do you think, I mean, could you..." her voice trailed off as she tried to formulate her thoughts. "Would it be ok if you held me?"

Porter let out, quite possibly, the biggest breath of his life. The love of his life was asking him to hold her while she slept. Relief coursed through him at her words and all he could do to answer her was hold open his arms. His relief was mirrored in her by the way her shoulders seemed to sag a little at his acceptance, as if a tight string that had been holding her up were snipped, allowing her to relax.

She came to him at the side of the bed and straddled his lap. Before he could reach around her she peeled away at the shirt she was wearing, letting it trail down her arms and float to the floor. Their eyes met for just a moment before she wrapped her arms around his neck and pressed her naked body into his chest. He felt her nose and mouth settle in the crook of his neck and he heard her inhale deeply. He used his hand to smooth the loose tendrils of her hair down and held her by the back of her neck, pulling her close.

After a few minutes, without breaking their connection, he slid to the head of the bed and laid them both down on their sides so their bodies were facing each other. She never let go of him and he didn't want her to. She kept her arms around his neck, snuggled into his neck. He continually used his hands to sooth her, rubbing his hands along her back, stroking the nape of her neck, gently kissing the top of her shoulder. He couldn't be sure how much time had passed, but he felt like they'd laid in bed for over an hour, and he was finally convinced that she had fallen asleep.

He kissed her temple, then gently and very slowly slipped out of her grasp. Her arms fell to the bed next to her and he took an opportunity to admire her while she slept. He examined the rough, red patch on her cheek that appeared after the incident down the hallway at the club. He traced a finger over it and it made him feel better to see that she wasn't actually cut, but just scraped. His eyes traveled down her body, partly checking for injuries, partly just taking in her beauty. Although her body was undeniably attractive, at the moment he didn't feel turned on by looking at her naked breasts or the creamy skin of her seemingly endless legs. Instead, he felt she was the most fragile and important being in his life. She was put in his path for a reason and he was going to do anything he could to remind her that if separated they would be undeniably miserable. The only way either one of them stood a chance at happiness was if they were together.

He climbed over her small body to lie behind her, trying his hardest not to wake her, although he figured with the valium and vodka in her system she was probably out for a while. He reached down and pulled the comforter up and over their bodies and then wrapped his arm around her waist, pulling her back to his front.

"You're mine forever," he whispered into her shoulder, then closed his eyes and let sleep take him away.

Porter woke to Ella thrashing in bed, her screams ringing through the silent and dark air. He ran to flip the lights on and was crushed by the sight of Ella curled up into a ball, hands gripping her hair at the sides of her head, screaming out pleas of mercy.

"Kyle, no! Don't hurt him!" She cried and tears streamed down her face. Porter wanted to help her but didn't want to add to her trauma by waking her suddenly. He crept over to kneel by her side of the bed. He tried to reach up and brush the hair gently from her forehead, but as soon as his fingers touched her skin she started thrashing around again, arms flailing, legs kicking. He was worried she was going to hurt herself. He saw an opportunity to restrain her so he jumped on the bed and pinned her arms down then flattened his body along hers, effectively immobilizing her. She still wriggled under him, crying out, and she sounded terrified.

"I'll leave. I'll go. Don't take him from me," she sobbed.

"Ella," Porter whispered in her ear as gently as he could. "Wake up, Baby. It's me. It's Porter. Come back to me." The only part of her that could move, her head, continued to thrash back and forth. She wasn't crying anymore, but her face looked pained and worried. He brought his mouth to her neck, trying to get her to hold still, and pleaded with her against the crook of her shoulder. "You're safe," he said. He felt her slowly relax against him, the tension in her arms eased, the muscles of her stomach went lax, and her breathing slowed. He still remained atop her, hoping the contact would sooth and calm her. He loosened his grip on her wrists and she slid her hands up his arms. He could still feel her hands slightly shaking, obviously the adrenaline still coursing through her from the nightmare.

He stilled as her hands continued down his back, slowly grazing her fingers down the canal that formed over his spine. She continued until he felt her hands cover his ass and she gripped him firmly, pulling him against her. He instantly hardened, but felt uneasy about it.

"Ella, tell me what you were dreaming about," he said against the skin of her neck. She raised her hips up to grind into him and shook her head at the same time. He was confused about where her mind was going, but his body was responding to hers. "Tell me what happened at the club," he said as he slid his teeth and tongue along her shoulder. Again, she shook her head, but her hands pulled his hips down into her again. A hiss left him as he continued to fight the urge to take her as she was offering.

She reached down in between them and palmed him, obliterating any restraint he might have been holding on to. He pulled back to look in her eyes, trying to figure out what she wasn't telling him.

"Did someone at the club hurt you?" He whispered. She answered simply by biting her lip. He took a deep breath in and rested his forehead against hers. His muscles went rigid at his next thought, and his blood pumped faster through his veins.

"Was Kyle there? Did he find you?" Silence was all he heard. He pulled back to look at her and her eyes were closed. He could see the wetness brimming through her fanned lashes, and she was still gnawing on her lip. "He was there, wasn't he?" He said with more insistence. "Did he touch you? Did he lay a hand on you?"

She opened her eyes, fighting back the tears in her eyes, and brought her hands to his face. She reached her lips up to his and kissed him.

"Please, Baby. Tell me what's going on." He slowly flipped his nose against hers, trying to convince her to trust him with whatever she wasn't telling him. "I can't help you unless you talk to me." She reached her hands down his back again, but this time slid her hands under the waistband of his sweatpants, her palms gliding over his ass, pushing the pants down his thighs. He growled in aggravation, knowing what she wanted – what she was doing. His mouth finally gave in and began to lick along her collar bone, splaying kisses along the skin that was salty from sweat. The sweet vanilla scent she always carried mixed with the tantalizing musk of sweat and sex was enough to cause his heart to beat powerfully in his chest.

He used his legs to kick his sweatpants the rest of the way off, and she helped, frantically trying to get his clothes off of him. She was naked except for panties and he decided to leave them in place for now.

"Even after everything we've been through, Ella, you still won't trust me," he said with an edge to his voice, just slightly masking his growing anger and frustration. "You make everything more difficult when you keep things from me." He moved down her body placing kisses and small bites along her abdomen. When he reached her belly button he kissed it lightly. His hands gripped her at her waist, his fingers digging in, trying to reign in his aggravation.

"Ah," she moaned, sounding to be a mixture of pleasure and a bit of pain from his grip, but it was the first sound she'd made since she woke and he viewed it as a triumph. He was going to make her talk, make her tell him. He continued down her belly, stopping at the border of her panties. He used his teeth to pull them down, but only until he could see the top of her mound. She ground her hips up to meet his face and he gave as good as she did, running his nose along her sensitive cleft still covered by her panties.

She whimpered at the contact, sending lightning bolts through his body, straight to his cock which was already straining. His hands slid back up her stomach and each one latched on to her breasts, pulling and palming her nipples, as his nose was still torturing her. He moved to the edge of her panties where her thigh met her hip, placing kisses up the bend in her leg. Kissing and sucking and nipping. She responded with worried groans.

"Tell me what happened," he said against her most sensitive skin, as he pulled his hands underneath her bottom and bit her through the lacy fabric of her underwear.

"I can't…" she breathed. Two words. He'd gotten two words from her, but he didn't like them. He brought her even closer to his mouth, increasing the pressure, kneading her ass with his hands.

"You can and you will," he demanded. He felt her shudder at his words and knew her restraint was crumbling. He moved to the other side of her, teasing the crease of her other thigh. As much as he was trying to break through her wall of defense against him, he was having a hard time keeping himself from plunging into her. He wanted to feel her damp and warm tightness around him. He wanted to feel close to her, but he wanted her to open up to him first, searching for a different kind of closeness.

He gripped the top of her panties and pulled them down her legs, trailing his mouth and tongue along behind them, his mouth devouring every inch of skin she had to offer. Under his mouth she writhed, pulsated. He could feel her coming apart with every flick of his tongue or press of his lips. He made his way back up to the heat of her core.

"Tell me," he said.

"Please, Porter, I can't," she cried, the sexual frustration evident in the timbre of her voice. He blew along her cleft.

"Oh God, Porter, I can't lose you. Please, don't make me tell you," she cried as she raised her hips up, searching for him, for the connection he was withholding from her.

"If you can't trust me, then you've already lost me," he said quietly against her thigh. The words rang true with him and he hadn't realized it until he said them. If she could keep something from him, then she wasn't fully his. Now, he needed her to confess or else he knew he'd lose her forever, one way or another.

"Please, Baby," he said pleading with her, nearly begging, as he nipped at the lips of her opening. "Let me in," he said, his tongue darting out just to tease. Her legs shook and he hoped to God he was whittling away at the wall she'd built in the last few hours, the wall he was sure someone else had helped her put up.

He sat up and brought his hips to press against hers, his cock just barely touching her. He maneuvered into her so that his shaft pressed against her clit, and she used her body to beg him for more. He felt her clit rubbing along the length of him as they used their bodies to torture each other into getting what they wanted, but he was sure he was going to win in the end – he had to. He took the tip of his length and ran it up and down along her slit. He watched her back arch and her mouth part, and moaning with pleasure mixed with fright.

"Promise me," she said through clenched teeth.

"Anything," he said, continuing to tease her, now reaching down and swirling his tip around her clit.

"Promise me we'll be safe, that you won't let him touch us," she pleaded.

"Tell me," he said, looking directly into her eyes, begging her with everything he had in his soul.

"It was Kyle," she sobbed. Porter stilled. "He told me not to go to the police or he would hurt everyone I cared about." Her admission was a whisper, but it blared through his body and through his heart. She was trying to protect him, to shield him from what she thought Kyle could do to him.

He sank into her heat in one long stroke and they both moaned at the contact. He collapsed onto her, scooping her up, wrapping his arms around her back underneath her, bringing her as close as possible to him. Her legs wound themselves around his waist, sinking him even father into her.

"I'm sorry," she whispered in his ear.

"Me too. I'm sorry I wasn't there to protect you." She pulled away quickly and looked right in his eyes.

"No, you aren't going to blame yourself for this. We're done with blame. You can't hold yourself responsible for him. Just..." She exhaled loudly.

"Just what, Ella?"

"Just don't let me go."

"Never." He bent down again to fuse his mouth to hers. The kiss was such a relief to him. More than ever before, in this moment, she was his. She had let him in, even when every bone in her body was telling her not to. His lips brushed against hers and his tongue slipped inside, seeking hers out. His hands came up around her stomach to cup her breasts, his thumbs found her nipples, rubbing and swirling until he heard her moan through their kiss.

"Tell me who you belong to, Ella."

"You, Porter, I belong to you."

He thrusted inside her slowly and fully. He reached down between them to where they were connected and pressed a finger against her.

"How much, Ella? How much of you belongs to me?" He ground the words out through his clenched jaw.

"Oh God, Porter," she moaned, gripping his shoulders. "All of me."

"Your body?" He plunged in again, feeling all of this shaft slide against her wet and clenching walls.

"Jesus... yes, Porter, my body is yours."

"Do I belong to you?" He asked, making sure she felt all of him as he continued to pump into her, still fingering her clit at the same time.

"If I'm yours – oh God, don't stop, Porter," she begged. "If I'm yours, then you're mine," she said looking right at him.

"I want your heart too." He slowed his pace and came back down to her mouth. Her hands came back to his face and held his gaze on hers.

"Before you had any other part of me, you had my heart," she whispered to him. "Please, Porter, love me." He rested his head in the crook of her shoulder and continued to draw in and out, all while using his finger to gently bring her to orgasm. He felt her legs tense around his waist, her walls clenched deliciously around his cock, and sent him over the edge into an equally shattering abyss.

They both panted and clung to each other, sweat was slick between their bodies, and he could hear feel her heartbeat through her chest. He went to move off of her and she gripped him even tighter.

"Please, just hold me for a minute more."

He kissed her forehead and moved back over her, resting his face against her shoulder. After a few minutes passed he felt her take in a breath as if she were bracing herself for something.

"Maybe we should decide what we are going to do now?"

Porter was reluctant to let the moment pass, enjoying having her body so closely and intimately intertwined with his. In this moment she was safe. She was in his arms and he was protecting her. But he rolled to the side and rested his head on a pillow.

"Why don't you tell me what happened in the club?"

"On one condition," she stipulated.

"What condition would that be?"

"No matter what happened, you cannot feel guilty or blame yourself for anything that he said or did." Porter's jaw clenched because he knew that would be difficult. From day one he was protective of Ella. He wanted nothing but to keep her safe and sheltered, but he seemed to be failing at every turn.

"Please tell me," was all he said in response. She stared at him for a moment, seeming to deliberate as to whether she would accept that as an answer.

"I was walking through the club, trying to get back to the table but there was a large group of people blocking the way so I decided to go around them. I was passing by the back wall and I felt someone grab my arm and pull me down the hallway. Before I could see him, he pushed me up against the wall, face first, and pinned my arms above my head, holding the rest of my body against the wall with his own." He could not control the immediate and immense tension that coursed through his body. The image of Kyle holding Ella against a wall was enough to make him want to kill Kyle. He wasn't sure that if Kyle were around he'd be able to control himself enough to let the fucker breathe another breath.

"Jesus, Ella," he said as he raked his hands down his face.

"He told me that he was the one outside your house that night."

"Shit!" Porter got out of bed, unable to sit still any more. She sat up and pulled her knees up to her chest.

"He also told me that I was to tell you all that I didn't want to press any charges against him for what happened that night at the apartment, outside your house, or anything else."

"What do you mean by 'anything else'"?

"The shooting."

"Did that motherfucker shoot you, Ella?" He nearly screamed at her. Her eyes misted over with tears and she wiped one away that slipped down her cheek.

"He said he didn't, but Porter, I just don't know what to believe any more," she said, trying to contain a sob. Porter moved to the bed, his anger and rage being pushed aside by his need to comfort her. He sat on the bed, leaning up against the headboard, then pulled her over to him and tucked her into his side.

"What else did he say?"

"He just said that if I did report him he would find a way to hurt the people I care about." She sighed and nuzzled into his chest. "I'm sorry, Porter. I was panicked. All I kept thinking was that I knew I wouldn't be able to keep this from you. I knew it. But I am so afraid that he'll hurt you, or Megan, or Kalli. OH!" She sat straight up and lunged out of the bed.

"Where are you going?"

"I've got to call Kalli," she said as she darted out of the room. Even though they were in the middle of a very serious conversation, it was hard not to notice that she was still naked. The sight of her walking back into the room with nothing on made him smile. She got back into bed and cuddled up to him again.

"Kyle is Scott." Porter gave her a confused look.

"Who the hell is Scott?"

"Kalli has been seeing a new guy, Scott, for a few weeks now, and it turns out it is Kyle. That's how he knew I was there last night and how he's been keeping tabs on me." Ella shuddered against him. "I can't believe she's been spending so much time with him, letting him in her apartment, letting him kiss her, all because of me."

"Hey," he said as he placed a finger under her chin and lifted it to look up at him. "No guilt and no blame. He did all of this, not us." She gave him a half smile and he knew she felt bad for having anything to do with the mess they all seemed to be in.

She dialed a number and he listened to her call Megan and explain everything again to her, and then again to Kalli, who had in fact stayed with Patrick and Megan. He could tell Megan was trying to convince Ella to go to the police and he agreed with her. The police needed to know that Kyle was back in town and responsible for the assault against her in her apartment and the night before at the club.

When she hung up, Porter brought her hand to his lips and brushed his mouth over her knuckles.

"Baby, we have to go to the police."

"But what if he finds out?" She asked with a worried expression on her face. "I can't risk anything happening to you. I just got you back."

"First of all, you never lost me. Second of all, he will find out – when the police arrest him and put him in jail." Porter looked over at the clock on her bedside table; it was a little after two in the morning. "I think we should go to the police tonight, Babe, the sooner the better." She let out a loud breath and looked up at him.

"You'll go with me?" He had to laugh at her.

"Babe, you'd be lucky to get rid of me until this whole thing is over. You're going to be getting really tired of me soon."

"I doubt it," she said with a small frown. "Ok, I'll go right now, but I'm wearing yoga pants and a sweatshirt." Porter smiled, glad she was agreeing to go.

"Good girl."

Chapter Sixteen
Ella

Ella was exhausted; utterly, completely, and ridiculously exhausted. Having been at the police station for nearly eight hours, it was now after ten in the morning. They had been questioned by every single officer in the Portland Metro area, or so it felt. All the officers who questioned her asked her the same questions and made her relive every horrible thing that Kyle had done.

She felt empty when she left and really stupid. In fact, stupid was the exact word to describe how she felt. She'd spent years of her life with a man who was capable of pure evil. She'd slept with him, been intimate with him, let him into her life and the lives of her family, and he'd hurt her in way that she could have never seen coming or imagined. No one at the police station went out of their way to make her feel badly or responsible, but it was hard not to question one's judgment when the person you thought you might spend the rest of your life with had, in the end, very little respect for your life at all.

When they were done questioning her, the police suggested that Ella not stay at her apartment until he was apprehended. They also suggested she hire private security for Poppy, which she agreed with. There was no way she was going to endanger the safety of Megan or any of the girls that worked there. Other than that, the police said she needed to be careful, report anything suspicious, and try not to go anywhere alone. She didn't think the last suggestion would be a problem. Porter had gone into caveman mode but, honestly, she didn't mind.

They were driving to her parent's house, who Porter had filled in on everything while they were at the police station. For now, it was a place she could rest until they figured out what steps to take next. She sat in the middle of the bench seat of his truck, his arm around her shoulders and she leaned into him, her eyes closed, very close to sleep.

"Babe," she heard his voice calling to her. "We're at your parent's house. Wake up, Baby." She opened her eyes, sat up, and started making her way to the front door. Her mom opened the door before they could even get to the top step of the porch. Susan tried to fuss over her, with good intentions of course, but Ella just wanted to sleep. Porter led her down the hall to what used to be her bedroom, but had been converted into a guest room long ago.

He helped her pull her sweatshirt over her head and pulled back the covers so she could climb in to the big, king-sized bed. She sunk into the heavenly mattress and almost immediately felt her eyes close. She felt Porter place his lips on her temple and then he whispered something about being back soon. She shot up, panicked.

"Where are you going?" She asked, all of a sudden she was awake and alert, not wanting him to leave her all by herself. He sat down on the bed next to her and pushed a piece of wayward hair back behind her ear.

"Babe, you're wrecked. Just go to sleep. Your parents are here. I'm going to go to your house and get some of your things. I'll be back in no time."

She threw the covers off of her legs and stood in an instant.

"I'm coming with you," she stated firmly.

"Ella, you're exhausted. I don't want you there anyway. I want you to sleep. You need to rest."

"Then stay with me, please, I don't want you to go there by yourself." He placed a warm hand on her thigh and squeezed.

"I won't be long and I'd rather you were here with your parents then at the apartment. It's better for you to be here. But I'll make you a deal," he said as he leaned forward and kissed her gently. "You rest right now while I go get some stuff for us, and when I get back I'll come straight to you and lie down until we both wake up rested." She wanted to argue, to get up and follow him wherever he went, but even she knew that she was worthless at the moment. She didn't even bother answering him; she just laid back down and pulled the covers over her face to block out the light from the window. She heard him laugh as he left the room.

When she finally woke up Sunday morning, she felt like she had been asleep for days. She opened her eyes, but only saw darkness. She waited, hoping her eyes would adjust to the lack of light, and eventually was able to make out the bedside table which had her phone on it. She checked the time and couldn't believe it was three in the morning. She'd been asleep for nearly seventeen hours. She heard the faint sounds of someone breathing and turned over to see the outline of Porter next to her. Warmth flooded through her to know that he was near her, as he promised.

She moved towards him, wanting to be as close to him as possible. When she felt the skin of his back with her hands she found him shirtless. She wanted to feel all of him against all of her so she quickly shucked off her shirt and bra and curled up against the warmth of his back, her hand reaching across his stomach. She burrowed her head against the back of him, content to just be in contact with him. She placed a few light kissed along his spine and felt him stir. His hand came to rest over hers and he twined his fingers with hers.

"Hey," she said against his back between kisses.

"Hey," he answered with a sleepy voice.

"Sorry to wake you."

"Don't be sorry," he said as he rolled over and pulled her into him, their faces inches apart. "Weren't you wearing clothes when you went to sleep?"

She couldn't see him clearly, but she knew he was smiled.

"I was. You are very observant," she said snarkily.

"I like your new look better."

"I'm sure you do," she said, trying hard to sound annoyed, but her small laugh got in the way.

"Are you feeling better?" He asked as he smoothed a hand down her hair.

"I'm feeling rested, but I'm still not sure what we're going to do, Porter. Everything is really messed up." She could feel herself start to tense up as soon as her brain tried to start processing everything that had happened in the last two days, two months even. It was all too much to take in and her body's natural response to the stress was panic.

"Breath, Ella. What do you want to have happen?"

"What do you mean?"

"What do *you* think we should do?" She thought for a moment about what would logically make the most sense. The police told her that she shouldn't go back to Poppy or to her apartment until Kyle was caught.

"Well, I can't go to work for a little while. And I can't stay at my apartment. You've already missed so much work. Maybe we should both stay in Lincoln City until they find Kyle and arrest him."

"Ok, we can go wherever you want. Are you sure you'll feel safe at my house? He's been there too."

Ella thought about his question. Did she feel safe there? No. But she didn't feel safe anywhere. Porter's house was one of the places she could be that wasn't one hundred percent tainted by Kyle. She was sure if he wanted to Kyle could find her anywhere and she refused to hide. She would be smart and safe, but she wouldn't hide. He'd stolen enough from her already; she wasn't about to lay down and let him win.

"Let's go to Lincoln City. We've got the 4th of July cookout coming up anyway. I'll hire private security for Poppy and I will just spend some time at the beach. I need a vacation anyway," she said with a forced smile, trying to downplay the severity of the situation.

"Babe, this won't last long. They'll catch him. He'll slip up soon and you won't have to worry about it anymore. But I'll do everything I can to make you feel safe. The Fourth of July is coming up, I can take a few days off and we can just relax – let the stress of the last couple days fade away. Maybe we should have some people over to the house for the holiday. We could grill and watch the fireworks."

"Thanks, that sounds like the best idea I've heard in a while." She said as she placed a small kiss on his mouth.

"Are you excited about the house?"

Ella knew he was trying to change the subject but felt a smile creep across her face reagrdless.

"Yes." Truthfully, she was more than excited. She was ecstatic. The idea of having a home to share with Porter made everything seem tolerable. Knowing that the two of them would be making a home together made her stomach flip in a deliciously anxious way. She wanted every part of their life together: she wanted to argue about who was going to take out the garbage, she wanted to drive him crazy asking him what he thought about patterns for curtains, she wanted to watch him sweat through a sexy baseball shirt while he mowed the lawn. Everything about a normal and mundane life, she wanted it all with him.

"Do you want kids?" She blurted out before she had a chance to think, surprised by even her own jump to a serious topic.

"Generally or specifically?" He asked. She knew he couldn't really see her, but she drew her eyebrows together in confusion anyway.

"What the heck does that mean?" She asked and heard him laugh.

"Well, I mean, in a very general way, I'd say sure, I want kids. I like the idea of having children. I feel compelled as a person to continue my lineage and all that. But specifically, with you, I want kids so badly I can hardly wait. To see you carrying our child, Ella, that will probably be the most beautiful thing I'll ever see. To hold our baby, to know that our love created a person, someone that will be a combination of *us*; it's the most important thing we'll ever do together, creating that child."

Ella's breath stole from her lungs at his words. His *words*. What kind of poet had he been in a past life to be able to weave words together in such a way that made her heart beat right out of her chest?

"Who are you?" She asked very seriously. "What made you the way you are? Why are you so kind and sweet? Strong and possessive? I can't even imagine what my life would be like right now if you weren't in it. How did you become so perfect?"

"Ella, I'm not perfect," he whispered.

"You're perfect for me," she quietly replied.

"I couldn't agree more. But honestly, we're just lucky I think."

"Lucky?"

"Think about everything that had to happen for you and I to be at my mom's bar at the same time that night: if her dishwasher hadn't broken, if it hadn't been raining, if you had decided not to go to the beach, if you hadn't left your lights on. There were a million different ways that night could have played out, Ella. How lucky are we that *this* is how our story ended up?" He emphasized his point by running his hands along her bare back, bringing goose bumps to the surface of her skin, making her shiver. "But luck only takes us so far. Now that we've found each other it's up to us to work at making our life together."

She smiled at his words, knowing that he pictured a full and complete life for them to share. As sure as she was about being with him, that he was with no doubt the only man she wanted to spend the rest of her life with. Her feelings of surety were only made stronger by the fierceness with which he believed in their relationship. He believed in their forever. And it made her love him even more for it.

"So," she said, trying to hide the fact that her cheeks were hurting a little from the giant smile on her face. "Tomorrow we go back to Lincoln City?"

"Sounds like a plan to me," he said, kissing the tip of her nose.

"Can I spend some time at the bar with your mom while you're at work?"

"I think my mom would really like that," he said sincerely.

"Good, I miss your mom."

"Let's go back to sleep. When we wake up we can get ready to go."

She stretched out along the bed, turning her back into Porter's chest as she felt his arm weave around her waist, pulling her close.

"I love you, Porter. More than I think I can even wrap my mind around."

"Don't worry. I know exactly how much you love me. It's just a little less than I love you."

She smiled and eventually found herself slipping away into sleep again.

Poppy remained closed for the day until the private security company could arrange for one of their security guards to be on site. Ella considered a one-day loss in sales to be a happy sacrifice to keep her friends and family safe. Megan was a little unhappy with the decision, offering to take Patrick with her to act as bodyguard, but Ella told her unequivocally no. That was not a risk she was willing to take.

Ella called Kalli, and even though Kalli was in no way holding Ella responsible for anything that had happened with Kyle, she couldn't help but feel the sadness that radiated off of Kalli. She knew Kalli felt used and stupid, hating herself for thinking that 'Scott' had wanted to be with her, only to discover that Kyle just wanted to get information about Ella out of her. In a phone conversation that morning, Kalli told her she felt responsible for everything that had happened at the club, as if she had led Kyle to Ella. This admission broke Ella's heart. Kyle was a bastard that had recently taken to ruining people's lives, but the last thing Ella wanted was her friends to feel badly about his psychotic ways. They had a lengthy conversation that really only solidified they were both really sorry and that Kyle was an asshole. She confirmed Kalli would be at the 4th of July cookout, and then Ella tried to convince her to invite the guy she'd met at the club before all hell had broken loose. Apparently, even in the chaos of leaving the club in a hurry, Kalli still managed to get his number. That alone made Ella smile and think something good had at least come out of all their drama.

Ella sat, once again, in the cab of Porter's truck as they drove to Lincoln City. It would be nice to live with Porter in Salem and she couldn't wait to start that portion of their life together, but she would always consider Lincoln City a special place for them. As they neared the ocean the scenery changed, trees became more spread out, the grass became a different shade of green. Her window wasn't rolled down, but she knew the air smelled different too. Pure. Fresh. Clean. She was looking forward to spending some time trying to relax at the beach, even if it was a forced vacation brought on by unimaginable circumstances. Ella would take it and make the best of it. She looked over at Porter and felt that any time spent with that man would be amazing, regardless of the situation.

Her belly did a delicious flip when he reached up and threaded his fingers through his hair, the brown locks always messy in a sexy way. His unconscious habit of running his hands through it made it impossible to remain styled, but it didn't matter because he looked edible with rumpled hair. He turned his head her direction, caught her eyeing him and gave her a sexy smile.

"Don't get me wrong, I'm not happy about everything going on with Kyle, but if I'm really honest, I am kind of glad that I get to spend the next two days with you uninterrupted," he said, turning back to face the road. Ella's chest filled with warmth at the idea of being alone with him until Wednesday when he had to go back to work. Spending their nights together was good for them and something she wouldn't have ever given up, but being with him all day was something she knew they both needed. She needed to have him near her, to be able to touch him if she wanted, to hear his voice and see his face.

"Mmm… me too. It will definitely be a nice change of pace."
She thought back to their first week together, how they had spent
the last few days of her stay holed up in his house talking, reading
and making love. She hoped the next two days would be a
repeat. She turned so her back was resting against the passenger
door and propped her feet up on his lap as he drove. She pulled a
book out of her purse and settled in for the rest of the drive to
Lincoln City.

The two days passed too quickly. When Ella woke on
Wednesday, she smiled as she stretched and felt wonderfully sore
from all the attention Porter had paid to her body since they'd
arrived at his house. True to his word, he never let her leave the
house and she was pretty sure neither one of them had put pants
on for at least thirty-six hours. It was wonderful. They had
ordered in food, watched movies, laid on the couch together with
their legs tangled around each other, both reading books. At one
point she'd gotten curious as to what he was reading so she
reached up and took his book, handing hers to him, and they spent
an hour reading each other's book. They switched back and forth
every hour for the rest of the evening, never commenting on the
books, just content to share them. Eventually he took both of
their books and tossed them on the coffee table and took her
mouth in a fierce and smoldering kiss. His tongue teased hers and
he tugged on her bottom lip with his teeth.

When he finally pulled away from her, he had a smug grin on
his face.

"What's so funny?" She asked, breathless from the staggering
kiss.

"I'm just glad I could put my research to good use."

"What research?" She asked, confused.

"All the tricks I just learned from your book," he said, his smile
growing wider. She blushed at his comment. "Don't get all
bashful on me now, Babe. I've got more notes and tips I want to
try out on you before this night is over." Ella tried to hide the fact

that she really wanted him to do all those things to her.

"That's not fair. Your book was only full of soldiers and battles," she said with a mock frown.

"Well, in that case, just to make it fair, you can call me Sergeant Masters while I do things to you that you've only read about," he said and gave her a self-satisfied wink. She couldn't help but laugh at him which continued as he hauled her up off of the couch and carried her all the way up the stairs to the bedroom.

As she thought about what happened in that bed the night before, she was sure that trading books would become a new hobby for them. The dull ache and pull of her muscles only made her remember the places Porter had taken her last night with his hands, his mouth, and every other inch of his body. She groaned out a smile and continued to stretch as she sat on the edge of the bed. She turned her head to look at Porter still sleeping on the other side of the bed.

He looked peaceful and young, his dark lashed fanned out against the tan flesh of his cheeks. He was shirtless and the chorded muscles that roped his back ran one into the other, making his body look more like a sculpture than a person. Every muscle was defined and prominent, even in rest. She shook her head, knowing he didn't even have a gym membership and all that rippled muscle and toned skin was just a product of his work. Ella was, by no means, out of shape, but she felt lazy and round when she looked at his amazing body. The thought was fleeting though because nights like the one before only cemented in her mind that he worshipped her body. Shivers ran through her remembering how he had paid homage every part of her.

She stood up and headed to the bathroom, hoping to shower and be ready for the day by the time Porter left for work. She thought she could spend the morning with Tilly at the restaurant. When she was done showering, she went back into the bedroom only to find Porter still asleep on the bed. Trying not to wake him, she dressed quickly and then went to the kitchen. She was almost done preparing some eggs and toast for him when he came down the stairs. He came up behind her and laid a kiss right behind her ear.

"Is this what I have to look forward to once we live together full time?"

Ella shrugged her shoulders. "I'm not opposed to cooking a meal now and then, as long as it's reciprocated," she said, turning to smile at him over her shoulder.

"You know I'm not a good cook," he said, almost pouting.

"How is it that your mom owns a restaurant and you can't cook?"

"Because my mom owns a restaurant." He said, like it was the clearest explanation he'd ever given. "I ate a lot of meals there and someone else always prepared them. My mom, for obvious reasons, never wanted to cook at home, so we ate out – a lot."

"Gotcha," Ella said as she slid over to prepare a plate for him. She handed him the plate and melted a little at his smile.

"Thanks, Babe," he said as he pecked a kiss on her lips and started eating. She couldn't help but imagine many more mornings spent this way: the two of them getting ready for the day, eating breakfast, small and not so small kisses. It was perfect and she wanted it forever. She smiled to herself, basking in the certainty of *them*. He was it for her. She'd had this thought before, a moment or two where she was reminded that he was most definitely the center of her universe. And every time her mind and body reminded her that she was irrevocably his, she was shrouded in a peaceful contentment. There was nothing as sweet and comforting as knowing you'd found the person that all your forevers were tied to.

Chapter Seventeen

Ella

She spent the morning hours trying to help Tilly around the restaurant. She cleared tables, did some dishes, but when she had tried to help a gentleman at the bar, Tilly shooed her away.

"You are not an employee, Ella. Sit down and relax," Tilly said with an exasperated smile.

"I hate just being in the way; I want to help," Ella said, trying to sound convincing.

"You could never be in the way, Honey. If Porter thought he'd let you spend the day with me to be wiping down tables and doing dirty dishes, I'd never get him to fix a darn thing around here again. You're simply here to keep me company and look pretty. Do you want a drink?"

Ella laughed because it was ten in the morning. "No thank you, maybe later."

Tilly shrugged her shoulders and gave a wink to Ella. "When more help gets here I want to take you out for lunch."

Ella was a little surprised by the invitation. "I don't want to be any trouble, we can just eat here."

"I've eaten ninety percent of my meals for the last twenty years here. Indulge me a little and go out to lunch with your future mother-in-law."

Ella blushed at the insinuation that she and Porter would inevitably get married – not to say that she didn't think it was true, it was just a little soon and Ella felt silly for believing in the fairy tale aspect of their relationship.

"No use getting all worked up about it. Facts are facts my dear and my son isn't going to let you get away again. I would bet anything on it."

"Well, the feeling's mutual," was all Ella could get out before she started to blush again.

When lunch time came around, Tilly drove them to a little café on the waterfront. The sun was shining and warm and it felt wonderful against her skin. She was pleased to see there was outdoor seating and agreed enthusiastically when Tilly asked her if she wanted to sit outside. There was a slight breeze coming off the water, bringing with it the salty-sweet scent of the ocean that she loved.

Both Tilly and Ella ordered a salad with crab, something Ella would only order while at the beach so she thought it a treat of sorts. Once they were left alone to wait for their order, Tilly asked Ella about her life before Porter: high school, college, parents, jobs. The conversation flowed easily and Ella found herself laughing more than once and Tilly's sweet and good natured interest in her background. Tilly's curiosity pushed Ella to talk about her first boyfriend, which got Tilly talking about hers.

"I was a senior in high school here in Lincoln City and he was a year older than me, working at the mill." Her eyes went hazy and Ella could tell her mind had drifted into the past. Tilly gave a small and quiet smile. "Andrew was so handsome: tall, dark hair with brown eyes. He was still young then, but he was so big and broad. His presence was imposing sometimes, all shoulders and chest, much like Porter." Ella nodded her head because she knew exactly what Tilly was talking about. "Everything about how we met was mundane and typical, no heroics or drama was involved, but it was perfect. I was a waitress at a diner in the evenings after school and one night he came in with a few friends. When I went to their table to take their order, I almost couldn't speak for how handsome he was. My brain went all silly and girly, but I managed to muddle my way through." Tilly's eyes twinkled with the memory and Ella could feel the love she still had for this man radiating off of her.

"He and his friends left the diner and I had this terribly rotten feeling in my gut that I would never see him again. My heart knew it was tragic. I watched him leave and get into the backseat of a car that drove him away. I tried to ignore the nagging from inside my brain, but even then I knew he was the one and that he had just driven away.

"Well, the next night he came back in, this time alone. He asked to sit in my section and when I saw him, I swear, I almost dropped a pot of coffee all over the floor," she laughed at the memory. "I had never dated any boys and had no idea how to flirt with one, so I just nervously walked over and treated him like any other customer even though my heart was pounding out of my chest and I couldn't take my eyes off of his mouth." She went quiet for a few moments and Ella let the silence float between them, allowing Tilly the opportunity to relive those exciting moments that Ella was so familiar with.

"He came in every night for a whole week before he got up enough nerve to ask for my phone number, even the nights I hadn't been working. My boss told me he came in, asked to sit in my section and then left disappointed when they'd told him I wasn't in. All the women who worked at the diner warned me that if I let him get away it would be a mistake. I knew that already and didn't need them to tell me."

"We were both still young but perhaps that made it all the more exciting. He was my first everything, my only everything," Tilly said with a hitch in her voice that brought the stinging of tears to Ella's eyes. She reached out and laid her hand gently on Tilly's, hoping to offer some comfort to a woman simply missing the man she loved. Tilly squeezed her hand and offered a small smile. She took a deep breath and then continued, seeming to push through the sadness.

"We married three years later and a few years after that Porter came along." A new smile filled with pride graced her face and Ella couldn't help but mirror it, having her own sense of pride in him. "He was such a good father: patient, loving, fun, firm. He loved Porter so much and wanted to teach him how to be a good man, how to be hardworking, and to have integrity."

"I think he did a wonderful job of instilling all of those traits in Porter," Ella offered. "And I think you did a wonderful job of raising him alone too. It must have been so hard..." Ella's voice trailed off, not sure how to finish the sentence, not sure she had to words to describe the loss Tilly had gone through.

"One day you'll understand the love a mother feels for her child," Tilly said turning her head towards the ocean, looking out over the seemingly calm waters of the harbor. "I was shattered when Andrew died, absolutely broken. Nothing could have prepared me for how it was going to feel knowing I would *never* speak to my husband again. Never hold his hand or kiss his lips. Never wake up next to him, never argue with him, never get excited when he came home again. So many things would never happen that *should* have happened. But not one ounce of my sadness mattered when I looked at my son who had lost his father." Ella saw a tear slip from the corner of Tilly's eye and she felt a knot forming in her own throat.

"Porter was at a very strange age when his father died. Twelve is old enough to understand death and how it works, but still young enough to have childlike thoughts about it. He was still a boy, trying to become a man. He took his father's death very hard," she almost whispered.

"Andrew had been driving to one of Porter's baseball games when that logging truck overturned onto his car. He tried to never miss a game, knew how important it was for Porter to see him in the stands, cheering him on, supporting him. The first words out of his mouth after I had told him what happened were, 'This never would have happened if he hadn't been on his way to my game'."

Ella's heart broke for the child who internalized blame for something so tragic and it broke for the woman who was sitting in front of her, full tears streaming down her face, still hurting twenty years later. Ella tried hard not to let her emotions get the best of her, feeling like Tilly needed someone to be strong for her in that moment, but her throat was stinging painfully with cries aching to get out. Tears welled in her eyes, but she was able, for the moment, to keep them at bay and just continued to rub and squeeze Tilly's hand on the table.

"He's always carried around the blame for his father's death, no matter how many times I tried to tell him it wasn't his fault. Even two of years seeing a child psychologist could never fully ease his mind that he wasn't responsible for the death of his father. It's something he'll carry around with him forever, I'm afraid." Tilly looked at Ella again. "When you were hurt, the first thing he did was blame himself. So many things he could have done differently, according to him, that would have altered the course of things, changed the outcome. It was just like when Andrew died all over again, only maybe a little worse because you were still out there somewhere and that made it all that much worse for him.

"I know I've told you this before briefly, but what he went through when you didn't remember him, it was terrible. I'm not trying to make you feel badly about it, because Lord knows you were the biggest victim of the whole debacle, but he was so sad, Ella. So... fractured. You can't ever question how much he loves you, ever, Ella. Promise me that. He loves you so much that the thought of being without you nearly destroyed him, quite possibly could have ended him for all the sadness that he was drowning in."

The tears she'd been holding in finally broke free and Ella pressed a hand to her chest to try and alleviate any of the pressure she felt building there. Everything felt wrong. The sun was shining but the darkness was taking over. Her skin was warm but she was chilled to the bone. "Blame and guilt are two things both Porter and I are very good at," Ella said, using her napkin to wipe away some of her tears, even though more were following. "I hate that he feels like he's to blame for anything that happened to me, but I understand it because I feel it too. I've got my own collection of "what ifs" that I replay in my head over and over, trying to make sense of what happened to us. But it's useless because nothing changes the fact that it happened."

Ella thought about all the ways that he was fueled by the blame he placed on himself. He internalized every feeling he had, analyzing it endlessly before opening up about it. He felt responsible for every bad thing that had happened between them, using that as a catalyst to wallow at times in the guilt. Ella shook her head a little at the helplessness she felt when she thought about Porter and the sadness that sometimes permeated him. But as soon as she thought about his sadness, she was forced to think about his happiness too. The guilt and blame also made him the possessive and protective man she'd come to love and appreciate. He would do anything to shield her from harm and even though she wished it sprouted from something else, she couldn't hate the passion and depth with which he loved her.

"Tilly," Ella began softly. "I've never experienced any kind of loss to the degree you and Porter have suffered, and I would never presume to understand all the complicated implications his father's death had on either of you. But I know, without one shred of doubt or uncertainty, that he loves deeper than any man I've known because of it." Ella tried to give Tilly a smile, but it was laced with sadness and tears that wouldn't stop coming. "He feels everything to the depth of his soul and holds on tighter because of it." Ella shrugged her shoulders and shook her head slightly. "Maybe he even appreciates things more because he realizes it can all be taken away." The words rang true with her. Porter had experienced more loss than any person should have to deal with. But instead of being afraid to lose her, it seemed he was afraid of not holding on tight enough, as if he thought losing her would be a product of his negligence instead of just their relationship not working out. How could she argue with loving someone too much? The thought made her smile.

"It's unfortunate that on some level he feels responsible for the death of his father, but that's not something that's likely to go away. His need to protect and love are so deeply ingrained in him because of it. It's a part of his DNA. The loss he's suffered is tragic, but he's gained a unique perspective from it." Ella did manage a smile at that point. "I've never felt so entirely and completely loved in my life. His ability to take his love for me and make it tangible – it's incredible." Ella shook her head and looked down at the table, removing her hand from Tilly's. "I'm sorry if it sounds contrite, but his love for me, it's almost like a blanket. I can *feel* it draped over me, keeping out the cold, wrapping me in warmth. It's the most wonderful thing I've ever experienced and I'll spend the rest of forever trying to make him feel one fraction of the love he makes me feel." Ella looked up to see Tilly smiling through tears, her eyes focused on Ella.

"I am so glad he found you," she said sincerely. "I have never seen him as happy as he's been since he met you. He's very lucky," she said softly.

"I think we're both lucky," Ella replied.

They were both done discussing sad and depressing topics, and the conversation organically moved back to lighter topics of Ella's store and her family.

"Will your parents be at the cookout for the 4th?"

"I think they're planning on coming," Ella smiled.

"I'll be glad to see them again," Tilly said mirroring her smile.

"It's going to be fun, I think. I'm excited to meet the people Porter works with. It will be interesting to see our two separate groups of family and friends kind of pushed together. Our worlds have been so separated lately. It feels like an either 'here or there' sort of thing, splitting all our time between Portland and Lincoln City. It will be nice to see everyone all together in one place."

Tilly gave her a big and genuine smile. "Everyone will love you, Ella. Now, I think we should head back to the restaurant and make sure it hasn't collapsed in our absence."

Porter

On his way to pick Ella up from the restaurant, Porter stopped to pick up some flowers for his mom. He wasn't around as much as he used to be and he wanted to see his mother smile. Not the obligatory smile, but the 'my son just melted my heart' smile. He'd worked hard for that smile before and wanted to make sure she knew he had been thinking about her. He also wanted to say thank you to her for staying with Ella all day while he was at work. He knew she probably didn't mind at all, but it still meant a lot to him that she was invested in Ella. His mother had done her fair share of shoving women in his face while he was single, trying to get him to settle down with someone, but she never showed the amount of love to any woman he'd been with as she had with Ella.

When he pulled into the parking lot of Tilly's, he saw Ella standing outside the restaurant talking on the phone. He parked and hopped out, flowers in hand, trying to hide his frustration that she was outside all by herself. He came up to her and slowed when he noticed the distressed look on her face.

"Yes, Officer, I understand," she said. "No, I'm not in Portland and I haven't been staying at my apartment." She looked up at him and gave him a sad look. He continued towards her until she was right in front of him and he kissed her forehead. He felt her lean into him and he took her weight willingly, wanting to be the one she always leaned on. "I hired private security for the store, but again, I haven't been there since the incident on Friday." She sounded worried and anxious. He began to rub slow circles on her back with his free hand. "I will Officer, and thank you for calling." She hung up the phone and he felt her shoulders slump.

"What's up? Was that the police?"

"Yes, they were just calling to tell me that absolutely nothing has changed," she sighed loudly and sounded frustrated. "He's still out there and I'm still hiding from him only, now, the longer he's still roaming around, the higher the chance is that he'll find out we went to the police and the more danger everyone is in." Her breathing had sped up and he could tell she was on the verge of panic.

"Ella, slow down. Take a breath," he said calmly. "First of all, just because they haven't found him it doesn't mean he knows we went to the police. Secondly, even if he did, he can't get to you. He had only come after you when you've been alone. By the way," he jerked his head back to look her in the eye. "What the heck are you doing out here alone?"

"There's some sort of game going on in there, Porter. I couldn't hear anything. I've only been out here for a minute."

"You can't be alone, Ella. Especially out here, out in the open. Next time go in the bathroom or the kitchen. Anywhere but outside by yourself, ok?"

"You're right. I'm sorry. It was stupid of me to come out here." She eyed the flowers in his hand. "You don't strike me as a *flowers* kind of guy," she said cautiously.

He smiled at her. "Good, cause they're not for you. They're for my mom." Her expression changed from questioning and softened into a more loving look.

"You brought your mom flowers?" She asked, her voice jumping an octave or two.

"Yes?" He was surprised when she leaned up and kissed his mouth, but it only took him a second to catch up before he wrapped his arms around her waist, trying not to flatten his mother's flowers in the process. Her tongue darted out and swept across his lips and he let out a groan, reaching down with one hand and grasping her ass. "Mmm," he said when they finally parted. "Wait a minute. Why don't I strike you as a *flowers* kind of guy?"

She raised an eyebrow at him and laughed a little. "Porter, you gave me a box of jumper cables with a bow wrapped around them."

"And?"

"And..." she trailed off. "Jumper cables are a far cry from flowers."

"What are you getting at?"

"Porter," she said as she placed her hand on the side of his face. "You are the most romantic man I have ever met. You say things that make my head spin. You make these sweet gestures, like picnics on the beach and in the hotel, that fill my heart with love. But I cannot say that you excel in the 'thoughtful gift' category." He frowned at her while racking his brain, trying to remember all the gifts he'd given her.

"I bought that ring on your finger," he said triumphantly. She looked down at her right hand, the tiny silver arrow ring starring back at the both of them.

"You mean this ring?" She said, holding her hand up so that he could clearly see it. "This ring right here that I was already going to buy?" She said laughing. "That's not a thoughtful gift. That's a nice gesture, buying a trinket for a woman you were trying to woo, but it wasn't a premeditated and thought-out gift."

"I wasn't trying to *woo* you," he said, pouting. "And what about the hotel and the lingerie?" He shifted, not liking the conversation and where it was leading.

"Babe," she said, now placing her other hand on his face so that she palmed both cheeks. "I love you and you are wonderfully romantic, sweet, and thoughtful. But the hotel and lingerie were just as much for you, if not more, than for me. I loved it all, but let's get real – you wanted to see me in that lingerie just so you could get it off me."

"You're making it sound like I don't appreciate you or show you that I care." His pout was out in full force now, and he just wanted to give his mother the flowers and go home to sulk.

"Are you...? Wait a minute, are you seriously insecure about this?" She asked, sincerely surprised, concern flashing across her face.

"Well, shit, Ella. I don't want you to feel that way about me. I want to give you everything."

She continued to look him in the eyes and she looked as though she was weighing her next words carefully.

"Porter, I don't need you to get me anything. I'm so happy just being with you. There's nothing you could buy or give me that would make me even half as happy as your touch makes me, or sharing books with you makes me, or even just sleeping in the same bed as you makes me. I'm not looking for flowers, or gifts, or large declarations of love here. I'm just looking for you. For us. I'm sorry if what I said made you think otherwise."

He looked into her eyes for a moment more, making sure he believed what she was saying. He knew she wasn't looking for material things, but if she had a need he wasn't meeting he wanted to know about it. "Promise me you'll tell me if I'm not giving you what you need. And…" he placed a finger over her mouth when she tried to interrupt him. "And I'm not just talking about gifts. I'm talking about more than that. I want to be your everything, Ella. I want to give you everything."

"Will you promise me the same thing?" She whispered against his finger which sent shock waves directly to his stomach, causing the familiar aching he had grown accustomed to. He nodded and she moved in to press her lips against his. "I promise," she said with her mouth brushing against his.

This kiss was slow and sensual, a promise between the two of them. Silent vows to give each other the reassurance they both needed. He would always be willing to promise her everything. His hand found its way into the hair at the nape of her neck, and he ran it's softness through his fingers. She whimpered quietly as his tongue slowly eased its way into her mouth and he knew he needed to stop torturing himself and get them home. He pulled away and heard her sigh.

"Where'd you learn how to kiss?" She asked breathily. He laughed out loud at her question.

"The summer before I turned eighteen, I spent many weeks tucked away in the sand dunes kissing a girl named Wendy."

"Does this Wendy still live around here?" She asked with a smile.

"Why?"

"Maybe we should be getting *her* flowers."

He groaned. "No more flowers. Let's go give these to my mom and get home. I'm not done with you." She turned and walked away from him towards the door and he heard a yelp as his palm smartly connected with her ass. She turned back to him, leering at him as best she could while hiding a grin, and he just flashed her his best satisfied smile.

"You're terrible," she said still trying not to smile.

"I'm amazing. Let's go," he gestured towards the doors. Once they were inside he found his mother and walked over to her and handed her the flowers as he placed a small kiss on her cheek. "Thank you for hanging out with Ella today. I appreciate it."

"Porter, these are beautiful," she said as she buried her nose in them, taking a big breath in. "But you don't have to get me flowers for spending time with Ella. I love Ella. I wish I could spend more time with her. Besides, we had a fabulous time today."

"It's true," Ella said as she plopped down on a stool on the other side of the bar. "Your mom and I spent the entire day talking about you. It was very educational."

"There's absolutely nothing my mom could have told you that I wouldn't have told you anyways. I've got nothing to hide."

"Maybe not, but I liked getting your mom's perspective on a lot of things about you. Don't worry, Babe, I'm teasing. I still love you just as much as I did this morning," she said, batting her eyelashes at him.

"Ella," his mother jolted them from their banter. "Do you still have that list we made?"

She reached down and patted the front pocket of her jeans. "Right here. Thank you for helping me make it."

"What list?" Porter asked.

"It's just a list of things I need to buy and make for the cookout for the 4th. It's the day after tomorrow," Ella reminded him. He knew exactly when the 4th was. He was looking forward to the cookout they had planned. A day to relax with friends and not worry about work or any of the craziness that seemed to be following them around.

"Do we need to go to the store tonight?" He asked, really not looking forward to going any place other than home. He really needed to be alone with her, wanted to feel her beneath him and use his hands to hold on to her.

"Nope," she said, looking pleased with herself. "Megan is going to come by tomorrow and we'll go while you're at work. Megan, Brittany, and Sarah all rented a beach house for a few days and Megan is going to come down early to help me get ready. Then after they close Poppy, Brittany and Sarah will come down too. They're all really looking forward to it." Porter was relieved that they could head home, but tried not to let it show.

"Well, Mom, thanks again for everything." He placed a kiss on his mother's temple and turned to Ella. "You ready to go home?"

She smiled at him. "Always." She got up and went to his mom and wrapped her up in a big hug that made him smile even wider.

"Thanks for such an awesome day, Tilly. And thanks for lunch too."

"Always," his mother said, repeating Ella's words back to her. They smiled at each other and then Ella headed towards him with her hand extended to him. He took it and led her out the door of the restaurant and to his truck. He helped her in and then jumped in himself. He looked at Ella sitting in the passenger seat, shook his head at her, and patted the bench right next to him, signaling her to move over. She grinned, but did as he asked. Once she was buckled she leaned into his side, nuzzling his chest.

"You smell like wood, and soap."

"One of the perks of the job," he said.

"It's ridiculously sexy, Porter."

He leaned down and kissed her gently before he started the truck and took them home.

Chapter Eighteen
Ella

Ella was pretty impressed with the culinary skills she had pulled out of her back pocket in the last two days. It wasn't complicated French cuisine, but the spread her and Megan had prepared for this cookout was no small feat either. Her and Megan had just finished setting up outside and Ella stood back to admire their hard work.

Picnic tables that, of course, Porter had built stood proudly in the middle of his large front lawn, draped with red checkered table cloths. Atop the tables were different varieties of red, white and blue foods. Strawberries, blueberries, and sliced bananas, cups with layered jello in them topped with whipped cream, deviled eggs dyed with food coloring, sugar cookies. They even had blue tortilla chips with salsa poured over a brick of cream cheese. They had basically prepared enough appetizers to feed an army and were leaving the main course of hot dogs and burgers to the men who insisted on running the grill. Patrick and Porter could stand in front of the hot grill all they wanted and she was fine with that. She wanted to sit in a lounge chair drinking the red sangria that Megan had found a recipe for.

"Well, Fella, I think we did pretty well. This is my first themed party and I am really impressed with our skills at the moment."

"I agree. It looks great. Just don't forget that we've got a lot more skills that are useful outside of the kitchen," Ella said, trying to sound like the older and wiser sister she was.

"Oh really?" Megan said while waggling her eyebrows. "What skills are we talking about and which room are they useful in?"

Ella rolled her eyes at her little sister. "Megan, you just single handedly set the women's movement back twenty years."

"Oh, Ella, on the contrary. The women's movement involves many theories of women taking back their sexual prowess in the bedroom as a way to challenge the dominant alpha male in the relationship. Seeing women as sexual equals is a very relevant and useful tool for the advancement of the equality for women in all realms of society."

Ella felt her mouth gaping wide open but couldn't help the astonished look that had taken over her face.

"That's right, Ella. I know you see me as just some silly twenty-something who might be getting married young, but I am not a delicate flower looking to stand in the shadows of her husband. I use my femininity and sexuality to assess my power, not to diminish it. You do too. You just haven't realized it yet. Patrick knows I get to be the boss when I want to. In fact, he rather likes it when I become the dominant," she said as she winked at Ella.

Ella closed her mouth finally and had a moment where she realized that, indeed, her baby sister was not as little, small, or fragile as she might have ever pictured her. She actually kind of admired her sister, and was possibly a little jealous of her and Patrick's life behind their bedroom doors.

Ella cleared her throat and let out a breath. "Well, Megan, you've left me speechless."

"Come on, Fella," she laughed, "Let's go set up the volleyball net."

As they were finishing with the volleyball net, she noticed cars pulling up the long driveway to the house. She felt the tiny rumble of nerves in her stomach as the thought of meeting Porter's friends and co-workers. She looked around hoping to spot him so that he could make introductions. As if he could read her thoughts, he stepped out of the front door onto the porch and Ella was, once again, overcome with the image of him and all the rugged sexiness that seemed to emanate from him. He was wearing khaki-colored cargo shorts that came down just to his knee making the large muscles of his calves stand out like boulders. And for the love of all that was holy he was wearing a baseball shirt, white chest with blue sleeves that came down to his elbows. His biceps were straining against the blue cotton and the simple image of him was wreaking all kinds of havoc on Ella's nervous system. Her lungs weren't working properly, her legs – useless, even her eyelids had forgotten their purpose so she just stood there – gawking. He continued towards her and she just lost herself watching him. The closer he got, the more rapidly her heart beat and when he was finally standing right in front of her, she noticed the smug grin the was plastered on his face.

His hand came up to cup the side of her face, always making her feel so small with his large hand against her. "You're staring, Babe."

She reached up and gripped his shirt in her fists, pulling him closer to her. "You knew exactly what you were doing when you put that shirt on," she grumbled as she looked up at him.

"Maybe," he said as he tugged on her ponytail, forcing her to look up at him. "If you're going to walk around in those shorts, showing off your long and sexy legs, I'm going to wear this shirt. Maybe," he said as he flipped his nose against hers, "after everyone leaves tonight, I can wrap my arms around you and you can wrap your legs around me." Electricity shot through her body and concentrated between her legs.

"You're terrible," she said as she rested her head against his chest.

"Get it together, Babe. Company is here," he said, smiling at her, obviously really pleased with himself and the effect he was having on her. She took a deep breath to steady herself and tried to think of really unsexy things and was interrupted by the sound of an angelic voice happily shouting from across the lawn.

"Uncle Porter!"

Ella watched as a little girl ran towards Porter, arms spread wide open, giggling and smiling. When she made it to him he picked her up under her arms and swung her in wide circles, her feet floating out behind her, her stick-straight brown hair flying in the wind created by their twirling. He must have spun her around twenty or more times and all Ella could see or hear was the smiles on their faces and the laughter coming from the little girl. When he finally put her down he was obviously dizzy, but she was anxious for more.

"Do it again!" she sweetly demanded.

"Maybe in a few minutes, Joy. I'm dizzy."

"Joy, if you break Uncle Porter your sister is going to be very angry with you." Ella turned and saw a couple approaching she assumed were the sweet girls' parents. The woman, who looked to be roughly the same age as Ella, held against her hip the most precious cherub-faced baby she'd ever seen. The baby girl gripped her mother's shirt looking around anxiously, but the tension faded from her face as soon as she laid eyes on Porter. She began reaching for him, opening and closing her fists, asking for him to hold her. He reached over and took the baby with ease, tossed her up in the air, making Ella's eyes go wide with worry. The baby, however, was having the time of her life, giggling as she flew up in the air and was caught in his strong hands. Ella looked over at the mother, expecting her to be having some sort of panic attack.

"Don't worry, he won't drop her," she said to Ella with a confident smile. "I'm Brook," she said as she reached a hand out to her. Ella took her hand and noticed that Brook had the softest looking ringlet curls framing her face. She looked fresh, happy, and exuded friendliness. Ella liked her instantly.

"Hi, Brook, I'm Ella."

"It's nice to finally meet you. My husband and I have been waiting for a while for this. We were starting to think that maybe you didn't really exist," she said laughing.

"Are you kidding?" She heard Porter say from behind her. "I couldn't imagine this perfection," he said eyeing her. Ella rolled her eyes and saw that Brook was doing the same thing.

"Ella, this is Brook, Matt's wife. Matt works on my team. I've told you about him. He's my second in command, so to speak. Ah, here he comes."

Ella looked to where Porter's eyes led her and saw a man walking towards them holding lawn chairs in both of his hands, somewhat struggling with the awkwardness of the large chairs, but with a determined look on his face.

"Leave it to Porter to invite us over for a cookout but require manual labor in exchange for food," the man said once he had put the chairs down at their feet.

"Matt, this is Ella," Brook said.

"Nice to finally meet you," he said shooting Porter a grin, as if he knew something she didn't.

"Likewise," Ella answered hesitantly.

"Uncle Porter," Joy said softly while pulling on the hem of his shirt.

"Yes?"

"Is this the girl my mom says you're gonna marry?" Brook immediately grabbed her daughter and placed a hand over her mouth as the girl smiled, knowing she'd said something she shouldn't have.

"You." Porter said pointing at Matt. "Keep your women in line," he said with a smile.

"Hey," Matt said holding up his hands as if in surrender. "I'm outnumbered three-to-one. Even the little one holds more rank than me."

Porter knelt down next to Joy, still holding on to the baby who looked right at home in his arms, and pinched her nose. "Joy, this is my girlfriend, Ella. She is very special to me and if you don't behave I might have to throw away the cake we made for you."

Joy's eyes went wide and a smile spread across her face. "I'll be good," she said excitedly and then ran away to play with the volleyball net.

"I swear, eight-year-olds have the biggest mouths and no filters. I'm sorry if she embarrassed you," Brook said to Ella.

"She's fine," Ella answered. Her eyes were still drawn to the chubby-faced beauty clinging to Porter's arms, obviously a baby after Ella's own heart. "Who is this little girl?" Ella asked motioning towards the baby with the perfect blonde curls coming down the nape of her neck.

"This is Faith," Porter answered before anyone else could, his eyes shining with obvious love for the baby. In that moment, Ella definitely felt her ovaries start to work overtime. The ache that seems to form in some mythical place in her body where babies lay waiting to be made squeezed her heart. Who would have thought that this strong man, who had no siblings, and seemed to lead such a solitary life, loved children? And they seemed to love him back. "I've worked with Matt since I started my business. I watched these two get married and have these beautiful girls. I'm their honorary uncle," he said with pride that radiated outwards, her ovaries clenching again. She hadn't been prepared to watch him sweetly interact with babies all day.

"Your family is beautiful," Ella said to Brook.

"Thanks, we like them enough," Brook joked as Matt laughed. It was obvious she was in love with her children and Ella enjoyed the laid-back attitude she exuded, hoping one day to get some parenting pointers from her. She had a feeling they could be great friends.

Another car pulled into the driveway and Porter handed the baby back to her mother, much to Faith's dismay. He kissed her curly hair as he handed her off and then took Ella by the hand to meet his mother at her car.

"Hey, Mom. We're so glad you could make it," Porter said as he took some bags from his mother's hands.

"It's the nation's birthday. I'll be damned if I'll sit behind a bar and serve drinks all day." Ella laughed, constantly entertained by Tilly's antics.

"Here, Ella, you might want to put this in the fridge."

"Ok, sure. What is it?" Tilly turned to her placing a round dish in her hands.

"My cheesecake," she said, smiling up at her. Memories flooded Ella's mind, bringing her right back to her and Porter's very first date. Tilly's cheesecake. Ella could feel the flush coming over her face as she tried to push away the images of Porter nearly taking her on the couch in his living room. Ella cleared her throat and tried to act nonchalant as she took the dessert from Tilly.

"No problem," she squeaked. "I'll just go put this away."

Ella hurried into the house, walking past the very couch that was being featured in her memory, set the cheesecake down on the counter, and tried to remain cool. She startled when she felt hands wrap around her waist from behind.

"Whatcha thinking about?" Porter asked right into her ear, doing nothing but stoking the flames she was trying to extinguish. The teasing tone of his voice made it obvious he knew exactly what was on her mind.

She cleared her throat. "Your mom brought cheesecake," she said, trying to sound like she was talking about the weather. "She wanted me to put it in the fridge."

"Hmm," he said as he nuzzled into her neck. "My mom makes the best cheesecake."

"Yes," she groaned, trying to agree with him, but sounding more like she was enjoying the attention he was paying to her body. "I remember."

"Maybe having people over to our house was a bad idea," he said as he nibbled along her shoulder.

"Why?" She asked as she let her head fall to the side, thoroughly enjoying the feel of his mouth on her skin.

"Because all I really want to do is take you upstairs and bury myself in you."

"Porter," she rasped out, trying to hold back the urge to turn around and open herself up to anything he wanted to do to her.

"Yes, Baby?"

"There are two small children in your front yard," she said and immediately felt his mouth halt. "And your mother."

"You make a strong argument," he said as he placed one more small kiss on her neck and stepped back from her. "But you best prepare yourself for what you've got coming to you later," he said, smoldering.

"And what's that?" She said, leaning against the island in the kitchen, very aware that she was taunting a caged tiger.

"Oh, Ella, if you have to ask, I haven't done my job properly." He stepped up to her again, his hard body pressed all the way up against hers, his hands braced on the counter behind her. His mouth came dangerously close to hers as he placed a kiss on the corner of her lips. "I'm going to fuck you until you scream my name as you come," he placed a kiss on the other side of her mouth. "And then," he pulled back and looked her in the eyes. "I'm going to do it again."

She swallowed the large lump that had formed in her throat and let out a pant of breath that had been caught below it. "Lucky me," was all she could manage. He laughed out loud and shook his head.

"I think the girls from your store pulled up a second ago. You should probably come outside and say hello." He said as he brushed away a strand of rogue hair that had escaped from her pontytail.

"I'll be out in a minute."

He smiled at her, knowing exactly why she needed to cool down.

"Ok," he said and placed a kiss on her forehead before he headed back towards the door. Ella turned around and faced the cheesecake again. Contemplating for only a moment, she finally took a knife and cut out a generous slice. She put it on a plate, covered it with a bowl, and hid it in the back of the fridge, fully intending for it to be for her and Porter later that night after everyone else left to go home. It felt sneaky and sexy all at the same time. She finished up in the kitchen and went back outside to greet all their guests.

The afternoon progressed and Ella had a great time. Her and Porter's worlds melded seamlessly as her parents chatted with Tilly. Brook and Kalli seemed to really get a long, and Porter, Patrick, and Matt guarded the grill with testosterone fueling the flames instead of propane. At one point, Ella found herself sipping sangria and just observing her life as it happened around her. Everything was more perfect than she really every thought possible.

A few more men that Porter worked with showed up throughout the day, and they all seemed nice and polite. A couple of them brought women, but they didn't stay long, having other plans. It was nice to put faces to names that Porter had used over the last couple weeks when they talked about work. Ella spent a good portion of the afternoon talking with Brook, and eventually little Faith warmed up to her and even allowed Ella to hold her.

Ella was smitten as soon as the baby reached out for her. The baby seemed more interested in the necklace around her neck than in Ella herself, but she would take anything she could get from the precious child. Brook took advantage of the baby's interest in someone else and asked Ella if it was ok if she got away for a moment. Ella agreed immediately, smiling at Brook.

Faith had a distinctly baby smell to her, soft, clean and powdery. Ella couldn't help holding her nose to the crown of her head and inhaling deeply. When she opened her eyes, she saw Porter watching her and the look in his eyes was something she'd never seen before, but she knew what he was thinking because she had been thinking the same thing when he had been holding Faith. He was picturing Ella holding their baby. She gave him a smile, knowing that whatever road they were on, babies were eventually going to be traveling with them. She hugged Faith closer and pressed their noses together, talking to her in simple words, making silly faces, trying to elicit laughter from her. Ella hasn't really known before the power a baby's laughter or smile could hold over a person. Once you are gifted with a smile from a baby, you spent all your energy trying to recreate that perfect moment the child deemed worthy of their precious smiles and giggles. By the time Brook made it back to Faith, Ella had no ovaries left. They had exploded and left her womb aching.

The day went fabulously and the evening continued much the same way. They set up a portable crib and Faith napped in the living room of the house. Joy sat on Uncle Porter's lap and all the adults sat around the table playing cards, sipping on various drinks. Ella was glad Brittany and Sarah came down, realizing when the new store opened she would miss seeing them constantly. They had such good heads on their shoulders, and had been integral in the success of her business when she had gone through all of her medical issues. It meant a lot to her that they viewed her as a friend as well as their boss. The fact that they came all the way to the beach to spend a holiday with her made her feel like she'd done something right in the way she ran her business.

Once the dark of night came, they all wandered down to the beach to get ready to watch the annual firework display. Ella watched as Matt carried a sleeping Faith cradled in one arm, holding his wife's hand in the other, walking slowly towards the sand. Joy skipped, and often fell, along beside them, clumsily trying to navigate her lengthy limbs that she was still trying to grow into.

Tilly walked next to Ella's parents, and her mom engaged in conversation with her, as they had all day. Tilly was so different from her mom, but she could tell the two women really enjoyed each other's company. Megan and Patrick walked hand-in-hand, Patrick next to her father as they spoke about the upcoming football season.

Porter held her hand in his and they silently walked behind everyone else, enjoying each other. He gave her hand a squeeze and she looked up at him smiling. Everything was perfect.

As everyone found a place to sit in the sand, Ella found herself nestled in between Porter's legs, leaning back against his chest. They watched Joy, surviving off the sugar rush of the cake she earned by behaving for Uncle Porter, as she ran up and down the shore trying to do cartwheels and sometimes succeeding. All you could see was moonlight, campfires, and flashlights as people swarmed to the sand, waiting for the fireworks to begin.

Ella felt Porter's finger pull her chin up towards him, and when their eyes met, he lowered his mouth to hers and she received the warmest and softest kiss from him. This was not a passionate kiss. He was not trying to seduce her. They both just simply craved the connection they shared, and the comfort that came with their kiss.

Ella startled as a loud bang rocketed through her veins. Her heart beat pounded in her chest. She laughed at herself as she realized what she heard was the beginning of the firework show and she saw Porter's grin as she was amused by her reaction as well. She gave him one more small kiss and then turned back around, snuggling her back into his chest, and enjoyed the rest of the fireworks.

Chapter Nineteen

Porter

Funny how thirty minutes can change almost any situation. The bundle of energy that was Joy, was now slung over her father's shoulders like a sack of potatoes. She made it about five minutes into the fireworks and she literally fell over with exhaustion. Brook now held tiny Faith and Matt grunted with effort as he hauled the not-so-tiny eight year old up the driveway.

"We better just put them in the car now," Brook said to Matt. She turned to Porter and gave him a small hug, then turned to Ella and gave her a longer embrace which made Porter smile. "Thank you for having us over today. It was so much fun."

"Thanks for coming," Ella said with an enthusiastic smile. After Matt placed a floppy Joy in the backseat of their car, he came around and shook Porter's hand.

"I'll see you tomorrow," Matt said. "Ella," he leaned into her and kissed her cheek, "I've been waiting for weeks to meet you and I'm so glad you've finally made Porter so happy. Keep up the good work," he said with a sneaky wink and then walked his wife to the passenger side of the car. Everyone else made their way to their vehicles and said their goodbyes. Luckily, all of the Portlanders rented houses or hotel rooms, so no one was driving very far. Once they waved to the last car leaving the driveway Ella turned to Porter and wrapped her arms around his waist.

"I think that was a very successful cookout," she said smiling up at him, the moonlight reflecting in the blue pools of her eyes.

"I think so, too." He looked around his yard at all the food and chairs strewn about. "This is going to be a bitch to clean up." Her hands slid down his back to cup and squeeze his ass.

"We can clean up tomorrow," she said in a very convincing sexy voice that had him straining against his zipper.

"Are you afraid of raccoons?" He asked, laughing.

"What?"

"Raccoons. That is what we will be dealing with if we leave this out here all night."

She rolled her eyes at him. "Ok, I will clear the food if you haul the tables back into your shop."

"Deal," he said, kissing her soundly. She moved all the food off one of the tables so that he could move it. He bent down and grabbed the table by the sides and picked it up, walking towards his workshop.

"You're a showoff," she teased. He knew she liked watching his muscles strain as he lifted the heavy table. He knew what he was doing. He walked towards the back of the house and his shop came into view. His truck was parked along the side of the house and as he walked passed it, his eyes squinted and seemed to be playing tricks on him. He put the table down and went closer to his truck to inspect.

The windshield was smashed in, cracks spider webbing out from the center where it looked as if a sledge hammer slammed into it. The same sledge hammer that probably put all of the crater-like dents along the sides of the bed and the giant dent on the hood. He walked to the back of the truck, still not really believing his eyes, and saw two words spray painted on the tailgate:

Last Warning

"What the fuck!" He yelled. Porter heard footsteps behind him and swung around only to find Matt walking towards him.

"Hey, Man, we left the portable crib in your house. Mind if I go – what the fuck happened to your truck?"

"I'll give you one guess," he said, seething.

"Fucking Kyle!" Matt had been the one person Porter felt like he could talk to about everything happening with Ella and Kyle, so he was well informed on everything that was going on.

"That son of a bitch was here, Matt. He was here while we were out on the beach. I'm going to fucking kill that bastard."

"Porter?" He heard Ella's voice coming from the front of the house.

"Shit, she's going to freak out," Porter said as he rubbed his hands on his face. "Matt, you need to leave. Get your family out of here. He could still be around."

"Fuck that, Porter. Brook can take the kids home. You need to call the police." Just then Ella came around the side of the house and saw Porter and Matt standing in front of the truck.

"Porter?" She said, her voice already starting to tremble. He walked up to her and took her face in his hands, making her look at him.

"Baby, I need you to go inside right now. Turn around and go in the house."

"Come with me," she begged him. He let out a loud breath, but turned her around and put a hand on the small of her back directing her towards the front door. Matt headed back to his car. He saw Brook get out and move into the driver's seat, backing out of the driveway. Matt came back up to the house and stood guard on the porch.

Porter took out his cell phone and called the police. Ella was curled up on the couch, her legs tucked under her, wringing her hands in nervousness. Porter wanted to comfort her, but he was so fucking pissed off he found it hard to even approach her. Once he hung up the phone, he looked at her. She stared at the floor, seemingly lost in her thoughts.

"Ella, are you ok?" She snapped her head up at him. "Everything is going to be all right, Ella."

"There were kids here, Porter. Our families were here. What if...," she lost her ability to speak as she began to cry.

"No, Baby. No." He said as he sat down next to her, pulling her into his arms. "Kyle is a fucking coward who will never have enough balls to actually do anything while I'm around. He wouldn't have hurt anyone, Baby. He's not capable. He just accosts women in dark hallways and vandalizes property when no one is around to beat the shit out of him." He tried not to the let the tension he felt in his body seep out onto Ella. He needed her to remain as calm as possible, especially since the police were on their way and would inevitably want to talk to her again.

"Why won't he leave us alone?" She continued to cry. That was a very good question; a question that had been plaguing him for quite some time. What the hell was Kyle getting out of all of this? Why wouldn't he just disappear? Wasn't it in his best interest at this point to just fade away? The more he hung around, threatening people, the more suspect he was. He was going to be caught, Porter knew it. He just wished it would happen sooner rather than later.

Minutes later Porter heard the distinct crunching of gravel as the police cars pulled into his driveway. He pulled away from Ella at the same time Matt called out from the porch.

"Porter, the cops are here."

"Ella, do you want to come out there with me?" She nodded at him and stood, walking behind him, but never too far away.

The police took their statements, took photos of the truck, which was eventually hauled away by a tow truck. They gave them the same speil they had given them before: don't let Ella be alone, report anything suspicious, be aware of their surroundings. Porter was nearly shaking with the feeling of helplessness. All they could do was sit around and wait for something else to happen. The police offered to patrol past his house overnight, but he was adamant that they weren't staying there.

"No, we'll go to my mom's house."

"Would you like us to patrol past her house, then?"

Porter nodded, not liking the idea of bringing this drama to his mother's house, but also feeling like it wasn't safe for Ella to be at his house anymore either. "I would really appreciate that," he said to the police officer. Porter called his mother, waking her up from the sound of her voice. He asked her to come and pick them up, telling her he'd explain the circumstances when she arrived.

Matt stayed and gave a statement as well, mumbling to himself and intermittently cursing and saying "Fucking Kyle" under his breath. Porter was angry that Matt had to be included in the drama, but glad for the support of his closest friend in the stressful situation. When everything was wrapped up, Porter slapped Matt on the back and thanked him for sticking around.

"Go home to your wife and kids," he said.

"I will, let me know if you need anything." Porter nodded and shook his hand, and watched as he got a ride home from one of the police officers they knew from high school.

Ella packed a bag for them, which they sullenly carried into the backseat of his mother's sedan and rode all the way to Porter's childhood home.

After they explained everything to Tilly and tried to assure her that, for the moment, they were safe, Porter led Ella down the hallways of his mother's small one-story house to the bedroom he used as a child. His mother hadn't really changed much in his room, just made it more neutral. His old queen-sized bed was still there, along with the desk he used to sit at to do his homework. Ella walked in the room, looked around for a second, and dropped her bags on the floor where she stood. Her hands came to her face, and Porter saw her shoulders start to move up and down in silent sobs. He moved to her quickly and wrapped his arms around her, using his hand to guide her head into his chest.

"Baby, I don't want you to cry. Everything is ok. We're ok."

"What if he had come while the kids were there Porter? What would he have done…"

"Don't do that, Ella. Don't play those games with yourself. He is a coward and he waited until we all left to do what he did. He was never going to hurt anyone, Ella. I promise you."

"Everyone was there, Porter. Everyone we love was there. He could have done anything he wanted and there wouldn't have been anything we could have done to stop him because we were so careless." She nearly hyperventilated and Porter knew she needed her pills. Soon she was going to go into a full blown panic attack and he didn't want that for her.

"Ella, breathe with me, I need you to calm down," he said as he held her face in his hands and looked her straight in the eyes. She pulled away from him suddenly, throwing his hands away from her face.

"I don't need you to help me breathe!" She yelled at him. "I need all of this to go away! I need to go away. I'm the reason all of this is happening. He wants me to stay away from all of you. I just need to disappear." He knew she was emotional, with good reason, but he didn't want her making decisions that were so drastic while she was upset.

"Ok, we'll go away. Tomorrow we'll drive to Portland and get on a plane and just go somewhere until this all blows over."

"We can't be together, Porter. As long as we're together, he thinks you're making me go to the police. If we're together he'll never stop. He'll keep harassing us and putting our families in danger. This will never be over. Can't you see that?"

Porter took in a deep breath. "All I see, Ella, is you running. You promised me you wouldn't run. We don't stand a chance if we're apart, Ella. He won't stop. He's a crazy son of a bitch and he won't leave you alone until he gets whatever it is that he wants." He took the two steps he needed to be in her space again, placing his hands on her shoulders, willing her to listen to reason. "Ella, if you go, if you leave me, it'll be so easy for him to get to you. You're not safe on your own. Please stay with me. I can protect you." He rested his forehead against hers, hoping she was hearing what he was saying, that she understood how much he needed her to stay with him.

"But if I leave, I'm protecting you," she whispered.

He knew, right then, he'd lost her. She thought she was doing the right thing. She thought she could keep him safe. It seemed that at that very same moment she realized she'd made up her mind. With her decision seemed to come some peace. He noticed that her breathing slowed and her cries ceased. They were still standing in the middle of his childhood room holding each other and he knew that she was going to walk away from him.

"I love you." The words left his mouth before he had even realized he'd said them, and it felt too much like a goodbye to him, so he pressed his mouth against hers, hoping the kiss would convince her to stay. He poured everything he had left in him into the kiss, his tongue taking wide sweeps of her mouth. She groaned into him like she had a tendency to do, and even though the situation was stress-laden and dangerous, he felt himself hardening for her. His urgency in the kiss brought on a new fever and he could tell she was wrapped up in it as much as he was.

She started clawing at his shirt, trying to pull it over his head. Once she pulled it off of him he went to work unbuttoning hers, but eventually just ripped it open, buttons splaying across the room, pinging on the hardwood floors. His hands moved up to cup her over her bra, the lace of it scratching lightly at his palms. He walked her backwards until her back hit the wall and he felt her hands running up and down his chest. He reached between them pulling her shorts off of her with lightning speed and his hand found a lacy thong was the only thing that stood between him and her heat. As his mouth ravaged her, he grabbed her panties and ripped them from her body. She pushed his pants and boxers down with equal speed. He grabbed her thighs and lifted her to wrap her legs around his waist, his cock perfectly aligning with her heat, and their bodies came together with such force and impact, he had to brace himself against the wall.

"You think leaving will solve all your problems?" He asked with a shaky breath, still rooted deep in her body, trying to control the shudders that raced through his blood, afraid this would be the last time he felt connected to her in this way, perfectly, wholly, and entirely. She was looking him directly in the eyes, her breaths panted out through her mouth which was still open in a wide "O" from his penetration.

"I'm not discussing this right now, Porter. You either make love to me or I leave. It's your choice," she said as she used her hips to grind into him, causing his breath to hitch in this throat. If those were his only choices, love her or watch her leave, his decision was already made for him. He walked her over to the bed, cupping her ass to keep their connection solid, and gently laid with her on the bed.

He smoothed her hair back from her face and kissed her lips. He was hungry for her, wanted so badly to take everything she had to give, but he was afraid that he'd never get the chance to show her again how much he loved her. So he took the slow route, the kind of love that had won her over in the beginning. His mouth wound trails up and down the contours of her body, pressing slight and feathered kisses all along her skin. He reached behind her arched back and removed her bra, using his hands to knead her breasts. His mouth worshiped the spot on her neck that would, regardless of what the future held for them, always belong to him.

"Please, Porter, I need more." She wiggled beneath him, trying to gain some friction from their connections. As much as his body wanted the same thing she did – to feel himself inside of her, the slow rub and grind of entering her over and over again – his mind just wanted him to burn the feeling of his body aligned with hers into her memory. She pleaded with him with her eyes, begging him to give her more, and he was stalled just watching her breathe in and out.

"Promise me you won't leave. Promise me you won't run."

"I'll never leave *you*, Porter. I'll never run from *us*."

He knew what she was saying, knew what she wasn't saying. Either way he wasn't satisfied with her answer. The only thing he had left to do was love her.

When he woke the next morning, he wasn't surprised when the spot next to him in bed was empty and he wasn't surprised to see her bags gone. It killed him, but he knew she'd be gone. When he finally braved a world without Ella in it, he noticed an envelope sitting on the bedside table.

Dear Porter,

It's funny, before I met you I never wrote anyone letters, yet here I am, writing one to you again. This letter is different, Porter, and let me explain why.

The last letter I wrote to you, I wrote it knowing that somewhere in the future we'd run into problems, that I would have doubts and fears, and that I would need you to come for me – to fight for me.

No one has ever fought for me like you did, Porter, and no one ever will. But now it's my turn to fight. This will never end as long as we're together, because you are so good at protecting me. There's nothing you wouldn't do for me and this is something I need to do on my own. I know you're hurt and possibly sad, but don't be.

I love you. Forever. I will never not love you. Never.

Give me an opportunity to fight for us. Trust in me, in us.

I will come back to you and everything will be fine. You'll see.

No one's ever loved anyone as much as I love you, except for you and how much you love me.

Wait for me. Never stop loving me. I love how you love me.
~Ella

Chapter Twenty

Ella

Megan picked Ella up early that morning. Ella gave her no explanation, just told her that she needed to go back to Portland, and to drop her off at her house to get her car. She never went into her apartment, but continued on to her parent's house, guessing that her childhood home would probably be the safest place for her to be.

Leaving Porter was excruciating, but necessary. It tore her up that he was repeatedly put in danger over and over again because of her. It made her feel helpless and fragile. She was tired of feeling like a victim. The only thing she thought she could do to regain some control was to take back the reigns and try to keep her loved ones out of harm's way.

She had a solid plan. Stay out of trouble and stay busy. The police had told her to stay away from Poppy, but at this point she figured if she had personal security at the store anyway, she might has well go to work. If Kyle showed up, at least he'd be caught and arrested.

She showered at her parent's house and tried to keep her thoughts away from Porter and how he must have reacted when he woke to find her gone. Hot water ran down her back, her head bent down so that her chin was resting against her chest. She hoped the hot water could release some of the tension that was building up inside of her muscles. She wondered about whether Porter would even want her after she pulled this stunt. Her plan, all along, included their happy ending. Kyle would be caught and they would be able to build a long and stable relationship. But she also had to consider that fact that after she left him, he could make the decision to be done with her.

She felt a tear spring from her eyes, but it washed away with the water from the faucet down the drain, swirling and circling until it was gone. It was hard for Ella to feel anything but sadness as she felt the ache that came with Porter's absence in her belly. They had promised each other they wouldn't be apart anymore, but now she had to stay away to make sure they had many more nights together. She was confounded by the thought of how much her life had changed in just three months. Ella got out of the shower, got ready for her day at Poppy, and made her way to the store.

It had been a while since Ella had been to Poppy, and while pulling up to the store brought, in one sense, a feeling of relief and normalcy, it was coupled with the constant flashbacks and panic that usually came with them. She took a few deep breaths in and when she felt like she had calmed herself down, she got out of the car and walked up to the store front. Once she made it inside the store, she turned off the alarm system and switched the lights on. She felt a wave of apprehension leave her body as she fell into the routine of opening the store. She threw herself into the familiarity of the tasks: checking stock, folding tops, returning emails. Everything was as it was supposed to be and as long as she kept herself busy, she could pretend that everything was fine.

Thirty minutes after she arrived, a very large and bulky man in a suit knocked on the front window of the store. Ella startled at the knocking, her hand flying to her chest trying to calm the raging beat of her heart. The man held a plastic id badge up to the window and as she approached she could see he was from the security firm she'd hired. She exhaled, silently berating herself for getting so worked up over nothing. She opened the door for him and he slid in, very stealthily which, for a reason she couldn't pinpoint, made her smile. She had a legitimate James Bond in her store.

"Hello, Ma'am. I'm John, the hired security guard." He reached out to shake her hand.

"Yes, nice to meet you. I'm Ella. I own this store."

"Nice to meet you too. I trust you had a good fourth?"

"Actually, John, I could have used you at the beach," she said as she sent him a faint smile.

"I'm sorry to hear that, Ma'am. But you're here now so I

assume everyone is safe?"

"That's what I'm hoping for," she said trying to stay positive but feeling drained already by the presence of another person. Perhaps she should have just stayed in bed at her parent's house. Ella's eyes raised to the door when she heard, yet again, someone at the door. Sarah stared at Ella through the glass with a smile as she put her key in the lock and let herself in.

"Ella, I didn't know you'd be in today! I'm so glad to see you. I had such a good time last night at your cookout."

Ella smiled at Sarah's bright and cheery disposition; nothing ever got her upset or made her angry. She was perpetually happy all the time.

"I'm so glad you had a good time. I just drove up this morning, hoping to get back to work and back to normal," Ella said, hoping that would dismiss the topic. No one but Matt and Tilly knew what had happened with Kyle the night before, and she didn't want anyone else to.

Ella and Sarah worked in companionable silence. Every once in a while Ella would catch Sarah giving her a pitiful look, but Ella knew she was just worried about her and tried to let it go. By midday Ella felt claustrophobic in her own store. With Sarah giving her concerned looks and John sweeping his eyes around the store constantly, Ella was sad to think that she couldn't be at the store anymore until everything was cleared up with Kyle. There was no way to forget what had happened when John the man-giant roamed around the store reminding her that nothing was safe anymore. Ella was about to leave when she heard her phone ring in her pocket. She saw the number of her real estate agent and answered as she walked into the backroom.

"Hello?"

"Ms. Sinclair, this is Rachel from Salem City Real Estate. I wanted to call you and let you know that the repairs to the rental house are complete and the landlord agreed to let you move in immediately. The house is ready for you whenever you want it."

Relief washed over her as she thought she had a place to go to just disappear.

"That's fantastic. Can I get the keys today?"

"Absolutely, I have them in my hand right now."

"Great. Can I stop by the office in a few hours to pick them up?"

"Yes, I will be in the office any time after noon."

"Thanks so much." Ella hung up, grabbed her purse, and informed Sarah that she would be leaving for the day.

"Ok, well, I hope you have a good rest of your day, Ella." Sarah was looking at her like she had so much more she wanted to say, but gave her a small smile instead. Ella returned the smile and gave a small wave too, not wanting to give her an opportunity to say anything more. She made it to her car and let out a frustrated breath as she rested her forehead against the steering wheel.

She tried not to think about the fact that everywhere she went caused her to panic. That everything in that store reminded her of Kyle and what she was starting to believe he did to her. She tried to pretend that none of it bothered her and that was more exhausting than she could have imagined. She sat up, pulled her phone out again, and dialed Porter's number. It rang a few times and she was afraid he wasn't going to answer. The thought that he could be angry enough with her to not pick up his phone made tears well in her eyes and that uncomfortable sting appear in the back of her throat. Finally, he answered.

"Ella," he said as a greeting. She couldn't determine if he sounded scared, frustrated, irritated, or perhaps a mixture of all three.

"Porter."

"Where are you?" He asked softly, sadness now the most prevalent emotion in his voice.

"Portland, sitting outside of Poppy."

He was silent for a moment but she could tell what he was

thinking. He was upset that she was at the store when they all knew it wasn't safe for her.

"The real estate agent called and said that the keys for the house in Salem were waiting for me, so I'm going to go there for the night and try to relax."

"Can I meet you there?" He asked her after a long pause.

"Porter, you know I'd love to be with you, but until Kyle is caught we need to be apart." He was quiet again.

"There isn't even any furniture there, Ella. Please, Baby, come home." She closed her eyes and leaned her head back against the seat of her car. She took in a deep breath, trying to control her emotions.

"I have an air mattress. I'll bring it with me."

"No. Ella, I know what you're thinking. You cannot go back to your apartment."

"I'm just going to run in and get a few things. It'll be ok. It's the middle of the morning."

"God damnit, Ella! Are you trying to get yourself killed? You run away from me, you leave me pretending it's for my safety, and you're spending all your fucking time taunting that fucking bastard by going all the places he knows where to find you? What was the point of all of this?" She heard a loud thud from his end of the phone and then the sound of metal crashing down. The sound was deafening on her end of the phone and she could only imagine the noise on his.

"You know what the point is, Porter," she said quietly, trying to combat his anger by staying calm.

"You expect me to just sit around while you're out there *baiting* him?" She almost flinched at his words, his anger now seething. She could feel his anger radiating towards her, even from two hours away. She'd never heard him so mad and it pained her that his anger was directed at her.

"I just called to tell you where I was going. I'm not asking you to do anything, Porter. And I'm definitely not asking for your permission. I need you to trust me and let me fix all of this. Everything will be ok."

"I won't be ok if anything happens to you," he said, almost a whisper and that affected her almost as much as if he'd yelled it in rage.

"And I won't be ok if anything happens to you because of me," she replied. He was quiet after that and she knew he tried to accept the fact that she was making the decisions, even if he didn't agree with them.

"Please let me come see you tonight. I don't want to be away from you," he said quietly. His rage she could almost handle, but the sad and dejected Porter was more than she could take at the moment.

"Oh, Porter," she cried. "I don't want to be away from you either. I will call you later and we'll talk until we both fall asleep. Just read my letter and, please, stay in Lincoln City. I need you to be there. I need you to be safe."

She'd made it in and out of her apartment in record time. The last thing she wanted was to spend time there at all, so she hurried through the apartment quickly, gathering the things she needed for a few nights. She was surprised when her panic wasn't an issue, but she figured that her determination and purposeful plan helped to ease her nerves. She knew what she was going in for and she had a plan. Once she had loaded her car and has everything she needed, she pointed her car towards Salem.

Ella was never really a fan of camping, but that's exactly what she felt she was doing at the new house in Salem. She'd set up her air mattress and made a little nest of pillows and blankets she'd brought from the apartment in Portland. She had a little lamp plugged into the wall and after everything had been situated, she laid on the air mattress and read for the majority of the evening.

The house was, as expected, entirely empty which only illuminated her loneliness. She tried repeatedly to push the thoughts of Porter alone at his house out of her mind. The ache she felt from the need to be with him was physical and real. She'd gotten use to always being with him and now that she was trying to keep him away from her, his absence was overwhelming. She waited as long as she felt she could before she called him, wanting to hear his voice but not wanting to spend a lot of time rehashing their earlier conversation and argue. She wanted his voice to wrap around her like his arms might do if they were together.

She dialed his number and at the same time heard a car door shut just outside the house. The phone started ringing and she got up to look out of the front window in hopes that she could see the car. As his phone kept ringing, her heartbeat sped up. She couldn't help but half wish that Porter was there. As if she expected it, her head snapped around to the front door as she heard a knock. She froze, unsure of what she should do. Something inside of her, a small voice or instinct told her not to open the door.

She breathed heavily and all she could hear was her lungs pushing air in and out, and then Porter's deep and sexy voice as he asked her to leave a message. Then she jumped and was startled by the pounding on the door.

She ran back into the bedroom, all of a sudden cursing herself for not having anything to protect herself with. She huddled in the corner of the room, turning the lamp off as she passed it. She heard a beep in the distance and realized that she had heard the tell-tale sound letting her know she should leave a message.

"Porter," she whispered into the phone. "I don't think I have much time. I think he's here." She heard another large bang, but this time it sounded like someone was trying to bust through the door, not just bang on it. "Oh, Porter, I'm so sorry for everything," somewhere along the line she started crying. "I love you so much and I don't want you to blame yourself for anything that's about to happen to me. I'm so glad that you're not here and that I could protect you this way." Her voice immediately ceased when she heard the distinct sound of the door finally giving in and breaking open. She cupped her hand over her mouth to keep herself as quiet as possible.

Footsteps could be heard roaming through the front of the house and all she could do was wait until they found her.

"I love you, Porter," was what she whispered into the phone before she placed it on the floor, readying herself to run as soon as she got the chance. She saw her door creep open and she knew before he said anything that it was Kyle. His silhouette so perfectly outlined by the light cast in form the hallway and she knew it was him.

"There you are, Ella," he said, his voice making her stomach roil.

"What do you want, Kyle?" Ella said, her voice sounding more strong and sure than she had anticipated.

"The same thing I've always wanted: for you not to be a problem for me anymore." He lunged at her and she tried to dart past him. He reached his arm out and grabbed her around her waist. As she yelled and screamed for someone to come and help her, she couldn't help but think that she'd made this too easy for him.

"Stop making so much damned noise, Ella," he said as he clamped a hand over her mouth. There was a cloth in his hand and panic came over her and she couldn't control the breathing that she now knew would bring on her own demise. As she felt herself slipping away, she heard him utter one last sentence.

"We're headed back to where this all should have ended months ago."

Chapter Twenty-One
Ella

The darkness had been all consuming. She remembered the darkness from before; it was the last thing she saw before she woke up in the hospital where the darkness turned into blinding light. Either way, light or dark, she knew she was in trouble.

She could tell she laid on a soft surface, but something was wrong with her arms. She tried to move to sit up but her hands were stuck together and when she tried to pry them apart she felt the cutting sting of the rope that tied them together.

Her eyes blinked open and she was glad to see that there was only a dim light in the room she was in. Her head pounded and she didn't need bright lights adding to her discomfort. When her eyes finally adjusted to the light and she could get a good look at her surroundings, she found herself sitting in the living room of the rental house at Lincoln City where she'd spent her birthday week. Her face scrunched up in confusion and she could feel the adrenaline start to move through her system. She tried to think back, trying to piece together how she had gotten here and why her hands were tied up behind her.

She heard a crash come from the door to the basement and heard his voice.

"Shit!" Kyle exclaimed from behind the door.

Her eyes grew wide with fear as the events of the evening came rushing back to her. He'd broken into the house in Salem and kidnapped her. She looked around frantically, trying to figure out her next move.

She clumsily got up from the couch, still wavering back and forth, concentrating on trying to keep her balance even though it felt like she was walking in a fun house with moving floors. Whatever he had used to knock her out was still affecting her, making it difficult to even walk in a straight line. She made her way to the kitchen but clipped her hip on the corner of the kitchen counter on her way in. She pressed her lips together like a vice to try and keep the painful shriek from coming out.

Awkwardly, she used her hands to frantically pull open drawers of the kitchen, trying to remember where the knives were kept from her stay all those months ago, trying to maneuver the drawer pulls with her hands tied behind her back. She tried to keep in the scared sobs, knowing she had only moments before Kyle came back into the kitchen to do only God knows what to her.

Finally she found the drawer with the knives and grabbed a small one by the handle and held it so the blade was hidden between her wrists and then darted towards the door, hoping to get outside. Once she made it to the door, she found it locked. She let out a small cry of frustration, her emotions starting to overwhelm her ability to keep quiet. The longer it took her to grasp the lock with her fingers, made nearly impossible simply by being tied up, the more frantic she became. Her fingers could find the lock, but she couldn't turn it in the right way to get it open. She was so focused on the door lock, she didn't notice the door to the basement open.

"So, you're awake." The sound of his voice made her blood turn to ice, her body freezing, and her mind racing. She looked up to see him standing a few feet in front of her.

"Kyle, let me go, please." He cocked his head to one side, examining her carefully, his brow scrunched as though he were considering her pleas.

"El, if I let you leave here, I'd be spending the rest of my life in jail. Why would I do that? I've got so much to live for," he said as a sickening smile spread across his face. She grimaced at the use of his old nickname for her. Nothing about the man in front of her reminded her of the man she'd spent four years of her life with.

"Who are you? What happened to you?" She asked honestly, still trying not to cry. He chuckled a little and rubbed his chain with his hand.

"I'm exactly the same person I've been since you met me. You are just a really bad judge of character. Now, get away from the door and go sit back down on the couch."

She didn't move. The farther she was from the door, the farther she was from escaping. She continued to stare at him, trying to emit an aura of fearlessness, trying to give him the impression that she wasn't afraid, even though she had never been more terrified in her life. His blonde hair was longer than she remembered and it looked dirty. In fact, as she took a moment to really look at him, he looked terrible. He was thinner, his cheeks hollowed out, dark circles were under his eyes, and his clothes were wrinkled and baggy.

"You look awful," she said before she could stop the words from coming out.

"What do you expect? I hauled your ass all the way in the house. Now go and sit on the couch," he said angrily.

"No," she said firmly. He reached behind his back and when his arm came forward he was aiming a gun directly at her.

"Say no one more fucking time Ella and I swear to God I will put a bullet in you so fast you'll never even get to scream."

This was the second time Ella had seen a gun pointing at her and in that moment something inside of her clicked on. She should be scared with the silver gleaming barrel winking at her, but instead she was angry. She was not going to let someone else determine what happened to her anymore. She was no one's victim. She calmly walked past him and his gun, not looking him in the eye, and sat back down on the couch. As she sat she slowly rotated the knife in her hands until she could tell the blade was against the rope. She began to slightly run the edge of the blade along the rope, hoping that she was putting enough pressure on the knife to make a difference.

She watched as Kyle came into the living room, the gun still in his hand but no longer trained on her. He paced in front of the coffee table, running a hind through his greasy blonde hair.

"You've always been more trouble than you were worth, you know that?" He looked over at her and she remained silent, not wanting to give him any ammunition to use his gun before she was ready for him. "When we started dating, you were cute enough, and inexperienced enough that it was exciting. You were so trusting and you never questioned anything I did. You were so stupid," he said with obvious disgust.

She continued to listen to him, or at least look at him, trying to pretend like she was taking in his words. He rambled and she tried to free her hands. He could say whatever he wanted about her. It didn't matter. She just needed to get loose.

"Why'd you stay with me if I was so stupid?" She asked to keep him talking.

"Well, Ella, that's a good question. How else could I continue to embezzle money out of Poppy if I wasn't dating you?" She froze at his words and looked up at his eyes. He smiled at her, his mouth turned up on one side, smirking, as if he'd just said something particularly clever.

"What are you talking about?"

"I'm talking about the tens of thousands of dollars I siphoned out of your business while I was distracting you with our pathetic relationship." Her heart hammered in her chest and her mind raced, trying to connect the dots he laid out for her. She blinked at him, her mind blank and empty. He walked over to her and bent down so his face was only a breath away from hers. "You never even noticed the money was missing. It almost became too easy."

Her breath shuttered out of her, anger starting to take precedence over any other emotion she was feeling at the time.

"You were *stealing* from me? What the fuck is wrong with you?" She screamed at him. Immediately she felt the contact of the gun hitting her against the cheekbone. The contact sent her reeling back, the sound of the gun meeting her face cracked throughout the room. She was stunned at first and then slowly she pulled herself back up to a sitting position. She shook the hair free from her face and was relieved to feel that she still held onto the knife. She looked at him with what she hoped came across as steely resolve and she resumed her efforts to cut the rope loose with the knife as she felt a trail of blood slide down her face.

"You were so stupid and trusting Ella. If you hadn't walked in on me and that stupid bitch Tiffany, all of this would be different. You'd still be at my side, working your ass off, and happily ignorant to everything around you. I'd still be happily milking your business for all it's worth, fucking every chick I got ahold of, and continuing with my master plan, which you royally fucked up by growing some balls and walking out on me."

She wasn't stupid enough to ask what he was talking about. She continued to try and cut through the rope on her wrists, hoping she was making progress. She would never be able to over power him without her hands. It would be useless to try and take him on with her hands still tied behind her back. She knew if she kept quiet he would continue his rant, giving her some time to get free.

"A few months before your birthday, I was getting real tired of dealing with you every day. I liked the money enough, but you weren't doing it for me anymore. I had a buddy of mine help me take out a life insurance policy on you. It took a few weeks to get everything squared away, to gather all the information we needed on you and forge your signature. But just before we were supposed to go to the beach, it went through." He got a far away and dreamy look in his eyes, and he began to look a little crazy to Ella. She had never seen this side of him before and almost couldn't believe that he was the same man she had loved for so long.Kell

"That week, at the beach, someone was going to break into this house and kill you. I was going to be lying next to you in bed and watch you bleed until you were empty," he said with a fire burning in his eyes. He said it with such passion and strange longing that it made Ella's stomach turn. "You were supposed to die and I was supposed to collect the five hundred thousand dollar paycheck."

At that moment she felt the rope finally break free, It took every ounce of self-control she possessed to keep the elation from her face. She slowly unwound the rope from her wrists and turned the knife so that the handle of the blade was fixed in her hand, ready to use it to protect herself.

"But you went and fucked everything up," he continued. "It took a little bit of planning and strategizing, but I managed to coordinate another hit on you that night at your store. The stupid kid had lousy aim and only hit your shoulder. Imagine how lucky I thought I'd gotten when you were in a coma with a brain bleed. Maybe things were looking up for me again. I hoped your body would give up and die already, but no, you still lived, which pissed the hell out of me." She watched him pace back and forth in front of her. She knew she couldn't go after him, especially if he still had the gun. Moving towards him would be a death wish at this range. She had to get him to come after her. She nearly laughed at herself, and perhaps that was a sign of how much stress she was under, but it was almost funny to her that at this moment she was trying to figure out how she was going to get her royally fucked-up ex-boyfriend to come after her with a gun.

"Then, when you woke up with amnesia and couldn't remember a damn thing, I almost let it go. I was so close to just fucking walking away from all of it, but then that pompous asshole you were dating just rubbed me the wrong way. He's a real piece of work, Ella. I can't believe you spread your legs so quickly for him – both times."

"You're just jealous," Ella said, sneering at him.

He laughed at her remark.

"I'm not jealous. What do I have to be jealous of?"

"Last time we were in the apartment you tried to get me to spread my legs for you and it didn't work, did it? As I recall, I kicked your ass that night. And you had to find someone else to shoot me cause you're too chicken shit to do it yourself." He came right up to her and placed the cold barrel of the gun against her forehead, and she immediately thought she had pushed him too far. She closed her eyes, waiting for whatever happens after you get shot in the head. Pain? The blinding light everyone was always talking about? Then she saw Porter in her mind. She saw his smile light up his face, she felt his hands on her waist, and his nose flip the tip of hers. She felt him all around her and knew that she couldn't give in this easily to Kyle. She owed it to Porter to give him their happy forever. She opened her eyes and all she saw was the hand holding the gun pressed into her head.

"You're just a coward. You need to hold women at gunpoint and rape them to get what you want out of them. I've got my hands tied behind my back and a gun pressed up against my fucking head, and you still wouldn't be able to get to me. I guarantee it," she said, spitting the words towards him, hoping he would take the bait.

"Fuck you," he said, his voice filled with quiet rage.

"You couldn't if you tried," she flung at him, hoping she hit her target.

Just as she was hoping, he reacted. She felt herself being pushed down on the couch as he climbed on top of her. He switched the gun into his left hand, pointing it directly at her chest, right in between her breasts. He held the gun on her, flush with her skin, and used his other hand to try and pry open the fly of her jeans.

"You're such a bitch. I'm going to show you what kind of a man I am and you're going to take it."

Her arms were still behind her back and she was still clutching the knife in her right hand. She waited for her one chance. She knew she would only have one shot to save herself, because with one pull of his finger she would be dead.

He still looked her in the eyes, telling her how much of a dirty whore she was and how badly he was going to fuck her up. She didn't really listen. She tried to concentrate on his eyes. When she saw him finally look down at her zipper, because the dumbass couldn't even get her zipper down without looking, she moved quicker than she'd ever moved in her life.

She pulled her right arm out from under her and plunged the knife blade into his left hand that held the gun. When all of this was over, she would think back about what it felt like when the blade sank into flesh, and the sudden halt the knife made when it hit bone and ground up against it. She would remember how the vibrations of the blade scraping along the tendons could be felt up her own hand through the handle of the knife. She couldn't think about it in the moment, she needed to keep moving.

He cried out in pain and let go of the gun, staring at his hand with a small knife sticking out of it. Ella couldn't be sure, but she thought she saw the other end of the blade poking through the palm of his hand. Using his pain as a distraction, she quickly grabbed a hold of the gun he'd dropped on her chest. He saw what she was doing and fumbled for the gun at the same time. She cried out, trying to find purchase on the one thing that was going to get her out of this alive. He struggled as well, one hand rendered completely useless. She sounded terrified, her wails only accentuating the fact that she knew everything could end right then.

Both of them had their hands on the gun and nothing could have prepared her for the loudest noise she would ever hear. The sound of the bullet leaving the chamber was more like a sonic boom than anything else. She could smell the gunpowder, smell the sulfur, and the hot steel raged in her hands. One thing she couldn't feel was pain. There was no pain and that was a blessing. If she had to die, she was glad there would be no pain. She closed her eyes and pictured Porter once more in her mind, the way he looked that night of their first date pressing her body up against his truck, kissing her for the first time. She would never have enough kisses with him. She felt the warmth of blood spreading over her chest, creeping into all the crevasses created by her body and her clothes. She never expected to feel warm in death, but was thankful at least for that small favor.

She also felt enormous pressure against her chest, a heavy weight pressing down on her making it hard to breath. She guessed, perhaps, she'd been shot in the lung and maybe that was why she was having a hard time breathing. She waited for her breaths to slow, to feel herself succumb to the death she had been fighting so hard to avoid, but it never came.

Her eyes fluttered open and all she could see was the ceiling. Her arms were being held to her chest and when she looked down to see what was pinning them down, she saw Kyle's body slumped over onto hers. Realization hit her as if she'd had a bucket of ice water poured down her back.

She pushed Kyle's body off of hers, rolling him onto the floor next to the couch. She saw his shirt covered in blood and when she looked down at her chest she was covered in blood as well. But looking at his pale face and the hole in his tee-shirt, she guessed the blood came from him and not her after all.

She stared at his body lying there, not moving, and wondered what she was supposed to do. She was afraid to do anything, fearing that if she made too much noise he might wake up. Unless he was dead. She watched his chest for signs of breathing, but saw nothing. She shook so badly though, she wasn't sure she would be able to detect such a small movement anyway. She took a few steadying breaths and then reached down to his body pressing her fingers against his neck to check for a pulse. She didn't feel anything, so she moved her fingers around trying to make sure they were located on the correct place on his neck to feel his pulse. Still nothing.

She sat back quickly and pulled her hand to cover her mouth as sobs poured out from her. She cried frantically as she tried to process the fact that she had taken his life. She stood up, but then sat back down when she realized her body was not yet ready to support her. Her legs were shaky, her hands trembling, and the room seemed to be tilting like she was back in the fun house again. She took a few breaths and steadied herself, standing up slower, but making it to her feet this time.

She wobbled to the door, made it to the porch steps and collapsed down on them, sitting with her head resting on her knees. She had no idea what to do next. She was just praying she'd someday be able to erase the image of her ex-boyfriend lying dead on the floor next to her.

Chapter Twenty-Two

Porter

Porter came in from his shop where he had been taking his frustrations out on his boat for the last two hours. He was sweaty and sticky and covered in sawdust. He walked into his bedroom and his eyes flashed to his phone sitting on his bedside table. He saw the little light acting as a beacon that signaled he had a message. He reached for the phone with antsy fingers, but before he could unlock it he put it back down. There was no use trying to hurry to see if it was Ella who had called or not. She wouldn't let him see her regardless. If it was a message from her, it would more than likely make the aching hole in his chest that much more painful to hear her voice. He put the phone down and continued into the bathroom to take a shower.

Of course, the shower was only a reminder of Ella, naked and waiting for him on that bench. He buried his head in the hot stream of water. It was no use. Again, she was everywhere. This is the same shit he'd gone through two months ago when he was being kept from her. He saw her all over his house and it drove him mad. He threw an entire plate in the garbage earlier when he'd found a piece of cheesecake hidden in the back of the fridge. He was sure she'd put it there with sexy intentions before all the shit hit the fan, and it was just taunting him, so he threw it in the garbage with more force than was necessary.

He'd had it. This was ridiculous. They promised each other no nights apart, and he'd be damned if it was him who was going to break a promise to Ella. She could shut the door in his face and he'd sleep on the porch for all he cared, but he was going to her. He was out of the shower and dressed in minutes, bounding down the stairs to get to his truck as quickly as his legs could carry him.

Before he put the truck in drive he pulled his phone out again and decided to listen to his message.

"Porter," he heard Ella's voice, but it sounded strange. She whispered. "I don't think I have much time. I think he's here."

His blood stopped moving in his veins, every part of him turned to stone at her words. His heart stopped beating, his lungs like giant boulders in his chest, locked in place not letting air in or out.

"Oh, Porter, I'm so sorry, for everything. I love you so much and I don't want you to blame yourself for anything that's about to happen to me. I'm so glad that you're not here and that I could protect you this way." He could hear her crying through the phone and he felt like he was turning blue for lack of oxygen. What was happening? Had he already lost her?

"I love you, Porter," was the last thing he heard her say before the muffled sound of the phone being placed on a hard surface. He continued to listen, hoping to hear something that would make him believe that she was ok. But instead he heard Kyle's voice.

"There you are, Ella." Porter nearly vomited at hearing him say her name.

"What do you want, Kyle?" Ella said, sounding far away and distant.

"The same thing I've always wanted: for you not to be a problem for me anymore." Porter heard a lot of shuffling and muffled cries, bringing tears to his eyes.

"Stop making so much damned noise, Ella," he heard Kyle shout. "We're headed back to where this all should have ended months ago."

Porter froze, in so many ways, he was stuck. Where did he go from here? What came next? There was so much nothingness surrounding him, it was hard to find even the will to think about his next move. He closed his eyes and willed his lungs to give him air. His brain needed air. Finally he was able to take a breath. He took a few deep pulls of the ocean air that surrounded him and begged himself to get it together. He turned back to his phone and looked at the call log to see when she had called him.

The log said she'd called two hours ago. Two whole hours had passed since she'd called him and since Kyle had shown up and done God knows what with her. He dialed the voicemail number again to listen to the message. It would probably haunt him forever, so listening to it one more time wouldn't make much of a difference. Hearing her scared voice, listening to her telling him that she was glad she could protect him, it took everything else out of him. Then he heard the last sentence Kyle had muttered. Back to where it should have ended months ago? What did that mean? Poppy? Their old apartment? Then, it came to him. He picked the phone back up and dialed 9-1-1. He threw his truck into drive and tore out of his driveway, relaying all the information he knew to the dispatcher.

The woman on the phone told him to stand down, that he should wait for the police to take care of it. He simply hung up on her. There was only a small sliver of a chance that Ella would even be there, and then he thought about the fact that if she were there, what were the chances that she was still alive? He didn't have time to think about it. He pushed back all his fears of the unknown and focused solely on the overwhelming feeling of protectiveness that he was so used to. He would find Ella, he had to. And he would kill Kyle. He would take pleasure in it.

He broke every traffic law driving to the rental, running every red light, passing cars on the 101, even driving on the shoulder when people wouldn't get out of his way. When he finally arrived at the driveway all he saw was an unfamiliar car, which only made him angrier. His door nearly came off with the force he used to open it, the engine still running, the headlights still on. He started to run to the porch but it felt like he hit a brick wall and he fell to his knees on the gravel.

Ella sat on the porch steps, her head resting on her lap. If he never saw anything, ever again, he wanted to remember the sight of her right in front of him. His hand found his chest and he gripped his shirt over his heart and he felt it pounding at an alarming pace. Tears sprang from his eyes and he breathed her name. "Ella." It was quiet, but she must have heard it because she looked up at him.

The fucking roller coaster he was on took another nosedive when he saw her drenched in blood.

"Ella," he yelled, suddenly on his feet and at her side, not sure how he made it to her when a moment ago nothing on his body worked properly.

"Ella, look at me," he said as he grabbed her face, making her look at him. "Where are you hurt? Baby, tell me. Where are you hurt?"

"Porter?" She looked at him with confusion. "You can't be here, you have to leave."

"Is he in there?" He stood up to go inside, but she grabbed his shirt.

"You can't go in there!" She yelled at him.

"Did he do this to you? Ella, tell me what's wrong?" Porter pulled out his phone to call 9-1-1 again, but then heard sirens coming and put it away figuring they would be here before he got through anyway. She pulled his shirt down with so much force he had no choice but to sit down next to her on the step. He wrapped his arms around her and wished she would just tell him she was ok.

The police cars pulled up and the same officers who had came to his house both nights were there.

"Are you two alone?" The officer asked. Porter looked at Ella for an answer.

"No, Kyle is in there," she answered quietly. Porter immediately moved to stand up. "No! Porter, please, don't leave me." The officer placed his hand on the gun in his holster and started to make his way into the house.

"You won't need your gun," Ella said with a distant and faraway look in her eyes. "I already killed him."

Epilogue
Porter

It had been three months since the incident with Kyle. The effects that night had on Ella were far reaching and still not quite resolved, and they might not ever be. Porter might not ever be fully himself again, either. But they were together and that seemed to be the overriding factor to their happiness. They both had issues to work through, but nothing was standing in their way of being together anymore. Their lives had become boring and uneventful in the most fantastic of ways.

He knew that night of their first date he wanted to marry her and he would have, in an instant, had he thought the timing was ever right for them. They fought so many battles together that he knew she would always wonder if their relationship was born out of some need to *fix* them or to bind them together in times of trial. So he waited. So many times in the last seven months he'd wanted to simply take her to Vegas and just get it over with, but he knew he had to wait for her to realize that all their obstacles were behind them.

Tonight he was going to surprise her at Poppy 2.0, as they jokingly referred to the new store in Salem. The store was almost therapeutic for her in that she had something to focus all of her nervous energy on and it was something brand new that hadn't been tainted by the events revolving around Kyle. It was a fresh start for her and for them together.

He opened the door to see Ella standing on a step stool, reaching far above her head, trying to reach the very top of the wall near the ceiling with a paint roller. Her tee-shirt was riding up and reveled the slightest sliver of skin above the waist of her running shorts. She was on her tiptoes stretching her long and lean legs even farther than should be legally allowed. He stood in the doorway for a moment and simply took her in. She belonged to him, in every way possible, and he was hers as well. He could look at her all night, but he wanted to feel her in his arms.

"Hey, Babe," he said as he walked towards her. She looked over her shoulder at him and smiled. He was secretly proud of her for not startling and jumping at his sudden appearance. It took her weeks to not jump at the sound of people's voices who snuck up on her. She was incredibly strong and he loved watching her grow stronger every day.

"Hey to you too. I thought we were going to meet at home."

"I wanted to surprise you," he said as he raised his head up for a kiss, smiling a little at the fact that for once, she was taller than him. She leaned down and gave him the kiss he was looking for. He took advantage of his height issue and wrapped his arms around her waist, placing his hand on her ass. "These shorts are nice," he said against her lips as he squeezed her through the fabric of them.

"You're a pervert," she said laughing at him. He gave a shrug, not willing to deny it. "You're not trying to take me anywhere are you? I am not dressed to go out in public."

"Nope," he said. He turned from her and started unloading the backpack he had with him. He pulled out a blanket and spread it out on the floor in the middle of the empty store. Then he pulled out a bottle of champagne and two plastic flutes. He looked at her and was rewarded with a smile so big his heart missed a few beats. He held up a finger to indicate 'one more' and he took out a paper bag that had dinner in it. "I got us some hot dogs from the food trucks down the street, since I didn't think the fire marshal would appreciate a campfire in your store here."

She stepped down from the stool and walked over to where he was kneeling on the floor and she knelt down next to him. "I love Porter picnics." She kissed him sweetly on the lips and he couldn't help but smile about it.

He patted the blanket next to him, indicating that he wanted her to sit next to him. She followed his instructions and took the spot next to him on the floor.

"Before we get to the gourmet meal I have brought you, I

wanted to give you something else first."

She gave him a questioning look and narrowed her eyes at him. "Ok…" she said slowly, drawing out the word in a way that made her sound unsure of what he was going to do. He reached into the small pocket of his backpack and pulled out an envelope. Her name was scrawled across the front of the envelope and she looked up from it and back to him a few times, trying to figure out what was going on.

"Open it."

Dear Ella,

There are so many ways I could tell you that I love you, but it seemed like it was my turn to write you a letter. You'll have to cut me a break though because, although I seem to do fine with words in general when I'm talking, there's more at stake when writing a letter like this – more on the line.

Every time you've written a letter to me, you've either been leaving me, or anticipating the fact that you were leaving me and preemptively trying to talk me into going after you. Well, although I will always love the letters you have written to me, both of them were entirely pointless and a waste of time and trees.

Not once did you leave me. It's impossible to be without someone who is so entirely engrained in your heart that you carry them with you wherever you go. So even though for weeks at a time you were across the state, you were never far away. Never. As I suspect I was never far from you either. The point being, there will be no more letters about going away or chasing after you, because as far as I'm concerned, you're mine, forever. The only thing left for us to do to cement the fact that I want you tied to me forever is for you to marry me. I should be down on one knee. I should be holding up a little velvet box with a ring in it for you, but that's not my style, Baby. I want to give you picnics on the beach (and anywhere else I can lay a blanket down), fireworks in the sand, waterfalls, kisses and many, many nights of us together.

I want to give you a house, fill it with babies, and I want to start now. Our life together starts now, Ella. Say you'll marry me. Give yourself to me and let me spend every day with the one person who makes me feel like I have every good thing I never thought I'd find.

Marry Me.

I love you even more than you love me, obviously,

Porter

When Ella looked back up at him it was with tears in her eyes. She had her delicate fingers placed over her mouth, but he could see she was biting her lip, probably to keep herself from crying. He moved closer to her and brought his hand up to cup the side of her face. She leaned into his hand and brought her eyes up to meet his. He held out a velvet box to her.

"I thought you said you didn't have a velvet box," she asked confused.

"Oh, this box?" He said motioning towards the very box in his hands. She rolled her eyes at him.

"Yes, that's the one I'm referring to."

"Oh, this isn't for you. It's for me," he said, as if it should be obvious.

"You bought yourself an engagement ring?"

"Months ago," he said as she opened the box. Inside the box was a silver ring, and when Ella saw it he watched as her nervousness and apprehension melted away. The ring was the same one they had seen at the jewelry vendor at the Saturday Market when they had gone together before she got her memory back. This ring was the male version of hers, which sat nicely on her ring finger at the moment.

"This ring was made as a companion to yours," he said as he took the ring out and slipped it on his finger. "The artist uses the woman's ring as a mold for the man's and so you'll see, all around my ring is the indention of where your ring would wrap around it." He said holding his ring up to show her. "Your ring, as you so eloquently stated when you saw it, represents you finding your direction, making your own way. Well, to me, my ring represents that whichever way you're pointed, which ever direction you're going, you will always be headed towards me." He watched as she took in what he was saying, and how her eyes kept darting back and forth between the rings and his eyes.

"Well?" He said with a smile. He was rewarded with her laughter.

"You want to marry me?" She asked with a squeaky voice, trying not to cry.

"Did you even read the letter?" He joked. She laughed again. "Well?" He asked again.

"I'll marry you on two conditions," she said, smiling and crying at the same time.

"I wasn't expecting to barter." He said with a straight face. "But I'm willing to hear your offer."

"At our wedding, I want your mom to make her cheesecake for our wedding cake," she said, also trying to keep a straight face.

"Hmm… interesting. What else?" Trying not to let on that he thought it was the best idea he'd heard all night.

"I would need for us to start making babies, like, immediately." She said, this time bringing her thumb nail to her mouth, worrying the nail in her mouth.

"Done," he said immediately. "You're not a very good negotiator." He said as he kissed her, laying her down on the blanket, covering her body with his, loving the feeling of her underneath him.

"Hmm… says the man who gave me everything I asked for without even one counteroffer."

He pulled back from her neck where he was placing small kisses.

"I don't need a counteroffer. If you agree to marry me, I'll give you anything you ask for." His face became very serious and he brushed her hair back from her eyes.

"Marry me, Ella." He said quietly, looking directly into her eyes.

"Forever?" She smiled.

"And ever. Never a day apart again."

"You're mine?" She smiled some more, obviously enjoying making him squirm.

"I'm yours if you're mine," he said.

"Then yes, I'll marry you," she said, placing a smiling kiss against his lips.

The End

Acknowledgments

There are so many people who have helped me through the process of writing this second book. It is the least I can do to offer up my thanks in the form of words on the page, which is why we are all reading this to begin with.

To my husband, Demian, I love you. So much. Thank you for everything you've given in sacrifice to help me see this whole crazy writing thing through. And thank you in advance for everything you will continue to sacrifice for me. You are the most selfless and caring man I've ever met and I'm so lucky that I'm the one who was smart enough to hold on to you. And thanks for your input on the word "boobs". Your knowledge on the subject matter was impressive and vast.

To Brook, you are the best "bestie reader" around. Your constant support and enthusiasm surrounding the books only serve to motivate me. Your feedback and love of Ella and Porter (mainly Porter) helps me in more ways than you can probably imagine. To Matt, thanks for always offering the important male perspective and for your eternal hatred for Kyle. I was so happy that you and your lovely wife made it into the book. If anyone deserves a cameo, it's you guys. And thanks for always making me laugh. This is stressful stuff, but you are always able to help me put aside the stress and just relax. I appreciate that.

To my mom, thank you for being the support system that you have always been. You always listen to me, help me weigh my options, and offer unwavering and unconditional love. That's all I'm going to write because I'm in a coffee shop and I don't want to cry in front of strangers.

To Krysta, where to being? Both of my books would be a complete disaster without your help. I am, without a doubt, the luckiest writer because I know that I've got an editor and a best friend wrapped up all together. One might think the combination might be worrisome, but I love it. You make my books one thousand percent better. I couldn't ask for a better editor and I wouldn't want to. You're my favorite. I appreciate and admire the time, effort, and professionalism you put into everything I task you with. Maybe one day when I'm filthy rich, we can arrange some sort of payment for every comma you have to cross out.

To Michelle of Once Upon A Crush Book Blog, your support of both books has been unreal. I didn't really know what to expect in the Indie Author world, but I never would have imagined there would be people like you who seem to take such joy in helping others. I will always be grateful to you and everything you've done for the books. I look forward to continuing to share all my work with you and helping you, in any capacity, any way I can.

To my awesome Beta Readers!!! I love you all dearly. Truly, I do. Rhiannon, Heather and Holly – you guys are the best. I so appreciate you three reading the book in fragments and giving me the encouragement I needed to get it done and do it right. To the betas who read the book in it's whole form – you guys helped me more than I can really put into words. You can't imagine how nerve wracking it is to write something and then put it out into the world for judgment and criticism. Hearing how you all love the book gave me a little more confidence and made everything brighter. Thank you.

To the readers and fans of Ella and Porter and The Never Series, I have no words. Absolutely no word can sum up how I feel about all of you. Every time you write me a message on facebook, an email expressing your love for the books, or leave a review, it makes my day. I can honestly say that Never Far Away might not have even happened if it hadn't been for the readers. Your support means so much to me and you are the reason I get to do this wonderful job that I never dreamed I would be lucky enough to do. I will always, *always*, be a reader friendly author. I promise. I will always make time for you and continue to be friends with you because I consider you all to be friends of mine. I hope you'll make the journey with me to other books and other characters as I am looking forward to you all meeting the other people who are in my head all the time.

Finally, to Ella and Porter, is it weird for me to write a thank you to fictional characters? I don't really care. To Ella and Porter, the two of you have brought me on such a wild, crazy, and wonderful ride over the last nine months. Thank you, Ella, for being the first character strong enough to make me listen to you and sit down at a computer and write. Thank you, Porter, for not taking a backseat to Ella and making me, along with many other women, swoon over your *words*. I'm not sure I can top the two of you, but I'm going to try. I will always have a special place in my author heart for the two of you, and I am so glad that you found your HEA. I am so lucky that I will forever get to know how your story continues because I will always be thinking about you both, wondering what you're up to, how you're doing, and watching your lives unfold. Hopefully, I will get to write about you again, but if not, I feel content.

Thank you ~ *Anie*

Made in the USA
San Bernardino, CA
12 October 2014